MOTHER?

There was something else in the house with her. The noise came louder now. Footsteps, going in one direction and then another, as if someone were looking for someone.

Ellen summoned up her courage and called out, "Who is it? I'm here! In my study!"

"Mother?" The voice sounded almost adolescent, plaintive and confused.

The long shadow of a male figure was now apparent in the next room. The air had turned very cold. The light seemed to change as if every bulb in the room were arcing brilliantly, ready to burst.

A young male stepped into the doorway, solid and substantial, sixteen years old and handsome.

"Mother?" he asked again. "I'm looking for Mrs. Wilder. Are you my mother?"

"Yes," Ellen said to her dead son. "Yes, Robin. I am."

"Are you ashamed that you had me? Do you want to hide me?"

She shook her head. "No."

"Then why won't you look at my picture?" He turned and walked away.

Ellen ran to the doorway, but Robin had vanished.

BOOK YOUR PLACE ON OUR WEBSITE AND MAKE THE READING CONNECTION!

We've created a customized website just for our very special readers, where you can get the inside scoop on everything that's going on with Zebra, Pinnacle and Kensington books.

When you come online, you'll have the exciting opportunity to:

- View covers of upcoming books

- Read sample chapters

- Learn about our future publishing schedule (listed by publication month *and author*)

- Find out when your favorite authors will be visiting a city near you

- Search for and order backlist books from our online catalog

- Check out author bios and background information

- Send e-mail to your favorite authors

- Meet the Kensington staff online

- Join us in weekly chats with authors, readers and other guests

- Get writing guidelines

- AND MUCH MORE!

**Visit our website at
http://www.pinnaclebooks.com**

THE LOST BOY

Noel Hynd

Pinnacle Books
Kensington Publishing Corp.
http://www.pinnaclebooks.com

For my good friends Paul and Michele Raley.

PINNACLE BOOKS are published by

Kensington Publishing Corp.
850 Third Avenue
New York, NY 10022

Copyright © 1999 by Noel Hynd

Pinnacle and the P logo Reg. U.S. Pat. & TM Off.

First Printing: October, 1999
10 9 8 7 6 5 4 3 2 1

Printed in the United States of America

For the thing which
I greatly feared is come upon me,
and that which I was afraid of
Is come unto me.
I was not in safety,
Neither had I rest
Neither was I quiet;
Yet trouble came.

Job

One

Ellen Wilder had never spent a day of her life in Georgia other than this one, the day she had come to bury the son she had never known. In her heart there was a hurt that threatened to never heal.

She stood at the edge of the funeral party, listening to a slender Methodist minister in a purple and black robe whom she had never seen before, and would never see again. She stood among people she did not know who said they were friends.

Ellen was a pretty woman of thirty-five, divorced, dark-haired, five and a half feet tall. Today she was hiding red eyes behind a pair of dark glasses that announced her desolation more than hid it. She wore a black dress, and was more alone than she had ever been in her life, having traveled to Stone Mountain in the suburbs of Atlanta from Massachusetts on a day's notice. Her eyes were pools of sorrow.

Dear God, she prayed silently, trying desperately to find faith and belief where she hadn't found them for years. *Have mercy on the soul of Robin Steven Duperry.*

Her late son.

In addition to the pangs of guilt, the flood of remorse, the avalanche of self-reproach and accusation, an old song kept turning over in her mind.

Midnight Train to Georgia.

Well, why not?

Midnight train, midnight plane.

She had taken a midnight plane and arrived at 2:00 A.M., so she could be at the church by 9:00 A.M., be at the cemetery by 11:00 A.M. She watched in torment. It had been sixteen years since she had given up her firstborn child, a boy. He would eventually be named Robin—and, just as eventually, she would lose track of him.

It had been 1983. She had been in her sophomore year in college and she had thought it was a safe day to have unprotected sex. A pregnancy had followed, and an eight pound ten ounce boy had been born nine months later, early on a November morning. She had given him up for adoption, gone back to university after missing a semester, and had regretted it almost every day since.

She knew he had been adopted into a family named Duperry, and she knew he had lived as an infant somewhere in New York State, the only child of a professional couple. That was all she had ever known, though somehow his adoptive parents had always kept track of her.

She regretted it, but beyond the first few years of his life she had never been able to successfully trace her son's whereabouts. Twice she had tried, most recently about five years ago. She had made slight headway, but then the trail, the location of the family he had been raised by, disappeared abruptly.

Nor had she ever known whether she *should* try to see him or meet him. Would it lead to further unhappiness? She knew he had been placed with a good family. She knew he was being cared for.

So why mess with it?

Again, she blamed herself. If she had loved him enough at the time he was born, if she hadn't given him up, he would never have lived his life separate from her.

Whose fault was that? Hers, she told herself. Who hadn't accepted responsibility? She hadn't, she answered. Why should she ask a son to reconcile for the failings of a mother? She shouldn't.

It was only in these last few days that the past had hurtled toward her with a huge rush. A man named Harold Duperry had phoned her late two afternoons ago from Georgia, his voice unfamiliar, his tone reassuring but somber, his accent of the old Confederacy.

It was a sad time, Mr. Duperry said, but he needed to ask. Was she, Ellen Wilder, the journalist from *The Boston Globe*, the same Ellen Wilder who had given up a child more than sixteen years ago?

"Who's calling?" she had replied, her journalist's instincts quickly kicking in.

Then, as steadily as he could under the circumstances, the man on the phone explained that his brother, sister-in-law, and their adopted son, formerly from Mt. Vernon, New York, had died the previous day in an auto accident while vacationing in Florida.

Adopted son . . . died the previous day . . .

Something in Ellen's throat, and in her soul, caught when she heard those words.

Adopted son . . . Mt. Vernon, New York.

Harold Duperry could barely retain his own composure. He was a decent man, trying to do the decent thing, at a time of enormous grief and pain.

Would Mrs. Wilder, he wanted to know, wish to attend the funeral services? She would be welcome if

she did, and Mr. Duperry would arrange for someone
to meet her at the airport.

In total shock, Ellen said she would call back.

She had put down the telephone and stared
straight ahead, feeling something hollow and ringing
inside her. Several minutes later she realized that
Martin Barnaby, another reporter on the same paper,
was standing near her, talking to her, leaning over to
see what was wrong. He had a hand on her shoulder,
comforting her.

Only then did she realize that her face was streaked
with tears, and her emotions had cascaded through
all those years when she had wondered about her
son.

"Ellen?" Marty had asked.

Barnaby was a big, kindly bear of a man, a veteran
of a thousand police stories on the city desk. He was
man who had never lost his eye for corruption, but
was endowed with great honesty and compassion.

"Ellen?" he asked again.

It was then that she broke down and cried openly.
Fifteen minutes later, she gathered herself together
and phoned Harold Duperry. She said that she could
take a late flight and would be in Stone Mountain
the next day.

After sixteen years, she felt it was the least she
could do.

Now, on a balmy April day in Georgia, Ellen stood
in the cemetery adjacent to an old, white, Protestant
church that somehow had survived Sherman's march
to the sea. There were about fifty people at graveside,
all torn with grief, burying three members of a family
that they had known well.

The sun was bright and there was a gentle breeze
across the churchyard. Ellen's gaze rose. Beyond the

old wooden steeple was a stand of six tall pines which seemed to act as honorary pallbearers. She tried to keep her imagination in check and lowered her eyes, looking back to the scene before her.

So this was where her first son, the one she had never known, would lie for eternity, she thought. She remembered the place where she had brought him into the world—eight hours of labor at Quinn Family Hospital in Norwalk, Connecticut—and now she stood by at the place where his journey would end.

Her conscience accused her second by second. If she hadn't given him up, would he have lived a much longer life?

Would he have found a woman to love?

Would he have raised a family?

Would he have found the spiritual peace that had always eluded her?

Had he been tortured by the unseen love of a mother he had never known?

Had he been a good boy?

Had he loved music? Had he played sports?

Had he been happy?

Could she ever put her life together after *this*?

The minister's words, the right ones, rolled onward with a gentle Southern inflection, but his words barely registered on Ellen. Her lower lip was clenched in her teeth. The purple and black clerical robes reminded her of the colors of a bruise, and she felt a great bruise upon her heart.

She looked away, no longer able to confront the reality before her. A stranger, a man whom she thought might be a Duperry cousin, placed a hand of comfort on her shoulder. He whispered something to her which she couldn't hear, and she assumed it was meant to

soothe her. She appreciated the kindness, but it fell
far short of being able to heal anything.

Not today.

Today was a day when nothing on earth would
heal.

If her boy Robin came back to her, she fantasized,
if she and her son could stand before each other,
just one time, what would she have to say?

What would they talk about?

How could she ever ask his forgiveness? The guilt
coursed through her like the jagged blade of a saw.

Three dark coffins slowly started into the ground
together, followed by flowers from those assembled.
When the coffins disappeared, Ellen turned away.

Harold Duperry found her. He embraced her. "He
was a beautiful boy, Ellen," Harold said. "We were
all so grateful to know him."

Thank you, she thought. Thought, but did not say.
She could not speak.

The Duperry relatives invited her back to Harold's
home for a quiet family reception after the service,
but she declined.

"Are you certain?" Harold asked. "There are some
things of Robin's. I've set a few of them aside for
you. Maybe there's something which—"

His suggestion was kind and consoling. But she
couldn't bear to look at the lifetime of momentos
from a boy she never knew.

"I'm sorry, Harold," she said. "God knows I appreciate it. Some other day?"

"I understand," he said. His own eyes welled.
Then, after a moment, he tried again. "Look," he
said. "There's one thing you *must* have. A photograph. A favorite photograph. May I . . . ? If not today, maybe I could mail it to you."

She nodded. "Please," she said. "Yes. Do that. Mail it." He already had her address in Massachusetts.

"I can't tell you how devastated I am," Harold said again, his own voice cracking this time. "You know, our whole family,"

He couldn't finish. Nor could Ellen. Two strangers brought together in tragedy, they hugged each other again. Then they said the brave things about staying in touch. Already, all she could think about was returning north. She had been through more than enough already.

The service was over.

If only she had kept Robin.

If only she had been braver.

If only she had been a more responsible mother.

If only . . .

The entire world bore the tone of the words *if only.*

A car and driver were waiting for her. She quickly slid into the backseat of a black Taurus, and a stone-faced driver in a dark suit took her to Atlanta International Airport. He drove steadily, and knew enough to not offer any fake cheer.

Involuntarily, she felt it had become a time for taking stock as she stared out the car window—a time to examine her life, what was right with it, what was wrong with it, a time to decide what she wanted to do with the years ahead. She had a daughter and a career. She loved her daughter, and wanted to make changes in her career.

Maybe the time has finally come, she thought later as she sat in a grimly bright airport room waiting for the flight that would take her back to Boston. She had always wanted to get out of big city journalism and run a small, independent paper; maybe somewhere in New England.

She felt shattered from this event. She sensed that she wanted her life to now proceed in a different direction. She felt ashamed in so many ways. Her daughter didn't even know that she had a half-brother.

She sighed.

She had some money through a small inheritance, and would receive a good severance package from *The Globe*. She had always thought that a move to ownership of a small local newspaper was fifteen years away—something she would do when she was around fifty. Many times, she told herself now that life was too short. The things that a woman wanted to do needed to be done now.

Not later. *Now.*

She knew several dozen people scattered around the east who were knowledgeable about small town papers. They always knew which ones were on the block. Maybe something was available.

Maybe she could make the move now.

Her daughter, Sarah, was nine years old. Maybe it would be a whole lot better for her to grow up with small town, traditional values than with the things she would be seeing in a jaded place like Boston.

Her flight was called, and as she went to her gate she continued this line of thought.

Maybe this way her daughter would grow up to—to what?

To not make some of the same mistakes Ellen had?

Well, yes. Wasn't that something that one hoped for with one's children?

The plane taxied down the runway and prepared for the liftoff. Then the engines roared and the thrust of four jet engines took the aircraft up into the sky. It was late afternoon, and early April's daylight was dying as she gazed out the window.

As time spiraled, so did her thoughts.

She leaned close to the window and shut her eyes. Meanwhile, one word, one thought, one notion, hung around.

Leaving.

Hey! Leaving what, Ellen? she demanded of herself. *You're leaving nothing behind. Not a son, not part of your life, not anything! Until you can confront the past, you cannot confront the future.*

Life was very simple like that.

She looked out the window of the jet. She looked upward toward Heaven, and wanted to see her son. She wondered where he was—his spirit, that essence within him that made him unique.

The aircraft banked and climbed on its journey north.

Deep in her heart, something wished for it never to come back down. She wished it would do the impossible, climb to the stars so she could see her son one more time.

She knew all too well that life didn't work that way. Yet there were many things about the space between life and death, Heaven and earth, that she'd also *thought* she'd known, but hadn't.

Two

On a bright morning in the middle of a spectacularly beautiful June, Maury Fishkin left his house on Poole Street in Wilshire, Connecticut, a town approximately two hundred miles from where Ellen Wilder lived with Sarah. He walked to his store in the town center.

Fishkin was seventy-one, fit and vigorous beyond his years. His family had operated the only hardware store in Wilshire since the Great Depression. Maury was perhaps Wilshire's best known and most popular citizen.

The temperature, like Maury, was in the low seventies. There was no humidity and Maury Fishkin walked briskly, as he always did, no matter which season. He was already wearing his summer uniform of a short-sleeved, no-nonsense white shirt, a red bow tie, and dark, lightweight wool slacks. His shoes were shined perfectly.

He was a fastidious man, intelligent and kindly. He was lean, with thick white hair. He said hello to everyone he passed and everyone cheerfully responded. He was in many ways an old-fashioned gentleman. Wilshire was in *some* ways his sort of New England town.

Two decades earlier, Fishkin had been the town's
First Selectman, the local equivalent of a mayor. He
had long since retired from the top political spot in
town, but still served on the five person Wilshire
Board of Selectmen—two Democrats, two Republi-
cans, and Mr. Fishkin, who had the endorsement of
both parties.

Because of who he was, and because his store was
a local fixture, Fishkin Hardware remained well pa-
tronized and busy.

Maury Fishkin had lived in Wilshire all his life, except for the time he had spent in the United States
Army from 1948 to 1950. To him, Wilshire wasn't Ca-
naan, but it would have to do. A thoughtful man as
well as Wilshire's most prominent merchant, he had
observed many things about his town.

Wilshire changed, for example, but it also didn't
change. People came and went, but they were frequently the same types of people. New buildings went
up where wooded lands and farmers' fields had been,
but in many ways the town retained much the same
personality in the 1990's as it had fifty or sixty years
ago. It was a quiet borough in central Connecticut,
midway between New Haven and Hartford, not completely suburban, not completely rural. For better or
worse, Wilshire was an "in-between" sort of place.

Many of the houses were older than the trees on
Main Street. And despite the fact that people from
both cities were always moving there, forcibly "gen-
trifying" the place, Wilshire still maintained an agricultural and mechanical link to the previous century.
The town was still home to six working farms, a cement foundry, and four factories: one that made wire,
one that made tableware, one that produced blown
glass and another, to the embarrassment of some,

that punched out cheap cigars: Vintage Connecticut
stogies, real stinkers, the type that used to give ball
parks and race tracks their acrid stench; the type that
Maury Fishkin's father, who had been born in Ger-
many but had lived in the Bronx, had smoked all his
life.

In its way, Wilshire was a town not dissimilar to
many others throughout the northeastern United
States. Then again, in many ways, it *wasn't* like any
other spot on the map of New England. Once again,
it was a place of in-betweens.

This was, after all, not the Connecticut of Fairfield
County, with expensive price tags, country clubs, private day schools and well-manicured lawns. Wilshire
was where the suburbs of New Haven collided with
old farming and manufacturing land, orchards, gravel
pits, foundries and construction depots, all of which
struggled for their economic existence. Some of the
orchards nearby had been let go in recent years, giving them a crowded, overgrown, unkempt look. The
one golf club in Wilshire, a big time enterprise back
in the fifties, had been closed and abandoned fifteen
years earlier. The land was now overgrown with weeds
and small trees.

"Wilshire is more Roseanne than Martha Stewart,"
sniffed a real estate broker from downstate Green-
wich in a much quoted remark a few years earlier in
The Hartford Courant. Many citizens of Wilshire were
left to wonder whether the remark was an insult or
a compliment, though it should have been obvious,
considering the source.

The central business district of the town of ten
thousand ran three blocks along Main Street, and an
equal three blocks up Center Street. The predictable
establishments were located there. A fire house and

a police station. Two banks. One local one, the Wilshire Bank & Trust Company, was as solvent as Fort Knox and hadn't changed its name for a hundred years. The other, an outpost of a large, scandal-plagued, deficit-ridden chain from Boston, seemed to change its name every season. Most recently, the Boston bank featured the logo of an 1840's style steamboat. Depositors were left to study the drawing of the steamboat, the symbol of their bank, and decide for themselves whether the ancient ship was sinking. It did have a slight imbalance on the waves, perhaps inadvertently reflecting the mother ship's relationship with the pesky Federal Reserve.

Also in the center of Wilshire were two sandwich shops. A furniture store. A pizza joint named Ferrara's done up with red, white and green Italian flags but run by a Greek family named Appopoppolis. There were two real estate offices, a flower shop, a small grocery store, the Wilshire Pharmacy, and a gas station that still featured an old Mobil gas sign with a red Pegasus. Also noteworthy was an old-style smoke shop, a place named Ritchie's, with perpetually dirty floors. The shop sold newspapers, magazines, candy, soda, beer, cigars, cigarettes, lottery tickets, and smokeless tobacco.

These businesses in town had been under relentless economic assault from a mall and a 24-hour K Mart located five miles away, but so far Wilshire had withstood the pressure. No one was getting rich in Wilshire, but everyone was making a modest living. It was a pleasant spot, particularly to those who didn't mind the town's militant insularity.

Just behind the center of town, adjacent to the firehouse and police station, was Lake Barbara, which covered about twenty-six acres and was open to swimming, boating, fishing, and mosquito breeding in the summertime and skating in the winter. Though shallow at one end, the lake was deep and cold in its center and it froze very nicely. Kids liked to skim flat rocks on Lake Barbara on their way to and from the middle school and high school, which were located adjacent to the lake and within view of the police and fire departments.

Like the woods that surrounded it, the lake was lovely, dark and deep—a Robert Frost sort of body of water—though what struck a lot of people about it was the eerie silence that always surrounded it, even when there was activity on it. Lake Barbara seemed to keep a lot of secrets. Perhaps the town did, too. There was often a strange silence about the town of Wilshire.

On that particular day in mid-June, Maury Fishkin arrived at his store at five minutes before nine. He swept his sidewalk and greeted two young women from the Wilshire Bank & Trust who were on their way to the post office. Then he went back into his store. Very recently, he had added a computer. His daughter, who lived in Virginia with her husband and children, had spent a week in Connecticut in April and taught Maury how to use a software that kept inventory.

Fishkin had resisted the computer at first, but was now one of its most ardent proponents. As he normally dealt with only a handful of customers on a Tuesday, he sat in the back at the computer screen and checked the store's finances. His longtime companion in the store was Pepper, an affectionate black Labrador who was ten years old and almost as much a local fixture as his owner. Pepper lay a few feet away as Fishkin worked at his computer screen.

The dog dozed gently. The dog did everything gently.

When working, Fishkin sometimes liked to patrol his hardware store with an unlit cigar in his mouth—one of the stinkers manufactured locally, naturally—and a New York Mets hat on his head, royal blue with an orange NY on its front.

The underside of the cap's bill had been autographed by Lee Mazzilli approximately fifteen years earlier. It was one of Fishkin's prized possessions. The decor of the store was in keeping with the baseball motif set by Fishkin's headgear: in the center of the store's back wall there were signed photographs of Tom Seaver, Ed Kranepool, Art Shamsky, and Ed Charles, plus pennants from the club's three most successful years: 1969, 1973, and 1986.

"Greatest team ever. The Sixty-nine Mets," Fishkin liked to tell customers who asked about the pictures. He particularly liked to educate Yankee fans and Red Sox fans on this point. There was always a twinkle in his eye when Maury talked baseball.

Fishkin was gruff-voiced and kind hearted. He kept a jar of old-fashioned candies on the counter with a sign reading, *Steal Some* on it. He extended credit to everyone and once—as a Christmas gift to the community during a bad local recession due to a lockout at the nearby Dinas Cement Foundry—wiped out every bill from every customer. His generosity had cost him twenty-five thousand dollars and nearly forced him to close the doors to his store. Then the foundry had reopened, the local economy had climbed back onto its feet, and Fishkin's Hardware had remained in business.

All that, however, was the past.

Shortly before noon, James Corbett, one of three remaining middle-aged males in the local tribe of thugs visited Maury Fishkin's hardware store. James was accompanied by his only child, a son named Isaac, a thin, demented teenager with bad skin, a narrow face, and a particularly unflattering haircut. He looked as if a bowl had been placed over his skull and then a lawnmower had been brought past. On his ear twinkled some chunk of metal that looked like the pop top from a beer can. Isaac had a piece of metal in his right eyebrow, too.

The Corbetts were a family of local bullies. They were solidly blue-collar, and had been a presence for more than a century in central Connecticut. They held just under a thousand acres of local land, on which they lived, farmed, and performed mechanical functions such as tractor repair and diesel maintenance. They owned a gas station, a truck stop, an oil delivery business, Ritchie's—the store that always had a dirty floor—land that other people farmed, and a parcel of otherwise useless woodland through which railroad tracks had run since 1887, and through which ConRail still hauled freight.

The latter practice was extremely profitable, akin to a license to print money, and had been for generations, though the family had resisted ever climbing to the middle class.

They liked being dirtballs and bullies. Rumor had it that they also had a thriving 'midnight auto' business, with chop shops in six contiguous Connecticut counties. They were bad news, all of the Corbetts, the three middle-aged brothers, James, Wilbur and Ritchie, in particular. No one in town liked them, and everyone eventually had to deal with them.

For example, builders of new homes knew better than to put in houses that didn't take oil heat, and no one else in Wilshire dared carry newspapers, magazines, beer, or cigarettes other than Ritchie's Smoke Shop. Someone else had tried to run a magazine and smoke shop back in 1965, but he had lost everything in a 2:00 A.M. flash fire, one that retained the suspicious scent of gasoline even after the Wilshire smoke eaters had extinguished it.

2:00 A.M.

That was another strange thing about the Corbetts. The men in the family were always moving around at night, doing God-knew-what. No one really wanted to ask—or know.

Maury Fishkin was one of the few men in town who wasn't intimidated by the Corbetts, and for many years the brothers had had something of a standoff with the former selectman.

"Bully boy bastards," Maury Fishkin used to call the Corbetts. "They ought to get themselves goddamn baseball hats with three B's across the top. Of course," he liked to add, "they're all so ignorant that they probably couldn't correctly spell three words in a row. Plus, their heads have points, so they couldn't wear caps."

James Corbett, a clan member in his early fifties, took the occasion of that summer morning to stop in at Fishkin's Hardware. Corbett was a '74 Buick of a man—bulky, overly muscular, laden with extra weight, heavily dented, and ugly to look at. All this in addition to being slow-witted.

He held the store owner in a pointless conversation while his son Isaac clumsily went through the adult tools in the back of the store. James intended for Maury Fishkin to be distracted by the conversation.

He wasn't. The shop owner's eyes followed the teen-ager. It was as crude a shoplifting exercise as it was calculated. The boy had wanted a hammer, so his Dad had brought him into town to steal one.

Isaac headed for the front door with his prize in-side his jacket. James cut off conversation with Fish-kin and left with his son. Nine dollars worth of petty larceny. That's what this was all about.

Maury Fishkin confronted the Corbetts on the side-walk outside his store.

"I want the hammer back," Fishkin said.

James Corbett looked at his son. Then his eyes raised to the shopkeeper.

"I don't know what you're talking about, old man," James Corbett said.

"You certainly *do* know," Fishkin answered.

A few frightened passersby stopped to watch.

"Your boy removed that hammer from my tool wall," Fishkin continued.

"I ought to kill you, you old fart."

"Before you try, I want my hammer back."

Fishkin extended his hand for the return of the tool.

"You're not getting it back," Corbett said.

Maury Fishkin's eyes narrowed into small, tight, in-dignant slits. "You might be able to intimidate every-one else in this town," he said to James Corbett, "but you're not intimidating me."

"No?" Corbett smiled.

"No. You're just a petty crook, and a lot of people in Wilshire are darned sick of it."

James Corbett's response was almost a chirp. He was enjoying this. "Well, we still have the hammer," he said. "It belongs to my son, and he's keeping it."

"In other words," Maury Fishkin said, "you *admit*

that you're raising him to be a no-good thief like the rest of your filthy family."

The mocking grin disappeared from James Corbett's face.

Now Isaac was getting scared. Just slightly. "Dad, it's okay. I'll give it back," he gloomed.

James Corbett whacked his son on the side of the skull. He ordered the boy to stand up for himself like a man. Then James Corbett turned back to Fishkin.

"Better take those words back, old man."

Maury Fishkin thought about it, weighed the words, then seizing the irony, misunderstood intentionally.

"I take back nothing from you except the darned hammer," he said.

Fishkin reached down quickly and pulled the hammer out of the teenager's hand with one strong snatch. First James Corbett and his son were shocked. Then Isaac Corbett, the spot on his skull still smarting from where his father had hit him, moved close and attempted to knee the old man in the groin. Fishkin was quick enough to lower a hand, the one holding the hammer, to partially protect himself. Isaac threw a punch at Mr. Fishkin, too, but when the teenager's hand struck the hammer, his young hand ended up worse for the contact. Isaac began to scream.

At that time, James Corbett responded with a punch to Maury Fishkin's stomach. Fishkin responded fiercely with the hand that clutched the hammer. Corbett's hand rose to block it, and the claw of the hammer struck Corbett firmly on the wrist, breaking it and leaving him to howl with pain. Bystanders across Main Street could hear the crack of the bone. When the teenager saw that his father had been injured, he retreated immediately.

Fishkin held the hammer tightly, bruised but temporarily victorious. He stood his ground for a moment, then returned to his store. Corbett, angrily clutching his broken wrist, withdrew to a pickup truck.

"You'll be sorry," he shouted to the hardware owner. He followed the threat with a string of curses interlaced with some anti-Semitism. "You just remember this day, you stupid old Jew fuckhead. You'll pay."

"Go to the devil," Maury Fishkin said.

Then he closed the front door of his store.

He walked to a rear counter, pulled out a shotgun, loaded it, and placed it next to his computer.

Once again, Wilshire was an in-between type of place: usually peaceful, but every once in a while at war; a place where traditional businesses now kept their records by computer, but also had a shotgun handy.

For a week nothing happened.

The old man had thwarted the family of local bullies, and the story circulated through Wilshire, as well as the nearby towns of Wallingford, Southington, Meriden, Hamden, and Cheshire. Each morning when Maury stepped into town wearing his well-shined shoes, white shirt, red bow tie, and dark slacks, as if nothing eventful had actually happened, more people came out to greet him. Their smiles were wider, and there was an extra edge of appreciation to their good morning wishes.

In return, there was an extra bounce to Maury Fishkin's step, an extra reason to smile, and maybe even a new reason to feel good about some of the things he had always worried about in Wilshire.

Fishkin was a local hero. The Corbetts hadn't even done anything in return, though the whole town expected it. A feeling of relief washed over Wilshire.

The conventional wisdom about the Corbetts changed abruptly. They had been considered dangerous. No one even knew exactly how many first and second cousins there were, counting marriages and degrees of consanguinity, and with their creepy pattern of intermarriage, an actual count could become problematic. If someone became his own uncle-in-law, for example, did he count once or twice? Nonetheless, the old belief had it that the Corbetts were to be carefully avoided.

The new conventional wisdom was that the family had long since shot their spunk as an intimating physical force in central Connecticut, despite the last people to deliver fuel in the area having had their trucks vandalized, and the rival smoke-shop-newsstand having been torched in the 1960's.

Both of those episodes went back years, it was now argued. The Corbetts were dying out, lived out on their old aggie-and-mecky complex in rickety buildings. They kept horses, sheep, and a smattering of other malodorous livestock, and stayed to themselves. The males in the family weren't very alpha any more; in fact James, Wilbur, and Ritchie had all entered a graying, paunchy, ugly middle-age. They weren't much to be feared unless you were a six pack of cheap beer, and the hammer incident only underscored the truth of that new assumption. It was possible that the provincial reign of Corbett terror had finally terminated.

So went the revisionist thinking.

Then things began to move into ominous territory. Isaac Corbett, the teenage hammer thief, started

showing up in town each morning and keeping a
strange, silent vigil across the street from the hardware store. He just stared at the place for an hour
or so, and left. Fishkin went out to talk to him once,
and tried to befriend him by taking him out for a
hamburger. The teenager cursed profanely at the offer and stalked away, only to resume his vigil the following morning.

Then, on the last day of June, Maury Fishkin's dog
disappeared in broad daylight. The Lab had been sitting peacefully in front of the store one minute and
was gone the next. Witnesses remembered seeing
members of the Corbett clan in town that morning—
Wilbur, James, and Isaac.

To Fishkin, there wasn't much question as to what
had happened to Pepper. If he did not *exactly* know
what had happened, he surely knew who had caused
his beloved Lab to disappear.

Fishkin didn't bother to go to the Wilshire police.

Chief Elmer Moore was playing out his twenty-five
years to retirement while the Board of Selectmen
wrung their hands over finding a replacement. Chief
Moore currently was looking to close out his tenure
in one piece and collect a monthly retirement check
well into the next millennium. He didn't want any
serious trouble with anyone. Plus, Chief Moore was
chronically ineffectual, and afraid of the Corbetts. To
make matters worse, two slow-witted Corbett first
cousins, DeWayne and Lukas, were patrolmen on the
twelve-man Wilshire force. They always knew when
something was imminent which concerned their clan,
the only bits of police work to which they paid full
attention. It was also well-known in town that De-
Wayne Corbett aspired to the job of police chief, despite having no qualifications for it. It was widely

rumored that the family was in the process of intimidating board members into voting DeWayne in.

As for the Connecticut State Police, Maury Fishkin wasn't counting on much help from them, either. Wilshire had long been a black hole for the Staties. The town of Wilshire police were known to be ineffectual, and the local Corbett clan dictated local law as they saw fit. Because of this, and because things had been this way for as long as anyone could remember, the state troopers' high command didn't like to waste much manpower on Wilshire. The results weren't worth the effort.

So Fishkin went out to the Corbett farm himself, with his shotgun in the car. He confronted James Corbett on the front porch of the farmhouse. James now wore a makeshift splint on his badly swollen wrist. The Corbetts didn't believe in doctors.

No one knew what words were exchanged, but the whole town could imagine. No shots were fired, and no one ever learned whether Fishkin went to the door of the farm with the shotgun or merely had it in his car. What was apparent was that Fishkin returned from the farm that day, and was in his store the next.

He said nothing other than to tell people that he had "had a talk" and that "things are being worked out with those bullies."

And Pepper?

"I'm going to get him back," Fishkin told people. "James Corbett promised."

No one bothered to point out that a verbal promise from Corbett was as worthless as the paper it wasn't written on. Maury Fishkin must have thought he was going to get the dog back, for one day he closed his store punctually at 6:00 P.M. and went to his car, a dark green Chrysler. Two witnesses on Sturgis Street said they *thought* they saw him driving toward the Corbett farm.

Fishkin was not seen again. Nor was Pepper. Nor was the car. Nor was the shotgun, which presumably had gone with Maury on his second visit to the Corbett farm.

So the conventional wisdom shifted yet again, this time reverting to the original presumptions and prejudices. The new conventional wisdom: the family was as dangerous as ever, as lethal as ever, and no one in his right mind ever stood up to them or courted trouble with them. It was clear that something horrible had happened to both nice Mr. Fishkin and his dog, Pepper.

The Connecticut State Police reluctantly joined the search. A docile, gray-haired uniformed trooper named Tom Sheehan, coasting through his final eight weeks on the force, was assigned to assist the local police. For a few days Trooper Sheehan's car was seen all over Wilshire, but the local police had nothing to go on, and thus nothing to offer the Staties.

An old man and his dog had disappeared. Things like that happened all the time. Some missing individuals turned up at the casinos or jai alai frontons. Some of them were found floating in the Long Island Sound. Others surfaced a few years later, with new wives and second families, in distant states like Oregon and Minnesota.

Maury Fishkin, however, didn't turn up at all that summer. At one point, four local cops and Sheehan drove out to the family farm to eyeball it. A justice in New Haven issued a limited search warrant for the barns and fields to see if Fishkin's dark green Chrysler could be located. It wasn't. The fact that DeWayne

Corbett was one of the searchers probably did nothing to help.

Fishkin's Hardware remained closed. Maury's daughter reappeared from Virginia to try to tend to some family business, then went back home. One night, around 2:00 A.M., some anonymous vandal put a rock through the plate glass window of the store. The police boarded up the window the next day. As a precaution, they boarded the door and the other window, also.

The effect created a major eyesore in the center of town, a little scar, a sign that the community had been wounded. Often, under the cover of darkness or very early morning, flowers were left on the front doorstep.

Signs showing affection blossomed. Some said, *Hurry back, Maury.* Others said, *We miss you.*

Conventional wisdom again emerged: Maury Fishkin was not coming back. Further rumors surfaced about the old family burial grounds out on the Corbett farm and some fresh tractor work that was being done there.

Tom Debevic, a local pilot, was talked into flying his Piper Comanche low over the farm to look for any fresh digging. He did, didn't find any, and when the right wing of his plane was hit with two bullets from a deer rifle on its second low pass, he took the hint and didn't invade Corbett air space again.

The back half of July scorched New England. Then came a very muggy August. Hazy, hot, and horrible were the meteorological signs of the times. Wilshire involuntarily broke a town record for consecutive ninety degree days, adding to the sultry, oppressive mood that gripped the town.

Many afternoons were punctuated by violent thun-

derstorms, and in one bizarre incident involving tur-
bulent weather the local firehouse was partially destroyed by a freak tornado. It was as if the
disappearance of Maury Fishkin had set off some
sort of atmospheric quirk, as if the gods were upset
with what had transpired in Wilshire.

The town's weekly newspaper, a struggling little
publication called *The Wilshire Republican,* ran a series
of articles in August about Fishkin's disappearance,
and mentioned the missing merchant's recent incident with Corbett *père et fils.* But then the paper
dropped the story altogether after they, too, had a
2:00 A.M. fire, and their one delivery truck was found
one morning with six broken windows and four
slashed tires.

The newspaper had been in a state of declining
circulation for a while, and the owners had had no
insurance since the week before the fire. The fire and
the vandalized vehicle put *The Republican* out of business. The paper—or what was left of it—was then sold
dirt cheap to a woman from Boston named Ellen
Wilder, a journalist, who was currently employed by
the big paper in Beantown and who had always
wanted to run a hometown paper.

The new owner knew no one in the area. To the
locals, this sounded like another disaster. A single
mother from a big city who thought she could come
in and be an expert on the Wilshire community. Collectively, the town cringed. What they really did not
need was an outsider bringing them their news. Well,
it barely mattered. Few people read that local rag,
anyway, and speculation was that Ms. Wilding or
Wildthing or Wilder would come and go in a year,
anyway.

September arrived. The hot weather remained.

There was one final event of note: The town realized that it had gained just what it did not need—another Corbett.

The new arrival was named Frank Corbett, a huge, hulking lug who looked as if he were in his late twenties or early thirties. Exactly which branch he swung from on the family tree was unclear. The central triumvirate of the family, James, Wilbur, and Ritchie, all referred to the new arrival as their nephew, and Isaac referred to him as his cousin.

He had come east from Ohio, and, according to those who knew the family, had run away from some foster home many years ago as a teenager. The Corbetts claimed he had lived on their farm as a boy for a short while, but no one outside the family recalled knowing him. No one even admitted to being his father. He was just there. No one asked the obvious questions. Frank seemed to be no one's child, and everyone's child—just another member of the happy, malevolent tribe.

Praise the Lord. Frank was six-and-a-half feet tall, and if anyone could have coaxed him onto the meat scale at the Wallingford Stop & Shop, he would have weighed in at about two eighty. He was a big, mean, vengeful looking man. His eyes were dull brown, and stared out at the world without curiosity. They sat in the middle of a thick head beneath a single band of dark hair that passed for a set of eyebrows. On his neck was a deep mesh of pink scars; it looked as if he had once gotten his neck caught in the blades of a lawn mower.

DeWayne and Lukas, the Corbett cousins on the police force, said they remembered him as a kid working on car engines, but at other times they said they didn't remember him at all. What everyone did know was that Frank was enormously strong, currently able to lift automobile engines by himself—much easier, he said, than using the hydraulic lift. He was strong as an ox, they said behind his back at Lorna's, one of the more popular eateries in Wilshire, and almost as smart. He was pumped up and looked like he used steroids. The one thing he didn't look was normal.

He even had a trick he could do with regulation handcuffs. His cousins DeWayne and Lukas stole a few sets of cuffs from the police department so that he could demonstrate.

Frank would put a pair on his wrists. Then he would jerk his arms apart with such sudden ferocity that he could break the manacles. This would silence any bar.

Frank Corbett. *Franny.* That's what people called him.

Franny.

The thing was, there was something significant about Franny that no one outside the family could quite place.

Franny had returned to Wilshire the summer that Maury Fishkin and his Lab had disappeared, but had he been seen before? Or after?

Were the events related in any way?

No one knew. As the hot, tense summer ground to a muggy conclusion, keeping in mind what had happened to the one man who had stood up to the family recently, no one had the courage to ask.

Autumn began.

And with autumn came a terrible series of events for the "in-between" sort of place named Wilshire, Connecticut.

Three

Motionless, barely breathing, Ellen Wilder stood a step inside the locked front door of her old house, her right hand brushing gently against the curtains that covered the window. Ellen watched the sudden, pulsating blue blaze of the police car as it moved down her street on the chilly autumn night. She turned her head slightly. Her eyes followed the blur of the cruiser's red taillights as the vehicle disappeared down Sturgis Road, leaving solid darkness behind it.

Town police, she told herself. *Not unusual to see them.*

The Town of Wilshire, Connecticut, did an okay job protecting its citizens, or at least making them *feel* safe, she had noticed. Whether or not they were safe was another question. It *was* unusual to see the local police go somewhere so quickly at this time on a Sunday evening. This was one stretch of rural-suburban America where Sundays were still a day of peace and rest.

Well, she reasoned, there were all kinds of people in Wilshire, including that little knot of troublemakers and petty crooks, the identity of whom were known to pretty much everyone. Then Ellen's attention and curiosity were piqued further. The first po-

lice car was followed by a second. The second car
was followed closely by a third. All three were going
as fast along Sturgis Road as good sense would allow.

This *was* unusual, and was surely more than a simple accident or domestic disturbance. She stayed at
her front door. The cars were traveling past her place
and, it occurred to her suddenly, in the direction of
Corbett Lane.

Corbett Lane led to only one place: the Corbett
Farm.

Well, Ellen reasoned to herself, God only knew
what went on in *that* place. Ellen had been in this
community for one and a half months, new owner
and editor of the only newspaper in the town, *The
Wilshire Republican,* and she knew already that there
was absolutely nothing normal about the Corbetts,
their family, their history, their relationship with the
town of Wilshire, or even their ancient farm.

She waited for more action out on the road. None
came. A little cloud appeared in the sky above the
trees before her house. She watched it pass in front
of a quarter moon and drift away.

Still no more traffic.

The late autumn night grew dark again outside her
home. For a moment she felt a surge of anxiety. What
was bothering her? she asked herself.

Something. An invisible, unbanishable something.
It was almost palpable. It bothered her all the more
because she couldn't identify where it had come
from.

She had spent a dozen years in journalism in New
York and Boston. Over those years she had won a
husband, gained a child, lost a husband, and honed
reportorial skills that had brought her a mixed bag
of trouble, controversy, and accolades.

And instincts. She had gained some keen instincts along the way, and at age thirty-five she felt they were working very nicely. Something within her always clicked in when something was up. Now, with these police cars speeding down a country road, she could almost smell it.

She sighed and closed the curtain.

She had spent her dozen years as a big city reporter, then as a contributing editor. Journalism had been in her family; her late father had won two Pulitzers in his career. As the single head of her household with a nine year old daughter, now recovering from the trauma of burying a son, she had been certain that the time had come to make a move.

Two months earlier, when *The Wilshire Republican* had come up for sale, Ellen had used every single resource and contact she had acquired over a lifetime to become editor, publisher, and full owner of a failed central Connecticut weekly newspaper.

The Wilshire Republican.

The paper wasn't necessarily Republican any more; editorially, it wasn't much of anything beyond congratulatory messages about the high school sports teams (who rarely managed to break even) and observations about the change of the seasons.

Ellen wanted the paper to serve more than Wilshire. Yet more than once, she had wondered what lunacy had taken hold of her to make such a move. The paper had suspended operations a month before she bought it, and Ellen had done well just to resurrect it enough to publish one issue in late September, under the bold headline:

We're Back!

In that issue, she introduced herself to the community and asked for patience and support to keep alive the only Wilshire paper. Her announcement seemed to have been met with a colossal yawn. What she had grossly underestimated before moving into this area was just how sleepy and complacent Wilshire was. A local fire, for example, was lucky to draw anything more than the six local firemen. Whether the volunteers even showed up depended on what—or who—was burning.

A second issue of *The Republican* had followed in the first week of October, then a third. Three Wednesdays in a row she had sold enough advertising to pay her small staff of part-time reporters, who also lent their opinions to the editorial pages.

Never mind paying herself. Often, Ellen was in the office alone, answering the phone, writing, or squeezing blood out of the ledgers. Increasingly, her paper was a one-woman operation in a town and county that had little appetite for a local newspaper, much less a liking for a woman with strong opinions. Fifty cents a week was too steep for most of the locals to care.

Sometimes, she felt like taking her newspaper and swatting the townspeople over the head with it. The local Board of Selectmen, which governed the town and had seats for five voting members, was down to four members following Maury Fishkin's disappearance. It would remain that way until the next election, a year away, or until Maury Fishkin surfaced. Meanwhile, as Ellen had witnessed herself at the most recent meeting, those four stubborn adults couldn't agree on anything—where to lay a new sewer extension, where to buy fuel for the buses for the elementary school, whether or not to buy new tires for the police cars.

They voted two to two on everything, then sat there and stared at each other—an old man and a young woman on one side, a young man and an old woman on the other, negative images of each other—perfectly offsetting each other's views, and greatly missing Mr. Fishkin, who had always led them past such impasses. They met two Mondays a month in a school auditorium, usually in front of an audience of fewer than a half-dozen townspeople. How, Ellen wondered, would they ever decide on a new police chief when they couldn't even surmount the trivial?

Wilshire was not exactly the most inspiring place she had ever lived. In fact, she was already missing the bustle of city life, even the proximity of it. And she had greatly underestimated the thick-skinned provincialism of the area before she had purchased the paper.

Yet the houses were fine, and the section of the country was prosperous. The location *should have been* excellent. There *were* other people like herself here who wanted more out of life than a lethargic, dirty-fingernailed day-to-day existence. Wilshire should have been more than the sum of its parts, yet somehow it was less.

On the same day of the third issue, the one that preceded the trio of police cars speeding down her street, she had sat down with Ken Karp, a blustery, sad-eyed accountant. At the end of a grim two hour session, she had felt like another misguided woman in business. It was doubtful, the accountant indicated, that the paper could survive another winter.

Thanksgiving and Christmas advertising would get her through December, the bean counter explained, but the first quarter of the following year would spin off thousands of dollars in losses. She could either absorb all that red ink, Karp told her coldly, or close down before she took them. There was no guarantee that spring and summer would be profitable, either. The bigger papers in Hartford and New Haven had recently cut their ad rates just to drive the smaller local weeklies out of business.

"It would've been nice for someone to tell me this *before* I bought *The Republican,*" Ellen said with obvious cynicism.

"No one's going to tell you something like that," Karp answered. "It's the type of question you have to ask for yourself. Didn't you take any business courses in college?"

"No."

Karp made a little smirk. "I can tell," he said.

At the end of the meeting, Karp also asked to be paid on the spot. She boldly wrote out his check. Afterward, she wondered why she was trying to fool Karp. He had just seen her books, the financial equivalent of having been seen naked.

And yet, even in the face of the dismal numbers, there was still another voice rattling away inside of her. This voice told her that she would see her way through this crisis just as she had many others.

She sighed again.

Well, the police cars were gone, and didn't appear to be coming back from their destination—not immediately, anyway. She put them temporarily out of her mind. She had done enough of her daily agonizing about the fate of her newspaper, and there was nothing more to do on that front on this day.

Instinctively, as a former reporter, she checked her watch and made a note of when the police cars had gone past.

11:14 P.M. It was time to call it a day. She would

look in on her daughter, Sarah, and then get some sleep herself.

Ellen turned and walked up the stairs to the second floor of her home. At the landing at the top of the steps she stopped abruptly, thinking that she had heard a strange noise: a knock somewhere downstairs, a vibration or a creak that she hadn't recognized or heard before.

Or had it been a gentle rap?

Mice? Squirrels?

It was the time of the year when the outdoor temperature was dropping precipitously. Small creatures always tried to move indoors and share the heat from the oil burner—rent free, the little pests.

Ellen intended to catch them live with Have-A-Heart traps, then get rid of them by turning them loose in the woods at the other end of town. From there, Sarah had laughingly pointed out, they could regroup and create a staging point for further invasions into other people's homes.

This hadn't sounded like a mouse or a squirrel. The sound had been, well, *larger*—if she had heard a sound at all.

Raccoons pillaging the garbage cans outside? Possums? A cat?

She cocked her head and waited to see if the noise came again. It did not. She felt a little wave of relief. She chalked it up as an "OHN"—an Old House Noise. That's how she described to her daughter those ominous things that go bump in the night. OHN's. Friendly "Old House Noises."

For Sarah's benefit, Ellen had transformed those inexplicable cracks in the dry floorboards and creaks in the old hallways into friendly sounds. Mysterious blips in the darkness were now signs that the house actually loved its occupants. That was the bill of goods that Ellen had cleverly sold her daughter. Sarah was now convinced, because she trusted her mother, but secretly, OHN's still made Ellen nervous.

She listened again, but the sound did not repeat itself. Ellen gratefully moved on.

Sarah would be sleeping soundly, as she always did. Ellen arrived at the doorway to her daughter's room and pushed the door open. A ribbon of light flowed into the nine-year-old's bedroom.

Ellen's gaze settled with reassurance on her sleeping daughter. Sarah's face was pretty, unspoiled, freckled, and pure, framed softly by her blond hair. Sweet as a sugar-coated dream, any restlessness settled by sleep. It was much like Ellen remembered her own face when she was a child, though looking closely at her daughter's features she also saw the likeness of Sarah's absent father—something that always bothered her.

The marriage that gave birth to Sarah had lasted eight years, and Sarah's father had been out of their lives almost as long. When Ellen had married Brian Kalman, he had been a commodities trader with a good brokerage house in Boston. He had been eight years older than she, once divorced already. Financially, he had been doing well, but he had had his secret side: a cocaine habit that took more and more time and attention, and an incurable thirst for skirt chasing. Ellen had given him more chances than she could count. Inevitably, the illegal trades, the drugs, and the endless adulterous affairs, including one with his ex-wife, collapsed around him. He became physically abusive at home.

One night, Ellen took two suitcases, filled the trunk of her car, and grabbed her daughter. She took her resumé to Boston and found a job at *The Boston Globe*. She reclaimed her maiden name and pursued the career she had begun in New York. Aside from the formality and brutal paperwork of the divorce, Brian Kalman had been out of her life since. So had most other men. Somehow, affairs had always left her shortchanged. She had learned to be independent and push romance and remarriage far from her thoughts. She'd conceded, defensively perhaps, that it would never happen successfully for her. So why look for it? Why seek what was not going to happen? Yet there were days when she looked at married couples who appeared to be happy, who appeared to be making a relationship work, and felt that there was something missing in her own life.

Only a few moments passed as she gazed upon her daughter's sleeping face. Another car drove by outside. The vehicle was moving faster than one normally might at that time of night. Usually only one or two cars passed in half an hour. Now there had been five, including three police vehicles. She wondered anew what was going on.

She glanced at her watch again. Eleven twenty-two.

A window in the upstairs hallway overlooked the front of the house. Ellen stood there for several minutes, waiting to see if any of the vehicles would come back. Or, she speculated with the experience of someone who had worked as a reporter, would she next see an ambulance going down the same road?

Or had she *just missed* the ambulance? she wondered next. For a few more minutes she waited to see if any vehicles would return. None did. That, too, was strange.

She checked her watched a final time. Eleven twenty-eight.

She glanced down the hallway of the second floor. There was a third bedroom, also. It was the disaster room in the house, painted a horrible brown by some previous resident and currently empty. She had to do something with that room, but she just hadn't had the time yet—or the inclination—or, with meeting payrolls at work, the extra dollars.

Well, okay, Ellen concluded, taking a final look out the front window. Someone somewhere in the baili-wick was having some excitement, but it wasn't her. If anything significant had happened, her own report-ers would tell her. Peter Whitely, an experienced local writer who was also her best advertising salesman, was on call this evening. It was his duty to keep an ear on the police radio.

Just in case.

For all she knew, Peter's car had been one of the two vehicles following up on the scene. Number four or five to zip by.

She went into her bedroom, leaving the hall light on as usual. Just above her head, a creak in the attic floorboards irritated her anew.

Cool October weather seeped through the shingled roof and permeated the attic. The weather forecasts were already touting a blast of unusually cold air heading in the direction of New England, but to-night, hot air from the skeletal heating system in the basement rose into the bedrooms. Should it have been any surprise that the attic floor creaked?

She washed and changed for bed, putting on a heavy cotton nightgown before sliding under the cov-ers. She picked up a book from her night table. She read a dozen pages until she felt warm, safe, and comfortable. A final drowsiness tiptoed up on her.

For a moment, Ellen closed her eyes with the room lights still on.

She felt herself nod. Yes, a soothing sleep was finally claiming her for the day.

Her eyes flickered open, and she glanced at the bedside table to the light and the clock radio.

Midnight. Exactly midnight.

Downstairs was a big grandfather clock that she had bought at a flea market in North Carolina while she was married to her crook-junkie-adulterer ex-husband. It was one of the few items that she had salvaged from her crashed marriage. The old clock chimed long and sonorously. It was also her cue to get herself to sleep. An odd, dreamy thought was in her head, half of a nonsense phrase. *Sixty minutes before the wolf.*

What wolf? What was that idea all about?

Ellen dismissed her dream fragment.

She turned off her lamp and settled in to sleep. Her thoughts meandered and twisted in various directions. Tonight, her mind waltzed backward through her lifetime. She mused about the brief affair she'd had in college. And her son, the one she had given up.

The one who's, you know, dead right now, Ellen, dear, said some irritating voice inside her. She wondered again about Robin, the son she had given birth to but not raised. She wondered about the life he had led. She wondered what things or photographs his surviving family members could someday show her. She wondered when she would have the courage to look at such things.

Of course, he'd be alive if he had stayed with you, the voice said next.

She felt a cold angry chill and turned over between

her sheets. She knew she wasn't the only woman who could torture herself with second guesses and self-doubts. She also knew she was very good at it.

She turned on the radio to some soft rock. Anything for a little night time company.

She had looked into the faces of a thousand children since her son had been born—every male child who looked at her, every young boy who in some way resembled her or her one-time lover.

How long, she wondered, would she be haunted by it? How long would it bother her? A lifetime? Even longer? If she could have traded everything material that she owned for the opportunity to have gazed upon him living again for only a few minutes, she probably would have taken the deal.

If only she could have spoken to him, had a conversation . . .

But such deals were not to be made. Life didn't work that way, and her departed Robin was often the last thing she thought about each day as she fell asleep.

She finally fell asleep, aided by the distraction of the music on the radio, and slept solidly for only one hour. Then the telephone rang.

She groped for the phone, clicked on the light again, and listened to Peter Whitely, her reporter.

All those police cars had been headed about two miles down the road from her, she learned. An anonymous phone call to the police had led to a body being found under circumstances that were, if anything, bizarre.

She sat on the edge of her bed, her desire to sleep fighting hand-to-hand with her old reportorial instincts.

She was then startled a second time. She heard footsteps in her house.

Distinct footsteps. In the hall. Coming closer.

She saw a shadow cast by the form of a body, back-lit by the light from the hall, the one light that remained on all night.

"Sarah?" she called.

"Mommy?"

Ellen exhaled. Her daughter stood in the door. Logic and common sense prevailed. Who *else* could Ellen have possibly expected?

"Did the phone ring?" the little girl asked.

"It rang, honey."

The little girl looked at her anxiously.

"Don't worry, angel. It's not anything bad for us," Ellen said. Then, thinking fast, she added, "How 'bout you grab a blanket, Miss Sarah? Take a snooze in the back seat while Mommy goes to look at a news story? Can we do that?"

"Can I miss school tomorrow?" Sarah asked impishly. Day or night, with the greatest of charm, Ellen's daughter was always trying to cut a deal.

"No-o-o-o!" Ellen answered, standing and scolding good-naturedly.

Sarah grinned, but with some fatigue.

"Who's gonna stop us?" Sarah asked.

"You're right, Miss Sarah," Ellen answered. "Who in the world ever stops us?"

They laughed. Moments later, mother and daughter were down the stairs, in the car, and out onto the unlit, winding road that traveled to the Corbett farm.

Four

What Ellen would remember most about her arrival at the stretch of Corbett Lane just before the bend that led to the farm was the eerie light cast by all the police cars. That, coupled with the fact that Sarah, good kid that she was, had gone right back to sleep in the backseat of the Honda.

Flashing red and flashing blue, the lights were all over the place. Ellen carefully lowered a window a crack but left her engine running. Her daughter needed air and warmth.

Ellen was greeted by the rumble and incessant crackling of an armada of police radios. Then Chief Elmer Moore, the senior local cop in Wilshire, a cigarette hanging from his lower lip, led her to something large under a big tree. Something large under a blanket with something long and narrow protruding from it. This was not the geometric pattern of anything she had ever seen before.

Moore was a thick, graceless man with a formless white face. He was nearing sixty, paunchy, and balding. He had the shape of a giant hamster. His sidearm hung at his side carelessly—he still packed one of the old-style six-cylinder Colts. Not that it mattered. He hadn't fired a shot on duty in seventeen years, and hadn't even been to the pistol range in Milford in the last three.

"You sure you want to see this?" the chief asked.

"Show me," she said, bracing herself.

"Show you?" he said. Repetition of questions was a Moore habit, one that wore thin on the unaccustomed listener fairly easily. "Okey dokey."

He led her to the spot. Under the tree, his body bent and broken at impossible angles, was James Corbett, now dead at fifty-three. It appeared that he had fallen—*jumped or been pushed?*—from the sprawling maple that he now lay beneath.

Somehow, to make the act complete, or at least add a memorable detail to it, he had landed on the teeth of an old pitchfork. The teeth had passed through his neck and throat. The jugular vein must have been pierced, because James was in the center of a mud puddle that was very red and very wet. He was facedown.

"So what's James Corbett doing in a tree in the goddamned evening with a pitchfork?" Chief Moore asked aloud.

"Eating cereal?" asked one of the uniformed men in a low voice. He followed this piece of wit with a schoolboy grin. A couple of officers looked up and discussed what branch James must have come down from. Neither DeWayne nor Lukas Corbett, the second cousins and family members who were on the force, were present, so their brother officers were perfectly free to not withhold their joy at seeing a local troublemaker meet his end.

Moore gave the officer a look of mild reproach, but made no other indication of disapproval. Surrounding the body was an array of beer cans. Five empties. Old Milwaukee.

"What's he thinking when he jumps out of the tree? Is he looking to kill someone, scare someone, or just kill himself?" Moore asked.

Then he thought it through a few steps further.

"For that matter," he growled, "what the fuck's he doing up in a tree with friggin' barn equipment? Goddamned fuckin' Corbetts. Always somethin', and always somethin' in the middle of the cocksuckin' night."

Ellen shook her head and averted her eyes.

"As if I care," Moore mumbled. He raised his eyes. "Sorry about the language, ma'am," the Wilshire Chief of Police said then, his gaze settling on Ellen. "I'm not real partial to coming out here in the middle of the night."

"That's all right," she answered. "I know all the same words you do."

Chief Moore gave her a weak smile, not getting her point. "These fuckin' Corbetts," Moore repeated. The phrase was becoming his mini-mantra for the evening.

Ellen had seen enough. More vehicles were arriving. She wandered over to Peter Whitely and saw that he was taking careful notes. She studied the scene and hated herself just a little for the thought that followed.

This, she involuntarily told herself, *will sell a lot of local papers. This we must cover thoroughly, and better than anyone in the state.*

She kept herself within earshot of the profane Chief Moore. This time, however, she gave no indication that she was listening. She had learned more than a few things in New York and Boston, and how to look like an innocent lady when she was scooping a story was one of them.

She glanced around, pleased to see that no other reporters were there. So she and Peter had the crime scene to themselves. She watched approvingly as Peter walked quickly back to his car and retrieved a camera. The police let him take photographs. In fact, they encouraged him, because none of them had thought to bring a camera.

"Jesus Christ, these fuckin' Corbetts," muttered the chief again. "At least now there's one less of 'em, so we got that to be thankful for."

Ellen made no response. The dead body was covered again.

Chief Moore's eyes rose in surprise to assess a new arrival.

"Michael!" Moore said, finally breaking into his first smile of the day. "Hey! Holy shit! Alive and in person!"

Michael Chandler, a detective with the Connecticut State Police, nodded in response. The two men knew each other casually, Chandler having worked a few cases in Wilshire over the previous few years.

Chandler was a sturdy, six-foot man who—against the odds—was edging into a dark, combat-weary middle-age. His once light brown hair was now graying mildly at his temples, but he exercised regularly and maintained good physical conditioning. His eyes were dark blue, his shoulders square. He had the classic American face and bearing that one might expect from a baseball player or a soldier, yet over the past year it had acquired the lines of stress and fatigue that inevitably befall any man. It was well-known among police in the state that Chandler had been shot during a particularly dicey operation in Bridgeport some several months back. The case had been all over the newspapers. Chandler had been pronounced dead, and then been raised from a gurney by an extra round of electric zapping and his brother's gentle pistol point persuasion of the doctors.

"What the hell are you doing here?" Moore asked. "You catching tonight?"

"I'm in statewide homicide now," Chandler said. With one deft motion he reached into his breast pocket and flashed the gold shield of a first grade detective. He clipped the shield to his jacket.

In his head something funny was happening. There was strange background noise to this whole place—a silence that was so still and so intense that it created almost a feedback effect, a ringing in his ears.

He shook it off and figured it was just one of the funny things going on in his head these days. Recently returned to active duty after medical and psychological leave—granted due to the so-called "shot and killed" incident—Chandler found that there were a lot of things in life that didn't make perfect sense any more. Fact was, a lot of things probably never had. He had just never noticed.

"That makes my presence here official," Chandler said.

"Statewide homicide now?" Moore considered it. "Well," he said. "Congratufucking-lations. Great place for someone who's been shot and killed himself. Must give you extra insight, huh?"

"Maybe it will," Chandler said.

"Anyway, Mike, if you get off on dead bodies, you've come to the right friggin' place tonight, that's for sure."

Ellen Wilder's gaze had followed that of the local

police chief, and she assessed the state homicide detective. She thought he was nice looking.

"Goddamn," Moore said. "If I'd known it would have took a pitchfork through a Corbett throat to get you out here again, Michael, shit, I would have done it myself. Sorry about the language again, Mrs. Wilder."

"It's not a problem, Chief," she said, a little air of fatigue slipping into her tone.

"That's good, 'cause I don't know no other way to chitchat. Ask my wife. If you fucking dare. Of course, my bride's got a worse mouth than I do." A couple of the officers smirked at that one. "Oh, and Mrs. Wilder? Do you know Detective Chandler?"

"No," she answered.

"Mrs. Wilder here now runs the local newspaper," Moore said. His cigarette was down to a one inch butt with an angry orange end. He dropped it and snuffed it.

"The Republican," Ellen said.

"Never voted for one. Ever," Chandler said with a wink. "Come from a long line of union and working people."

"Do you ever read my paper?" she asked.

"Sorry. I didn't know it was still published," he said.

"We're off to a great start, aren't we?" Ellen answered.

She smiled, the best smile she could muster under the circumstances. "I won't hold it against you," she said, "even if I thought I should." She paused. "I'll send you a copy," she said. "That way you won't have to forage through a newsstand."

"Thanks," he said. "I'd like that." He meant it.

He reached into his shield case and pulled out a business card.

Detective Michael Jude Chandler
Connecticut State Police

It bore his office address and telephone number as well as his pager number.

"Looks like you've got your front page for the next edition," Michael Chandler said. He eyed the corpse. "So who *is* the victim?" he asked, looking back to Moore. "Everyone seems pretty happy around here."

"Who's the victim? Shit! You've never heard of the Corbett family here in Wilshire?" Moore asked.

"Corbett?" Chandler asked.

"James Corbett."

"Uh oh," said Chandler.

"Yeah," the chief said. "Right."

"One of *the* Corbetts, huh?"

"That's two in a row you got right."

"That narrows it down to a few thousand people who'd want to do this, huh?" Chandler asked.

"A few thousand who'd want to do it. Finding the guy with the balls to do it is something else." Moore paused. "Unless he done it to himself. Know what I mean?" The old cop had a hopeful look in his pink eyes.

Chandler shrugged.

"I've heard of the clan," he said. "That doesn't mean I know everything about them or recognize them when I find them dead."

Chief Moore laughed, a sharp, little ironic snort. "Lucky you," he said.

Moore turned to Ellen. "State police don't like to

come into Wilshire none too much," he said. "Ain't worth their time."

"Why not?" she asked.

"Nothing good happens here, so why should they want to get involved in it?"

"Why does nothing good happen here?" she asked, uneasy with his statement.

"It just don't, lady. That's all there is to it."

"We also don't come in because there's a certain protocol," Mike Chandler told Ellen. "Chief Moore can tell you about that."

"Protocol?" she asked.

"Huh? Bullshit," Moore said.

"It's a matter of territory," said Chandler. "If the town police don't ask us in, we don't come, unless the situation warrants it. We need to be invited."

"Bullshit," Moore said again. "You flat hats don't *want* to come to Wilshire."

Chandler crouched down and looked at the body. He made sure Corbett was dead: no pulse. He glanced up.

"So maybe it's a little of both," Chandler said, seeking to conclude a meaningless discussion. He counted the beer cans and looked at the specifics of James Corbett's death attire—oily overalls and a greasy white T-shirt, no jacket.

"Territory, huh?" Ellen asked. "So it's a male thing? Like dogs with trees?"

"You'll do well here, Mrs. Wilder," Chandler said, not looking up.

Chief Moore stood by, almost lost now in the exchange.

"So tell me about the Corbetts again. Local farmers, right?" Chandler asked. "Or mechanics?"

"What?" Moore answered.

Details again. Chandler motioned to the dead man with a nod of his head. He reached into a pocket and pulled out a pair of rubber gloves. Ellen admired his professional approach, particularly at that hour.

"He's wearing mechanic's overalls and he's got motor oil all over his hands, wrists and shirt," Chandler said, his gloves in place. "But he's dead with a piece of farm equipment. So which was he?"

"What's the farm equipment?" Moore asked. "Six beer cans?"

"There are only five cans," Chandler said without re-counting. "And a man's dead here, Chief," Chandler answered as Ellen watched him. "It's the middle of the night. Could we get to the point? Mechanics or farmers?"

Moore sighed. It was the sigh of exasperation of a man being dragged to work.

"Yeah," he finally answered. "The Corbetts are farmers sort of the same way John Dillinger was a disgruntled farm kid, and they're mechanics in the same way that the Unibomber was an electronics geek."

"Real bad guys," Chandler said aloud as if to fix it in his own mind, or for Ellen's consumption. "No good."

Moore lit another cigarette. He filled the chilly air around him with a thick haze. He hacked a thick, rich guttural cough and spit out the results.

"The worst," he answered. "You've got a bit to learn here, Mike," Moore said. "Local clan of backwoods bully boys. Won't be an awful lot of tears at the funeral for this piece of scum."

"Did he have family?"

"He's got three," Moore answered. "Third wife. First two left him when they got tired of being beat up before sex. Not like his brother Wilbur, the family capon." Chief Moore glanced at his men again. They provided a wonderful captive audience for his late-night humor. "I like to think that maybe Wilbur don't have no kids thanks to a fancy accident with a threshing machine, but there's probably some other reason."

"Yeah," Chandler said. "Probably."

"Take a look at the crime scene, if you want, Mike. We got to get the body ready for the cadaver caddies," Moore said.

"Aren't you going to give it a look?" Chandler asked.

"Give it a look? Already did," Moore said without much interest.

"May I do this?" Chandler asked.

He motioned to the head of the corpse. He indicated that he wanted to move it slightly to take a better look.

"Take it home with you if you want," Moore said.

Gently, respectfully, Chandler lifted the deceased's head. The face of James Corbett, which had been buried face down in the wet ground, came into view.

"Hey, that would be one of those late-night movies that plays on the UHF stations, wouldn't it? If cops started taking home heads?"

"Lord . . ." said Chandler slowly. He recoiled from the face of the dead man. Instinctively, Ellen and Chief Moore moved to a position where they could see, too.

Ellen winced. Moore only stared, but both noted what Chandler had found. The dead man's face was still contorted in a look of terror as well as agony. His eyes were open and bulging. His face was twisted. His mouth was open in a scream that no one could hear any longer. It was as if, in the final seconds of his life, James Corbett had seen something hideous from another world.

Chandler laid the head down carefully. He had seen enough. He stood and removed his gloves.

"Cold night, don't you think, Chief?" Chandler asked, standing.

"Yeah. I suppose so. Why?"

"Are we supposed to think that he was sitting in a tree without a coat or a jacket when rain is possible and the temperature's in the forties?"

"See those beer cans, huh?" Moore asked.

"I saw them."

"That's Irish anti-freeze."

"I'm just saying the scene here doesn't add up," Chandler said.

"And I'm just saying that it's no big fucking deal if it don't," Moore answered. "When it comes to the Corbetts, don't look for things to add up. 'Cause they never do. And you'll only get yourself further bent out of shape if you try to make 'em add up."

"I hear you," Chandler said. "I don't necessarily agree. But I hear you."

"That's all you got to do as long as I still wear the star in Wilshire," Moore said with uncharacteristic annoyance. "Hear me."

Ellen found herself looking curiously at Mike Chandler, wondering if he was up for what was before him. And, as the next few minutes unfolded, she also felt another wave of instincts kicking in.

Every single one of them scared her.

When she looked down and carefully studied the dead man, she noticed that his eyes were still wide open. Chandler *had* noticed something both horrifying and intriguing. What was it that James Corbett had seen in the moments before he had died? It must have been truly hideous.

Were they both overthinking? She wondered if it had been the nearness of death itself that had so frightened him. Had it been the agent of his death? or the fright itself that had done him in? And the pitchfork through the throat? Had it been simply a quaint rural afterthought, designed to throw the police off course? She knew that even if Chief Moore wasn't thinking in these directions, the state police detective was. She carefully slid his card into a pocket and stepped back from where the body lay.

Absurdly, every once in a while there was a flash of light at the scene, creating a weird, strobe-like effect each time. The origin was Ellen's reporter, Peter Whitely, and his camera. Each picture reminded Ellen that her paper was still in business.

A few moments later, a truck from the state medical examiner's office arrived. Chief Moore authorized the body to be removed.

Once again, Ellen's cynical streak kicked in. *The Wilshire Republican* had been the only paper on the scene, and she had more of the story than anyone. Sometimes getting a scoop was just being in the right place at the right time.

Chief Moore turned back to Detective Chandler.

"Know what, Michael?" he said. "We're going to have to take a trip to the fuckin' farm. Someone's gotta tell the family and get some papers signed on Brother James."

"You want me to go?" Chandler asked.

"It would be good if I had a Statie with me," he said. "Less chance that one of those morons would vent their grief with a shotgun."

Chief Moore thought about it some more.

"On second thought," he said, "to hell with it, Michael. I'll send DeWayne or Lukas out there. It's their damned family. Doubt if they'd blow their own kin away, although you'd never know."

"I'll go if you want," said Chandler.

"The more you stay away from that place," the chief said, "the happier you'll be." He drew hard on his cigarette. "Just remember that," he said. "The less time at that filthy old farm, the better. And whatever happens out at that place, don't get too involved."

Sometimes children tumble into a sleep that is too sound and too deep. Sometimes their bodies slip into a state that frighten parents. If sleep is death's counterfeit, is death also sleep's counterfeit?

Ellen had once written a feature for *The Boston Globe* on a subculture of photography in Massachusetts in the early 1900's. Families who had children who died in infancy or early childhood often dressed the child in his or her best clothes for burial, lay the body on a bed, and hired a photographer to record the child's passing.

Ellen had examined several dozen haunting, old black-and-white photographs. She had been struck by the manner in which the children appeared so much at peace.

Little angels. Actually, little corpses.

Sometimes it chilled her when she saw her own daughter asleep, particularly in a deep, cozy slumber. The look was as beatific as those ghostly old silver nitrate jobs from 1903, of kids who had missed their entire lifetimes. Now, because she had lost a child recently, the memory of those photographs chilled her all the more.

Ellen returned home almost an hour and a half after she had left.

Sarah was breathing steadily but would not awaken. She was getting to be a big girl, and getting heavier as she grew. Ellen managed to carry her upstairs and put her back in bed.

She tucked her in and kissed her.

It was only then that Sarah, as if to confirm her mother's wishes, opened her eyes very slightly and smiled.

"Thank you, Mommy," she said.

Then she rolled over and slept. Deeply and soundly. Ellen joined her in sleep. It was 2:00 A.M. exactly. The grandfather clock downstairs, with its portentous heavy chimes, tolled the half hour.

Five

Earlier that same Sunday evening, before jumping into a green Jeep Cherokee to travel to the location of James Corbett's death, Michael Chandler had sat alone in a small new house in the town of Meriden, fifteen miles north of New Haven. It had otherwise been a quiet Sunday evening, and Detective Chandler had attempted to relax.

Relaxation did not come easily. These days, he was given to dark moods which could get progressively darker until no light was visible. Mike Chandler was a man who now lived with badly frazzled nerves, diminishing patience, and a mind that was poised to travel through doors and windows that had never been open to it before.

Tonight, however, he *had* successfully relaxed on a leather sofa in front of a wide-screen television, a prized possession into which he had just sunk a crazy two thousand dollars. The projection picture on the television was as sharp as a scalpel, and was the size of the rear end of a small truck. The sound system, when tuned to sports, gave him the feeling of being not just *at* the game but *in* it, so while Chandler wasn't exactly in Heaven, he did feel as if he were approaching it, not for the first time.

It was late evening and he had not been home for long. Chandler hoisted his feet onto the sofa and kicked off his shoes. The sports came on the television as he removed the cap from a bottle of Pabst Draft. His other hand rummaged through a dish of potato chips. One from each important food group, he figured.

This time of year, sports to Chandler meant ice hockey, and the news was not good. His beloved New York Rangers had scored twice in the first period, then stood by as the hated Philadelphia Flyers filled goalie Mike Richter's net over the next forty minutes. Final score: Infidels from Philadelphia Six, Rangers Three. Well, at least there had been a good brawl in the third period.

Chandler sighed. What kind of world was this? He was not too far from his fortieth birthday. He had spent almost fifteen years working in plainclothes and carrying a gold shield, yet now he was having a tough time figuring the world around him.

The sports news broke for a gaudy commercial from a local tribe of Native Americans who were running a gambling hall in central Connecticut. What made them a fortune in 1998 would have sent them to the federal slammer in Danbury in 1978, and there they were advertising it on the tube.

Then came a message from a Chevrolet dealer named Hy in Milford, who claimed to own the biggest lot of "previously appreciated" automobiles in New Jersey. Hy now promised, as a gesture of his limitless good will, that he would sell any customer a car without a single dollar down. He was a regional celebrity by now, thanks to his ads.

"You know Hy! He don't lie!" proclaimed Hy, himself. "If you have a pulse, I can sell you a car!" Convenient, Mike Chandler thought, in case the viewer had just blown his last few paychecks at the nearby roulette wheels.

He sighed again. He could remember a more orderly time in Connecticut when gambling was illegal, people went to church on Sundays, not local casinos, a used car was called a "used car," and vehicles were sold primarily by local dealers, not carpetbaggers from Trenton.

He could also remember when most people in Connecticut spoke English, even the immigrants who worked at Sikorsky Aircraft in Stratford. Back then, Spanish and Korean were not languages of which a state cop like his father—the man who had urged him into a police career and then been his early mentor—would occasionally need to know.

His father, Captain Peter Chandler.

His father, who had loved to dispense advice. A piece of favorite advice returned now to Mike Chandler: *Help put the lives of other people in order, and you'll put your own in order at the same time, huh?* He could almost hear the old man's voice.

Car dealers and casinos. Koreans and con artists. In addition to being an edgy, moody man, Michael Chandler remained an observant one. He saw not just these people, but the little details by which they defined themselves.

Details, details. Chandler was always focusing on them.

The details of a man or a woman told so much. The way a man lit a cigarette—was it with confidence or with an air of guilt? The car a man drove—was it clean and new and orderly, or old and ill-maintained? The way a woman brushed her hair, wore her skirt, or crossed the room frequently told him whether she was looking for a suitor or trying to avoid one, whether she was confident, with a settled life, or was unhappy and seeking changes.

Eye contact said a lot. So did physical bearing.

Chandler's father, a respected captain in the state police who had pushed two sons toward police work, had been one of the finest instructors in watching for details. Now Mike was a lifelong student, whether he wanted to be one or not.

He finished his beer and decided not to open a second. The late local TV news concluded.

Chandler channel-surfed to some beach volleyball via ESPN. The sun! The California shore! Yeah! Hard-bodied five-foot-eleven babes in bathing suits. Now *there* were some details he didn't mind dwelling upon this evening.

He smiled and turned off the television.

For a moment he sat in silence.

Damn!

Why didn't he just admit it? Something was bothering him, and he could not put a finger on exactly what it was. Deep down, however, he had plenty of suspicions:

A recent romance had broken up, one that he thought would lead to marriage. Then there was the impending second anniversary of his father's death. Both contributed to a disturbing loneliness that he felt increasingly these days. This, coupled with the looming prospect of his fortieth birthday, seemed to be weighing upon him heavily.

Granted, on paper his career was going just fine. He had recently been moved to homicide after injury leave for several months early in the year. He had picked up the advancements and promotions that he wanted within his department. He was respected among his peers and by his commanders. It was obviously, he figured, the *personal* situation that troubled him.

The *injury*. The incident with a local ne'er-do-well named Tito Mareno that culminated in gunfire earlier this year. The incident that the psychiatrist kept telling him to put out of his mind which he couldn't—not completely.

But then, catching a bullet, flirting with death, and coming out of it with a partially wrecked left shoulder and upper arm were not things that a man could easily ignore.

How he wished he could—but he couldn't.

So he opted for the second beer, after all, even though the solace he found in alcohol was a little danger signal in and of itself—particularly since being shot. Over and over that incident with Tito Moreno played in his mind, like a movie on a single looped reel. It seemed to be *always* at the edge of his consciousness, repeating itself.

He shoved it away for the evening, even though the reminders were there—even opening a can of beer, or unscrewing a bottle of beer, brought with it a twinge of pain in the area of his wounded nerves.

He knew all the stories about cops who hit the bottle too hard after traumatic injuries or near-death experiences. The booze provided solace, but he was battling to keep it in check. Every day was a struggle. Sometimes he felt himself very much on the edge of things. He kept his own counsel on all of these. There were state police offices in Hartford just looking for men like him to furlough and retire. When Mike Chandler retired, he promised himself, he would do it on his own terms. He didn't want to be let out to pasture by the bureaucrats. That was a lousy fate, second only to being gunned down on the job.

He straightened his living room and kitchen. Unlike many men who lived alone, he kept a neat, orderly home. It disappointed him that other aspects of his life couldn't fit so appropriately in place.

He went upstairs and settled into bed.

Still, his mind was working.

He lay perfectly still and finally isolated what was bothering him. It was a deep down, inexpressible sense of *imminence*. His nerves were wound as tight as a drum, because he had an overwhelming notion that *something* was about to happen.

Something big.

Something horrible.

Something unlike anything that had ever happened to him before.

He lay in the darkness just before ten and felt as if he were being enveloped by a major league premonition. He wondered whether this was part of aging—a creeping sense of mortality, a little pathway from a man's youth to middle-age through which everyone travelled. No wonder the booze sometimes helped.

For many minutes sleep refused to descend.

He could hardly have described this feeling to even his most trusted friends, this spooky sensation hanging on the other side of his subconscious. What was going on?

His shoulder began to trouble him again. The pins and needles feeling, the tingling sensation that could become pain or become numbness.

So fitfully, impatiently, he turned in bed. The tingling eased. He wondered how psychosomatic the discomfort was. Was the pain in his mind, or was it like a divining rod, sensing trouble before trouble was even visible?

Finally, sometime before eleven, sleep did come. He lay in peace in the dark silence of his home until nearly 1:00 A.M. He had a dream. A nonsense dream about a plain woman with brown hair. She had a funny name. A name formed in his mind for the first time. *Janine Osheyak.* Never heard the name before.

He had never met her. He figured it was one of those funny sex fantasies which made no sense. The name only stayed with him because the sound of the telephone split the night and ripped him out of his sleep. He turned on the room light as the phone kept ringing. Insistently. Rudely. Demanding. Calling him to the scene of James Corbett's death.

When he answered, his sleeping senses beginning to unscramble and the voice on the other end of the line beginning to make sense, he realized that his premonitions had been uncannily accurate.

He set down the phone, paused for a moment, and felt the sweat settle on his brow.

Back before the image of brown-haired Janine, he had been dreaming of—

That part of the dream had been quizzical, even in its horrific nature. He was dreaming of a dead man standing by a tree in a forest, looking at him.

Looking *for* him.

A dead man who was gradually introducing him to other dead people, all of whom were standing, moving and communicating, otherwise seeming alive, in a worldly sense.

God Almighty! What an image!

He tried to deduce what location they had been in, where that dream was set, but he couldn't.

He struggled against the vision, fighting off the

dream as best he could. He dressed quickly, picked up his weapon and his badge. Within a few minutes, he was in his dark green Jeep Cherokee, which was specially modified and equipped with a police radio beneath the dashboard. Through ice, snow, and mud, he had crashed along more than one impacted country road in this vehicle.

Tonight, the obstacles were not those of weather. Tonight, Mike Chandler was nursing his darkest fears on his way to work, drawn by both his commanding officer and a set of long buried events that he could not yet understand.

In the Cherokee he realized that he had just entertained a vision that was refusing to go away. At the core of that image of dead people waiting for him, there had been a certain brightness and light.

He gave a deep, shudder of horror. He knew immediately where he had seen it before. His shoulder gave him a pang of pain, another of those sharp spasms, and then the tingly numbness followed. He wondered if in some bizarre way, that bright light was drawing him back.

And he knew that this woman he kept picturing, this Janine Osheyak, was all part of the tangled puzzle.

Six

DeWayne Corbett had drawn the assignment of informing the other family members of James's worldly demise, a task that he had set to shortly before dawn that same morning. Meanwhile, the medical examiner in New Haven had the body, performing his usual voodoo against the family's wishes, seeing if there were any telltale clues that might distinguish a murder from a suicide from an accident.

A very tired Michael Chandler stood in Chief Moore's office at the Wilshire Police Department.

"The Corbetts have a way of dealing with their enemies," Moore said. He sat at his old desk at the rear of the Wilshire police station. The desk was long and broad, with ball-and-claw legs. It had been picked up at the local Goodwill twenty years ago during one of the budget rampages by the Board of Selectmen. Despite the predictable flags, photographs, and congratulatory certificates, it made the chief's office look like the back room of a faded movie theater.

Elmer Moore spoke through a carcinogenic tobacco haze. He coughed, a big loose ugly cough.

"What way is that?" Michael Chandler asked, sipping coffee. A thorough fatigue rattled through him, not surprising on one hour's sleep.

"Which way is that?" He laughed. "Oh, they murder them," Chief Moore said simply. His tone was routine. Matter-of-fact. He might just as well have been talking about livestock. *Oh, they feed them. Oh, they sell them. Oh, they murder them.* Chandler was already understanding why the state police were so frustrated in this town.

He turned back into the chief, who was still speaking. ". . . so it wouldn't be a real shocker to learn that some godfearing bastard had come along and murdered one of them back. Heh?" Moore asked.

There was laughter around the room. The laughter was partly nervous. There were three other Wilshire cops in the room, and Michael Chandler was the only one not laughing.

"You're not serious. Right?" Chandler asked.

"Not serious? I wish I wasn't," the chief said. "Oh, hell. Maybe they don't always murder. But they always go about trying to intimidate. They're a whole fuckin' clan of bullies. No one can do nothing about them."

"Give me an example," Chandler asked.

"An example of no one doing nothin'?" Moore asked. "Or an example of them being bullies?"

"Either. Both," said Chandler.

"Shit," said Moore, to the amusement of his men. "You got all day, or just the afternoon?"

The men around the chief laughed again. Then the recent stories began, including some of the lesser known ones, incidents in which the Corbetts were only *suspected* of their usual forms of retribution. There had never been any arrests.

"There was a horse farmer down the ways," Moore said. "Name of Benjamin Miller. Got in some fight with the Corbetts over the price of fuel oil. Someone went out in his stables one night and broke the right front legs of his best five mares."

"That was a typical thing," a Wilshire cop named Wes Kelly added. Kelly was a big man with high blood pressure and a red, craggy face. "Ben Miller had to have his horses put down by the vet. Know what I mean? The Corbetts don't just come around and *kill* your livestock or burn your house. They make you do it yourself. There's always a sinister touch."

"Yeah, that's their trademark," said another cop, named Tom Forsythe. "The sinister touch."

"Like a pitchfork used in a murder?" Chandler asked.

"You could look at it that way," the chief said solemnly, "but only if you wanted to."

Forsythe mentioned another case.

James Corbett, the very late Jimmy Corbett, got into a fight in O'Casey's Bar over in Waterbury with a man named Snead who worked for Southern Connecticut Telephone. A week later, Snead's repair truck was sabotaged. The lug nuts on his rear tires were loosened—not removed, just loosened.

"A lot of punks would just slash the tires and be done with it," said Forsythe. "Or just pull the hubs off, so that the car wouldn't go nowhere."

"But that was pure Jimmy Corbett," Moore said. "The lug nuts wouldn't fly loose until the truck hit sixty miles per hour. So Snead was guaranteed a high speed accident."

"The timing was even such that it was at the end of the workday in the winter," Forsythe added, recalling the case. "That meant the truck would be on Interstate Ninety-one or Ninety-five at rush hour when it spun out."

"How bad was the accident?" Chandler asked.

"Two people killed, one woman paralyzed," Chief Elmer Moore recalled.

"And you investigated?" Chandler asked.

"Couldn't hang anything on anybody," Moore said. "The whole damned clan vouched for the fact that no one left the fuckin' farm all afternoon."

"That's what they always do. Vouch for each other," someone else said.

There was agreement around the room. The topic jumped to the case of Maury Fishkin, who had stood up to James Corbett and then disappeared along with his dog a week later.

"Nice man, that Maury," Forsythe said. "Used to wander around his store in a Mets cap and chomping a cigar. Gave my family credit when Dinas Cement was laid up."

There were nods around the room about poor Mr. Fishkin. Then the topic arose of the two young Corbett males, cousin Lukas and DeWayne, who were on the Wilshire police force.

"Spies," said Chief Moore. "Spies and pricks. They never make good arrests, never put in extra effort, and probably commit as many crimes as they make arrests."

"Why keep them on the force?"

"Why keep them? I got grandchildren, and I'm five years away from retirement. Think I want to end up impaled on a pitchfork, too?"

The other deputies laughed. Behind his back, Elmer Moore's nickname was "Fudd." His men took him that seriously.

"Plus, what the hell, at least I know where they are when I got them on the force."

"Aren't you sort of copping out on your duties here, Chief?" Chandler pressed.

"Copping out? I'm staying alive!" Moore retorted. He took a final drag on his cigarette-in-progress and leaned forward. "Know that scene in that great cowboy movie?"

"Which one?" Chandler asked.

"Uhh," said Forsythe, rising as if to leave. "Here comes the chief's *High Noon* sermon."

"Listen, you guys shut up!" Moore snapped.

He turned to Chandler, the only one in the room now paying attention. "You know that *High Noon*? That great Cary Grant movie?" Moore blustered.

"It was Gary Cooper, Chief," Kelly said hopelessly.

"What about the movie?" Chandler asked Moore.

"Well, it's the same here!" Moore said, snuffing his cigarette angrily. He was indignant, and suddenly very serious. "You think the town is with you, you think people will fuckin' stand up. Then on the day you want support, you're out there all by yourself. Alone."

"So you don't get the local support against these people? Is that it?" Chandler asked.

"That's only part of it. They're scared. With the Corbetts on the force, you can't even count on secrecy here. DeWayne and Lukas always know when something's up."

Chandler sighed. "I hear you," he said. "But it seems as if the town police force is at least a little intimidated, too."

Moore bristled.

"Intimidated? Bullshit!" he snapped. "Let me tell you—after Maury Fishkin went missing, we went in and tossed that fuckin' farm. Went in with a search warrant. Brought four state cops with heavy weapons and had Tom Debevic fly over in his goddam airplane. Didn't find shit. Where were you for that?"

"I'd just come back on the force. Disability."

"Oh, yeah. I forgot. You got whacked, didn't you?"

"Tell me about the search," Chandler asked.

"We even looked in their damned lakes," Moore said.

"Looked in? You didn't drag them?"

"You know how much that costs? Think I'm going to get money from the town for that?" Moore asked. "Look. There's this theory, too," Chief Moore tried. "Maybe Maury Fishkin was just scared. Maybe he went away. Took his dog and went away until things cooled down."

Kelly was shaking his head.

"Nah, that ain't what happened, and we all know it," Kelly said. "Does Fishkin walk away without clothes? Does he walk away from a profitable store?" he asked. "And he'd been in the community here all his life. Where's he gonna go?"

More nods around the room as Chandler made mental notes.

"Yeah, I guess it doesn't make sense, does it?" Moore said, retreating.

"Hey, old Maury's dead somewhere. We all know that," Forsythe chimed in.

"Well, too bad," Chief Moore said. "Because Uncle James is gone now, too. Hey, well at least they now have Franny out there."

"Who's Franny?" Chandler asked, glancing around the room, seeking to be included.

As soon as he asked, he knew he had hit upon something. The room fell very quiet.

"The latest thug to emerge from the clan," said Chief Moore. "He appeared several weeks ago after living out in the midwest for a while. Right about the time Maury Fishkin disappeared."

"Is there a link?"

Chief Moore shrugged. "Don't know," he said.

"Was Franny interviewed on Fishkin's disappearance?"

"The only cops he'd talk to were Corbett cops. Lukas or DeWayne again. Both officers said Franny had an alibi."

"Let me get this straight." Chandler said. "This one family has this whole police force quaking in its boots? Am I correct in this?' "

Chief Moore's self-righteousness rose quickly. So did his defensiveness.

"Listen up, Chandler," he said. "I'll give it to you real straight here. The Corbett clan's been an albatross for this town for longer than anyone here's been alive. Jimmy falls out of a tree and lands on a pitchfork. Well, fine. Who the fuck cares? If someone pushed him, they should get a medal. If it was a family member, we'd never be able to prove it. So you know what we do? We leave it alone."

"What if a Corbett was involved in the death of Maury Fishkin?" Chandler asked.

"Probably was. But we'll never be able to prove it."

"No body, either," Wesley Kelly chimed in. "No body."

"Where do you think he went?"

"My own opinion?"

"Sure."

"I think old Maury's probably planted out there on the nine hundred fifty acres somewhere. But I can't prove it, and I can't find it, and no one ever saw his car."

"So then?"

"So then we don't have a case yet. What are you gonna do?"

Chandler thought about it. "I know what I'm going to do," he said.

"What's that?"

"Have a drive out to the farm," he said. "You've got a death and a disappearance, and the link is the Corbett family. Where would they dispose of a car and a body?"

Moore shrugged.

"Almost anywhere."

"Maybe they took it to New York State or somewhere," Kelly said.

"They wouldn't do that," Chandler said. "People like that are like cockroaches. They never move too far from where they're born." He glanced around the room. "If Mr. Fishkin was murdered, he's buried somewhere locally."

Shrugs all around the room—the prevailing sentiment of the entire local constabulary.

"I want to go out to that farm," Chandler said. "I want to take a look."

Chief Moore sighed.

" 'A look'? A fuckin' *look?*" Moore shook his head. "Hell. Go out to that farm and you know what you'll find? Nine hundred fifty acres and probably nine hundred fifty questions, and probably nine hundred fifty answers you don't want to know."

"I still want to see it for myself."

"Michael," said Moore, trying to talk sense. "We're going to mark James Corbett an accident, okay? That means you can go home, go back to the barracks, and work on something useful. If someone killed James Corbett, he should get some sort of medal. I'm serious. Not a pair of fuckin' handcuffs."

"I still want my look," said Chandler.

The police chief grimaced. "Don't say I never

warned you," he said. "You go out there, it's like
sitting in a closet and shaking a hornets' nest."

"I'll let you know how I did," Chandler said. "Unless someone here wants to ride backup."

Everyone rushed to not volunteer at once. If the
death of James Corbett remained unsolved for the
next hundred years, it appeared, that would have
been just fine for all the local officers in the room.

Chandler got to his feet and gathered his things,
in preparation for taking the ride by himself from
the Wilshire town center out to the Corbett farm.

For more than a century, a narrow road in central
Connecticut led past a lake and through a wooded
area and arrived at the Corbetts' farm. The road was
called Corbett Lane by the locals, even though there
was not a single street sign to proclaim it such, and
on maps it either wasn't there or existed as a thin
blue line. It wasn't such so much a lane as a country
road. In some ways, the path was also a state of mind,
as were many things involving the Corbetts.

Regional lore had it that the Corbetts had named
the road Corbett Lane back in the 1880's, and no
one had been in any position to object. There had
been some scandal at the time. There had even been
rumors that the family, setting their claim to a perverse sense of brutality and inhumanity, had buried
one of their male members, Jethro Corbett, under a
winding stretch in the road, instead of in the family
cemetery located in a wooded area on the edge of
their farm, a family burial plot that remained active
into the present day. The centerpiece of the cemetery, and the oldest grave there, was the tomb of Jeremiah Corbett, a Civil War soldier who had become a

hero by getting in the way of Confederate artillery at Cold Spring Harbor.

Jeremiah's son Jethro had been different, and hadn't been included in the family cemetery. The Corbetts liked to say that they had planted Jethro Corbett there on Corbett Lane as a sentry.

A ghostly sentry.

His spirit would maintain a vigil against visitors or intruders for eternity, or so they said. It was common for families to plant such rumors, if not actual bodies, back in those days. Rumors of that sort produced a sort of northern voodoo, and a fearful distrust of evil sprits kept superstitious immigrants, freed slaves, and robbers away from one's property.

According to local legend, there had also been "sightings" of Jethro in the early 1900's. So people had thought, though no one took into account that there were fifteen living Corbetts at that time, eight of them male, five of those adult, and they all looked alike. They were thick-browed and stoop-shouldered. They were rugged and gloriously slow-witted.

All of them.

So who was to say, on a dark summer evening just past dusk, or on a winter afternoon, when night arrived before 5:00 P.M., exactly who had seen whom? Not back then, and not any time since.

The road, and the naming of it, was a small but stubborn metaphor for this family. It had loose dirt, branches, and dead leaves piled at its shoulders, as if the pathway had recently been excavated out of the earth. It could have been in any of the surrounding Northeastern states, Massachusetts, or Rhode Island or New York. On colder days it could even have been farther up, in New Hampshire or Vermont.

The rumor of the ghostly sentry had never been

supported by any reasonable thinking people, even though it had its appeal to local superstition. The same ancestor, either Jethro or Jerome—the name varied depending on whose family bible one looked at—had also been seen out in one of the far western states, Nevada. Persistent stories had it that in the 1900's he had gone into the claim-jumping business, drawn by the riches of silver, become wealthy, and worked out a common law marriage to a Carson City madam, with whom he raised either his family or someone else's.

So never mind the part about him being buried under the road. Never mind the part about him having made pregnant—forcibly the police said—the daughter of a New Haven banker, which may have expedited both his trip west and the supposed "burial" beneath the road. And, while in the business of forgetting about things, never mind the part about the confusion over the name, also.

Jethro. Or Jerome.

Who cared?

Back then the whole family was illiterate, anyway. They made their cramped spidery X's on pieces of paper to conduct the business of their farm and, when all else failed, to honor their financial obligations.

A century and a decade had passed since all that, and not much had changed. Even the Corbett farmhouse had not transformed much over all those years. In deference to the twentieth century, modern convenience and the odd health code, plumbing and electricity had been installed.

There had been several new roofs on the white farmhouse and the two red barns. Some iron supports had gone into the basement of the family homestead, to keep the structure standing. And God knew, the bully-boy attitude of the family hadn't changed much, either. Why would it?

The back road that was known as Corbett Lane was the only road that led to the Corbett farm. It had originally been a dirt path between dairy farms, and the farmers of central Connecticut in the 1830's had driven their cows from one pasture to another along this route. The modern paterfamilias of the family, John Tillings Corbett, born in England in 1848, had annexed all the local farms around his own. He joyfully watched neighbors go into bankruptcy due to water that was suddenly polluted and streams that suddenly ran dry. In a few isolated cases, when all else failed, John Corbett acquired his neighbors' land by the means he favored least—outright purchase— though usually for a sum so low that it was believed that some sort of extortion was involved. Gradually he owned a 'devil's dozen' of thirteen farms and combined them all into one six hundred acre expanse of land in the center of the state.

The family also liked to put forth the notion that they were related to "Gentleman Jim" Corbett, the great nineteenth century boxer who had defeated John L. Sullivan, the last of the bare-knuckle heavyweight champions. As evidence they pointed to the James Corbett, 1845-1907, who was buried in the family plot. A few people believed the claim, but none who had consulted a sporting encyclopedia to learn that the real Jim Corbett, or actually the other and better known Jim Corbett, had lived from 1866 to 1933, and was buried in Binghamton, New York.

Heads of the Corbett family in the twentieth century behaved similarly to their founder. Each time a contiguous farm fell to their possession, new neighbors became targets. Often they bought adjacent land and subleased it back to the family from whom they had purchased it, making former neighbors their tenants.

By the 1930's, the family was both wealthy and militantly rural. None of the men went past the eighth grade. Some of them liked to tinker with trucks and tractors, so the family opened a machine shop for agricultural equipment, but hired other people to run it. Corbett males continually assaulted local women and beat the charges in court. Corbett men usually served in the armed forces of the United States, obeyed the draft, went off to all the major wars. To much local disappointment, they always came home unscathed and meaner than ever.

Rumor also had it that Corbett men had committed a handful of murders over the decades. Local enemies had a way of disappearing, including a Connecticut magistrate named Benjamin Finkel who had upheld a speeding violation—eighty-two miles per hour through a 15 MPH school zone at 7:30 A.M.—against James Corbett in 1955. Who had any idea, since the Corbetts owned all that land, including a cemetery, where the bodies of the 'departed' or 'missing', including Judge Finkel, might have been planted? The family was cut a wider berth than ever as the 1980's rolled through central Connecticut.

Then something funny started to happen. The Corbetts began to diminish. Not in wealth. Not in menace. Not in their sinister nature. But in numbers.

Dixon Corbett, who was head of the family in the 1940's, had only four children, all sons. Dixon, Jr., Wilbur, James, and Ritchie.

Number One Son, Dixon Junior, died in April of 1970 when a tree crashed into his speeding car. He was on his way back from Manhattan at the time, where he'd spent the day beating up anti-Vietnam-War protesters. He had had no known wife at the time.

Wilbur married, but was the family steer. He didn't breed, though not for lack of trying. He married three times, most recently to a thick-jowled foul-tempered woman named Lizzie who had only two passions: anchovy pizza from Louie's in Wallingford, and the UConn women's basketball team.

James, the third son, ran the oil delivery racket and was also an expert on car parts. He had a son, Isaac.

The youngest of the four boys, a wiry little stiletto of a man named Ritchie, was the brother who ran the newspaper store. Married, he'd had one daughter. He spelled his name with a "t" in the middle because that's how it had appeared in his father's hand on the birth certificate: Ritchard—a unique name for a unique and quarrelsome individual.

He was thin and weasel-faced and, in an act of vanity that often afflicts middle-aged men, had recently purchased a toupee. The fake top was a dark, wavy, inappropriate rug that had locally earned him the nickname of Liberace, though he was never called that to his face. When he wasn't wearing his wig, Ritchie affected a red bandanna around his skull—a central Connecticut white guy do-rag, which, in keeping with its owner, was one of the ugliest sights in Wilshire. Ritchie also drove a big, obnoxious red-and-white Chevy Impala. It was sixteen feet long, got eight miles to the gallon, and was said to have once hit one hundred and forty on the stretch of I-91 North from New Haven past Montowese Avenue, and a hundred and ten on the Merritt Parkway between Orange and Wallingford. Ritchie thought of these as something akin to local records, matters of distinction. Strictly speaking, they were.

There was even an irony involving Ritchie's operation of a newspaper establishment, as signs in his store were usually rife with apostrophe problems and misspellings. Ritchie had never read a book in his life—something he was frequently proud to tell people—not even a dirty one.

He did have some skin magazines at the back of his store, however, not far from the biker mags and the guns 'n' ammo publications. Breezing through the pictures from these three literary groups was enough to feed the intellectual drive of the youngest Corbett brother.

Ritchie's daughter had been a charmingly slutty girl named Gracie Lynn, best remembered in town for wearing pink micro-mini skirts, black anklets, and Doc Martens. Gracie Lynn had died of a drug overdose while in her third year of high school. Her boyfriend, who was reputed to have provided the drugs for her, disappeared one night two weeks later, either for his health or as the victim of a highly suspect accident. His Harley disappeared at the same time, and had never been re-registered in another state.

Gracie Lynn's death the previous November had left four living Corbetts. The family population was thus at its lowest ebb since the old original bastard, James Tillings Corbett, first started poisoning his neighbors' water supply in the 1870's.

Four living male family members, three of them middle-aged and one of them a teenager. Apparently, that had created a temptation that was too great for someone to ignore.

So on a cold Sunday night in October, things be-

gan to happen. Police cars started to fly down Corbett
Lane, and telephones began to ring in bedrooms
where people were sleeping.

Seven

Chandler drove slowly along the country road that led to Corbett Lane. It was the afternoon following the grisly discovery of James Corbett's body. Although the sun was shining, Chandler could see that a weather system was developing, one likely to bring cold rain and cold weather to the area.

In the meantime, however, smells of autumn filled his car, of dead leaves wet along the road and dry dead leaves illegally burning in someone's backyard incinerator. Well, that was a problem for the town cops, he mused. It wasn't his job to play bloodhound and track down the penny-ante amateur polluters.

He drove by the wooded areas on Sturgis Street and came to Corbett Lane. He passed the maple tree from which James Corbett had swan dived, for reasons yet unclear, onto a pitchfork. There was a car with a couple of teenagers driving slowly past it, the occupants gawking and looking up. A pretty girl of about sixteen was smiling, and the boy who was driving, baseball hat reversed, pointed to the branch that James had used as a diving platform.

Chandler looked at the kids and then at his watch. One o'clock in the afternoon. Didn't anyone go to a full day of school any more? An uneasiness filled him when he thought of the citizens of the America of the next century; the kids he saw these days didn't seem to know or learn anything.

He reached an open field just before Corbett Lane. Strands of mist hung over it—James' spirit, he assumed facetiously. The sunlight lay in bright strips across the field. He wished it would lay in similar strips across his mood.

He turned onto Corbett Lane. After two hundred feet he hit an unpaved mixture of gravel and dirt, followed by a series of bumps. A suitable welcome, he was sure. Nailed to a tree was a wooden sign that said simply *Corbett*, and spiked high to the trunk of another tree farther down the lane was a metal No Trespassing sign from a hardware store.

He slowed his car as he came to a closed gate. There was an intercom attached to it, heavily rusted and with the wires pulled from it. Chandler could see that it didn't work.

He got out of his car and undid a chain that held the gate shut. He looked at a grim, white farmhouse that seemed to be bathed by a heavy shadow. Flying off to the east and west from the farmhouse were a pair of rambling additions, several extra rooms of living space that had once been intended to keep this whole family under one tattered roof. The attempt had failed, as Brother Ritchie had his own depressed-looking gray cottage off on his own quarter acre. There were also two red barns adjacent to the main house, and fields that rolled back in each direction.

Chandler stepped back into his car and drove toward the front of the house, instinctively knowing that his arrival had probably already been noted. He stopped the car, stepped out, and heard a pair of large dogs barking angrily from within.

The detective paused long enough to look for the inevitable array of used appliances and found them on the north side of the house—two washers, one refrigerator, plus something large and rectangular that was rusted so badly that he couldn't tell what it once had been. The collection of dead appliances sat next to a pair of propane gas tanks. Beyond them were two long-retired vehicles, an old Cadillac with huge, rusted late fifties style fins, and what appeared to have once been a milk delivery truck for a now defunct dairy. The former had grass growing through it. The latter was four different shades of rust and had no unbroken windows. It matched Chandler's overall mood.

Farther back, behind the main house, most likely untouched by human hands for many years, were a set of broken, rusted swings and a sodden sandbox, its wooden perimeters rotting away—more of the little depressing details of life, the little hidden voices that told him so much.

Chandler turned his attention back to the business of the day. He went to the door, knocked, and stood to the side of it.

He had gone to a thousand doors in his career if he had gone to one. One time a barrage of bullets had greeted him, though it had missed. He had never stood flush before a closed door again.

As he thought about the incident, his shoulder suddenly began to throb, the tingling having intensified into a small, acute pain. God in Heaven, he was fortunate to have a friendly pharmacist in Meriden who would issue painkillers without a prescription to police and fire fighters. Then again, it was when he had been successfully *through* the door, that time in Bridgeport, that he had been whacked from ambush.

Chandler grimaced slightly and waited. He wondered about his own sanity, living his life like this, traipsing to door after unfriendly door, pursuing conversations and inquiries focusing upon man's inhumanity to man. He wondered if a sniper were following him right now.

He scanned behind him, the barns and auxiliary buildings in particular. He felt his heartbeat heighten. He listened to what was going on behind the door on which he had just knocked.

One of the big dogs inside acted as if it were going crazy. A frenzied, angry concerto of howling, snarling, and barking played through the door.

Then a woman screamed profanely at the dog, and Chandler distinctly thought he heard the woman take a strap to the animal—that, or she kicked it. He definitely heard the dog yelp. Then it whimpered and wisely shut up. Well, at least this was a little bit of a switch: today he could witness man's inhumanity to beast.

He seized that moment of comparative tranquillity to knock a second time.

A few seconds later, he heard a latch fall within, and a chain come undone. The doorknob rattled and the door opened. Chandler wished he had brought a backup.

A sullen, thick woman with a round pink face loomed into view as the door opened halfway. Lizzie Corbett.

Lizzie, the third and current wife of Wilbur was thirty-five going on fifty. She wore no makeup, and her hair was pulled straight back. She looked as if she had been about to receive an emergency face pack. Disturbingly, her hair was its natural ratty brown color.

No fancy cosmetics here. No cosmetics at all. And rarely were they so much needed.

"Yes?" she asked with a disapproving glare. "Who are ya, and whaddya want?"

Lizzie's left hand, holding a lit cigarette, hung at her side. She wore a pale green tank top with blue trim and stains. A complicated blue-and-red network of tattoos crept beyond her shoulders and a few inches down her arms: snakes intertwined with hearts and daggers, and a bare-chested sailor with a Hitler-style mustache.

As she spoke, she raised her wet, pinkish eyes over Chandler's shoulder, taking a quick census of any others that might have come calling. When she had scanned adequately, her censorious gaze came back to Chandler and thumped him smack in the eyes.

Chandler had his shield ready. He showed it.

"Detective Michael Chandler. Connecticut State Police," he said.

In the background now, from within the farmhouse, he heard the plaintive voice of a male country singer. Chandler was not deeply versed in redneck music, but he thought he recognized the husky, mellow twang of Dwight Yoakam covering a Willie Nelson tune.

"So?" she snapped. She eyed his state police shield before he flipped it back into its case. "I'm supposed to be impressed? Kiss my ass." Even the Corbett women had a certain primitive charm, he thought, probably gained by osmosis.

There was a foul smell in the house, and it now wafted forward. Too many dogs, too enclosed a space. Chandler noticed that her tank top was a basketball jersey.

Chandler felt as if he had come to the door of a

barn, one that hadn't been mucked out quite as thoroughly and hygienically as one might hope. To some degree the aroma was also redolent of death. Before his eyes flashed the many times he had come calling on the homes of missing persons, people who hadn't been seen in the normal places for a week, and had been met by the rotting scent of human decomposition even before he had the door open.

Meanwhile, Lizzie's long dry fingers gripped the door frame and she tried to push the door shut in his face. As delicately as possible, he didn't let her. He pressed a foot forward to halt the closure of the front door.

"Hey, asshole," Lizzie Corbett said. "What the fuck is this all about?"

"I'm here in connection with the death of James Corbett," Chandler said. "I'm sorry for the loss you've suffered in your family."

His words and thoughts had only traveled that far before she burst out in an even more intense anger.

"I'll bet you are," she said acidly. "Real sorry. Everybody is real sad, ain't they? Bet we can't die off fast enough out here to keep people happy, huh?"

Absurdly, Chandler found stock phrases of solace and consolation coming to him.

"I understand how upset you are," he said. "I really do sympathize. But I wonder whether you or Wilbur or James's other brother, Ritchie, could shed any light on what happened to James last night."

"Nobody here knows nothing," she said again. "'Cepting the fact that one of our family members got took down."

"Do you feel someone might have murdered him?" Chandler asked.

"I'm not talking to you," she answered.

"It would be helpful if you would," he pressed.

"Look, we work real hard here," she said, switching the topics as quickly as possible. "Nobody here at this farmhouse was born rich or nothing, nobody went to no fancy schools like Avon or Loomis or Choate over the ways, and nobody buys no fancy clothes or talks with ten dollar words. Corbetts get what they get from fighting for it, specially since everyone else fights to keep it from them, all right?"

"I need to talk to Wilbur," Chandler insisted. "Or maybe Frank."

Wilbur was out in the rear of the house, she said, and Chandler could walk around the house if he wanted to take his chances with her husband. "Drag your ass around back yourself," she said. "I ain't letting you walk through."

"What about Frank, Mrs. Corbett?" Chandler asked with endless courtesy. "He around?"

"You mean Franny?" she said, easing a notch.

"Yes. Franny."

She laughed. No, Lizzie said in response to Chandler's inquiry, she hadn't seen Franny at all recently—hadn't "hardly seen him none for a couple of days."

"Isn't that unusual?" Chandler asked.

"Nah," she answered. "I didn't see him none for eight years, neither."

"But Franny's living here now, isn't he?" Chandler pressed. "I would think he might be more visible."

"Franny's like that," she said, cooling down even more. "Sometimes he don't find his way home so good. I think he goes whoring in New Haven. How the fuck do I know what he does?"

"Well, this is important, Lizzie," he said, trying to keep the conversation as elevated as possible. "Eventually I really need to talk to Franny."

"I don't think he wants to talk to you none."

Chandler took her understatement under advisement. "Then maybe you could fill me in with the answer to a very easy question," he said.

"What?"

"I'm new in this area. Who's son *is* Franny?"

She paused and snorted. "Dixon," she said.

"Dixon was James's father, wasn't he?"

"Dixon, *Junior,*" she said. "The dead brother. The one who died in sixty-nine or seventy."

Chandler blinked. "But I thought Dixon never married."

"He didn't. He knocked up some woman in Ohio and had a bastard kid. The bastard kid is Franny."

"Ah," Chandler said, appropriately enlightened. "I see."

Somehow Wilbur must have known there was a visitor, because a few moments later he hulked quietly into the door frame beside Lizzie. He pulled her away from the partly opened door and replaced her in Chandler's view. She stayed at his side and watched their unwelcome guest with a dopey, fishy stare—eyes wide, mouth open, breathing noisily.

"You're a state cop, ain't you?" Wilbur asked.

Like the rest of the male members of the clan, Wilbur was big, burly, and pale faced. He was unshaven, a smattering of white whiskers sprinkled across the dark shadows of his jowls, and he wore a flannel shirt bearing extensive grease marks, both new and permanent. Matching marks were on his hands, and Chandler guessed he'd been beating up on the farm equipment out back. He smelled of sweat, petroleum, and—if Chandler's senses were serving him properly—a trace of marijuana.

Strangely enough, this bulky, craggy man before

Chandler had once been the family Adonis, a handsome, low rent Lothario in his younger years. Now he was all porked-up, and he came equipped with the self-hating, defensive nastiness of a man whose youth and good looks had gone all haywire. The qualities now fit so well that they seemed to have been factory installed.

Chandler flashed his shield and identified himself.

"So what the fuck do you want?" Wilbur asked. "We're in mourning here. We had a death. My brother."

"Could give me any insights into what might have happened last night?"

"Jimmy fell out of a fucking tree."

"Try this one, Wilbur. What was he doing in a tree at eleven P.M.?"

"Jacking off, maybe. How do I know?"

"Maybe you could try to help me a little more than that, Mr. Corbett," Chandler said. There was a sinking hopeless feeling within him.

"Maybe I could spread my ass and you could kiss both cheeks and the fucking hole, you dumb cop," Wilbur offered instead.

"And maybe I could come back with a warrant," Chandler said, his patience gone.

"A fucking warrant for what?"

"Anything I damned well want," Chandler finally said. "You might have the local police afraid of you, but I'm not local and I don't give a crap about you and your farm and all the people you bully in Wilshire. You'll answer my questions, or you'll wish you had."

Wilbur blanched.

A delay of three seconds followed as he digested Michael Chandler's words. Then, in response, Wilbur

angrily pushed the door. He shoved it almost shut—
almost, because Chandler put his shoe back in the
door frame and blocked it. Wilbur glared through
four inches of opening.

"I'm also looking for Franny," Chandler said.

Gradually the door opened wider. Wilbur filled the
space.

Chandler took one step backward, keeping a distance between himself and his adversary. He kept his
right hand near his weapon. Wilbur was wearing extra
poundage around his middle, but he was the type of
central Connecticut dirtball who, at age fifty-four, had
worked with heavy farm machinery for forty-five years.
Wilbur was solid as a tree trunk, even if his bark was
comprised of suet. If he came directly at Chandler,
it wouldn't be a good situation. Lizzie, baseball bat
in hand, moved next to her husband.

Chandler felt he had no alternative than to stay on
the offensive.

"I can come back with twelve backups and a warrant, and we can pull this place apart, Wilbur," Chandler said. "Do you want that? Or will you cooperate?"

The answer was swift.

"Ain't no judge around here that'd give you no
warrant," Wilbur Corbett said. "So get off our land."

He grabbed his wife by the shoulder and pulled
her backwards. As the door slammed shut, Chandler
could see her elbow her husband back. The sound
of another punch and a yell from within accompanied the slamming of the door. Then everything was
quiet.

Chandler stood his ground. He stepped back to the
door and knocked again.

"Mrs. Corbett? *Mrs. Corbett?*" he called.

Chandler had reasonable cause to call for backups

and enter the premises. He would have liked to.
Spousal abuse. He could have smashed the door
down and given the damned farm just the thorough
tossing that it had long deserved.

Then her voice came back.

"It's all right, Mr. Chandler," Lizzie yelled. "Just
go the fuck away."

Just go the fuck away.

It should have been the Corbett family slogan.
They should have had a mat on their front step bearing that sentiment. They should have had it in Latin
on their coat of arms, along with a busted appliance,
pigs, pitchforks, and a hand with an upraised middle
finger.

Grudgingly, Chandler walked back to his car, not
knowing exactly how to proceed next, half-waiting for
a shotgun to emerge from a lower window of the
farmhouse. These people lived as if in another century, he reminded himself, and by their own warped
rules.

He walked to a position near his car from which
he could see into the nearer barn. He turned and
looked at the farm house. He felt several sets of eyes
upon him. He had no idea where they were, but he
figured that since he was here he might as well give
the place as good a look as reasonably possible.

So he strolled to the barn and looked in.

The open area was big and yawning and cavernous.
Distantly, he had hoped that it would yield a suggestion about the death of James Corbett or the disappearance of Maury Fishkin, but that would have been
too easy, too obvious. The Corbetts, he was already
learning, were deceptively sneaky and sinister, considering there probably wasn't a triple-digit IQ on the
premises, unless it belonged to one of the livestock.

Chandler turned back toward his car.

Upstairs in the farmhouse, a curtain shifted quickly. A face was there for half a second and then gone. For some inexplicable reason, the vision gave Chandler a thrill of fear. Chandler thought he had seen an adolescent boy.

Chief Moore's words echoed. *Nine hundred fifty acres, and probably nine hundred fifty questions, and probably nine hundred fifty answers you don't want to know.*

And probably a few answers he *would* like to know, Chandler told himself as he climbed back into his car. Whatever those answers were, they were not forthcoming on this particular visit.

Driving back into the town center and thinking back on the Corbetts' qualities of cooperation, Chandler wondered how any answers would ever emerge.

In a fit of post-trauma paranoia, it occurred to him: The answers he wanted would probably *never* emerge. Wilshire was a black hole for the state cops, he recalled, and no one really expected real answers in Wilshire. His commanders had thrown the case of the dead man on Corbett's Lane to him, because no one else wanted it, not because it was his proper time to catch a case.

More accurately, no one else merited it. The case was a throwaway. Just the type of thing the department would give to a man who had just returned from an injury, and probably wasn't fully fit to do his job, but insisted on being back, anyway.

In his car, he cursed long and low. The department probably knew his arm, his shoulder, and his psyche weren't all meshing together in first-class running order. The bastards knew because the state police bureaucracy knew half of what it should and all of what it shouldn't, and they were jerking him around—patronizing him. They, in the person of his commander Captain Steve Lindemann, had given him a case that no one really gave a rat's ass about.

He continued along Sturgis Street back into town. Well, he'd damned well show the bastards, he concluded, Lindemann in particular. He'd show them that a difference could be made, even in a creepy place like Wilshire. He'd unearth so much in this place that *everyone* would wish he'd been assigned somewhere else.

Then he realized further: sometime during the visit, his shoulder and left arm had stopped aching. He wondered why and when exactly it had happened.

The package had traveled more than two weeks and a thousand miles to get to her. It arrived on Ellen's desk, postmarked from Georgia, simultaneous to Mike Chandler's driving away from the Corbett farm.

For several seconds, Ellen stared at the return address.

Harold Duperry. Stone Mountain, Georgia.

She ran her finger along the edges of the large bulky manila envelope. She could tell what it was, not that she didn't remember Harold's pledge. There was a picture frame within the brown paper and brown box, and the frame would contain a favorite photograph of the son she had never known.

The arrival of the parcel knocked Ellen out of Wilshire, Connecticut, and the world of small town newspaper publishing. She drew a breath and summoned her courage. She opened the package.

There was a handwritten letter from Harold on a

plain sheet of white paper. The framed picture was in a separate box, individually wrapped.

She read the letter.

> *Dear Ellen,*
>
> *Many months have passed. The pain of our loss has eased only slightly. I'm sure you feel much the same way, and Robin's passing weighs as heavily upon you as upon the rest of those of us who loved him.*
>
> *Nonetheless, I did promise you the enclosed and do want you to have it. Maybe it will be easier to accept now than in April. This was a portrait of your son taken during his tenth grade year of high school, about one month before his passing. I know you—*

As if primed by some external force, Ellen's tears began. She folded away the letter. She held the framed portrait of Robin unopened in her trembling hand for several seconds. No, she realized, she did not yet have the courage to open it and look at him.

She wondered if she ever would.

She pushed the wrapped portrait back into its envelope, along with Harold Duperry's letter. She put both in the middle side drawer of her desk. She closed the drawer resolutely, clasped her hands before her, and thought about it.

No, she realized yet again. She was not yet ready to accept what she had done in giving up Robin, and she was not yet ready to accept his passing.

She was angry with herself. This was real life. These were situations that she had created for herself. Why couldn't she come to grips with it? She felt as if she were wearing a badge that told everyone how weak and deplorable her behavior had been.

She drew a breath.

She steadied herself and turned her thoughts to the failing advertising revenue of her newspaper. It was too late to save her son, but maybe, she reasoned, she could still save her newspaper.

Eight

With mounting interest and a mounting sense of dread to accompany it, Michael Chandler continued his journey through the details surrounding James Corbett's death, and the regional reign of small-state terror over which the Corbett family had presided for generations.

The office of the state medical examiner in New Haven had declared the death an accident. The post mortem had been conducted by the ME, himself, an enormously obese man named Norman Verdi. Dr. Verdi had grown up in Madison aspiring to be a Shakespearean actor and gone to Quinnipiac College in Hamden. Then he had chucked the stage after starving in New York for five years and somehow maneuvered himself into medical school in Mexico. He still played the bard in summer theater, specializing in Falstaff, Hamlet—in which he played the King—or any comic variation on all of these.

And what a piece of work was Dr. Verdi's report in this case. To Chandler, the conclusions of the medical examiner's report made for high comedy and low motivation. Something in Chandler's gut told him James Corbett's death hadn't been much of an accident.

Suicide, maybe, Chandler thought two days later as

he sat in his car overlooking Lake Barbara in Wilshire, eating lunch and looking at the bright fall day that surrounded him.

His attention focused on something on the far edge of the lake—something moving. He reached for the binoculars that he kept in his Jeep and raised them to his eyes.

A beautiful October scene: a large deer without antlers emerged from the woods, followed by a slightly smaller one—a doe and her nearly grown fawn. They walked for a moment by the lake and drank some water. Then something must have scared them, because they turned in unison and retreated to the safety of the woods. It was almost hunting season, Chandler reminded himself. Time for the animals to make themselves scarce, and time for at least one case where someone blew away some local farmer's cow, or worse. A season without human fatalities was a successful one, he had always felt. He wasn't much on hunting, himself. His father had been a hunter, but Mike had hated the blood of the sport, the butchery of the animals, and the horrible sight of the carcasses hanging in front of rural Connecticut homes after the annual kills.

Fatalities. Fatalities in the woods. Animals and people.

The thought pattern sent him back to the late James Corbett—Pitchfork Jimmy, as the kids at Wilshire High now called him.

Suicide maybe, Chandler mused, but an accident, *no.*

"Might as well mark it natural causes, Doc," Chandler had said to Verdi when he had visited in person that morning.

"Want me to?" the doctor had inquired conspiratorially. "It wouldn't be the first such request I'd had on this job."

Chandler's curiosity piqued immediately. "Yeah?" he asked. "Who else contacted you?"

Sensing trouble, Verdi abandoned that line of conversation.

"No one," he said tersely.

"Come on, Norman. I want to know."

"No one."

"Family? The Wilshire police?"

"No one."

Norman Verdi slipped into a pair of yellow headphones—he used a "splatterproof" Walkman, as he called it—and turned to his next slice-and-dice job, leaving Chandler to wonder: Who had influenced the ME, or sought to?

Had it been the Corbetts? Did they know something about the death, and were they planning to settle things via their own traditional thuggery?

Had it been the Wilshire police? The town cops hardly seemed interested in launching a murder investigation over James Corbett. A finding of "accidental causes" suited their purposes as if custom-tailored.

Or had it been someone else? Was there a third party, perhaps the murderer or murderers, whose purposes an accidental ruling would serve equally? And if there were a third party, who was it?

Chandler turned over all of this in his mind as he munched a sandwich and knocked back a Diet Coke between noon and one. So far, he subscribed to the middle theory.

After all, he had discovered that the pitchfork that impaled James Corbett had been wiped free of fingerprints before landing in the state police lab. Not even James's prints could be found. So how had he held it to impale himself? Similarly, the beer cans that had formed a magic little circle around the fallen were equally free of prints. The New Haven lab had attested to the fact that James's stomach had been free of beer when he died, and his blood alcohol level had been almost nil. That pretty much shot to hell the theory that he'd been sitting in a tree drinking beer. What other drinkers would have wiped Old Milwaukee cans free of their prints?

It wasn't just that the case didn't make sense, Chandler mused, but the sense that it made pointed to some sort of cover-up, and a remarkable lack of desire on the part of everyone to confront the facts of James's death.

The more Chandler thought about it, the more the whole enigma spun apart and re-formed in various kaleidoscopic patterns of deception.

The Wilshire police *and* the Corbett family were together on this one, he'd decided briefly, but the theory collapsed of its own absurdity. Wherein lay any common interests between the Wilshire town cops and their most frequent lawbreakers?

Still the enigma remained, complete with all its shadings. At one point, keeping all this in mind, Chandler had phoned Dr. Verdi and put to him his thesis about why the findings of an accidental death simply didn't follow from a pitchfork wiped clean of prints, a bloodstream with no booze in it, and pristine empty beer cans.

Dr. Verdi was an educated man, and could spot an inconsistency as quickly as the next rational human being. He could also spot consistency in other forms, such as receiving a paycheck from one Friday to the next.

"It's still an accident, and will remain one," Verdi said.

"Why?" Chandler demanded sharply.

"There are more things in heaven and earth than you are aware of in Central Connecticut," Verdi threw back. Then he hung up the phone, his brief cameo as the Hamlet of the steel-and-guttered table concluded.

Chandler, however, did have one important audience. He took his notions to his commander in Fairfield, Captain Jack Lindemann.

Lindemann shrugged. "What's the ME say?"

"Someone got to him. I don't trust the report."

"Stay with it. See what you find," he said.

Lindemann had no love for the medical examiner's office, and had locked horns with Chief Moore in a jurisdictional squabble six years earlier, so he didn't mind the chance turn a double play: show up the ME's office and make the Wilshire gendarmerie look bad, too. Fact was, Lindemann *always* liked to make any local town police look bad across the state. Lindemann figured that a bad reflection on the locals only shined up the image of the Staties. It was, he deeply felt, part of what his budget was for. So he proceeded accordingly, and so did the men under his command.

The funeral of James Corbett was in progress as Chandler finished his lunch. The ceremony took place at the small family graveyard located within the confines of the Corbett's property. No outsiders attended. None, obviously, had been invited.

To top things off, since the local police weren't speaking much to the local reporters, Peter Whitely from *The Wilshire Republican*, was phoning Chandler twice a day, sniffing around for something on which to build a story. So far, Chandler wasn't giving him much that he couldn't figure out for himself. Hell, Chandler figured, smiling to himself, the new owner of the paper was a lot more attractive than Peter Whitely. She could come around in person and be as nosy as she wished. He smiled at the thought.

Chandler leaned back in his Jeep and placed his hands on the steering wheel. The police radio under his dashboard crackled intermittently. In his rearview mirror he watched a man in a suit unlock an over-powered BMW and climb into the driver's seat. Chandler guessed the driver was about fifty. The car was black and gleaming. On its rear window was a red-white-and-blue Grateful Dead sticker, and on its license plate holder was the logo of a dealer down in Fairfield County. Details, details. They gave away so much. Deadheads had more than a touch of gray these days, and they often had more than a touch of cash, too. They were also moving farther up into exurbia, where half a million bucks could buy something more than the cheapest house on the block.

The BMW pulled away, taking with it the specter of an aging millionaire ex-hippie. A vision of James Corbett appeared again in his mind, replacing that of Bob Weir and the late Jerry Garcia.

Corbett: What was it about this case that Mike Chandler couldn't stay away from? he wondered. He'd had other cases like this that he had easily walked away from when progress was not possible. Now here he was investigating a murder, which is how he thought of it, that officially was no such thing.

What was the feeling within him that was tugging him along?

As he searched the knowable details about the Corbetts, he felt himself desperate for any little inference, hungry for any small connection of facts, however oblique, that would draw even the smallest details into focus, but he had nothing. He barely had a context for James's death.

And as he turned all this over, he found the front part of his mind working at odds with the back. His eyes had settled on Lake Barbara before him and he was watching something else unfold by its shore.

Two boys, each about twelve years old, had darted away from school during lunch hour. They now stood on the edge of the lake skimming rocks across the water, about fifty feet in front of Chandler's vehicle. Chandler recognized both of the boys. Andy Rourke, was the son of a diesel mechanic who worked for a truck dealer down in Hamden. The other boy, Matthew Souza, was the son of two teachers at Wilshire Junior High.

Two good kids. Andy raised his hand and waved when he realized that Detective Chandler was watching them. Chandler waved back, then, playfully, gave a toot of the car's siren and a flash of the red light.

Both boys laughed.

Their voices were animated, and they joyfully skimmed the rocks. Chandler took time to watch and count—four, five, six, skips—before the stones sank. In the summer, he recalled, there were boats on this lake, and even swimmers in two sections, but Lake Barbara had closed to water sports on the fifteenth of September. Nonetheless, there seemed to be some sort of game or competition going on. The boys had one baseball hat bearing a Mets logo and they passed it back and forth between them, depending, Chandler guessed, on who had best skimmed a rock.

Chandler smiled.

When he had been growing up, he used to go to

the state park down at Sherwood Island in Westport
with his father. His father liked to walk a mile or two,
particularly in the cold weather. Even on bitter winter
days, his father took him to skim rocks into Long
Island Sound.

Chandler watched the boys for several minutes.
Then there was a call on his radio for any available
assistance. Accident on Route 34 in Derby. The officer on the scene needed assistance.

The detective flipped the beacon onto the roof of
his car and went to assist. What the hell, he figured,
the state had straightened out its ledgers recently,
and Chandler could use the overtime.

He never arrived in Derby.

Chandler had traveled to the outskirts of Wilshire
and was passing the parking lot of a farm supply
warehouse when he spotted the hulking form of the
one man in the world to whom he most wished to
speak.

He hit his brake hard and cut into the parking lot.
He pulled the car to a stop and looked at his subject.
He kept his engine running.

There was Franny Corbett, all six and a half feet,
two hundred odd pounds of him. Chandler had
never seen him before, but was certain from the description everyone had given him—the size, the
shape, the bulk and the truck, it all fit together.

Franny stood next to the cab of his red pickup
truck and put the key in the lock. He was dressed in
a pair of tan trousers and a denim jacket over a black
T-shirt. There was some sort of gold chain at his
neck, and he wore dark glasses. He seemed impervious to the cold, as if the mere fact of his height and
weight made him larger than the weather.

Chandler stepped out of his own car. He walked

toward the big man, stopping ten feet away. He watched Franny carefully. Chandler was as uneasy with this potential interview as he had ever been. He kept a careful eye on Corbett's large hands.

"Franny Corbett?" Chandler asked.

The big man turned and glowered at him.

"Maybe," Corbett answered.

Chandler reached for his shield and showed it to Corbett. "Connecticut State Police, Franny. I'm Detective Michael—"

"I know who the fuck you are," Franny said. His voice was like heavy stones being dragged across cement.

"We've never seen each other. How do you know who I am?" Chandler asked.

"I know things."

"That's good. I like to ask questions."

Franny looked his way through the dark glasses. It was only a glance, but it contained a carload of contempt. Franny spit on the pavement in the direction of Chandler's shoes.

"Fuck you," Franny said.

Chandler let it pass. He was too busy looking for details. Corbett's hands and arms told Chandler that this man was powerfully built. The heels and fingers of his hands were thick and callused. Franny had probably worked as a laborer for much of his life. At least that's how he looked.

"Why don't you go away? I don't got nothing to tell you," Franny said.

"But *I* need to talk to *you*, Franny," Chandler said. "About your Uncle Jim."

Corbett remained quiet. He unlocked the cab and opened the truck door. Chandler looked at his work boots. They were covered with the same color of pale brown mud found on the Corbett farm.

"How come you're not at the funeral?" Chandler asked. "Big family affair like that. I'd think you'd be there."

"Fuck off."

"Must be a reason."

"Didn't like Jimmy," said Franny.

"Who didn't?"

"Who the fuck do you think? *I* didn't."

"Did you like Maury Fishkin?"

"Who?"

"Don't bullshit me, Franny. You know who I mean."

"Do I?"

"I have the feeling the body is stashed around here somewhere. Why don't you help me find it?"

"I can't help you on that one," Franny drawled.

" 'Can't, or won't, Franny?"

"Yeah," Corbett said. "Both."

Then something peculiar, frightening, and astonishing happened.

Franny reached to his dark glasses and removed them. He folded them away and turned. Chandler watched his hands carefully. Then their eyes locked— Chandler's on Franny Corbett's, and Franny Corbett's cold brown eyes on the policeman's.

Chandler froze.

The vibrations that Michael Chandler took from this man were unlike any other he had ever picked up from any living human being. He sensed something that he knew contained fear, but was much, much more than that. It was something deeper and darker. Chandler wasn't just feeling it because Corbett was a head taller and four inches wider. No, there was also something very wild and immeasurable within this Corbett in particular.

In making close eye contact, in fact, Chandler experienced something resembling an electric shock. It was *that* powerful. There was something here that reminded Chandler of the night he was shot, and the sensation that he had felt of tumbling into that resolute brightness that was his seven minute death. His old wounds even started to hurt, the spot where the bullet entered his body, and the inside areas through which the projectile had ripped. A mini-vision of the brown-haired woman who seemed to be his princess of mortality showed before him like an acid flash. Then it was gone.

Chandler couldn't shake the overall discomfort he felt in Franny's presence. The sensation made the policeman shudder. He felt a disgust, a shakiness, and almost a sickness. Next there was a certain breathlessness. Then he reacted to something else very visceral within Franny Corbett. He felt as if he were confronting something that wasn't entirely human.

An animal in human skin, he thought to himself. *Or something . . . something supernatural.*

God Almighty, he mused. *Where are these thoughts coming from?*

Again, he had no answers to the question he posed to himself. At the end of all this, Franny Corbett, sensing the policeman's extreme discomfort, smiled.

"You should listen to them spirits," Franny said in another low rumble. "The spirits'd tell you stuff."

Perplexed, Chandler blinked. "What?" the policeman asked.

"Spirits," Franny said. "Can'tcha see them? All over the fucking place. They'll tell you a lot of shit if you'd listen."

"I don't see anything," Chandler said. "Not today. Just you."

"The other spirits'd bite you on the ass if they could," the big man said. "But today they can't."

Chandler held Franny in his view for several seconds. Was he a nut case, the detective wondered, or just trying to come across as one?

"I have no idea what you're talking about," Chandler answered, knowing how feeble he sounded.

"And so far as the pitchfork through Uncle Jimmy's fat throat," Franny continued, ignoring Chandler's response and moving on to his next topic of choice. "No fucking big deal, huh? Look at this."

Franny pulled back the collar of his shirt. There was an ugly gash along his own throat, scar tissue that looked as if it had been sewn by an unskilled backwoods sawbones. It had never healed properly and—God forbid!—no Corbett had ever seen fit to get Franny some plastic surgery to lessen the ghastly appearance. The scar ran about five inches across the neck, as if Franny had survived some bizarre knife fight or a suicide attempt, or a slash from a broken beer bottle in a barroom brawl.

Chandler curled a lip and steadied himself anew. "What the hell's that from, Franny?" he asked.

"I cut myself shaving." The big man grinned.

"Tell me what it's really from."

"Fuck. Don't matter," Frank Corbett said huskily. "Shit happens. Accidents and stuff. Farm equipment's sharp. It cuts. Hey, we butcher pigs on that farm, too. Make our own ham. You know the pigs piss when you cut their neck, did you know that?"

"I knew that."

"Yeah. Well, you'd piss, too, wouldn't you? I pissed when they cut *my* throat."

"When *who* cut your throat?"

"Don't rightly remember. Least not today."

"Uh huh," Chandler said, seeming to have been led to a dead end. He studied his adversary and waited to see what Franny might volunteer next. Franny must have known the tactic, and he wasn't going to go for it.

"So what do you have to say to me?" Corbett finally growled. "Are you fucking going to stand there and stare, or do you have a question?"

"I want to talk to you about your Uncle James. And how he died."

"Fell out of a tree. Fucking pitchfork through his throat. What the hell more is there than that?" Franny asked. His eyes narrowed. "If'n Uncle James'd lived, every time he'd of taken a slug of beer, the beer woulda come pissing out the holes in his throat. So it's a good thing he died, huh?"

Franny grinned. "So there," he added.

Chandler groped for something to ask next, but he was suddenly aware that his preparation for this moment had mysteriously disappeared from him. Something about the presence of Franny Corbett had thrown him that far off.

"Why don't you tell me where you were when he died?" Chandler tried. "How's that for starters?"

Franny climbed into the cab of his truck. Chandler wanted to raise a hand to stop him, but some instinct told him not to.

He just plain didn't dare.

"I was at home in bed dry-humping my pillow, for Christ's sake," Corbett said. "Where the fuck were you?"

Franny put the key in the ignition and turned it. The truck turned over with a clank. It gave a long blast of sooty exhaust. The interview expired in much the same way.

Franny started to pull his door shut. Chandler, in a sudden bold move, stepped forward and held the door with an extended left arm.

Corbett's eyes landed upon his again. Another smile crossed the big man's face. If this were going to be a test of strength—not wits, but *strength*—the smile seemed to say, there wasn't much question who would win.

Corbett sat in the cab and slowly pulled the door shut with one arm. Chandler was helpless. He felt as if he were trying to stave off a machine. Having barely exerted himself, Corbett used his other paw to reach to his side and push Chandler away.

Chandler was so stunned, so overwhelmed, by Corbett's raw physical strength, that he allowed himself to stand there helpless for several seconds.

Corbett gunned the accelerator.

"Asshole," Franny said. "Stay the fuck away from me."

He hit the gas and pulled away.

Franny Corbett's interview was concluded, the first of several meetings between the two men. All Mike Chandler could think of as Franny rode away was how much the big man disturbed him, and how much he could use a drink.

Chandler found that drink two hours later at his home in Meriden. He sat in his living room before the large screen television, but the set was not on. Chandler was deep in thought.

He had sensed an eerie connection with Franny Corbett, and couldn't place what it was, or didn't want to admit what it was. For all that Chandler could think about since encountering Franny face-to-face was the night when he had almost died.

More accurately, the night when Chandler had died . . . and come back.

He sipped directly from the bottle of beer in his quiet home. He tried to make an assortment of thoughts fit into some comprehensible pattern.

Over and over, he replayed the moments when he had been shot and killed and then—through the miracle of wires, tubes, and electric shocks—been brought back to life again.

Dead, and then returned to the living. The complete round trip, all in a few hours.

If not legally correct, that was clinically correct. It had happened on a freezing morning in Bridgeport, on the previous January tenth.

He and his partner, Martin Schoor, were working undercover narcotics, hot on the trail of a sleezebag Colombian powder importer named Tito Moreno.

Chandler and Schoor received a tip that Moreno was holed up in a two-story housing project four blocks south of St. Vincent's Hospital.

Dressed in flak jackets, they responded and requested backups. When they arrived at the address, however, they found a town house style unit with an open front door. Inside, they saw a cluttered staircase leading to the second floor.

They waited. The early morning was quiet. No cars. No activity, even in a notorious project where the pharmaceutical commerce usually went on around the clock.

It was 1:00 A.M.

Chandler volunteered to enter the premises for the first look. Schoor would follow. They had worked on the arrest for two months, and were hungry for the collar.

Chandler entered the first floor of the unit.

Nothing happened.

So he went quietly up the staircase with his partner behind him. He entered a room at the top of the stairs. It was cluttered with a large mattress in its middle, two lamps, and drug paraphernalia. If Chandler had five dollars for every cockroach he saw, or twenty dollars for each one he stepped on, he could have retired wealthy on the spot. Instead, he nearly died poor.

He went into the first room. Nothing. There was a closed closet. He passed the closet and went to a back bedroom. Again, nothing but rubble.

His partner stood at the door, weapon ready.

Then everything happened.

When Chandler emerged from the bedroom, Tito Moreno emerged from the closet, his finger tight on the trigger of a Glock-9. The first two bullets hit but failed to penetrate Chandler's flak jacket, and sent him sprawling. The third, however, found the lower edge of the left-side armhole and hit flesh.

A searing, overwhelming pain slashed through Chandler. The bullet severed an artery and lodged near his heart even before he hit the ground. His partner, meantime, emptied his own weapon into Tito Moreno—three shots while Tito was standing, and another five after he hit the floor. No one complained.

In the twenty minutes in took medics to respond. Michael Chandler lost consciousness and two pints of blood. The hemorrhaging wasn't fully stanched until he was at the hospital. By that time, on the operating table, his heart had stopped.

Electric shock was applied to his chest.

Enough voltage flowed to kill a man if he weren't already dead, and more than enough flowed to zap him back to life, if he were. Nothing worked. The doctors gave up, and were pulling the sheets over Michael's body when David Chandler, Michael's younger brother and also a state trooper, arrived. David had been roused from bed at 2:00 A.M.

"We lost him," said the doctor. "I'm sorry."

"When?"

"Five minutes ago."

As an army reservist, David Chandler had been a medical corpsman in the army. He had seen action in the Gulf War and had witnessed strange things, things just short of miracles.

"Is he still on the respirator?" David asked.

"We haven't flicked the switch yet, so, yes."

David again: "How long's the heart been down?"

"It's been flatlining for seven minutes," said another ER doctor.

"Seven's a lucky number."

"Not today, I'm afraid."

"Try it again, Doc."

"It won't work. Waste of time. And I have other emergency patients."

According to local lore, David Chandler drew a pistol. The state troopers who were there to donate blood did nothing as Michael's younger brother pointed it toward the intern.

"Do it again," he said softly. "Now."

Seven minutes turned into eight. During the eighth minute, the heart fluttered. Then it started again. Michael Chandler was back from the dead. Incredibly, brain function returned unimpaired. His flesh and internal organs were stitched together. The hospital stay was less than a month. Tito Moreno was had been buried for three weeks by the time Chandler went home.

The department offered him retirement on full disability. He didn't want it. What he wanted was his job. The department gave it to him, but not without six months of rehab, physical and psychiatric.

Therein lay many recent irritations.

Having been shot, killed, and then brought back to life drew attention. For example, a battery of questions from the psychologists. The shrinks. The psychic researchers. The busybodies. The priests.

What did you see while you were dead?

God?

Eternity?

The Future?

The Past?

Long lost relatives?

Now, on this evening in his home nine months later, with the rumble of the television in the background, he spoke aloud.

To no one. To everyone.

"I'm sorry," he answered, as he had many other times. "I didn't see anything. I was conscious, but I didn't see anything. I was just *there.*"

And, he might have added, if he had wanted to see long lost relatives he would have hit the family picnic in Willamantic each year. He took a pass on that, too.

What did you feel? Everyone wanted him to feel something different.

Jesus.

Enlightenment.

Liberation from worldly concerns.

A soaring sense of flight.

A "higher state of being," whatever that meant.

He spoke again, the words coming to him easily but defensively, as they always did on this subject.

"I'm sorry. I saw nothing. I was conscious, but I saw nothing. I felt a certain brightness, but I was just *there.*"

"Where?" they had all asked.

"It was very bright. That's all I know. That's all I remember. Everything was very bright."

"Did you see God?" a psychiatrist once asked him.

"I saw a woman with brown hair."

The shrink raised a single eyebrow. "Was she naked?"

"I gave you a serious answer, Doc."

"I asked a serious question."

"She was clothed."

"Did you know her?"

"I didn't recognize her."

"An hallucination, perhaps."

"A memorable one," Chandler allowed.

"Well," one doctor from Yale New Haven Hospital ruminated at a subsequent interview session, "your heart had stopped. No blood was being pumped. So, if you please, that sense of brightness *could* have been from the very preliminary stages of chemical decomposition of the brain."

That doctor was an Indian in a turban, a brilliant, bearded weirdo from the pysch ward in the old elm city. His name was Dr. Christyashani, and he was five feet two inches tall with a long slightly pointed nose that gave him the facial qualities of a wolverine. He had an irritating voice to match, particularly when he was prowling around about metaphysical questions.

The doctor pressed the point.

"Now, if you please, did you notice if this was a yellow brightness or a white brightness?"

"Yellow, maybe," said Chandler, starting to feel exasperated.

"Did it remind you of anything?"

"What do you mean?"

"The color? Associations, if you please."

Chandler shrugged. "Dog urine on snow."

Dr. Christyashani blinked. "I see," he said.

"Do you?"

"Yes."

Chandler waited for a moment.

"It's a joke, Doc," he said.

"Joke? Please? Meaning?"

Chandler sighed, and his thoughts drifted again. He hadn't much wanted to share his private ruminations with strangers. He missed his father, the man who died before Mike could put his life in order. He missed not having a particular woman in his life, someone to be there when he came either home each day, or even out of surgery. He was not the type of man to share such thoughts with shrinks.

At this juncture of his life, Chandler became intensely private and introspective. His hunch was that if he had lived, survived a bullet meant for his heart, he was back on this planet for a reason, and he knew there was no way anyone could wrap any science or psychiatry around a theory like that. Whether the reason presented itself now or thirty years in the future, or ever at all, remained to be seen.

So he had cut a few corners to get back on the force. No one could tell, but the bullet in his left shoulder had diminished his feeling in his left side, as well as his mobility. A left-handed draw, he was a half-second slower than he used to be in drawing a sidearm. His shot, as demonstrated at the range, was only eighty percent as accurate. And there were various pains and discomforts that came and went, though almost always there was something.

A tingling numbness, for example, frequently came up out of nowhere in his shoulder and spread down to his arm. Sort of a little mini-paralysis, it lasted for only a few seconds. It was accompanied by an intense pain. Sometimes it deadened all feeling in his fingers. The doctors couldn't trace it, but threatened to keep him off active duty until he stopped complaining about it. If it didn't go away at all, they would "retire" him on disability—meaning take away the job in police work that he loved.

He was having none of that.

So he stopped mentioning the paralysis, and he refused to admit the pain persisted. No one knew it was there if he didn't tell anyone. So he lived with it, and told the docs that the symptoms had vanished. And with that went the final hurdle to getting back on active duty, but the incident and the situation had left him very much a man on the edge.

On the edge of giving himself over to heavy drinking.

On the edge of finding a true terror in having almost been killed.

On the edge of walking into yet another situation which would finish what Tito Moreno had begun. Sometimes, a violent death seemed to be just one false step away, just one doorway that he didn't need to walk through.

Nor was it ever far from his thoughts, not with the pain in his upper arm and shoulder, and not with that damnable brightness that flashed relentlessly back on him. Not when there was already the heavy whiff of homicide in the air, and the irrefutable feeling that there would be more to follow.

As he sat in his home and finally guided his thoughts away from the night he died, the strange mood that was upon him began to lift.

He drained his second bottle of beer, but resisted opening a third. He also resisted making any preliminary conclusions about Franny Corbett. He would have to study the big lug up close again and reconsider what it was that was "wrong" about Franny.

For better or worse, he felt himself drawn to the man, and the reason why was just one more thing that Chandler was incapable of understanding. He closed his eyes for a moment.

He thought back to that intense brightness that had accompanied his near death. Then a startling rediscovery was upon him.

In the midst of the brightness, he saw now, was a human figure.

It was a light, ethereal figure, and he had the sense of having seen it all along, yet never realized it until now. The name Janine Osheyak came to him again, and the vision of a pretty woman with brown hair again materialized.

In abject fear his eyes flashed open.

The room was quiet. He was alone. And he felt more lost and confused than at any moment since he had left the hospital.

Nine

"Ellen?" the familiar male voice asked.

She was startled. Far away in thought, working at her desk, she had thought herself to be alone. She looked up from her desk at the offices of *The Wilshire Republican* Wednesday afternoon.

Peter Whitely, her best reporter, stood at the door to her office, an apologetic look across his face.

"Peter?" she asked, relaxing.

"I'm sorry. Did I take you by surprise?"

"I was getting ready for the accountant again," she said with a rueful smile.

"Ken Karp?"

"Who else? Mr. Bearer of Dreadful Tidings," she said. "I think I'd just as soon get ready for some root canal work. At least the dentist is cheerful."

"May I come in?" he asked.

"Of course."

She folded the ledger that she had been working on, the one showing the subscription rates down again, advertising down again, newsstand circulation rate not improving—a trifecta of bad fiduciary tidings. New ownership, she was learning quickly, was doing nothing to help this paper. The meeting with the accountant later that day wasn't promising to be any more uplifting than the last one had been.

"I know what you mean," he said in his usual kindly way. He paused and seemed to gather his nerve. "I wonder if you have a minute?"

"Of course," she said. "What's up? Something on the Corbett article?"

"Well, no, not exactly," he said.

Peter finally eased into the room and found a chair. He was looking thinner than usual, a little cadaverish, in fact, and his hair was much too white for a man of fifty-five. Then again, even when he was in a good mood Whitely looked like a Yankee mortician. Like the accountant who would follow him, he did not look as if he were there with pleasant news.

"As for the Corbett article," Peter said, "there's really nothing new. I've been talking to Chief Moore each day. He keeps referring me to that young policeman."

"Michael Chandler."

"That's right," Whitely said. "But Chandler's a laconic soul. Doesn't have an awful lot to say. Won't even tell me if he has a suspect or not."

Ellen shrugged. "Have you asked around town? Do you have a handle on the story for the week?" she asked.

"Well, no," he said hesitantly. "That's actually what I came to talk to you about."

"In what way? You need a handle?"

"No. I need more than that, Ellen."

Now she looked at him in a new and unpleasant light. She felt startled. "Don't mince words, Peter. Let me have it."

"Ellen, you know I've been with this paper for eight years, and what I have to tell you now is nothing personal. It doesn't have anything to do with you or your ownership."

She knew right away. "You're leaving," she said.

"I'm leaving," he answered.

She sighed. "You're my best reporter. And you generate thirty percent of our ad sales. "You know that, right?"

"It doesn't guarantee food on my table," he said. "I know you're doing everything you can here, but—"

"I understand," she said softly.

She understood, yes, but was hurt and disappointed, too.

The tension lifted slightly. Peter managed a meager smile. Outside, something happened to the sunlight for a moment. The brightness disappeared, and an overcast held their section of central Connecticut. In the change of light, a strange shadowy darkness crossed Peter's face. Suddenly, only for a few seconds, he looked two decades older than his years.

Ellen had never seen such a change in a man's appearance from one moment to the next. It was as if he had traveled twenty years right in front of her, then come back again. It was creepy.

Surreal.

She almost recoiled from the vision. Then the sunlight returned, she blinked, and Peter Whitely looked normal again.

". . . and you know," he said, in the midst of explaining as she tuned back into his conversation, "when I was in advertising in New York, back in the late eighties, I was making sixty-six grand a year. That was my high mark. Nineteen eighty-seven, I think it was. Then came all the downsizing. Hell, they cut *me* down in size, all right."

"Do you have something else lined up?" she asked.

"I think I do," he said.

"Do you need a letter of recommendation?" she asked. "Your former editor might be a better person to write it, but I don't mind—"

"I won't need it," he said.

There was a slight pause as she realized. "Oh," she said. Then she asked, "You've already been hired?"

"I have."

"May I ask where?"

"You won't be happy," he said.

She thought about it for another moment. Then it occurred to her, and whacked her hard.

"Oh, Peter," she said. "Which is it? *The Hartford Current,* or *The New Haven Register?*"

"The *Courant,*" he answered. "In their business office."

"Their *business* office? My God, Peter!"

"Sorry," he said again.

"What are you doing in their business office?"

He was silent till she twisted it out of him.

"Selling advertising," he said.

"Ah," Ellen answered.

It was a yet another blow. She leaned back in her chair and felt as if she were sinking. "My best writer and best ad salesman defects to the business office of my mortal enemy." She groaned. "Peter, it was already a bad day before this."

"I know."

"And you'll probably be trying to take some of your accounts with you, right?"

He said nothing.

"Right?" she asked again.

"It's business," Peter said softly. "I'm sorry."

"Me, too." She was getting angry, but reining it in. He exhaled deeply. "I'm afraid that's the way it is,

Ellen," he said, trying to explain it away. "I'm, uh, not happy to do this. But, you know, I'm fifty-five. They offered me four twenty-five a week to start, plus health care and pension after ten years if I stick. I have to consider my own position."

"Peter, I suppose I'll try to understand," she said evenly. "You have to do what's right for you."

"Thank you," he said.

She tried to assess her own thoughts and maintain her composure as her publishing venture crumbled around her. She gathered herself, then tried to put on the best face possible. By God, she told herself again, she had always wanted to run a small independent paper, this had been the only one available that she could afford. She would be *damned* before she let her dreams collapse in the first few months.

Her resolve stiffened.

"Well," she said, "whatever you do, I still have that space on page one for you for the next issue. We hate to lose you, but I suppose your final thousand words will be . . ."

Peter was already shaking his head. "I'm not going to have time, Ellen," he said.

"Not even for your final article?"

"I have to be over in Hartford for an orientation this evening at six. They want me to *start* tomorrow morning."

"This *evening*? *Tomorrow*? So you can't even finish the week here?"

After an uneasy pause, he answered simply, "No."

There was a chill in the room as the monstrosity of this sank in on her.

"Well," she said. "When you abandon ship, you do it quickly and efficiently, don't you, Peter? You even leave a few detonation devices on board, it seems."

He said nothing. She filled the silence for him.

"You'd better let me have your office keys and your press card, Peter. And good luck."

He stumbled.

"Yes, of course," he said. "I'm sorry, Ellen. I really am."

"I know," she said flatly.

His fingers were no longer nimble, and he had difficulty getting the office keys off his ring. It took a minute. He handed them to her. She accepted them without speaking.

Then came a final bit of business.

Peter already had a final expense report made out. He handed it to her. Twenty-eight dollars.

"If you can put a rush on that, I'd appreciate it," he said. "The *Courant* won't cut me a check for three weeks, and—"

"I'll take care of it, Peter. I promise," she said, wondering why she was subsidizing her competitor's employee after they had stolen him from her. Another of life's injustices. At least this one would only cost a couple of dozen bucks.

Peter Whitely apologized again and then was gone.

Ellen leaned back in her chair and wondered what insanity had possessed her the day she had quit her job in Boston and bought this paper. Financial ruin, that's what it would bring her.

Not a local Pulitzer or the fulfillment of any dream. Just ruin.

She felt like crying, but was too busy. Too busy, and too resilient by nature. She had been through the loss of a child, she reminded herself, and a divorce. Somehow she would live without this specific reporter. She was amazed sometimes at how resilient she could be when getting nailed to the wall.

She took a moment before she went back to the figures that she would have to discuss with Karp. She tried to put this loss in perspective. And yet, there was no getting around the fact that this was a bad one.

Yes, she had one less name on the payroll, but Peter had been her most dependable writer. The only one on her staff who didn't use the words *there* and *their* interchangeably. The only one who could get the *who, what, where, when,* and *why* into a news article in the first paragraph and still be interesting. And now he was gone.

Worse, as she thought it through, was that Peter had gone and would be taking all his personal contacts for selling local advertising with him. More immediately on the down side, she had eight inches to fill on the front page. The last thing she needed was for the paper to be late on the stands. That would cause a further drop in advertising and circulation, and would feed the rumors that *The Wilshire Republican* was on its way to the graveyard.

Eight inches. And no one to write it.

No one who had anything extra to write on the Corbett slaying. No one with any insight on the whole damned paper. Peter had been the only local reporter who wasn't scared out of his socks by the family.

Oh, Lord, she thought, what had she done buying this newspaper? How would she ever recover from a mistake like this? She glanced at her watch. Karp the Wampum Tabulator would be there in half an hour. "Spreading more gloom," she muttered.

As the afternoon progressed, she was proven correct. The newspaper wasn't just being run on a shoestring. It was being run on a Velcro sandal strap.

Karp arrived at five o'clock and was at his funereal worst.

The accountant predicted that without a sharp upturn in advertising and circulation—and he made a dramatic point of saying he had no idea where *that* might come from—the paper would be out of business by the end of the year. With the payroll reduced by the loss of Peter Whitely, Karp reckoned with one small positive aside, there would be a previously unforeseen savings of four thousand dollars over the final quarter. That *might* allow the paper to teeter past Christmas into January or February, he theorized, months that were traditionally bleak for small market papers. Of course, he added, *The Wilshire Republican* would be teetering toward the millennium at a weekly net loss. The paper just wouldn't be out of business quite yet.

The certainty of his tone, cheerful in its morbid way, irritated her no end.

"Then I'd have to use our line of credit with the bank to get us into the spring," Ellen said.

Karp hesitated before he answered. Instantly, Ellen knew she'd hit upon another negative.

"I don't think so," he said.

"Why?"

"The bank has reduced your line," Karp said.

"To what? And *why*?" she demanded.

Karp drew a breath. "They're afraid *The Wilshire Republican* is going to go under," he said. "So they've reduced your line from fifty thousand dollars to twenty-five thousand."

"That's about what's owing now, isn't it?" Ellen asked.

"That *is* what the debt is now," Karp said. "Twenty-four thousand, eight hundred fifty nine, to be exact."

Her anger was brewing. So was her sarcasm. "How about the pennies, Ken?"

"Okay. Twenty-four eight fifty-nine, plus sixty-two cents."

She could only stare at him. "Well, as we pay it back we'll have to borrow it back," she said.

But the accountant was already shaking his head.

"No," he said. "Once again. I'm afraid not."

"What are you saying, Ken? They've *canceled* us? We've never missed one damned payment! This is the local bank, for God's sake! How can they do that?"

"Local, shmocal. Banks are banks," Karp explained. "They play by their own rules, and the first rule is that they make up their own rules as they go along. The Bank of Wilshire is no different than any other. They have so much bad paper out that they're tightening on everybody."

"But why *us?*"

"Because you're here."

"Why *now?*"

"Because you're vulnerable. They're afraid of your going into bankruptcy," Ken Karp explained. "They're not being unrealistic. I'm afraid of it, too."

He sighed.

"You need to pay them one thirty-sixth of the total debt each month. Otherwise, they could call in the whole balance."

"Why the hell are they doing this?" she asked.

"Like I said, they're bankers. And they're *scared,*" he repeated. "They think you'll be gone by early next year. And unless you do something drastic, you will be."

Ellen gave it some long hard thought. She quietly seethed. She would go into the local bank, she told herself and hash this out, *mano-a-mano.* She tried to be positive, but she had a hunch that as a single woman in business, her hurdles were being set significantly steeper, and a little closer together than they otherwise might have been.

She looked back to Ken Karp.

"All right," she said, her resolve tightening. "I'm not going to replace Peter Whitely. I have experience writing, I'll cover his assignments. I already don't have as much time as I need, but I'll do his job."

"What about the ad sales that he provided?"

"I'll have to do those, too," she answered.

Karp shrugged.

Nothing ever animated Ken Karp other than a six figure profit margin. If she had said that she was embarking on a trip to Mars, he would only have asked about the cost of fuel or whether she had purchased her ticket twenty-one days in advance to get the best fare.

Ellen was terminally sick of him and his doubting attitude.

"As for the future accounting, Ken," Ellen announced, "my sister has a degree in it. She'll do it for me free."

For a change, *he* looked surprised. "You've already spoken to her?"

"No. I'll call her this evening."

"Then I'm gone?"

"You're gone. I'll mail you a check tomorrow."

He shrugged. "I think there's just enough in the account before the weekend receipts," he said.

"And as for the Bank of Wilshire and *The Hartford Courant,*" she concluded, "screw them both. I'm here to stay."

"Well, I do accounting and finance for both of

them," Karp answered routinely. "So I'll tell them you said so."

"Be damned sure you do, Ken. Be damned well sure you do."

Before leaving the office, Ellen phoned her sister Gretchen in Boston. Gretchen agreed to do the books for *The Republican*, to keep them juggled properly as long as the paper stayed afloat.

Then Ellen searched through her pockets and found the business card that Detective Mike Chandler had given her. She placed a call to him. She had already figured out that Chief Moore in Wilshire wasn't the most articulate and informative, much less the most helpful, of peace officers. She hoped for better from Chandler.

She got what she wanted.

Detective Chandler returned her call fifteen minutes later. He patiently and courteously answered her questions about the case. They talked for forty minutes.

Several times Ellen asked him to speak more slowly while she took notes. She was horrified to learn that the Wilshire police had dropped their investigation almost altogether. And the state police, aside from Chandler's presence, weren't falling over themselves to give an investigation into James Corbett's death a high priority.

When she hung up, she was impressed. She taped Chandler's business card to her telephone so that she would have it handy, until she had his numbers memorized. For now, she had more than enough of what she needed. One thousand words. She brought

up a new document on her computer screen and
went to work.

Despite her dismay over the sleepy way things were
being done locally in Wilshire, much of the old excitement of shoestring journalism started to kick in. She
was on a story, but she was on her own newspaper. *The
Republican* was small and struggling, but by god it was
hers! It would go as far as she could take it.

She felt a rush of excitement. She soon had fifteen
hundred words, good and sharp, succinctly recreating
the crime scene and calling upon quotes from witnesses. Unable to leave well enough alone, she then
pulled together a sidebar article on the Corbetts and
how trouble had plagued them throughout their tenure in central Connecticut. She tried to be as objec-
tive as possible.

She reorganized her front page, incorporated a
suitably lurid picture from the crime scene, one that
conveyed the scene's horror, but which shied away
from being too graphic, and continued the story on
page two. Two more pictures accompanied the page
two material. Her sidebar went on that page, also.

She settled back. She should have been pleased.
Instead, she sat at her desk with her hands linked,
one on top of the other, a left hand finger tapping
on the back of her right hand.

Something about the paper was still bothering her.

Suddenly she knew what it was. She couldn't believe that even as an experienced newspaperwoman,
she had taken this long to isolate the greatest problem with *The Wilshire Republican.*

The paper had no character. No spine. No *cojones,*
as some of her male counterparts on papers in New
York and Boston would have said. The content was
squishy soft, and so were the opinions.

She looked back to the editorial page. On it was a final offering from Peter Whitely on the impending sewer construction and her own ramblings on the beauty of the autumn season in Wilshire.

"Oh, the hell with that," she muttered to herself.

She reedited Peter's thoughts and dropped them from three paragraphs to four sentences. She did the same to her own thoughts on autumn foliage. She dropped Peter's opinions to the second slot on the editorial page, and moved her own to the bottom. That opened up space of three hundred words from the masthead of the paper downward.

A phrase came to her. She entered it as the title of her editorial:

A TIME TO WAKE UP

This past Monday, I was one of three spectators at the Board of Selectmen's meeting as the board spent three hours deciding absolutely nothing. Not totally unrelated, I've also noted that the missing Selectman, the departed and beloved Maury Fishkin, vanished amidst rumors this past summer, but no investigation continues into his disappearance. Now we have witnessed the death of a noted citizen in what may or may not have been a criminal act on Tuesday night. Our police department seems content to label this an accident and let it disappear. Meanwhile, businesses close in Wilshire and new ones don't open. The whole town seems to be hamstrung by its ineptitude.

Maybe it is rash for someone so newly arrived to come to such conclusions, but it seems to this new arrival, that this town could be a wonderful place to live if only someone would shake it awake.

It will thus be the role of this newspaper to issue

*wake-up calls where needed. It will be the role of you,
our readers, to tell us when we have overstepped, and
why.*

    *All this, I hope, will happen, before Wilshire dies
off of its own neglect.*

Too severe? She wondered. Maybe, but at least it might
provoke something. Perhaps it would get people talking. Maybe, she fantasized further, there were even
people out there who agreed with her. Everyone local
wasn't brain dead, were they?

She polished her words and then locked her editorial and her story in place. At least for that evening,
and on that evening, she was in business as her own
woman and her own journalist.

The rush of excitement carried her out the door
to her car and across town to meet her daughter just
as the after school play group was ready to disband
for the evening.

Ten

Home offered Ellen no relief from either her large or small problems. What bothered her most was the empty room on the second floor of her house, the room down at the end of the hallway at the rear.

It had been Ellen's intention to spruce up the room and use it as an extra bedroom. It would have been a perfect room for a second child, a thought that plagued her in light of Robin's death, but a second child didn't seem like much of a possibility these days. Another possibility was a guest room—or a "whatever" room, as she thought of it. She could use it for "whatever" she and daughter Sarah wanted.

But that wasn't what Ellen called the room now. The previous owners had painted the room an unusual shade of deep dark brown. Perhaps they were aiming for an earth tone or some soothing New Age hue. Maybe the deep brown had even looked good with the right furniture, though Ellen doubted it.

"The brown room," she now called it, in reference to the glaring physical characteristics that gave the room its odd feel.

Ellen felt as if she had to do something about the brown room. It bothered her. She had lived in cities, where space was always at a premium, long enough to feel a pang of guilt about an unused chamber.

Getting the time to attack the brown room was another matter. Running the newspaper was turning into an eight-day-a-week proposition. Well, she thought, she had brought *that* situation on herself. She was certainly not ready to back away from the challenges of a small independent newspaper, difficult as it was becoming. Nor was she willing to back away from the brown room much longer.

Long range, she was still wondering what to do with the room, how to set it up, what furniture to put in into it. She stood by herself for several minutes in the center of the room. Thinking. Wondering.

Down the hall, meanwhile, Sarah was busy finishing her homework.

Damn! Ellen thought.

There was something *distressing* about being in that brown room, something unsettling that changed her mood whenever she entered the chamber. She was sure it was the color, though there was also a strange scent in the room, an irritating persistent mustiness that she had noticed even when she had first walked through this house with Mrs. Walker, the real estate broker.

She wondered whether there were the remains of a dead animal somewhere nearby, or lodged between the walls. The smell changed from day to day. Some days it got better. Other days it got worse.

Maybe it was due to weather, perhaps humidity. She wondered again if there were a squirrel's nest somewhere within the walls, but she had never seen or heard any evidence thereof. Why didn't the darned smell just dissipate, once and for all, rather than repeating itself? Was there some bird or animal—like an owl or a hawk—that constantly dragged small fresh carcasses onto the premises?

Well, she decided, no need to agonize about it any more. It was time to do something.

Ellen set to work with a broom, sweeping the floor. Then she donned rubber gloves and poured some disinfectant into a bucket of water. She went to work on the walls, using a large sponge to clean every inch of wall surface. It took twenty minutes.

Although concentrating on what she was doing, she noticed that the furnace clicked on in the basement. "That will probably cost me twenty more dollars that I don't have," she mused ruefully, a not so kindly reference to the local oil dealer's price quote of a buck twenty-seven per gallon. Every time the furnace clicked on, it was like listening to money hemorrhage out of her checking account. In the back of her mind, she made a mental note to contact a discount fuel oil dealer sometime very soon.

She sighed and continued with the walls. The local weather forecast was calling for some very cold air to come into the area overnight, a nice icy blast from Ontario and points north. The temperatures would be heading toward the thirties. Well, she mused, if she was going to stay alive, she might as well stay warm, too.

She pulled on a sweatshirt to cover her T-shirt. She could have changed to jeans, but she stayed with a pair of shorts. She had caught a glimpse of herself in the mirror earlier that evening. She was pleased, or at least she'd thought she was. At thirty-six, she felt she still looked good, though she also knew she spent too much time each day looking at her own flaws. Well, she could still turn male heads nicely, sometimes even when she *didn't* want to. It gave her a feeling of confidence. Absently, she wondered about Michael Chandler and what his love life was like these days.

She smiled. Maybe it was time to date someone again. And maybe not. She mulled this over and stayed at work, humming to herself as she battled the brown room.

"What are you doing, Mom?" Sarah asked from the doorway.

Ellen jumped. She had been lost in her own thoughts—about the house, about the newspaper, about the bizarre death of James Corbett—and Sarah had taken her by surprise.

"Oh, sorry," Sarah said.

"It's okay, Sarah," she said, recovering.

"What are you doing, Mommy?" her daughter asked again.

"Washing walls, washing floors," she answered. "Maybe washing my hair if I get it caught in the bucket by accident."

Sarah giggled.

"I'm trying to make this room habitable for humanity," Ellen said. " 'Humanity' means me and you, babe. Want to help?"

"No." Her daughter playfully folded her arms in mock insolence. "I hate cleaning!"

"Think *I* enjoy it?"

"No. But you do it well."

"Thanks." She winked at her daughter. "That means I ought to throw the bucket at you."

Sarah playfully stuck out her tongue. Ellen made a fake motion of hurling the bucket at her, and they both laughed.

"Okay. What do you want me to do?" Sarah finally asked.

"Have you finished your homework?"

"I finished it."

"You actually don't have to help, honey. I'm just kidding."

Sarah watched her mother scrubbing.

"I'll do something," Sarah said next. "Just tell me what."

Ellen leaned back, assessing the floor, wondering how to put her daughter to work. The room remained chilly, despite the rumble from the furnace two floors directly beneath her—music to the ears, Ellen thought idly, of the international petroleum cartel.

"Tell you what, Miss Sarah," she said. "Go downstairs and take a look beneath the sink in the kitchen. There's an extra bucket. It's red. Fill it with warm water and bring it back to me, okay?"

"Okay."

Sarah disappeared promptly. A few feet away from Ellen, the old window shade gave a rattle, as if from an unseen hand.

Ellen eyed it critically. The shade was partially torn. The lower section was yellowed with age, and the upper part was white. The shade looked as if it had been hanging untouched at one length for many months, if not years.

Ellen went to it and pronounced the shade beyond repair. She reached to it and tried to remove it. For some reason the shade stuck, as if that unseen hand were now holding it in place. It was the strangest feeling, as if she were struggling against something she couldn't see.

What the—? she thought.

She felt as if she were trying to pick up a book that some man had a strong heavy hand on. She couldn't budge it. Then whatever had been securing the shade gave way. She lifted the shade easily from its bracket.

Ellen took the shade from the window and rolled it up. She stood it outside the door to the brown room. The old shade was now officially trash.

Ellen set back to scrubbing, rubbing the brush hard against a section of the floor, on which a sticky substance had formed a deep stain. For a second she was startled. She thought a large shadow passed through the room, as if someone had stepped quickly and quietly past the doorway to the brown room.

She turned. "Sarah?" she asked.

No answer. She frowned. Now *that* gave her the creeps. If she had to swear in court, she would have said that the shadow had seemed to have belonged to a man. A large man.

"Sarah?" she asked again.

Ellen climbed to her feet and went to the door. No one at all. Cautiously, she even walked from room to room. She stood and listened, but all she could hear was the sound of Sarah downstairs running the water in the kitchen.

She thought of her OHN's again—The Old House Noises. She sighed. Now, she reasoned, she had OHS&S's—Old House Sights and Shadows.

Or Old House Shouts and Screams, something maliciously playfully suggested from the far edge of her consciousness. *Or maybe Old House Shrieks and Shivers.*

She smiled.

Some people *did* find old places to be rather spooky, but she wasn't one of them. God knew, she reminded herself, that she had known plenty of people with misfortune and horrible events in *new* houses. So what was this all about, other than fatigue and a hyperactive runaway imagination? Hollow-eyed Ken Karp and his accountant's Ledger of Impending Fiscal Doom were far more threatening than a few shadows in a sixty-year-old house, she figured.

Sarah returned a few minutes later with the correct bucket and the right amount of water. Ellen gave her daughter's hand a squeeze, and wondered if Sarah would still be such a help as a teenager or an adult. For a moment, Ellen realized what a beautiful young woman Sarah would become.

Something unpleasant surfaced again from the nastier edge of her consciousness. It was an unconscious thought in the direction of the male child she had given up years ago.

And where was *Robin* now? something evil asked her. He had already lived his life. What did *he* look like as a young angel?

God! These bizarre thoughts!

An extra shudder went through her. Fortunately she was able to dismiss these notions. They didn't seem real enough to entertain.

But he is a young angel! something else said to her.

"Shut up!" she said, and her thoughts were somehow purified.

Sarah emptied the full bucket into the upstairs bathtub. When she came back, Ellen was scrubbing again.

Sarah stood in the doorway and watched her mother work for several seconds. "Mommy, I think this room is yucky," Sarah said.

"We're going to paint it, Sarah," Ellen said. "Tomorrow evening. Once we get the color changed and the smell gone, it'll be as nice as any other room in the house."

"I hate it," Sarah said.

Hate. Terminology she had never heard her daughter use before.

"That's not a nice word to use, Sarah," Ellen said.

"What word?"

" 'Hate.' You shouldn't 'hate' anything."

"I do hate this room."

"Why?"

"It's bad."

Ellen stopped what she was doing.

"What do you mean, 'it's bad'?" At the base of her neck she felt a little shiver start to creep up. Then it was gone.

"It just *is*," her daughter insisted.

"Why?"

"It makes me feel bad. It makes me feel all sad and unhappy to be in here."

"Why?" Ellen asked again.

"I don't know. It just does." She paused. "I don't want to be here. Can I go watch *Friends?*" the little girl asked.

"I don't know. 'Can' you?"

"May I?" Sarah corrected herself, a slight pout on her delicate lips.

Ellen thought about it. She thought about a lot of things. Downstairs the grandfather clocked chimed solemnly.

"Sure," Ellen finally answered. "If you want to, go ahead. Hey, Miss Sarah?"

"What?"

"See that broken shade by the door?" Ellen asked. Sarah put her hand on it.

"Please put it in the garbage in the garage, okay?"

"Okay."

"Then you can watch television. Say Hi to Rachel and Monica for me."

Sarah laughed again. "Thanks, Mom."

Ellen leaned back. What *was* it about this chamber that was so unsettling? she wondered. Was Sarah feeling the same thing as she?

She sat quietly for a moment.

She had heard about houses with bad vibrations, or bad overall auras. She had even heard of houses where crimes had been committed which seemed to have left some funny impressions in the rooms—some sort of psychological imprinting or electrical something. She had never thought of such things in terms of her own home or even this particular room—until now.

She even thought back to that bizarre situation on Long Island, the one where the house had been the subject of a grisly, family multiple murder in the 1970's. Amityville, Long Island. The so-called haunting of the house had turned into a bestselling novel and horror film in the 1980's.

The brown room was very still as Ellen worked her way through the memory of the Long Island horror house. Then something way back in the recesses of her memory told her that the Long Island story had been ultimately shown to be a hoax. Well, at least none of the other residents had a problem with the place except the people who had cashed in on the book.

Ellen looked around. Time to come to grips with her creepy feelings, she told herself.

"Come on. *Rationality,* Ellie W.," she insisted. "We are dealing with four shit-brown walls, a wood floor, a plasterboard ceiling, a window, and this damned cold. Nothing else."

Hey! *The cold?*

Yes. Even with the physical work she was doing

there were goosebumps appearing on her bare legs. What the heck was going on? she wondered. The furnace had clicked on ages ago and was chugging away like a tugboat down under the living room. However if she opened her mouth wide and breathed really hard, she could practically see her breath.

"Hey, at a buck twenty a gallon, I want to be warm," she thought. She went to the heating grate.

The grate was closed.

She put her hand on the iron lever that should have opened it, but now *it* wouldn't budge. She pulled it hard. It wouldn't move. She peered down into the grate and couldn't see an obstruction. It was obviously stuck in a closed position.

In an oblique way, this sort of made sense. The people who lived in this house must not have used this room. *And why not?* she wondered immediately. So they kept the heat off, and probably kept the door closed. Opening the grate would be a project in and of itself. So she let it go.

She returned to the center of the room and looked around at her work. Well, the walls looked brighter.

Sort of.

The floor looked cleaner.

Sort of.

And she felt better.

Sort of? Well, no.

She didn't like to admit it, even to herself, but she liked the room even less now. The brown room was starting to give her almost a sick feeling. She wondered if the previous occupants of the house had felt that way, too.

Well, she was a reporter. She would find out. In fact, she told herself, she would trace the ownership of the house at town hall. The place had been built in the 1930's, so how many owners could it have had? She'd see if anything strange had ever happened on the premises. Surely if anything major had ever happened, the local library or historical association would have material about it.

She grimaced. Why hadn't she thought of *that* before she had plunked down her money and moved in? Why hadn't the real estate guides suggested *that* for every new buyer coming into a home? Nothing like blood-spattered walls to wreck the resale value of a place and—

Oh, God! What an unfortunate thought! Brown paint! Horrible stains on the walls! Surely that was the reason for the—

Of course! Her mind raced. She could see a brutal ax or knife murder taking place right there, right where she stood in shorts and a sweatshirt!

Probably a woman had been the victim! Or a child!

The flesh, the blood, it had all flown against the walls as the hacking and stabbing continued. Why hadn't she asked the real estate brokers?

Brown paint! Of course! The dark tone covered the bloody aftermath of the most horrendous homicide.

"Aargh!" she said aloud. She shook her head vigorously.

"Come on, Mrs. W.," she said. "Tune out the nonsense and just come to grips with reality. You're way overtired and—"

Her rambling thoughts were interrupted by a horrible scream—her daughter's anguished voice from the garage!

For an instant, Ellen's blood felt as frigid as if she had been drenched with a bucket of ice water.

She heard her frightened little girl yelling again.

"Mommy! Mommy, come quick!"

"Sarah! I'm coming! I'm coming!" Ellen yelled back, turning and racing toward the stairs.

She heard a door slam, and knew a frightened Sarah had retreated from the garage to the kitchen.

Alone? Was someone else there?

"What is it?" Ellen called back in a frenzy.

"Mommy! There's something there! Something in the garage!"

Ellen arrived in the kitchen. Sarah was barricading the door with her thin arms.

"What? What's in the garage?"

"Something!"

"A man? A stranger?"

Ellen reached for the portable telephone. And a butcher's knife.

"An animal," Sarah said.

Ellen, easing slightly answered, "A what?"

"It's under the car," Sarah said.

Ellen blinked, going from a sense of fear to a sense of the absurd practically within a heartbeat. "Well, what the heck is it? A mountain lion?"

"It's gray," said Sarah.

"How big?"

Her daughter opened her hands and gestured. It was, she indicated, slightly larger than a four-slice toaster.

Relieved, Ellen gave her an ironic smile. She sighed and calmed her raging nerves.

"Let's take a look," she said. A moment passed as she gathered herself. She traded the knife for a broom and a heavy flashlight.

Ellen opened the garage door. The old window shade was exactly where Sarah had dropped it. There was no movement in the garage.

"Under the car," Sarah repeated.

Ellen got down on all fours, her bare knees cold against the concrete of the garage floor. She shined her flashlight under the car.

At first she saw nothing.

Then there was a flash of gray, and two reddish eyes reflected the beam of light. Huddled near a tire was an opossum, trembling slightly, a refugee from the plunging temperatures outside.

"It's a 'possum, Sarah darling," Ellen said. "And it's more scared than the two of us put together."

"What's a 'possum?" her daughter asked.

"You *did* live in the city too long, didn't you?" Ellen said. She coaxed Sarah into getting down and taking a look with her. The frightened creature tried to make itself small before the rear of a tire.

"The little gray guy couldn't be more harmless," Ellen said of their unannounced visitor. "But I'm not inviting it to spend the night, either."

"Oh," Sarah said. She thought about it. "Should we feed him?" Sarah asked.

"Not a good idea, Sarah. If we feed him he'll take up residence here, and we'll never get rid of him."

Sarah looked disappointed. A potential new pet was in and out so quickly. "So what are we going to do?" the little girl asked.

"We'll send him back to the woods where he belongs," Ellen said. "He's wild. He shouldn't be depending on us, or he'll forget how to find food for himself."

"Oh," Sarah said. Her mother's logic seemed impeccable.

Ellen opened the garage door. A blast of cold rushed in. When the animal refused to leave and even resisted being chased with the broom, Ellen sent

Sarah indoors for her car keys. When Ellen started the car, the animal shot out of their garage.

Ellen watched the animal trot toward the street, then disappear into the woods on the other side of the road. Her daughter stood next to her, and she placed a hand on Sarah's shoulders as they watched the small, gray beast depart.

Ellen looked up at the trees around her house and the stars beyond. It was a sharply colder night, but a clear one. The cold air on her legs now felt suddenly invigorating. She closed the garage door within a few seconds. No point letting any more creatures in.

"Hey," she said to Sarah. "Enough excitement for one evening. Bedtime."

"Aw—"

"Bedtime," Ellen repeated. "I'm not getting enough sleep as it is, my dear, and if you don't turn in, I can't, either."

"Aw—" Sarah said again in playful protest.

Ellen took a gentle swipe at her daughter's backside, but the little girl was too quick. Nimbly, she sped away to get ready for sleep.

Ellen went back upstairs and collected her cleaning equipment. She would paint the walls white, she decided, to neutralize the brown. Then she would paint the room a comforting light blue, or maybe even a cheerful yellow—anything to change the character. She again dismissed the horrendous vision of a murder in that room. She closed the door to the brown room and left it for the night.

She put her daughter to bed. Half an hour later, she, too, was asleep.

* * *

Ellen's second unannounced visitor of the evening arrived five hours later. It was the time of the night that he liked to wander.

The intruder bypassed every lock in the house. He stood downstairs in the living room just as the grandfather clock chimed three. His heavy breathing and his heartbeat played counterpoint to the tick of the clock in a strange symphony.

For several minutes, he stood in the middle of the living room, like a huge, hulking, misplaced armoire. He wondered what he would do if the little girl woke and saw him, or if the woman who headed the household was a light sleeper and came down with a gun.

That would be trouble, he mused in his simple way. That would cause him to change his plans. Women were unpredictable like that. He had always had problems of misunderstanding with women.

He took several minutes to get his bearings. On a side table, there was a figurine of a dancer, a small likeness that Ellen's father had brought back from Europe when she had been a girl. The figurine looked like something from a Degas painting. The intruder picked it up, examined it, and kept it in his hand.

His brown eyes drifted to the big grandfather clock. It was now four minutes after five. The pendulum in the old clock swung methodically, and the ticking from the clock was loud and resolute.

The visitor ignored it. He set down the figurine on a coffee table before the living room sofa. Then he walked to the steps. He moved very quietly for such a big man. His footsteps on the old steps might have caused creaking for normal men of his weight, but his touch was like a feather—almost unreal. He was upstairs in a few seconds, having made no sound.

A bathroom light was on.

Obviously, Mrs. Ellen Wilder kept something on in case she or her daughter wanted to move around in the night and see their way to the bathroom.

The light bothered him. He didn't like it, and didn't need it. He could see very well in the dark.

He took two steps toward the bathroom and then pushed the door open, throwing a larger ribbon of light into the hallway. He saw the switch on the wall. Switches made noise, so he moistened his fingers and reached for the bulb. It was a hundred watts, and it had been on for hours, yet he barely felt the heat as his large, thick, strong fingers turned the bulb slowly until the light was extinguished.

He entered the woman's room first. Her door was open. He moved very quietly and approached her bed. He looked down at her. She must have been very tired, for she was sleeping soundly, so still that she almost appeared to be dead.

The huge man extended an arm. His fingers went to her mouth. The tips of the fingers stayed just above her lips. Yes, she was alive. His fingers, the ones that had just touched the lightbulb, picked up the feeling of her breath.

His hand moved slightly. It was right at her throat. Mrs. Wilder was very pretty. He wondered what it would be like to have sex with such a woman. What were educated women like in bed? Did they do the things that whores did, or did they do the things that farm girls did? Were they compliant? Did they take orders? Were they submissive?

A long smile passed across his lips as he fantasized. *Well,* he told himself, *maybe someday.*

He lowered his hand to his side. Ellen rolled in her sleep, and the big man recoiled slightly. Very qui-

etly, he backed away from her and went to her door.
This was not the time for her to see him.

He passed quietly from her room.

The other bedroom door was also wide open. From
the hallway, he could see the little girl sleeping. Sarah
was his real interest in the house. If only her mother
knew! His frame filled the doorway to the little girl's
bedroom. He stood for several seconds watching her.
She was a sound sleeper. That was good.

He slowly entered the room, his huge feet moving
quietly across the carpeting. He moved to within six
feet of the bed, then three. His eyes were absolutely
feral. He had excellent night vision. The little girl
had a smile on her face, which must have meant that
she was in the midst of a wonderful dream.

He wondered what a wonderful dream could be to
a little girl like that. He wondered about all the unknowable things in heaven and on earth, and fantasized that someday he would have the answer to that,
too.

He was beside her bed. Her angelic face was still
uplifted with a smile. He gazed down and moved his
hands to her head. He touched her hair. It was soft
and silky. She smelled very sweet.

He was mesmerized by her innocence, her vulner-
ability, her defenselessness. He knelt, like a man before a religious shrine. He caressed her hair for
several minutes. At one point he stopped when he
thought he saw her eyes flicker open slightly. But they
closed again.

He had the urge to pick her up, but he resisted.

In the darkness of the child's room, a big dumb
smile crossed Franny's face. He was happy there. He
decided to stay.

Franny sat down on the edge of Sarah's bed and

gazed at her for several minutes, hoping she would not open her eyes, see him, and start to scream.

He would have to do something unpleasant, after all, if she screamed.

An hour passed. The huge man kept his nocturnal vigil. Then he rose. Outside, the sky was still black. It an hour or so, it would turn a very deep blue, signaling the advent of dawn—the birth of a new day. His primitive thoughts drifted to the Corbett farm and all those places, both magical and mundane, contained in the family's nine hundred fifty acres.

Franny looked at the child for a final time. Something caught his eye. There was a mosquito buzzing near the child's head in the dark.

Franny's eyes flashed. So did his powerful hands. He caught the insect out of the air with a thumb and forefinger. He obliterated it.

Franny could obliterate anything he wanted. He knew that. And anyone who encountered him should learn that very quickly.

He receded slightly from where Sarah Wilder slept peacefully. He smiled again.

At ten minutes before seven that same morning, Ellen's eyes flashed open with horror. This rarely happened. She had overslept.

Oh God, she thought. "Oh, God!" So early in the morning, and already she was behind.

She had forty minutes to get her daughter fed, dressed, and off to school, as well as herself fed, dressed, and off to the office. The procedure usually took seventy minutes. There was nothing, she concluded quickly, quite like being under the gun from the moment she rose in the morning.

"Sarah? Sarah?" she called, bursting from her own bedroom, sleepiness still hanging in her eyes. She went toward her daughter's room.

"Sarah, honey, I overslept," Ellen said. "You have to—"

She looked into her daughter's room.

No one was there. No Sarah.

In fact, the room looked surreal. Her daughter's books and schoolbag were gone, and the bed had been made.

Well, the bed had been crudely and roughly made, as if by hands not used to making it.

"Sarah?" she called out.

No answer. The house was still. Her daughter was nowhere in sight.

"Sarah?" she called out with urgency. "Where are you?"

Still nothing. A terrible feeling came over Ellen. She went to the stairs and ran down. There was a slight noise from the kitchen: A man's voice, rumbling low.

"Good God! What the—?"

She felt a terrible sudden sense of fear. A mother's gut feeling of intrusion and violation, not to mention the burning, searing fear of something having happened to a child.

Again!

She ran to the kitchen door, gasped, and stopped short. Ellen could barely believe what was before her.

"Sarah?" she said.

Her daughter, fully dressed for school, turned and smiled.

"I wanted to surprise you," Sarah said.

Ellen caught her breath. She exhaled a long low breath of relief. "Well, you did," she said.

"I wanted you to sleep a little more," Sarah said. "I was going to come up and wake you at seven, Mommy. Was that okay?"

The man's voice was from the news on the radio: WCBS in New York.

Sarah had poured cereal for the both of them and had put the orange juice and milk on the breakfast table. Four slices of bread were in the double toaster, ready to descend. For a nine-year-old, she had done an excellent job at making breakfast.

"That was fine, Sarah," she said. "Just fine."

Ellen went to her daughter and hugged her, relieved and happy in more ways than she could count. In the living room, the unstoppable old clock chimed 7:00 A.M.

Half an hour later, Ellen pulled up the garage door and stepped out to take a breath of morning air before taking Sarah to school.

She was almost shocked at what she encountered.

There had been plenty of fall color in the trees the day before—all of the reds and oranges and yellows that she had loved as a girl—but during the night something extreme had happened to change the appearance of the world that surrounded Ellen's new home.

The cold wave that had come through with a vengeance had icily assaulted the landscape. All around the house, the beautiful leaves had been stripped from the trees, and now the branches remained as skeletal arms, hands, and fingers. The trees stood like tall, silent sentries of winter, announcing the death of the harvest season and, when the wind moved through them, pointing in their rickety, clattering way toward the deep chill and resonant cold of winter that would follow.

The change was shocking in its suddenness. It was as if October had turned to December, without the buffer month of November in between.

Ellen put an arm protectively around her daughter. Some maternal instinct told her that protection was necessary. She took her to school, afraid to glance in the rearview mirror as she drove.

Sarah arrived at school and Ellen was at the office by nine. In the confusion of the morning, no one noticed in the downstairs living room that the small figurine had moved overnight from one table to the other.

Eleven

Detective Michael Chandler was engaged in a never-ending battle against paperwork from previous cases. Thus he found himself at his office in the state police barracks in Westport, Connecticut on Wednesday night, trying to close out several previous investigations.

There was a small bin that contained unfinished but still open cases—police investigations that Chandler and others had put in weeks on without results. Chandler attempted to make progress with this bin. It was late in the evening, a time when he might have been home.

Many of the cases were incidents which he had worked with the local town police, Bridgeport, Milford, Hamden, and Wallingford, in particular. Included were numerous housebreakings, car thefts, and store thefts, punctuated by a smaller number of assaults. There were a pair of bank robberies that were part of a series with the same signatures up and down the east coast. The Feds had become involved in that one and they hadn't been able to resolve it, either, though they also had airport police involved. The theory was that the robbers were jetting into the area, hitting, and running—or, more literally, flying.

Several different law enforcement agencies in the area were waiting for the robbers to strike again, and make a mistake. Every airport was going to be covered.

He went through his files.

Constant reviewing kept him familiar with each case. Many of these investigations were matters on which he had spent hours of thought on his own time. The most aggravating part of police work, aside from the risk of getting killed, was to have doped out a case, know how it had been perpetrated, sometimes even know who had done it, but remain unable to bring it to conclusion. Anything that was on his desk and couldn't be closed bothered him, but he knew the world was gloriously imperfect. That had been demonstrated many times by now.

Being alive was a bonus, he reminded himself. Being able to come to work was a bonus. Why bitch about some unresolved cases?

Besides, he mused further as the hour grew later, unresolved meant unresolved *as yet*. It was never out of the question to close one far down the road.

Most of these dossiers, as he sorted through them, were returned to the right hand corner of his desk. A few, perhaps one in every six, he managed to put into a deeper section of his department's files, the one for cases that were likely to remain static forever. Some of these were still kicking around from the time before he had been shot. Every such case, every crime that he released to the department's version of Siberia, pained him. An unresolved case was like a riddle which, having been asked, has no answer. Such happenings violated his sense of fair play. He took some small consolation from the theory that in at least some of these cases the perpetrators were prob-

ably already in jail, having been nailed for other un-
lawful acts.

At a few minutes before midnight, he reviewed his
memorable 'Cemetery of Angels' case. It was an incident from a few years ago, having to do with an
assault in a supermarket parking lot in Westport. The
victims had moved to California, where the case had
been picked up by an L.A. detective named Ed Van
Allen. The suspected perp, Chandler knew, was dead.
Chandler was able to relegate this file, too, and
should have long ago.

Then he decided to spend a few more minutes on
the immediate business before him—The Corbett
Case, as he called it. He picked up the file and
leaned back in the chair at his desk. His arm gave
one of those irritating twinges and began to radiate
pain.

The pain reminded him of getting shot, and
thoughts about getting shot reminded him of being
dead, or having been dead for a few minutes, anyway,
and then coming back.

He shuddered. The barracks were quiet. He raised
his eyes for a moment and saw Franny Corbett standing there in front of him: Solid and substantial. Clear
as a bell. All six and a half feet.

Then Mike Chandler blinked and the image was
gone.

Now Franny *wasn't* standing there, and neither was
anyone else. It was as if Chandler had picked up a
split second flash from a projector, or had caught a
peek at something from another reality, something
loitering on the edge of his consciousness, and then
it had flashed away again.

Eerie. Creepy.

He stared at the spot in front of his desk. His

shoulder gave a further tingle, and he grimaced. The image before him had been, for some immeasurably short space of time, so clear and forceful that he had difficulty rejecting it. Yet by all that he had been accustomed to believe in, there was no one in front of him.

He was alone.

Gradually, he lowered his eyes. He looked at the front of the Corbett file. He flicked his line of vision upward again to try to see if he could recreate the circumstances that had thrown the image of Franny before him.

He couldn't. It didn't happen a second time. Then he realized that he had broken a slight sweat. Something within him had reacted fearfully to what he had seen.

Instinct? Impulse?

He breathed deeply and tried to wish away the pain in his shoulder. It wouldn't obey the command. He reached into his desk for some ibuprofen tablets, quaffed a pair of them, and tried to ignore the pain.

Chandler held the Corbett file in his hand for several seconds, then opened it. He reread and restudied everything he had on the death of James Corbett, taking twenty minutes. When he finished that material, he opened an accompanying file, containing photographs and background information on the Corbett family. That took another ten minutes. When he was finished with it, he pushed both files to the right corner of his desk and left them closed.

He folded his arms in front of him and thought intensely. His eyes found the old-fashioned, round wall clock. He noticed that the minute hand had passed the six, and the hour was on the upside toward 1:00 A.M.

Damn!

Something about this Corbett investigation bothered him intensely. He couldn't quite put a finger on what it was. Maybe it was the absence of normal logic. Nothing in the case ever added up properly.

Mike Chandler didn't like cases that contradicted themselves. There was something, he felt, inherently evil about them—something "off kilter," as he thought of it. Even in the infinite capacity of human beings for mayhem or deception, there was usually a skein of logic, but it escaped him here.

Given: Two suspicious deaths, and very probably two murders, in the same small Connecticut town in four months. How did they tie together, if at all?

Point: The logic of the two cases imploded on itself, or at least it seemed to. Franny Corbett might not even have been in Wilshire when the original incident with Maury Fishkin had occurred.

So why would Franny have felt compelled to kill Fishkin, as had been suggested?

To "earn" his membership in his old clan? Maybe.

Had he been brought east to do the job so that James would have a cover story? Was Franny a jagged-fingernailed family hit man? Maybe. But why bother to import someone? The family had never felt obliged to bring in outside help before.

Point: But then again, if Franny were a murderer, why would he now be murdering his own family? *That* made no sense. That suggested that the crimes had different killers, even though the deaths might have been linked. If Franny was the second killer, was James the first? And who was the second? Franny again?

Where was the method in that? Where was the logic?

And for that matter, where *was* Fishkin? Chandler held to the theory that the hardware dealer, if he was dead, was submerged from view locally.

Somewhere.

Somewhere sinister.

Somewhere right under everyone's noses.

But where?

A boozy craving welled up in Chandler. He wished he had a brew with him. Against department regulations, sure, but who was going to bitch? He could have concealed it in his hand, kept it low near his desk. Hey, there had been a time before Tito Moreno when he would never have *dreamed* of quaffing a brew on duty. Now he had the urge all the time.

He thought of a beer vendor whom he had once seen at Yankee Stadium earlier this past summer: a guy who called himself, "Cousin Brewski."

Get a buzz from The Cuz.

Chandler smiled and went back to work.

Corollary: James Corbett still could have died accidentally. Maybe there was no first and second murderer—only a killer of Fishkin, *if* Fishkin was in fact dead.

Maybe, Chandler further reasoned, Fishkin and his dog would come floating to the surface somewhere, alive and well, and in the end Chandler would have no murderers at all. Just a piece of white trash who fell out of a tree onto a piece of rusty farm equipment.

He reasoned this point, but he didn't believe it.

Then again, the two deaths could have been totally unrelated. And yet, and yet. It didn't make complete sense. Like much of life, it refused to tie neatly together.

As he thought anew about the two cases, it preyed

on his mind all the more. Chandler shook his head. There was something about the Corbett case that had eluded him. Something he couldn't see.

Something big.

Further point: Over the years, he had learned to trust his gut. His instincts. His feelings.

All of these were on a sharp edge now, keenly honed. Everything within him told him that Franny Corbett was the linchpin of his investigation.

Follow Franny. Find the solution.

That simple. That elusive. Even his shoulder seemed to be telling him that. His shoulder cried out in pain every time Franny crossed his mind.

Which led to a final point. What *was* it with Franny? What was that fearsome, unearthly quality about him?

And why, why, *why*, did so many details repeat on him about the day he had been shot whenever he was in Franny's presence or thought about him? Why did his shoulder bother him? As it did right now, for example, as the clock said ten of one.

Why?

The Corbett case, he told himself as his thoughts rambled further, was like a bad dream.

Yes, indeed, he decided as he rose from his desk and prepared to go home, the Corbett case was *exactly* like a bad dream.

Another thought came to him from somewhere: *Like your usual bad dream, Mike?*

In his usual bad dream he was back in that housing project in Bridgeport, standing there helpless as a scumbag drug dealer shot him from ambush . . . then he was falling, listening to the shouts and screaming surrounding the second round of gunshots . . . then he was dead in the hospital . . . drifting . . . drifting . . . drifting . . . toward whatever bright light it was he had sensed when his heart stopped and his brain had flatlined.

In the dream, he continued to drift. He never came back from the dead. Not until he woke up.

Your usual bad dream? The question repeated itself. Then it amplified itself. *Was there some linkage between what had happened to him from gunfire in Bridgeport and the Corbett case?*

Well that was sure as hell a funny thought, he told himself. Where had that come from?

Why *would* there be a connection?

How *could* there be?

Because he felt funny in Franny Corbett's presence? *And what about Janine Osheyak?*

"What?" he said. That name had popped into his mind again, straight out of his subconscious. Where was it coming from?

He had no answer to that question, or any other. That was part of the enigma of the Corbett case. The more he posed questions, the more other questions suggested themselves. Some cases were about narrowing things down so that an investigator could understand them. The Corbett case seemed to be about widening the scope of the whole episode, looking for possibilities that he might not have believed existed before.

Words came to him on wings. Like a voice whispering in his ear. *Accepting the supernatural?*

His head shot up. He spoke aloud.

"What?" he asked.

"Accepting the supernatural."

This time the words repeated themselves with the tone of a statement, not a question.

"Where in hell did *that* come from?" he asked.

He waited for an audible response, but all he heard was the quiet walls of the police station late at night. He heard a sergeant talking on the telephone somewhere in the distance, and then the crackle of a radio.

Nothing else.

Then he stared at something on the corner of his desk in abject disbelief. The folder containing Corbett material was wide open! He did not remember reopening it, but conceded that he might have. It was open to the Polaroid picture of Franny, as if in response to his mental inquiry, and the fleeting, acid-flash style image of the big hulking man *had* wafted before him several minutes earlier.

Franny gazed at him—this time from a photograph.

In return, Chandler stared and stared, and stared some more. What unseen force had passed near his desk and opened the file? Had someone walked by, and had he been too wrapped up in his work to even notice? He didn't think so. Had he accidentally knocked a file open, or inadvertently left one open? He didn't believe that, either. So what was the explanation?

Now his brain was *really* playing nasty tricks on him!

What was the only conclusion?

Franny Corbett had been talking about spirits during their one conversation. Had someone, or some spirit *some way*, in a manner that Chandler didn't understand, managed to slip past his desk and—

"You should listen to the spirits," Franny had grumbled. *"The spirits'd tell you stuff."*

Perplexed, Chandler now thought back on the exchange and turned it over in his mind, working it from a different perspective.

"Spirits," Franny had insisted. *"Can'tcha see them? All*

*over the fucking place. They'll tell you a lot of shit if you'd
listen."*

Mike Chandler drew another breath, then pushed
himself back from his desk. He rubbed his tired eyes
and backed off from this line of thought, too.

Another voice in his subconscious chimed in. A
frighteningly familiar one.

"It's true, you know. The spirits *will* tell you things,
Mikey Boy."

His late father's voice. His eyes shot open and he
looked around. The words had seemed so clear, so
distinct. It was almost as if he had heard them audi-
bly, as opposed to in the stressed-out memory cham-
bers of his mind.

He looked around uneasily. He heard his heart
pumping. He was thirsty as a man in a desert.

He was also overtired, stressed, and getting into a
delusional state, he told himself. That was why his
thoughts were becoming irrational.

1:00 A.M.

Hell. What was any reasonable man doing at work
at 1:00 A.M. He had come in at 8:00 A.M. the previous
morning.

He pushed himself back further from these strange
ruminations. He reminded himself that he was a man
who dealt in the physical word, the world of tangible,
empirical proof.

Fingerprints.

Gunshot wounds.

Times in the day.

DNA tests.

Clear-eyed, clear thinking godfearing witnesses.

The answers to his questions, the resolution of the
Corbett case, the riddle of Maury Fishkin's disappearance, were anchored in this tangible world. It was not

floating around among the stars. It was delusional to think otherwise, or to pose questions better left to the astrology columns.

No, no, no, he insisted to his subconscious.

He was *not* ready to start postulating on other-worldly explanations for things. He might have been to death and back, but he was a rational man.

He repeated that. It was his mantra for the evening, his morning prayer. His catechism.

He was a *rational man* who believed in the empirical logical demonstrable things!

That was what he told himself. Why was it that he hadn't *convinced* himself?

He blew out a long, tired breath.

He rose from his desk. Time to go home. He was due back at work in another seven hours. He sometimes felt as if he were on a treadmill, and the treadmill never stopped moving, day after day. Nor did his feet.

Michael Chandler turned the light off on his desk and departed from the main work room of state police headquarters. It was 1:10 A.M. His eyes were red-rimmed, and his cheeks were lined with fatigue.

A moment later he was in the parking lot. He felt very cold when he walked to his car. His shoulder spasmed and jabbed him with pain when he placed his left hand on his car door to open it. As he drove home, he passed a big time-and-temperature display that overlooked the turnpike, a bank logo parked on top of it, the logo with the listing steamboat.

He winced. Twenty-nine degrees, the temperature read.

The cold rush of air from Canada that had crashed across New England had apparently settled in. It had torn all the colorful leaves off the trees, and now it was placing its grip on the central part of the state.

He shuddered. The first freezing weather of the season. He took it as a signal of the early winter to come, and felt more discomfort than usual at that thought.

On Sturgis Road, Ellen Wilder was passing what seemed to be an uneventful night. The package that she had received from Harold Duperry had sat in her desk drawer at work for long enough. At six o'clock that day, she had taken it from the drawer, piled it in with all the other work she was bringing home, and had taken it from the offices of her newspaper.

At home, she had not yet been able to open it, either, but when she came home, she laid the package flat upon the far right hand side of her desktop in her downstairs study.

In the evening, comfortably changed from work clothes into jeans and a sweatshirt, she helped Sarah with some homework. Then she did some newspaper work on her computer. Most of her remaining staff writers were downright awful. There wasn't one who turned in text that didn't have to be cleaned up. Cleaned up, Ellen grimaced ruefully, meant rewritten. Key facts were buried at the ends of stories. Entire paragraphs meandered through one, long, runon sentence. Half of her staff was computer illiterate, and handed in material on lined paper torn from notepads. One reporter's handwriting looked more like hieroglyphics than English.

She sighed.

Once again, these were the nit-picking, aggravating,

time-consuming things that slowly killed her. How could she have known that she was also going to be the top rewrite woman on the paper, in addition to owner, publisher, editor, and advertising manager?

Well, thank God in one way for the oncoming winter, she mused as she tried to decipher the submitted text for a note on the obituary page. A few of the local stores had taken out advertising for winter storm equipment: Snow blowers. Snow shovels. Fifty pound bags of rock salt. All the other wonderful accoutrements of winter in New England.

Her ad pages, with some surprising late purchases, were better this week than any previous week. She had an idea as she cheerfully worked the obits. There were two funeral parlors in neighboring towns. Why weren't they placing ads with her paper? She made a mental note to drop by both over the next day. She would entice them with a free ad if they bought one. People had to die, didn't they? She would go in there the next day and turn on all the charm she had to try to nail some advertising. She wondered what was an appropriate skirt length for hawking favorable ad rates to a mortician. She smiled, remembering when she used to work city hall in New York when she was in her twenties. The shorter the skirt the more politicians tended to talk.

As she closed out the small column, she flicked her computer screen back to page one. There was nothing new on the death of James Corbett, and her front page coverage said so. In fact, the whole investigation, to the extent that it even *was* an investigation, seemed to be going nowhere fast.

She leaned back for a moment and studied her coverage. There had to be *something* new, she reasoned. Some new angle. Something to at least catch people's attention and sell more copies of the paper. She wished something would happen within the next day, before she had to close her story.

She wondered further about the disappearance of the hardware man back during the summer. She made a note to call the state police about that one. Did the Fishkin family have an idea about what to do with the store? It seemed to be sitting there, inert, waiting for its owner to return.

Where was a potential story? she asked herself. Was there *some* special angle somewhere?

A line of doggerel came to her, playing upon her own words: *Was there some special angel somewhere?*

Probably not. Who believed in such things?

Flap, flap. The only winged beings around Wilshire were the crows and the grackles, which probably should have been the town mascots.

Angels. Hell, she could use a few.

Finally, she studied the composition of her back two pages, sports and ads. *The Republican* would run ten pages this week, which wasn't bad. Three and a half pages were advertising. Calculating mentally, she figured that losses that week might be minimal. There might even be a tiny profit of a hundred dollars or so, depending on how the accounting was done.

Tiny profits, she mused, could be cause for a large celebration. At least the flow was going into her pocket instead of out.

Sarah was ready for bed at nine-thirty. Ellen went upstairs and talked to her daughter for a few minutes before kissing her goodnight. She closed the door three quarters and left the room.

For some reason, she then walked to the brown room. As usual, it was intensely cold inside. Worse, with the low temperatures outside the cold seemed to be seeping through to the adjoining rooms.

Ellen went back downstairs and worked till eleven. When the grandfather clock struck that hour, she turned out her desk light and went upstairs, leaving the unopened photograph of Robin on her desk. She slept soundly.

The next morning, she found the unopened package on the left side of her desk, which startled her. She was sure she had put it on the right.

It was stacked neatly with her other things, so she decided that she must have moved it herself.

In any case, she placed it in a drawer and locked the drawer. She also made a deal with herself. It was foolish to deny what was in the package and to keep putting off looking at it. Better to get the heartbreak over as soon as possible. So the deal was, she would open it before the weekend was over.

One more issue of the paper, and she would try to reconcile herself to her past.

It sounded reasonable, and she felt comfortable with that decision.

Twelve

The next morning broke bright, cold, and clear, but it wasn't the morning that would prove memorable. It was the afternoon, when Mike Chandler dropped by the police station in Wilshire.

He received the same, increasingly chilly reception that he was getting in this town. No one on the local force had made any further effort to resolve James Corbett's death, other than to keep it parked in the suicide file. Lukas Corbett, one of the slow-witted Corbett relatives on the force, was sitting at Chief Moore's desk when Chandler came calling, drawing a salary and watching television.

Lukas was a thick man with a round face, oily dark hair, and a shaggy mustache to match. He wore jeans, a police shirt halfway in and halfway out of the uniform, and gray boots. He barely looked up when Chandler appeared at the door.

"The chief around?" Chandler asked.

"Day off," Lukas Corbett answered. He belched softly.

"Anything new on your cousin?"

That caused Lukas to turn. "Which cousin?"

"The one who swallowed a pitchfork."

Not a flicker of anything came from Lukas as he

answered. "Nothing." He looked back to the television and sat in his own haze of cigarette smoke.

"Tell the chief I came by," Chandler said.

"Yeah," Lukas said. Chandler knew he wouldn't, and left. On his way to his car, he encountered Andy Rourke, one of the two schoolboys who liked to throw stones across Lake Barbara.

"Hey, Andy," Chandler said.

"Hello, Mr. Chandler."

"How are things going?"

"They're okay," the boy said.

"Still skimming rocks up at the lake?"

"Yup."

"What's that I see you doing with Matthew Souza and the blue baseball hat?" Chandler asked.

The boy smiled.

"The hat washed up on the side of the lake," Andy said. "Matthew and me, we found it when we was skimming rocks. So whoever wins the competition each day keeps the hat."

"Like a champion keeping a title belt? Like in boxing?" asked Chandler, following this along.

"Yeah. Or like in the pro wrestling, 'cepting the pro wrestling is most probably fixed."

"Yeah," Chandler smiled. "It most probably is."

"And in boxing you have to bite somebody's ear off."

"You're a smart kid, Andy. A little bit of a smart-ass, but you're okay."

They both laughed. Then they fell into stride with each other.

"So what do you do? Count the skips?" Chandler asked idly. "Most skips wins? Or is it the longest skip?"

"Not neither. It's most points."

"How do you get a point?"

"Three skips and kerplunk," said Andy.

"You mean, splash? It sinks?"

"No. It hits something."

A little cloud scudded over them and left them in a chilly shadow. A breeze kicked up to accompany the shade. "I'm losing you, Andy," Chandler said.

"There's something in the water," Andy said again. "You can't see it, but like, it's there? When you hit it with a stone it goes 'kerplunk'," the boy explained.

Chandler stopped short, feeling a chill not associated with the weather. He looked at the boy. "It does *what?*" he asked.

"The stone skips through the water and makes this kerplunk sound?" Andy said. Like every other kid in town, he had a habit of ending his statements with an upward interrogatory inflection.

"Then it's hitting something. Wood? A log floating?" Chandler asked.

"Nope. It's metal. It looks sort of flat."

"It *looks?* How big is it?"

The boy shrugged. "You can't see it so well from shore. Maybe it's four feet long."

"And it moves?"

"Not very much."

"Color?"

"Same as the water. Dark."

"So it could be a dark green?"

"Maybe." The boy paused. It was a long pause. It was a should sort of pause.

"What is it, Andy?" Chandler asked. "What do you know?"

"Can I tell you a secret?"

"Sure."

"It's just sort of kid talk."

"That's okay. Go ahead."

Andy drew a breath. "Kevin McCarthy—he's this kid in the fifth grade at St. Agnes? He's this real good swimmer. He swam out there to the kerplunk spot when he was off from school during the Jewish holiday. No one else was at the lake. And he claims that there's a doorway to this whole underground city under the lake."

"Why does he say that?"

"Because of when he swam out to it, that's why. He says he saw like the top of a window. He swam out and he comes back, and the next day he's going, 'Wow! You can't believe it! There's this monster's face pressed up against a window, with big monster eyes.' "

Again, Chandler had a very cold feeling.

"I think it's just bullshit," Andy said softly. "Know what I mean? I mean, it's like haunted houses. There's like no such thing, right?"

"I haven't seen a real one yet," Chandler said, uneasy with the question and equivocating carefully. "At least not that I knew at the time."

"Yeah, well, I don't believe in no underground city. But Kev's afraid to go to the lake. He swears he saw something."

"Andy," said Chandler firmly. "Take me and show me."

"Aw, you don't want to."

"Yes, I do."

"Do I get to ride in the police car?"

"I think we'd better walk."

The boy shrugged again. "Okay," he said.

Chandler engaged the boy in small talk as they walked from the center of town out to the lake. The sun was bright, and hung in the sky to the west when

they arrived. There was a breeze, and the surface of
the water was rippling. Chandler was wearing a wind-
breaker, but the breeze cut right through it. He
looked at the water about fifty feet off the pier.

"I don't see anything, Andy," he said.

"Sometimes you can't hardly," the boy said. "But
it's there. I know it's there. Something's there. I figured it was some old boat."

"Anyone ever report losing a boat in this lake?"

"Nah, not that I know. And anyways, it's only been
there for a few months. I figured it might have
shifted around a little."

"Like from late summer?"

"Yeah. Maybe."

"Show me exactly," Chandler said.

Andy pointed. The object that he had described
still was not visible, not to the eye.

While Chandler struggled to see something, anything, in the water, Andy ambled back to the land
and picked up a handful of flat stones. He walked to
the end of the pier.

"Follow me. Watch," the boy said. "This is like
pitching against the Yankees." He was a southpaw
with a good delivery.

"Exactly," said Chandler.

The boy's first stone skimmed past the spot. The
second one hit something hard just beneath the
water surface.

Kerplunk, just as Andy had described it.

Kerplunk. The sound of a stone hitting a heavy
metal container that was probably filled with water.
An image flashed to Chandler of a time in Bridgeport
when he'd been on homicide down there. The harbor police had fished an oil drum out of Long Island
sound, opened it, and found a local loan shark who'd

been missing for a year—or what was left of him. His hands and his head had been buried somewhere else.

Chandler had the same sickening feeling now, though this time he had a pretty good idea what he would find.

Andy skimmed a third stone. This time Chandler could see exactly what was happening. There was a constant breeze across the lake, forming little waves. Sometimes the waves washed over whatever was in the water just enough to leave its top, its roof, exposed. And sometimes the waves covered it. It was almost imperceptible to the eye. And sometimes Andy's stones missed it.

Kerplunk. The boy nailed it again.

"Good shot, huh?" he asked.

"Great shot," he said. "Now you get to ride in the police car."

"Why?"

"I'm giving you a lift home. Then I have to come back with a boat."

"Can't I stay?"

"Bad idea, Andy."

The boy was disappointed, but accepted his exclusion from the mystery. Adults were always ending the fun like that. This was nothing new. Damn them all.

Chandler drove Andy Rourke home and radioed for a state police boat and a backup in a car. The car came right away, bearing a big, dumb trooper named McMichael from Southbury. It took another hour to get a boat there, during which Chandler took a moment out and phoned Ellen Wilder at the newspaper.

"If you have a strong stomach but want the next part of your story," he said, "better get here."

"Where's 'here'?" she asked.

"We're on the lake," he said. "And there's something in it."

A moment of silence. Then, "Oh, Lord," she said.

Chandler already knew that the next thing he would need was a tow truck with a one hundred foot chain, something big and muscular for pulling a heavy vehicle out of the mud at the bottom of the lake.

Two state cops, Tom Vincent and Ethel Berry, arrived with the boat and launched it. McMichael stayed on the shore, where he would prove to be happier. Ellen Wilder arrived, and stood not too far from him.

Chandler, Vincent, and Berry motored out to the spot of Kevin McCarthy's underground city and Andy Rourke's four-foot metal target. The three cops sat together as the afternoon died and the trees to the west sent long, spindly shadows across the lake.

Chandler directed them through the water.

Within a few feet of the proper spot, the cops still couldn't see anything. They turned lanterns on and looked through the water. They navigated past an armada of beer and soda cans and a multicolored school of floating condoms. A white plastic Clorox bottle clunked against their vessel. Nothing much else was immediately visible, so where was the gate to the mysterious underwater city?

Chandler knew he was within a few feet of it. He knew it was there.

"Are we fishing, or is there something here somewhere?" Vincent asked.

"There's something here somewhere," Chandler said.

"You'd better be sure. I'm missing my weekly handball game to fuck around on this lake."

"I'm sure."

The woman trooper remained quiet. She kept looking over the bow of the boat, an expression of anxiety across her face.

Chandler took an oar from the boat, poked around in the water and found what he was looking for. When he had it, as expected, it was clear that what they had found, what the boys had been bouncing rocks off. They pulled the boat close to it and looked down. They were directly above the roof of a submerged car.

Chandler banged his oar respectfully on the roof of the vehicle.

"What the fuck is this?" asked Trooper Vincent.

"My guess is it's a dark green Chrysler with Connecticut plates MYG Eight-Seventy-eight," Chandler said. "We'll need that towtruck to get it up, and I got a hunch that we'll need a call to the state medical examiner, too."

"Oh, shit," Vincent said. "What makes you so sure?"

"Because the car, its owner, and the owner's dog disappeared at the same time. What does that usually tell you?"

"Nothing good."

"We're going to find a present in the car," Chandler affirmed. "Not a nice one." He looked at the female trooper, who blanched. "You okay?" he asked.

"You telling me there's a body down there?" she answered.

"I'm telling you I think there's a good chance," he said. "And we're going to need to find out."

He paused. She looked, in the warm glow of the pink sunset, as if she were going to throw up. "You okay with that?" he asked.

"Just fine," she said softly. "Just hunky dory."

"I knew you were."

The towtruck with the winch arrived just past dark. By then there was a substantial portion of Wilshire's people standing by the lake watching—men who worked in town, people just passing through, a photographer from the Wilshire paper, and, incredibly, mothers with children.

A chain was attached to the sunken car, and the tow truck laboriously raised the sunken vehicle from its wet tomb.

The remains of Maury Fishkin were found in the front of the car, the decomposing dead face that had looked up from the depths when Kevin McCarthy had seen him two months earlier. The remains of Pepper, Maury's Labrador retriever, were found in the trunk.

The state of decomposition was extreme, but the medical examiner, Norman Verdi, that amiable fat man who was the local prince of corpses, was able to tell a few things very quickly.

Gentle Mr. Fishkin had been dead for a few months. Most likely he had died shortly after he had disappeared. From the condition of the body, Dr. Verdi believed that the hardware man had been alive when he had been bound and gagged and had gone into the water inside his car.

Mercifully, however, Pepper had been shot.

The funeral service for Maury Fishkin was held in Bethel, Connecticut, at a reform temple the next day. The interment followed at a new cemetery in the same town. Four hundred residents of Wilshire traveled to the neighboring town to attend. There was not a single Corbett among them.

The Wilshire police followed with the usual light-weight interrogations. The prime suspect, of course, was James Corbett, who was already dead and thus even more unavailable for comment than usual. The theory put forth by Chief Moore was that James must have killed Maury, and then some anonymous do-gooder snuffed James by pushing him out of a tree one night.

The theory worked, but it was too convenient. Nor did it answer the questions of who might have helped James in the commission of homicide, and who that special person was who pushed James out of a tree.

If Moore was concerned with these things, though, he was not taking trouble to show it.

Mike Chandler sat in on Chief Moore's token investigation, and augmented it with some of his own. Not that Chandler's work accomplished much. Brother Wilbur had little to add when Chandler paid a visit to see him, other than the admission that he had always considered Maury Fishkin "an old Jewboy wiseass." Ritchie Corbett, the youngest brother, sitting behind the dirty counter of his smoke shop, presiding among the skin mags, cigarettes, smokeless tobacco, and other products highly prized by Wilshire youth, had even less to say than his sibling.

"Never liked the man," narrow-eyed Ritchie said to Chandler. "Maury was an old crook."

Isaac Corbett, teenage son of the late James and perpetrator of the incident that may have led to Fishkin's demise, didn't have much to volunteer, either. He even claimed he had never tried to shoplift anything from Fishkin's store.

Chandler found Lizzie Corbett in the Wilshire CVS that afternoon, buying, of all things, soap. He asked her a few questions, too.

"I don't know nothin', and I ain't got nothing to say," she informed him. "Not one fucking word. Don't want to get involved none."

Despite the cold weather, despite the time of year, Lizzie was overflowing a tight pair of black shorts that day, and had topped them off with a Rebecca Lobo-WNBA T-shirt beneath a massive down vest.

Franny Corbett was nowhere to be found.

The Wilshire Republican was a coincidental beneficiary of Fishkin's death and Ellen's coverage of it. The paper printed two thousand copies the day after the body was found, sold every one, then printed another five hundred before the evening of the next day.

The Republican had the scoop coverage and all the pictures. The resale of photographs and the picking up of the story by the Associated Press put the paper into the black for the month, and even covered the shortfall of cash from September. It was a bitter way for fortune to be turned around, though it was stunning at the same time. There was no congratulatory phone call from Ken Karp.

Ellen Wilder sat down on Saturday evening to keep her secret promise to herself. She opened the side drawer of her desk at home. It was late and Sarah was already in bed asleep.

Ellen held the wrapped portrait before her for several minutes, then summoned her courage and opened it.

The wrapping paper pulled away and she turned the framed photograph into her view.

The sight of her son took her breath away. She bit hard on her lips and kept her eyes dry—that is, almost dry.

Robin had been a handsome young man. In the picture, he wore a school blazer and a light blue shirt, open at the collar. His eyes were blue, and his hair was sandy brown. His face was handsome, distinctly echoing the combined features of both Ellen and his biological father.

For several long minutes she gazed at the photograph. Then she drew a long breath and set it down. Her eyes were now dry, and her nerves were steady.

There, she told herself. She had gotten past that.

She was braver than she thought she was, she reasoned. She wondered what she would ever have said to Robin, had she and her boy come face-to-face in his lifetime. This, too, was a question that would never be answered.

She kept the photograph out for an hour, perched on the side of her desk. At one point she felt like talking to it, but she decided that this would not be a good idea or a good habit to get into, so she didn't.

When she was ready to go upstairs to sleep, she put the portrait back in its paper and back into the desk drawer.

The next morning when she awoke, she knew she had dreamed, and she knew she had dreamed of her late son. The feeling was very palpable.

She was unable to recall exactly what the dream was. She only remembered that she and Robin had been together.

Perhaps, she figured as she quietly and thoughtfully made Sunday breakfast for herself and her daughter, that was the only thing important in the dream. She gave up trying to recall the actual events, figuring that it just might be best not to know.

Thirteen

Five days after the burial of Maury Fishkin, driving home across Route 68 in Wilshire, Mike Chandler spotted Franny Corbett's GMC pickup truck outside a bar called Lorna's. The temperamental clock in his car told Chandler it was half past five. A dull Friday afternoon had almost completely expired, the day having been cold and wet, and there had been no trace of sunshine for the last forty-eight hours.

The lot outside Lorna's was still half empty, but as the bar was only half a mile from the nearby foundry, the parking lot was filling up with Dinas Cement workmen in gimme caps with *DC* across the front. It was a Friday and the 'DinCem' boys, as they were called locally, couldn't quite bring themselves to go directly home with their paychecks.

Lorna's was a ramshackle, red-shingled roadhouse right by the highway. It had a black roof. Above the entrance, atop the roof, there was a sign that was at odds with proper grammar and punctuation but nonetheless proclaimed,

Lornas'
Bar Restaurant

The establishment had a primary reputation as a cheap place to get drunk after work, and did a secondary business as a blue-collar pick-up joint. Its tertiary reason to exist was the spaghetti and meatball dinners which sold for $6.95, and the house specialty, hot chicken wings with Italian seasonings and "blue cheese fra diablo" sauce.

Chandler pulled his car into the lot and parked a few places from Franny's truck. Then he sat for several seconds looking at the vehicle.

Out of instinct, and because a little voice kept telling him nasty things about Franny, he took a moment to call in the license plates over his police radio. As he waited, he noted a fresh dent on the rear door of the vehicle, a round dent about the size of a man's head. He wondered who Franny might have backed into.

A few moments later, the police radio crackled a response. There was nothing wrong with the registration. There weren't even any outstanding moving violations, and the one parking ticket that Franny had picked up in Cheshire he had paid within four days. Franny even had paid up car insurance, which was more than could probably have been said for twenty percent of the other cars in the lot.

Chandler sighed. As far as his truck was concerned, Franny was an upright citizen, pillar of the community. Still, Chandler's gut was telling him something. There was something badly bent about the biggest Corbett. Chandler liked to think that he had developed *some* instincts over the years. How could he be so wrong here? *Goddamn!* he thought. *Something* was wrong with Franny Corbett. Like a dog, he could sense it, the same way he felt Franny probably could sense that he was onto it.

Michael Chandler stepped out of his car. He felt the wet cold of the late afternoon against his face. Daylight had expired half an hour earlier, but it seemed even longer ago. An irritating cold rain was also beginning.

Involuntarily, he felt himself give in to a little shudder. Fall and winter evenings, their coldness and length, hung heavily upon him. Chandler had learned from experience over the last few years to hate the shortened days. They always led into the bleakness of winter, and winter had always, for some reason, put an extra edge on death to him. He felt it even more since getting shot, that extra proximity that mortality now had for him.

These thoughts pursued him like little furies. His shoulder ached suddenly. Then he tried to set his thoughts straight again. Two violent deaths locally in the last six months and he was, as of this morning, the primary on both cases. Where in hell was this leading him? The pain in his shoulder and upper arm wailed.

He made a point to walk by Franny's truck so he could eyeball it.

Once again, even on close visual inspection, there was nothing out of the ordinary about Francis Corbett's set of wheels. The inspection sticker on the front window was up-to-date, and there were live registration stickers properly affixed to the battered blue-and-white Connecticut license plate. Had he not been certain that someone somewhere was probably watching him, Chandler would have noted the little numbers beneath the renewal stickers and checked them, too. He would have checked the Vehicle Identification Number, also. He was that sure that there was something "wrong" with Franny, and just catching on to a little of it would to lead him to the rest of it. Something in his gut kept telling him this, but for this fading afternoon, he would have to content himself with a glance at the big man's front windshield. It didn't look as if had been punched out and replaced—a sure sign of tampering with the VIN.

Chandler continued into the bar.

Lorna's. In every mid-sized, blue-collar town in New England there is at least one joint of borderline respectability like this one. Lorna's was a mildly threadbare dive which looked like a hundred other such places that Chandler had visited around the state.

There was a long mirror behind a worn bar. Plenty of cheap whiskey and the predictable national name brand beers on tap. An explosion of NFL, NBA, and local high school sports memorabilia and pseudo-memorabilia on were on the walls and a noisy jukebox blared a tune forgotten in most other sections of the country.

Usually on the premises was an irritating little man named Dick Dugan, who tended bar. Dick had locked horns with Chandler many times. Dugan liked to get drunk with his customers and then, after work, go driving through Wilshire, Cheshire, and Wallingford. Fast.

Twice Chandler had arrested him on DWI's, once while driving with a suspended license. On a fourth encounter, Dugan had no insurance, no valid registration, no state inspection sticker, and no chance of passing the breathalyzer test that was put before him, in addition to having driven seventy miles per hour through a school zone.

Dugan was a short, wiry man with a crushed, misshapen nose, the result of a collision with a DinCem's foreman's fist one night. He had a square jaw and jet black hair that was always so stiffly in place that it looked as if it had been combed with a T-square. He was also blessed with the kind of belligerence and irritability that some small men elevate to predominant traits.

Lorna's had something else that no other beer joint in Connecticut had—Lorna herself, the proprietress, who sometimes tended the bar with Dugan, the queen of all she surveyed, night after night.

Lorna DiBernardo was a sturdy woman of thirty-five, with very Big Hair and an Eighties look. She was almost always on the premises somewhere, as she kept the books, baked the chicken wings, and broiled the artery-clogging burgers. No one knew which she cooked better, the books or the chow. Her father had owned the bar and named it after her. He had also supplemented his income with a successful and locally renowned sports bookmaking operation. Her grandfather, Long John DiBernardo, had been a Wilshire legend, a big, pleasantly profane man, an enterprising soul from Amalfi, who had been a popular bootlegger during Prohibition. He had been a hardworking man right up into the dark day in 1932 when his competition from Boston caught him, bound him, then gagged and handcuffed him within the cabin of one of his loaded delivery trucks before tossing in two sticks of dynamite. The loss had weighed heavily upon several local policemen who had children in college at the time.

Lorna never knew Grandpa, but had heard the stories. She had once been a high school cheerleader in West Hartford, had been married to an electrician for three months, then had three children by two different men whom she never married. Once, she had been very pretty, but too many men, three children, fifteen years, and twenty additional pounds—mostly from her own cooking and beer—had taken their inevitable toll. All things considered, however, Lorna was still a local woman to be reckoned with, and not at all ineffective as a local seductress.

There were only a handful of tables going when Chandler walked in, populated mostly by men, with a few women sprinkled about. There was also a little knot of half a dozen Dinas workmen involved in a lively discussion-transaction at the south end of the bar. A few wore the torn, stained T-shirts from their previous summer's softball team, bright orange T's with the word *Cementheads* across the chest.

A moment after Chandler made his appearance at the door, the music ended. Dick the bartender walked down to the men and said something softly, then pumped the jukebox again

Collectively, the six workmen's eyes rose and fixed on Chandler. Their discussion ended abruptly. Their whole end of the bar fell strangely silent, and their little knot broke up. Temporarily. Chandler knew the drill; whenever a state cop walked into a place, a lot of activity ceased.

Chandler chose to ignore them, spotting his quarry.

Franny was sitting alone at the north end of the bar, the usual sullen expression across his face. The hulking frame, the clear, high forehead, and the ragged hair weren't hard to find. Franny was the largest moving object in the room. He had four inches and maybe forty pounds on the next largest male.

Franny's brown-eyed gaze slid in the direction of Chandler's reflection in the mirror just as Chandler entered the room. He wondered whether Franny had seen him through the window, thus accounting for Chandler's sense of being watched in the parking lot, and had expected him.

There was eye contact almost immediately, back and forth, Chandler to Franny and back again. An obvious connection.

Chandler walked slowly to Franny's end of the bar and sat down next to him. The bartender gave Chandler the usual welcome, which was to ignore him, which was fine, since Chandler didn't feel like drinking.

"Hello, Franny," Chandler said.

The big man did not answer. Conveniently, the entire bar had run out of quarters, and the infernal jukebox came to a temporary rest.

Franny Corbett's gaze slid away from the cop and back to the half-consumed bottle of Budweiser in front of him.

"Franny, I need to talk to you," Chandler said.

Another few seconds of silence. "So fucking talk," the big man finally said.

"I want to know where you've been for the last few days. I want to know where you've been, *and* what you've been doing."

"I been here for the last few days."

"I want some specifics, Franny," Chandler said.

"Can't you find that out by yourself?" Franny answered.

"I want to hear it from you."

"Why?"

"I just do."

"Suppose I lie?"

"I'll find out and we'll have to talk again."

"Find out without asking me. Then I don't got to lie to you none."

"Come on, Franny. Let's do this the easy way."

The big man snorted. "Fuck it," he said.

Franny's six-six frame was bent over his drink. His left hand was clamped around the beer bottle like a vise. The twelve-ounce mug in his right hand looked like a shot glass in a normal man's.

Chandler waited.

"You're not drinking?" Franny asked.

"I'm on duty."

"Maybe you drink too much," said Franny.

Chandler recoiled very slightly. What had Franny meant by that? How could he have known?

"I drink what I want, when I want to," Chandler said. "I'm not drinking now because I'm here to talk to you."

"You're not drinking now because you have a problem," Franny said, glancing Chandler's way very slightly.

Chandler instinctively wanted to stay out of his gaze. He felt as if he were being caught in floodlights every time Franny fixed him in his view. How had he known Chandler had had a booze problem? Was that all over town, too?

Franny's dull brown eyes looked away again, perhaps hoping that if Chandler left his sight he would actually disappear. The gaze also found something invisible in the middle distance and returned, disappointed to find that the policeman was still there, waiting patiently.

Several seconds passed. Franny spoke again, his voice a low, unpleasant rumble. "So I'm a suspect, huh?" he asked. "In which murder? Uncle Jimmy's? Or is it the other you want to blame me for? The hardware man?"

"Why do you think I'd want to blame you?"

"Because Uncle Jimmy fell out of a tree, and no one knows who did it. Same with the Jewish guy and his dog."

"How did you know there was a dog down there, too?"

Franny snorted. "The whole fucking town knows, you kidding me?"

"But why would I blame *you*?"

" 'Cause it would be easy."

"Why would it be easy?"

" 'Cause you don't like me. Nobody likes me. I'm an outsider. Even among the Corbetts I'm an outsider."

"Did I say you're a suspect?" Chandler asked.

Franny sipped directly from the brown bottle. "No," he finally answered.

"Then you're not. I just want to talk to you."

"Fuck," Franny said. "I know what you're thinking."

"What am I thinking?"

"You think there's something wrong with me. But you can't tell what. So you like me for a couple of killings."

Franny turned toward him face-to-face, and Chandler felt that same surge of fear, of anxious discomfort, that he had felt the previous time. He had never known anyone to give off such an *aura* as Franny Corbett. The big man stared him down. Franny had a way of hammering an adversary with his eyes, alone.

Chandler blanched slightly and exhaled slowly. In his primitive, low intellect way, Franny had it doped out with unerring precision. Chandler even knew that Corbett recognized his fear. The pain in Chandler's shoulders was as loud as a choir of demons.

"Let's just talk, all right?" Chandler asked. "Let's just get to know each other."

"Fuck," Franny said again. "That's a laugh, too, ain't it? Who the fuck wants to get to know a state pig?"

The right corner of Franny's mouth moved slightly, as if with a nervous tic. Actually, he'd formed a nervous smile, one that was visible and then gone very quickly, as if he had taken a moment to appreciate his own wit.

"I ain't so stupid as some people think," Franny said, continuing on the same point. "If you're questioning me, I'm a suspect."

"I didn't say you were stupid. And if you were a suspect I'd have to warn you of your rights," Chandler said with unflagging patience. "But you work on the Corbett farm. You come and go from the place. You were *there*, Franny. You know your uncles. You know what goes on out there. I want to know how you fit into the whole picture."

"I don't fit into no picture at all," Franny answered.

"Then maybe you can help me understand a little about your family," Chandler suggested. "That would help."

Franny grunted. "You'd do best to just ignore me completely."

"Sorry. Can't do that. I've got a pair of suspicious deaths."

"Suspicious. Yup. That's what they were," Franny said.

Dick Dugan had placed his cigarette in an ashtray within Franny's reach. The smoke was bothering Corbett. Chandler watched what followed with disbelief.

Franny reached to the cigarette and took it between his thumb and forefinger. He worked up a small pool of saliva between his lips and pressed the lit end of the cigarette to the moisture. Then he snuffed the burning end between his wet lips.

He set the butt back in the tray and looked toward Dick Dugan. As Dugan watched impotently, he then abruptly shoved the ashtray over the back edge of the bar, sending it noisily to the floor.

Dugan chose to and ignore it, turning away.

"You have quite a number of ways to make yourself popular, don't you, Franny?" Chandler asked.

"Bar tricks," the big man answered. "It's just bullshit bar tricks."

"Like breaking a pair of handcuffs. I hear you're good at that."

"Handcuffs," Franny snorted. "Yeah."

"I hear your cousins provided you with a few that you broke just by jerking them apart."

"Yeah, maybe," Franny snorted again. "I done that. Fuck handcuffs. Ain't no pair of handcuffs that can hold me none."

"So you're real strong," Chandler said. "Of course, the prisons are filled with men who are all pumped up. It's not such a big deal."

"I'm strong mentally, too," he growled.

"Yeah?"

Franny looked back to Chandler. He frowned ominously. His eyes rolled like powerballs in their sockets, connecting again with the detective's. "Want to see another bar trick?" Franny Corbett asked.

"Sure."

"Watch close."

Franny turned and looked across the room. Chandler tried to follow Franny's gaze, but failed to detect anything significant. The jukebox across the room came to life and started to play.

Gladys Knight. "Midnight Train to Georgia."

Franny turned back to Chandler.

"See?" the big guy said. "I done that."

"You did what?"

"Made the jukebox play."

Chandler eased slightly and leaned back. "Come on, Franny. That's horseshit."

The music filled the room—a mellow, bittersweet ballad on the best sound system that Lorna DiBernardo could keep nailed down.

"No, it ain't. I done that. I started the fucking music."

"Yeah?"

"Hey, it's a true fact, Fuckface. I done it!" Franny insisted.

"Yeah?"

"Yeah! I done it for you. You ask the lady who runs the newspaper here about Georgia. She's got a boy down there!"

"What are you talking about?"

"That's all I'm telling."

"Who are you talking about? Ellen Wilder?"

"That's the lady. She's got a boy down in Georgia. So I played the music so you'd ask her about it."

"Uh huh," Chandler said.

Franny looked away, still very calm. "Your loss if you don't believe me, fuckhead."

"How would you know anything about Ellen Wilder?"

"I'm telling you. I know things."

"And how did you make the jukebox play that song?"

"Jesus Christ on the fucking cross, man. I can do

things, Chandler. In my head. I can do shit that you can only dream about. I get them to happen."

"Get me a million dollars," said Chandler, making a joke of it.

"Only *some* things. Things that are important to me."

"Why is a song important?"

"I like this song. I like midnights."

The music continued. Now it was "A Rainy Night in Georgia."

"You been to Georgia, Franny?" Chandler asked.

"Maybe."

"Show me another trick," Chandler said.

Franny brooded about it for a moment. "Okay," he said at length, a low growl of agreement.

Chandler followed Franny's gaze a second time. As Chandler moved his own eyes, something beckoned at the fringe of his vision. Something quickly jerked into motion behind the bar.

A bottle of Canadian Club, just set in place by Dugan on the ledge at the base of the mirror, fell hard from its perch. Dugan turned and stared at the wreckage of glass and booze. Chandler, deeply startled, stared, too.

Then Dugan's sight arrested angrily and accusingly on Franny.

"Accident, huh?" Franny asked. He smirked. "Guess that wasn't so secure where the barman put it down."

Chandler now looked at the broken bottle and the wasted liquor in shock. Franny's expression didn't change an iota. His sipped his beer. Had the big guy done that? Chandler wondered. Or had he seen that the bottle hadn't been place on its perch that well, and was set to fall?

Had he timed it just perfectly?

Had there been something else? Was there some *other* more complicated explanation of how Franny could have done that?

"Did you do that?" Chandler finally asked, breaking a sweat.

"What the fuck do you think?" Franny answered.

"I don't know."

"You're a detective," he grunted. "You figure it out."

Dugan walked to the spot, still staring suspiciously at Franny Corbett. He picked up the broken glass and threw it into a wastebasket. He mopped the liquor with a bar towel, then threw that away.

"You ought to be more careful with the booze, asshole," Franny said in a low voice.

Dugan heard the remark and didn't react to it. Chandler heard it, too, and wasn't sure how it had been meant.

Was Franny intentionally giving him a double meaning? *Who* should be more careful? Dugan? Chandler? It was almost too sophisticated a locution for such a lug of a man.

But Chandler had heard it. Hadn't he?

Dugan cleared the area and walked away to the other end of the bar. He couldn't wait to get away from Corbett.

"Everybody's fucking afraid of me," Franny continued almost routinely. "It's sort of funny. I don't mean no harm to no one who don't deserve it. Yet they're all afraid."

"Why do you suppose that is?"

"Maybe everyone deserves something bad, huh?" Franny suggested.

"Did Maury Fishkin deserve something bad?"

Franny seemed to take the question under advisement. "No," he said softly. "The Jewish guy was a nice old man. That really sucks what someone did to him."

"How do you know? Did you ever meet him?"

"I *know,*" Franny insisted.

"Then you wouldn't have hurt him?"

"I wouldn't have hurt him. Whoever hurt him got into deep shit with me." Franny thumped the center of his chest with a dirty-fingernailed thumb to punctuate the point.

"What about your Uncle Jimmy?"

"Uncle Jimmy was a cocksucker," he said bitterly. "Uncle Jimmy was a bad man. Like the whole fucking family."

"Then, does that mean—?"

Franny turned toward the policeman again. "You know there's this old family burial yard out on the farm," said Franny, interrupting. "You ever been there, state pig?"

"No."

"You should."

"Why?"

"You could listen to the fucking spirits," Franny said. "I keep telling you, the spirits would tell you shit if you'd only listen."

Chandler was having difficulty following this. "Be more specific," he asked. "What would I find in that graveyard? Where would I look?"

"Shit. You figure it out."

"Would I see spirits?"

"Maybe."

"Do *you* see spirits?"

"Sure," Franny answered flatly. "All the godamned fucking time."

Then the big man's gaze shut Chandler out again.

Franny's hand moved across the bar like the paw of a hungry bear. There was a dish of pretzels, nuts, and Rice Chex that was half gone. Franny scooped it out, grabbing the contents in one ursine clutch. He shoved the mixture into his mouth.

"I don't fit into no real picture for you, and I don't got nothing more to say," Franny said.

"But you told me that you see things that I don't," Chandler said. "I want to know what."

"I see things, all right," Franny answered. "I see all sorts of things."

"On the farm?"

"On the farm."

"Tell me about them," said Chandler.

"I thought you wanted to know where I been the last few days."

"Tell me that, too."

Franny sighed. "Bullshit," he said. "I'm bored with that."

Chandler followed Franny's gaze yet again, and then saw what he was watching. A pair of pretty local women in their twenties, who Chandler recognized as secretaries from a local insurance agency, were seated by themselves at a table for two. It was the end of their work week and they were having a drink before they went home.

They were still dressed for work. Their attire was unfashionably short and tight. In the back of Chandler's mind, he placed them. A young woman named Lisa Ann Petrillo and her co-worker Nella. The girl on the left, Lisa Ann, was showing plenty of both legs. The display had nailed Franny's attention.

"See that girl," Franny said. "I like her."

There was something chilling about the way he said

that, too. Meanwhile, Ray Charles came on the juke-box. "Georgia On My Mind." Franny smiled slightly as if he were still doing tricks.

"Is that right?" Chandler asked.

"Yeah," Franny answered. "That's right."

"Do you know her?"

"I overheard. Last time I was in. Her name's Lisa Ann. She works for Nationwide or State Farm. One of them car places."

"Car insurance," said Chandler.

Franny's eyes narrowed, and he was still watching the girl. "Yeah. That's it. She works for the guy up on the hill."

By that, Franny meant the insurance agency that was up on the hill at the crest of Route 68—John Tyler Insurance, no relation to the former president. It was Mr. Tyler's habit to constantly hire high school girls and eventually try to hit on them. Lisa Ann was older and had a husband, on paper at least, but that didn't mean she was hit-proof.

"Am I right? Is her name Lisa Ann?" Franny asked.

"I don't know," Chandler lied.

Something else clouded over on Franny's expression. He somehow knew every time Chandler lied. "I think you know. You just don't want to tell me none."

"Franny, both those women have husbands and families. I don't think you should bother them."

"Who said I was bothering them?"

"No one."

"I'd like to do sex to that Lisa Ann someday," Franny said. "I think I'd like that."

"She has a husband," Chandler repeated, fighting off a sinking sensation.

"Those little tiny girls like Lisa Ann, I'd like to do

sex to 'em real hard," Franny continued. "Make 'em squeal when they come."

"I don't want to hear this from you, Franny."

Franny wouldn't let it go.

"A lot of married women let you do it to them, I hear," Franny pronounced. "Think I don't know what goes on in Wilshire during the afternoons? All these horny housewives got to get it some, you know."

"Do us all a favor and stay away from married women, will you, Franny?" Chandler asked.

The big guy grunted.

He gave the girls another glance. Chandler followed it. Something silver twinkled on Lisa Ann's ankle—an ankle bracelet. Then Franny looked back to the bar and Chandler's gaze returned with him.

Franny finished his beer in a single gulp and motioned for another from the bartender. Dick Dugan appeared quickly and brought a fresh bottle. Chandler could tell that, for the time being, anyway, Franny's thoughts had already moved on.

"Tell me where else you worked on a farm," Chandler repeated.

"Checking up on me, huh? Want to see if I killed anyone out west, huh?"

"Did you?"

"Did I what?" Franny asked, his voice lower and more gravelly than usual.

"Kill someone out west?"

"No. No one. Not yet."

"How 'bout in Wilshire? You kill anyone here?"

"I got my plans. And you can't stop me."

"Cut the crap, Franny, or you *will* be a suspect."

"And if I do become one," he asked with an angry

scowl, "who the fuck's gonna run me in for questioning, huh? You? You and what army?"

Chandler's gaze remained steady. "I'll call for as many backups as I need, Franny," he answered. "Is that your question?"

Corbett stared back and then seemed to ease slightly, as if a little wave had washed over him.

"Out west. I worked on a farm out there, too," Franny announced.

"Where?"

"Out west. Like I said."

"*Where* out west, Franny?"

"Ohio, I think."

"You don't know?"

"No. It didn't mean much. It was somewhere near a state border. Part of the farm was in one state, the other part in another. You know, they got big states out west. Big farms, too."

Franny grinned again, dumbly, sheepishly. His mood seemed to change yet again.

"Know what? You could go up to the top floor of the farmhouse and look around this widow's walk, or whatever you call it. And you know what? When you were up there, you could see three different states."

"Three different states?"

"That's what I said," Franny answered.

Franny grimaced again slightly. He found something in his pockets—a few sunflower seeds. He worked them into his teeth, then expelled the husks with a swift blowing motion, across the bar. As Dick Dugan refilled the bowl of nuts, pretzels, and Chex, he shot both Chandler and his drinking buddy a filthy glare.

"Tell me about the farm," Chandler said. "Pigs? Chickens?"

"Yeah. Some of those."

"Crops?"

"Yeah. Sure."

"Cows?"

"I dunno. Probably."

"You're not talking to me, Franny. You're not telling me the truth."

"I told you the truth about being able to see three different states."

"It's not what I wanted to know about."

"And you're just fishing for answers," Franny said loudly and with sudden, extreme petulance. "I don't know what the fuck you're giving me all this botheration for. I ain't done nothing I shouldn't have. So fuck you! Hear me? *Fuck you!*"

Franny's eyes were blazing and he was in a sudden rage.

Others in the bar turned and stared.

Dugan stood back and waited for the first punch. At a door a few feet from the bar, the familiar figure of Lorna appeared. As was her habit at the first sound of animated voices, she was holding a baseball bat—one of the Black Beauty specials that George Foster had once autographed personally for her when he played for the Mets.

Lorna, seeing who the potential combatants were, said nothing. She watched and held her breath.

The moment passed, but just barely.

Franny angrily picked up the fresh beer and stood, towering above everyone. He drained the bottle. He reached into his jeans and grabbed a cob of folding money. Peeling off a bunch of one dollar bills, he put them on the counter. The bartender was wise enough to stay away.

Then Franny slammed down the bottle. He had

finished his drink and the unwanted meeting, too.
He gave Chandler a look of contempt and then
swung a lustful final look at the two girls at the table.
Then he stormed for the door, arriving there just as
a bunch of cement workers were on their way in.
Franny roughly shouldered his way through them.
None were dumb enough to react.

The bartender seized that moment to amble over
to the dollar bills. Dugan silently picked up his tip
and retreated. There was a line of sweat across his
brow.

Lorna appeared beside Chandler.

"That big ape comes in here three or four times
a week, Michael," Lorna said. "He drives a lot of the
good customers out."

"What do you know about him?"

"Everyone's scared of him. He gives everyone the
creeps."

"Everyone including me," Chandler answered.

Her gaze remained on the door, and her hands on
the George Foster, until she was certain that Franny
wasn't on his way back in for an encore.

"I don't believe that," Lorna said, placing a hand
on Chandler's aching left shoulder. "You're not
scared of anyone, are you?"

Chandler ignored the question.

"How 'bout if I fix you some dinner, Mike?" Lorna
said, her tone of voice changing. "It's on the house.
I hate to see you going home alone. You need a
woman to keep you happy."

Chandler made five minutes worth of the proper
excuses and said good-bye.

Back out in the parking lot, something made him
look for new tire tracks from Franny's truck, but
there were none. No tire tracks, nothing to indicate

that the vehicle had ever been there at all, though the rain and other traffic had eradicated a lot. In fact, the very parking place that Franny had vacated had already been replaced by a van from the cable television company.

Chandler cursed. If he had known which way Franny had driven, he would damned well have given him a tail—followed him—seen where in hell he went. Who did he hang out with? Where did he spend nights? What did he *do*? Chandler thought of asking his superiors for a couple of extra detectives, to put Franny under a twenty-four hour watch, but rejected the notion. A detail like that would stick out like a well-manicured thumb in this town. Also, Chandler's own interest—or was it an incipient obsession?—in the case dictated that he would handle everything himself.

He, Chandler, wanted to discover what made Franny tick, who had killed Maury Fishkin, and who had put a farm tool through the neck of Franny's Uncle James.

The rain was steadier now, and Chandler stood in it. The water was starting to seep through his clothing as he unlocked his car. The air was also turning colder, even giving a hint that the precipitation could turn into sleet with a drop of another two or three degrees. Sleet this early, Chandler remembered, was the reliable forerunner of relentless New England cold and another horrible winter.

This thought was in his mind, and the key to his own car was in his hand, when he heard a female voice call to him through the rain.

Petite Lisa Ann Petrillo, from the Tyler Insurance Agency, waved at him from under a red umbrella. She hurried toward him, a lovely flurry of trim female arms and legs in the rain. There was even a little wink from the silver band around her ankle.

"Lisa Ann?" he asked.

She arrived next to him, raindrops sprinkled across her skin. "That man," she said. "The one who just left?"

"What about him?"

"He's a Corbett, isn't he?" she asked.

"Apparently. Why?"

"He won't leave me alone," she said. "It's not that he's actually *done* anything yet," she said.

"What's he do?"

She was at a loss to explain it.

"He . . . he just hangs around," she said. "He stares at me. He just . . . every time I look up, he's there. Watching me."

Chandler thought about it for a moment. "Ever had a problem with any other Corbetts?" he asked.

The girl blanched for a moment. "I could never go into that smoke shop without the owner making a sexual remark," she said.

"Ritchie's Smoke Shop?"

"That's the one. He's a Corbett, isn't he?"

"He's one," Chandler affirmed.

Lisa Ann shuddered and shivered. "Ritchie doesn't bother me because I don't go in there any more," she said. "But now *this* one?" She made a face of disgust.

"I saw him looking at you while we were at the bar," he said, editing the events slightly. "I reminded him that you were married."

"I'm not sure it will make much difference."

"Did you mention it to your husband?" Chandler asked.

Her expression clouded over.

"Mike, I already have enough problems at home

with my husband. I'm not looking to add one." She paused and added, "We're not getting along. Not at all."

"I'm sorry," he said.

She waited.

"Look," Chandler said, "next time I see Franny Corbett I'll make it as clear as I can he's not to bother you, okay? Meanwhile, if you have a problem . . ." He reached into his shield case and pulled out a business card. It bore his office number. On it, he also wrote his home phone number.

"Any time, day or night, if you have a problem," he said. "Just call."

"You after him for something else?" she asked.

"Maybe," he answered. "Can't tell."

She sighed and looked much relieved. "Thanks," she said. She tucked the card into a blouse pocket under her raincoat. She was, even in the rain, a very pretty young woman. He wondered what the problem was between her and her husband. Some men, he reasoned, didn't appreciate what they had until they had lost it.

Then she surprised him. She leaned forward and kissed him on the cheek in the rain, her lips warm against the cold of the evening.

"Thanks," she said again. She gave him a smile and trotted back into Lorna's. Chandler was so surprised that he said nothing and merely watched her go. She had even made his arm feel a little better, unless the absence of Franny that had accomplished that.

Once again, Franny in his crude, ham-fisted way, had been correct. There were an awful lot of single women out there longing for attention, though perhaps not quite the attention that Francis Corbett might have in mind.

Fourteen

Mike Chandler was a troubled man when he returned home to Meriden that evening. He parked himself in front of his television, but barely paid any attention to the ice hockey he found on ESPN. He made himself some sandwiches and opened a quart bottle of Carling Black Label to accompany the food. Hockey wasn't on his mind that evening, though, nor was the food.

He drank straight from the bottle. The entire night was as dark as Franny Corbett's presence in his life.

He broke a sweat when he thought of the man. What was going on?

What was that strange feeling that inhabited him when he was in Corbett's presence? Why had the image of Franny flashed before him at police headquarters?

Why did he relentlessly have in mind the time he was shot and killed every time that he came into contact with Franny? What was that extra shiver that Chandler felt?

More beer. A second quart bottle. More thoughts.

Why had he heard his father's voice? He caught himself—why had he *imagined* that he had heard his father's voice, acting as Franny's advocate, or an ad-

vocate of the spirits? What were these spirits with
which Franny claimed to commune?

He thought back several weeks to the night when
he had first been called into the Corbett case. He
thought of the nightmare he had been having, of the
images he'd had, of conversing in a dark open space
with people who were dead.

He shuddered.

What was Franny trying to tell him about Georgia?
And Ellen? What could the big man know? How
could he possibly know it? Where was the connection?

Chandler couldn't even control his own thoughts.
And his shoulder was killing him. He lifted his dam-
aged arm. The tingling went into the shoulder and
down toward the elbow. Sometimes when he did this
he couldn't even feel to grip.

And that's how it will end for you, some voice within
him told him. *You will go to draw your weapon and there
will be no sensation in your hand. You will be unable to
draw your weapon and you will be murdered by some hunk
of street scum.*

He finished a quart of beer. He went and found a
third cold bottle. He opened it and went to work on
it. Time passed.

He leaned back, and closed his eyes. The brightness started again, that yellowish white light that he
had seen when he had been dying.

Or was it when he had been dead? A dark figure
started to take form in the middle of it, a figure that
seemed, from the feeling he had, to be beckoning
him. But Chandler didn't want to see the figure. Or
meet it. He felt that the encounter would be too terrifying, so terrifying that it could stop his heart.

He cried out. "No! No!"

His words echoed in his empty home. He opened his eyes and looked around, wondering where he had been. He must have drifted off, because the hockey, which he had last seen in the middle of the third period, was now over. The wrap-up show was on.

His sandwiches were finished. Did he even remember having eaten them? He couldn't tell, and he was halfway through the third quart of beer.

He put his hand on the bottle. It was warm.

God, he thought. An hour had disappeared somewhere. He stood up and understood where the time had gone. He was drunk. *Very* drunk.

No wonder he was seeing funny things. Thinking funny things. Hearing funny things. Doing funny things.

"Quite drunk," he said.

He giggled, making the crystal clear sense of any inebriated man.

Then his mood shifted mercurially, and he cursed to himself. The damned Corbetts had driven him to the most disgusting of all boozing, one quart bottles. It was incredible, the destructive nature of those people.

Well, he'd get his revenge on them, he decided. He'd keep kicking butt on the cases before him. Inevitably, all trails would lead to the Corbett clan. Clear 'em out and lock 'em up.

He attempted to stand again, and failed.

With the help of the armrest of his sofa, he tried a third time. Success. He was on his feet. Unsteady, he staggered to the stairs in the center of his house. With a major assist from the banister, he managed to pull himself up the stairs.

He lurched into his bedroom and in the darkness crashed onto his bed. He managed to pull off his weapon and lay it at his bedside. His fumbling hand found the light switch, and he put himself in darkness.

He lay there, listening to himself breathe. Listening to the quiet outside his home.

He thought about his late father. Where was *his* soul tonight?

He thought about Lisa Ann Petrillo.

Her husband was out of the picture. Maybe he should put a move on her. Random thoughts of women also led him to Ellen Wilder, the new owner of the newspaper. *There* was a lady closer to his age and his speed, he mused as the room swirled round him and he closed his eyes. He wondered what her marital situation was.

Hell. He was a detective, and he didn't even know that?

"Shame," said a voice.

He realized it was Franny's.

In his mind, at least.

His eyes flickered again. They found the luminous dial of his watch, inches away from his face, in the dark.

11:12 P.M. A nice orderly number. Easy to remember. One, one, one, two.

He giggled and closed his eyes again, a contented drunk at last.

A few minutes later, Chandler was aware that he was falling asleep. He managed to relax, to take himself out of the day's events. He could feel his mind, his body, and his thoughts drifting.

Then something took hold of his psyche, and he experienced the sensation of tumbling, as if he were free falling through some magic realm. The feeling was a pleasant one.

A sense of contentment washed through him, a notion of well being. It was combined with a sense of psychological travel, almost as if he were visiting a part of his mind that he had never previously known to exist.

The sense continued, as if he were a kite or a man on a hang glider, traveling wherever the wind wanted to take him.

The feeling was almost liberating, as if he had broken free of earlier ways of thinking.

Actual hours passed, and seemed like only a few heartbeats.

A noise jarred him.

His eyes flashed open. His heart was beating loudly. He wasn't sure whether the noise had been in the dream or in his home.

His brain sorted through things, and he recalled where his weapon was. Hot on the heels of that thought was the concern about his arm. Would *this* be the moment that his left hand failed on him?

He saw the dark bedroom around him, searched it and found nothing amiss. He closed his eyes quickly, searched for the pleasant feeling that had gripped him, and sought to recapture it.

He found it, and sailed with it for what seemed like several minutes but was probably much less.

Something happened. He had felt odd sensations before when entering the land of sleep, but never quite in this way. Abruptly, something felt different.

An odd chilliness overcame him and he felt himself shudder in his bed, as if some cold current of air had come from somewhere to surround the room.

He opened his eyes. The room was filled with an unusual light. He didn't know where it was coming from, and it cast strange shadows through his sleeping area.

He lay perfectly still, starting to sweat. He felt as if he had sensed something evil in his subconscious, as if he had felt something change within the room.

It was the atmosphere. The tone of the room.

Something.

An undeniable *something* was different. Then Michael Chandler knew what it was. He had involuntarily reconnected with a feeling of anxiety that had gripped him during the day, that free-floating anxious feeling of disquietude that had plagued him for the last few weeks.

What *was* it? He had the sense of being emotionally very naked, as if someone were seeing into his soul.

Into his thoughts.

He closed his eyes, tightly this time. There was a lightness around him, then a darkness. He felt as if he were traveling somewhere.

He turned in his bed. Now he was being transported involuntarily. Wherever he was going, it was to a place he didn't like. A place he feared. A place he did not wish to visit.

Oh, God! Here it comes again! The dream. *My own worst nightmare. No, no, no, I don't want to go there!*

His dead father was standing before him, pointing to the door to the housing project, the stairways that ascended to the chamber where he would be shot again and again and again, until maybe someday he had a heart attack while asleep and stayed in that room to die.

Tito Moreno would get him, after all—if Franny Corbett or some other white trash dirtball didn't get him first.

"Dad, I don't want to go up there," Chandler insisted in the dream.

"Oh, but son, you have to. You're a policeman. You have to be brave."

"I don't want to go."

His father's image turned very grave. "Don't disgrace the family, son. I was on the force, and so is your younger brother. Go."

"But—"

"Go," his father said in a kindly voice. "Go up there and get shot. That's your fate. To get shot."

He was back in Bridgeport. Roger Schoor was raising a handgun and blowing bullets at Tito Moreno, and Moreno was spinning, falling, and Chandler was going along and firing a final bullet, and in the dream Chandler screamed, threw off his flack jacket, his bad arm failed him, and he was riveted in place while Tito Moreno emptied an automatic pistol into his chest.

The nightmare. A black beauty of a nightmare.

He spun in his bed. Awake. There was not one part of him that was not soaking wet from sweat.

Then something even newer and even darker was upon him. Something current.

He felt his eyelids waver and stay open. He looked into his bedroom and thought he saw movement right at the doorway to the hall.

He *knew* he had seen movement!

A cold fear gripped him. In the darkness, he definitely saw the figure of a large, hulking man in his doorway, partially concealed by the door.

Oh, Jesus, he thought. *Oh, holy Jesus!*

Chandler's eyes opened wider. He reached for his service weapon, keeping his eyes focused on the shape behind the door.

Then an even greater fear was upon him. The body of the man behind the door took on a recognizable shape, the one he feared the most.

Six-foot six, big and hulking.

Unquestionably, Chandler was looking at Franny Corbett. Suddenly, the entire room was the color of Franny's spirit.

Chandler's gaze rolled through the darkness. His tingling left hand found the weapon. He latched his grip on it and pulled the weapon to him. His gaze went back to find the intruder. Franny must have understood the movement in the dark, because his figure withdrew slightly.

Chandler readied the weapon.

Then he spoke. "Franny?"

There was no answer. The figure seemed to waver in the hallway.

"Franny?" Chandler asked again. "I know you're there. Answer me, or I'll shoot you."

Still no response.

"What are you doing, Franny?" Chandler asked. "Why are you here?"

Now the figure withdrew. In the dimness of the room, Chandler could no longer be sure he saw the physical shape, but he thought he heard a floorboard creak.

"Franny! Answer me!" Chandler demanded.

With his other hand, Chandler reached for his light switch.

He turned on the lamp at his bedside table. The light flashed on, filling the room with an infuriating, yellowing illumination. In a moment that was so brief that it couldn't be measured in real time, the sensation reminded him of the recurring flashes of his "death light."

Then it was normal again. There was nothing beyond the doorway—*not* where Chandler had thought he had seen a body. That, he was certain, was because Franny was trying to leave.

Chandler came to his feet. He walked to the door and abruptly pulled it wide open. It clattered and rattled as it struck the wall. As it made that sound, Chandler suspected—no, he was certain!—that it covered another sound, that of an outside door closing downstairs.

He was so convinced that he called out. "Who's there? Come on! Who's there?"

No answer, other than a distant echo in his empty house.

Chandler felt the wetness of his palms against the weapon. He walked slowly through the second floor of his house, waiting for something, looking for something else to happen.

His shoulder throbbed. His left palm now tingled with the acute pins and needles feeling that suggested a mini-paralysis.

He went cautiously downstairs. He moved to his front door.

It was locked, just as he had left it. He turned and searched the downstairs. He found no one. He picked up the almost empty quart beer bottle that he had left in his den. He carried it with him.

He moved to his front window and peered out into the darkness. He saw nothing. He remained at the front window and threw on the large outdoor light. The light swept across his front lawn. There was no one there.

No Franny Corbett.

He checked his back door, too, and the door that led to the garage. All had been locked and bolted

from within. All remained that way. No window had
been penetrated. No one human could have entered
the house and departed.

The phrase repeated on him: *no one human could
have entered . . .*

Chandler stood very still by his front window.

He thought about the evening at Lorna's, his
dream, and what he thought he had just experienced.
He tried to put it in perspective, and failed. Just as
he could not explain to himself what he felt when
he was in Franny's presence, he was unable to explain
his feeling on waking up from another horrible
dream.

He felt the need for air—a lot of it, even the real
cold stuff. In fact, after an evening of boozing, the
cold air might do him good, he reasoned.

He reached in his front closet and pulled on an
old coat. He unlocked his front door—*it was now almost impossible for him to walk through a doorway without
thinking of being met by a hail of bullets*—and stepped
out into the night.

The cold assaulted him. Hard. It was probably
thirty-five degrees. He glanced at his watch and saw
that it was almost 5:00 A.M. A completely inhuman
hour to be awake, he figured. Then he recoiled from
that word.

Inhuman.

Chandler settled onto the front step of his home.
He sat perfectly still and listened to the night. He
set the bottle of beer down next to him and slid his
weapon into his coat pocket.

Nothing. He saw nothing and sensed nothing. Just
coldness and blackness. He let his eyes adjust to what
there was of moonlight and starlight. His thoughts
traveled, and in his mind he saw himself as a much

younger man, half his current age, walking young women home on chilly winter nights, his arm around their waists, their gloved hands in his.

He heaved a sigh.

This whole episode tonight, realistic as it had seemed, must have been the product of a hyperactive imagination. There could not possibly have been any Franny Corbett in his house. The door was *chained* from the inside. Franny, big, hulking weirdo that he was, simply hadn't walked through a locked door.

Had he?

Chandler wondered why he had even asked himself such a question. Of course not. Franny was live, flesh and blood and muscle and bone, not a spirit. To even entertain the notion of anything different was ludicrous!

Wasn't it?

Mike Chandler's eyes settled. He could barely see into the darkness beyond his lawn. Then, when his eyes did adjust, and when he could focus on a dark stand of trees across the street, Chandler suddenly thought he saw movement.

He couldn't be sure, but slowly his hand moved for his weapon. What was this all about, anyway?

He kept his eyes trained on the place where he thought he had seen something. From somewhere the figure of Franny Corbett inevitably came into focus.

Franny was standing across the street watching him. Staring back.

"Franny?" Chandler asked softly. "Talk to me. What do you know? What are you leading me to?"

The vision was about fifty feet away, but Chandler was convinced that he saw Franny smile.

No spoken response followed.

"What do you want?" Chandler called out into the darkness. He felt diminished by the scale and the blackness of the night that had embraced him. His voice was meager as it tried to fill the night.

Again, no answer.

Minutes began to pass, then a quarter hour. A bluish hue finally came up across the wiry network of branches that were formed by the rattling, skeletal tops of the trees behind Franny.

Chandler grew impatient. He drew his weapon and brandished it, moving it from one hand to the other, pretending that he might suddenly go psycho and start firing. Franny was unmoved. Distantly, Chandler thought he heard laughter.

A mocking, haunting laughter.

As Chandler would recall it later, it was almost a hypnotic, dream-like state that he had entered. Quarter hours seemed to pass as single minutes. Chandler was next aware of the sky becoming much lighter. With the advent of daylight, Franny was still there, not stationary, but a solitary pacing figure on the opposite side of the road, one who seemed to be waiting for Chandler and yet oblivious of him at the same time.

Was this where Franny spent his nights? Chandler would remember thinking. Out there at the roadside like some feral beast? Or was Franny waiting to summon Chandler somewhere?

To his death? Or to some other state of awareness?

Chandler kept his eyes trained as the first fingers of morning embraced the road and the woods. Franny remained there. If the big man was there as an emissary, as someone to guide Chandler somewhere, the detective had decided: he wasn't going with him.

Not quite yet.

The words of Chief Elmer Moore returned to Chandler. *Those Corbett men. Always out all night. Who knows what the hell they're doing after dark?*

Who knows, indeed, Chief?

Chandler kept watching across the road. He felt as if he were in the realm of magic. Something fantastic and inexplicable happened then, at least in the context of everything else Mike Chandler had been taught to believe in the course of his forty winters.

Franny turned toward him, arms akimbo, a look of anger and frustration on his face. He stared at the policeman, who stared at Franny in return.

Then Franny gradually faded. Right before Chandler's eyes, the figure of Franny Corbett faded into nothingness. He was gone.

Chandler tried to convince himself that Franny had walked away, had disappeared among the trees while he had blinked, but he knew that wasn't the case.

He knew it in exactly the same way that he knew Franny had been in his home, and for that matter, in his head.

Now the words from Chandler's father came back: *Help put the lives of other people in order and you'll put your own in order at the same time. Huh, Mikey Boy?*

Mikey Boy—his father's childhood name for him. He hadn't thought of that one for years.

His head was swimming.

Mike Chandler was left alone on his front step with disbelieving eyes, a trembling hand clutching a pistol, a worn car coat, nerves rubbed raw, a quart bottle of beer that was seven-eighths dead, and everything he had ever believed in complete chaos.

The new day, as it happened, broke with an astonishing brightness.

Fifteen

Ellen could see the street in front of her newspaper office from her desk in the back room. She also could see that she had trouble when she looked up and saw the ugly red-and-white Chevrolet parking outside her newspaper's office. The two remaining Corbett brothers stepped out of Ritchie's Chevy and turned toward her door.

She held her breath. Ellen was alone, and she knew the Corbetts were not there to buy extra copies.

Wilbur came though her door first, his thick shoulders filling the door under a car coat. Ritchie, the thin, mean one, followed by a few feet. Ritchie kept looking around, as if to see who might be watching them.

Ellen remained at her desk and watched them from where she sat. "Yes?" she called out. "May I help you?"

The brothers closed the door behind them. They studied the front office like a pair of tourists, looking critically up and down. Then they turned toward her and walked in her direction. Wilbur said something to Ritchie that Ellen could not hear.

They arrived at the door to her office, filling it.

"You the secretary," Wilbur asked, "or are you the Boston lady who prints this shit paper?"

"I'm Ellen Wilder," she said, leaning back. "I'm the publisher."

"That mean you're responsible for what gets printed?"

"I'm responsible," she said.

They looked at each other, then at her—long, icy, intimidating stares in Ellen's direction.

"You know who we are?" Wilbur asked.

"You're Wilbur Corbett, and that's your brother Ritchie behind you."

"Then I guess we don't have to waste no time on no frigging introductions," Wilbur said, a nasty smirk crossing his face.

"I guess not," Ellen answered.

"We don't like some of the shit you been saying," Ritchie said. At the moment, and out of nowhere, he was the hotter of the two.

Ellen folded her arms and decided to attempt reason.

"What exactly didn't you like?"

Wilbur answered. "Everything you said about our family."

She drew another breath. "I don't think we printed anything untrue," she said. "I wrote the stories, myself."

"Yeah?" Ritchie asked. "Ever think about unwriting a story? Printing a rejection?"

"You mean, a 'retraction'?"

"Yeah. That's it," Wilbur said.

"No," she said. "Not if what I printed was right the first time."

Ritchie looked at Wilbur in exasperation. He shook

his head. "She don't get it," he said. "I told you she wouldn't. And she don't."

The brothers were starting to spread out a little in her office, picking things up, putting them down, constantly moving in directions in which she couldn't watch them both. They drew nearer to her at the same time, like a pair of wolves moving in on their prey.

"Let's go back to the beginning," Wilbur said. "You wrote them, huh? Both articles that made us out to be a bunch of shits?"

"I wouldn't describe them that way, but I wrote them, yes."

"How *would* you describe them?" Ritchie asked.

"Accurate," she answered.

"Well, accurate or no, lady," Wilbur ranted, "don't do nothing like that again!"

"Why not?"

" 'Cause we don't like what you said about our family, fuck it," Ritchie said. "Don't you understand that?"

Ellen blanched slightly and needed to steady herself, but very quickly her fear started to give way to another sentiment, indignation. How dare these imbeciles walk in here and tell her anything!

"This may come as news to both of you," she said boldly, "but as long as I'm running this newspaper, I'll decide what I'm going to print."

"Shit, lady," said Wilbur. "You just don't know how it works in Wilshire, do you?"

"Why don't you tell me?"

"It's real simple. You either do what we tell you, or we make you wish you had."

"And how are you going to do that?" Ellen asked.

"Something real bad happens to you."

"Such as?"

"Well, the last owners had a fire. And their friggin' trucks had accidents."

"Are you were responsible for them?"

The brothers laughed.

"And Mr. Fishkin? Who owned the hardware store?"

"Hey, he brought trouble on hisself," said Ritchie.

"So that's the type of thing that would happen to me?" she asked.

"No. Because you're being a bitch, something worse would happen," Wilbur said.

"Much worse," Ritchie said.

"Like what?"

Ritchie thought about it. Then he picked up the picture of Sarah from Ellen's desk.

"This your kid?" Ritchie asked.

Ellen felt a sensation of fury zing through her, fury riddled with fear. Fortunately, her indignation covered her.

She reached for the photograph and put her hand on it. Ritchie tightened his grip and grinned.

"Give that back to me."

"Maybe I will."

She yanked it. It wouldn't budge from his grip. Ritchie Corbett laughed.

Ellen yanked it again and Ritchie, toying with her, released his hold. The picture flew from Ellen's hand to clatter noisily onto the floor. For a moment Ellen thought the frame had broken. She reached down to pick it up. The men stared at her lecherously. Wilbur was trying to see down her dress. She was close enough to Ritchie to see the cirrhosis-induced yellow of his eyes and smell the foul booziness of his breath. From Wilbur, she caught a splendid whiff of a Walmart cologne. For the first time, her prevailing sentiment was pure fear.

"You got a husband, lady?" Wilbur asked.

"None of your business."

"She ain't got one," Ritchie said.

"Too old and ugly. Nobody'd be interested," Wilbur added.

"Get out," she said again.

In the back of her mind, she was wondering what she had in the desk drawer for protection. A pair of scissors. A letter opener. There were two brothers, each of whom must have had seventy pounds on her. She felt incredibly vulnerable.

"Your girl?" Ritchie asked, turning his attention back to the photograph. "She walk home from school?"

"None of your goddamn business!"

"Your kid? She have her time-of-month yet?" Wilbur asked.

Ellen slapped at him. She swung hard. Wilbur held up a beefy, workman's hand and deflected her best shot. He only laughed again.

"Whoa, you got a real attitude, lady," Wilbur said. "A bad one."

Ellen stepped back to her desk. She put her hand on the telephone.

"Now what are you doing?" Wilbur asked.

"Calling the police."

The Corbett brothers laughed. She dialed 911.

"Shit, lady" said Ritchie. "That ain't gonna do no good. Who do you think's gonna come over? Cousin DeWayne or Cousin Lukas?"

"Maybe both if we're lucky," Wilbur said.

Ellen glared at them. "We'll see who comes," she snapped back.

The 911 operator was on the phone. A flat male voice. It sounded dumb.

"This is Ellen Wilder at *The Wilshire Republican*," she said. "I've got two Corbett brothers in my office threatening me. I'd like them removed."

"What?" the voice asked.

Ellen repeated.

After a pause, the 911 operator hung up.

Were they rushing over? Or ignoring her? She broke a sweat as the negative answered suggested itself.

Ellen said nothing. She moved her fingers and pushed down the button on the phone. Her hands weren't as steady as they might have been.

"They're sending someone," she said.

"I doubt it," Wilbur answered.

"They ain't coming," said Ritchie. "They probably hung up on you."

"Well, how do you like that?" Wilbur mocked. "You pay tax money here in Wilshire, and you can't even get a cop."

"Not even a Corbett cop."

"Someone will come," Ellen said. "I'll call the police station directly."

The men laughed again.

"Well, hell. Don't wake up Lukas. He sleeps in the back when he's drawin' a paycheck."

"If Oprah's on, Lukas won't answer, neither."

"Hell, maybe Chief Elmer will come over," Wilbur laughed.

"Think he can find the way?"

Ritchie laughed at what passed for Wilbur's wit.

"I'd love to see that. Fudd ain't made an arrest for twelve years. And I don't think he'd make one today."

"Shit, he watches that colored woman every damned day."

Carefully, Ellen put her hands back on the telephone. She tried to think her way past this moment. She tried to think of *something* that would help. She saw Michael Chandler's business card on her desk.

She dialed his number. No answer, but the call kicked through to his pager number. She entered her calling number.

"Hey, what the fuck you doing?" Wilbur asked after a few seconds.

"I want you out of here," she said. "I called the state police."

"State Police don't come into Wilshire," Ritchie huffed. "It ain't allowed."

"It *is* allowed, it should happen more often, and one of them does."

A silence descended for a moment upon the brothers. They looked at her quizzically.

"You don't know what you're messing with, lady," Wilbur said, growing very angry.

She kept the desk between them and her. She felt her heart thundering. She felt angry and helpless at the same time.

"Leave," she said. "He'll be here in two minutes. If you're still here, I'm going to have you arrested."

Wilbur turned very serious and immensely threatening. He stuck a thick forefinger toward her face.

"Listen, lady," he ranted. "I don't want to see our names in that shit-assed paper of yours again. You understand that? You're new to this fucking town, so maybe you don't understand. People die for fucking with us. Follow?"

"Like Mr. Fishkin?"

Wilbur eased back, almost pridefully.

"Well, shit goddamn it," he said, as if in a revelation. "Maybe the little bitch *does* understand."

The two men straightened themselves up and glowered at her a final time. Wilbur turned slowly and sauntered toward the door. Ritchie picked up the picture of Sarah and looked at it as if to remember what Ellen's daughter looked like. Then he contemptuously shoved it back onto the desk as Ellen lunged for it.

"I'd watch your ass if I was you, lady. For your kid's sake, huh?" Ritchie said.

"That would be pretty careless of you, wouldn't it?" Wilbur said. "To do somethin' that would make your kid get hurt?"

"Get out," she said again in a low voice. "Get out and stay away."

Ritchie and Wilbur laughed, then left.

Furious, but frightened, Ellen remained at her desk. After the Corbett brothers had passed through her front door, she waited for a moment, staying purposefully at her desk, her arms folded across her chest. When the Corbetts started to pull away, she strode to the front door and locked it. She watched their car back up and pull away. Ritchie was driving. Wilbur, in the shotgun seat up front, stuck his paw out the window and gave her an upraised center finger as they pulled away. She felt like flipping him one in return, but chose not to even dignify him with one.

Ellen waited by her door, distracted from her work and greatly shaken. The more she thought about the events that had just transpired, the unwelcome visit from the unlovely Corbett brothers, the more frightened she became.

Her maternal protective streak arose, also. It

crossed her mind, as she waited for any form of police to arrive, that the bully brothers might have continued on to her daughter Sarah even as she stood there. One instinct told Ellen to lock up her office, get into her car, and rush over to her daughter as quickly as possible. Another told her to stay where she was until the police arrived. Patience was something she had learned a long time ago. She was already planning her counterattack on the Corbetts, with a good detailed account of this incident prominently printed in her paper. This was one more story, she told herself with irony, on which she could not be scooped.

Traffic passed her office without stopping. The local police remained invisible. Five minutes crawled by interminably.

Then Ellen saw a high beam of yellow lights sweep quickly through her parking lot. The headlights were distinctive, and she knew they were from a Jeep. Mike Chandler's red Jeep Cherokee pulled directly before the newspaper's front window and parked.

Just watching him step out made her feel better. She unlocked the door. He walked to it, and could tell from her expression how distraught she was.

"Trouble?" he asked.

"Enough of it," she said. "Corbetts. Ritchie and Wilbur. Came here to threaten me."

He felt himself stiffen with anger. "Did they touch you?" he asked.

"Not physically. And not this time," she answered.

"Why don't you sit down?" he suggested. He glanced at the clock. 6:20 P.M.

She felt some emotion welling inside her. She fought with it for a moment and won.

"So it was an intimidation visit?" he asked.

"You could call it that."

"Tell me what happened."

She described the details and contents of her unwanted visit. He listened patiently and calmly, asking
a small question here or there, growing angrier with
each moment. Working police beats in Boston, Ellen
said, she had experienced intimidation before, but
nothing quite like this—a pair of inbred, half-crazed
brothers turning up in her office while she was working alone. The intimacy of it in a small town setting,
where everyone knew everyone, and where the intimi-
dators knew exactly where she lived and of what her
family consisted, made it all the worse.

At the end, Ellen heaved a long sigh, feeling better
at least for having vented her tale. Some of his calm
had spilled over to her. Chandler felt worse, having
heard her story.

"Just the two brothers. Wilbur and Ritchie," he
confirmed when she concluded.

"That's correct."

"No Franny?"

"No."

"See a teenage boy at all?"

The question struck her as strange, with an eerie
echo. "What teenage boy? What does that mean?"
she asked.

"The last couple of times people have had troubles
with the Corbetts, the uncles posted their teenager,
Isaac, on the victim a few days in advance. That's what
happened to Mr. Fishkin. Isaac apparently watched
him for a few days before anything happened."

"I didn't see Franny, and I didn't see a teenage
boy," she said.

"Maybe that's good," he said. "My guess is that
this was meant as a warning."

"Maybe," she answered.

"And you called the local police?"

She motioned toward the empty door and parking lot. "Twenty minutes ago," she said.

"Jesus Christ," he cursed, shaking his head. "Their headquarters is five minutes away even if they walked." He pondered the point for a moment. "Who did you talk to?" he finally asked. "A man or a woman?"

"Man. A dispatcher, I'd guess," Ellen recalled.

"Maybe not. Wilshire's funny in more ways than one. The nine-one-one is antiquated. Probably intentionally. The calls kick into the local police station instead of a county dispatcher."

She grimaced. "I might have known," she said. "And, of course, what does that tell us?" she asked.

"It tells us that when there are Corbetts involved," he said, "the law in Wilshire works differently."

"We knew that already, didn't we?" she asked. "I've been here two months, and I'm sick of it."

"I knew that the day I came into Wilshire," he said. "It's so well known among the state police, that it's almost a throwaway that they sent me in here."

"What's that mean?" she asked.

"It means that I just came back onto full duty after a temporary disability leave. My commander sent me here to look at a possible homicide, but they didn't expect me to do much."

"Is that right?"

"Last summer, when Maury Fishkin disappeared, they sent in a broken-down old cop named Sheehan. All Trooper Sheehan did was punch a time clock and pick up a check until retirement. No wonder Mr. Fishkin's car is in the lake and no one finds it."

"So you're not *supposed* to accomplish anything here?" she asked. "Is that it?"

"It's vague. It's more like I'm not *expected* to accomplish anything." His eyes settled on hers. "This is off the record, right? I don't want this turning up in print."

"It's off the record," she said. She was pleased that he trusted her enough to talk.

"I was supposed to look at a dead body, fill out some forms, and get out of town. But it turned out the body belonged to a Corbett. That was the first complicating factor. Now we have *two* homicides, in my opinion—Maury Fishkin and James Corbett—but I can't string them together. So the department still doesn't expect much."

"Nor do the people in this town, it would seem," she said.

"*Some* of the people," he said. He managed a slight smile. "Then there are the stubborn ladies who come in from out of state. They run newspapers, expect a bit more out of life, and don't understand how things have worked here for a century."

"So you've finally read one of our issues?" she asked.

"The one you sent me," he said.

"And?"

"What can I say? You spelled my name right."

She managed a nervous laugh. "Is that all you can say?"

He shrugged. "If I say too much more, I'll find myself quoted again."

"At least I do it accurately," she said.

"Sure. But sometimes that can cause trouble, too."

She sat back at her desk and managed to relax further.

There was a slight silence between them, which Ellen felt obliged to fill. "Thanks for coming over," she finally said.

"I didn't mind at all," he said. He motioned to the picture of Sarah.

"Don't you need to go get your daughter, however?"

"How'd you know?"

"After school day care ends at six-thirty. It's the type of thing I do know," he said.

She frowned. "You have children?"

"A nephew and a niece. My younger brother's a state trooper, also. No kids of my own."

"Oh," she said.

"Not married," he said. "Came close about a year ago, and have been recovering ever since."

"Too bad," she said.

"Maybe," he answered, looking at her.

She took a long pause, and watched him as he picked up the picture of Sarah and gently set it down again. "Very pretty girl," he said. "My guess is she's your only child."

"Why do you guess that?"

"Wouldn't I see evidence of another?" he asked.

She had a burning impulse to tell him about the son she had lost. Somehow she felt comfortable talking to him. She battled the impulse and controlled it.

"You're either very perceptive or nosy," she said.

"This from a former reporter?" he asked.

"Point," she said.

She laughed again. "Come on," he said. "If you're closing up here I'll walk you to your car."

She accepted the offer. She turned out all the lights except one. When she got to her car, she found him looking it over, checking it. He had heard enough of the stories about how the Corbetts booby-trapped and sabotaged vehicles of those against whom they bore a grudge.

"Should I be nervous?" she asked, watching him.

"Just be careful," he said. He pronounced her car safe to enter and drive. "I'm going to go have a talk with both of the brothers."

"What are you going to say?"

"Depends on what they say to me first," he said. "I expect that they'll deny that this incident took place. In that case, something might happen to them that *I* might deny took place. I don't know."

"Handle it properly," she said. "I don't want you overstepping on my behalf."

"They overstepped," he said. "And *they* broke the law. Now they need a receipt or they'll move it one step higher."

"Meaning I *am* in danger?"

"Just be careful," he said again. "And call me again if you need me."

Ellen said she would. She thanked him a final time and pulled her car out of the parking lot. She knew Sarah would be waiting impatiently.

Chandler followed her car by a hundred feet as she drove to the school. When she had picked up Sarah safely—she was the last child there—Chandler also insisted that he follow her home.

He went to the door of her home with her, examined it again for intrusions, and made sure that she was safely within.

"You don't trust those Corbetts at all, do you?" she asked.

"They need to learn that they can't do things like this," he said calmly. "I think this might be something they might eventually regret." He paused. "Well, you're safe at home," he said. "Now it's time for me and them to have a little chat."

"Be careful," she said.

"I promise," he answered. "By the way, what page were you planning to put it on?"

"Put what on?" Ellen asked.

"The account of what happened this evening. I'm assuming you're planning to print something about your visit."

She gave him a smile. "You *are* perceptive," she said.

"I try to be."

"Page one. Next edition," she said.

"Don't look for Ritchie to carry that edition in his smoke shop," Chandler said. "And don't expect the Corbetts not to retaliate. Stay in touch with me regularly."

"I'll do that," he said.

He left, and she watched him walk back to his Jeep. He stepped into it and waved. She waved back, and she let the curtain withdraw to where it had been. She had no way of knowing that Michael Chandler was inordinately angry, and now had exactly the type of weapon that he wished to use against the Corbetts.

Sixteen

Detective Michael Chandler drove angrily from Ellen's home back through the center of Wilshire, not knowing exactly in which direction to vent his rage.

He went into the local police station, but the officers whom he wished to confront were not there. No one was there, in fact, other than DeWayne Corbett, who was in the chief's office in the back room, watching television.

Chandler appeared at his door.

DeWayne looked up. "Yeah?" he asked.

DeWayne Corbett, the aspiring future police chief, was seated at Chief Moore's desk. He was getting a feel for the job: eating macaroni salad out of a plastic container and potato chips out of a bag. He had a pack of Merits lying on the desk and had a couple of cans of beer lined up.

"What can I help you with?" DeWayne asked, not evidently wanting to help with anything.

"I'm looking for Elmer," said Chandler.

"Fudd went home," DeWayne said.

"How about Lukas?"

"How about him?"

"Where would I find him?"

"Don't know."

"Who took a call from the newspaper half an hour ago?"

"What's it to you?" DeWayne asked.

DeWayne turned his attention back to the television.

Chandler walked to the television set and knocked the cable box off the top of it. It flew noisily to the floor.

DeWayne stood quickly and angrily.

"Hey, what the—"

Chandler was ready. With his good arm he shoved him hard and sent him awkwardly back into his chair.

"You tell Moore that I need to talk to him."

"Talk to me," DeWayne said. "I'm the future chief here."

"Not if I can help it, you're not," Chandler snapped. "But you can tell your thug family to stay the hell away from the newspaper or anyone involved with it."

DeWayne steadied himself, his eyes narrow angry slits.

"I don't know what you're talking about, Chandler. And you're way out of line here."

"You took the call yourself, didn't you? And you hung up because your cousins told you they were going over to the newspaper."

There was just enough of a pause for Chandler to know that he'd nailed it perfectly.

"Fuck off," DeWayne Corbett said again.

"If anything happens to the newspaper or anyone who works there or any family member, I'm holding *you* personally responsible, DeWayne. *You!*"

"You can't hold nothing, Chandler, other than your own dick. You're a single state harness bull. You ain't got no juice here in Wilshire."

"We'll see." His shoulder was killing him again. He

felt as if he had aggravated something by shoving De-
Wayne.

"The Corbett family's the law here," DeWayne continued. "Thatsa way it's always been. As soon's you
get back to your barracks, the confusion'll end."

"We'll see about that, too."

Chandler turned his back to DeWayne and walked
out, feeling better in terms of mood. He slammed
the door and went to his car. When he glanced
through the window of the police station, DeWayne
was tending to the broken cable box.

Angrily, Chandler climbed back into his Cherokee.
His upper arm and shoulder throbbed now, but he
started to settle down. He wondered whether the confrontation with DeWayne would be forgotten the next
day, or was just the first gauntlet down between him
and the Corbetts.

He drove to Lake Barbara for a moment and
thought things through. The only thing that two-bit,
hick dirtballs like the Corbetts understood, he told
himself, was force. Action, reaction. They could not
be allowed to think that the episode at the newspaper
was going to pass without a response. That would
only move them to their next step.

Chandler checked his weapon as he sat in his Jeep.
The weapon was loaded. He flexed his arm and hand.
His arm was in bad shape, with lack of feeling in the
wrist today and nasty, persistent pain in the upper
left shoulder, even before jostling a Corbett. His fingers seemed to be working, and he hoped they would
work if he needed to pull a trigger. Day by day, he
could feel the nerves and reflexes degenerating.

He started to wonder how long he could hang on
to his job. The pain was now constant. Little tasks
like opening a door or taking the lid off a jar or

popping a cap off a bottle—mundane things that re-
quired a grip in two hands—could cause a jabbing
pain, then several minutes of paralysis or lack of sensation. How could he ever draw a pistol if he had to,
or squeeze a trigger to defend himself?

He felt like a duck with a broken wing—vulnerable,
vulnerable, vulnerable, an easy target for the hunters
out there—but to seek medical help for his arm and
shoulder would be to call attention to it. Then his
case would be forwarded up to the state police medical affairs office in Hartford. There they would write
his retirement papers from the disability. He cursed
a body that was failing him, then reminded himself
that in another sense he was lucky to be alive.

Dead and back. That's where he was. He sighed.

He pulled his Jeep from where it was parked,
turned, and drove toward the Corbett farm.

He broke loose from the town center and traveled
the Sturgis Road. He passed Ellen Wilder's house and
slowed down. The house looked safe and secure. On
an urge, he stopped and went to her door.

She came to the door, and brushed the shade aside
from the inside. She smiled and opened the door to
the cold night.

"I was going by. Just wanted to make sure you were
still all right."

Sarah appeared behind Ellen. The little girl looked
mildly frightened, as if she knew something was going
on. She stood close to her mother.

"We're fine," Ellen said.

"You have my number."

"I have it," Ellen said.

"I'm taking a ride out to the farm. Keep your
doors locked unless it's me."

"Are you expecting trouble?" Ellen asked.

"You never know."

He continued the rest of the way out to the farm. His thoughts rambled again.

Death. Killing. The Corbetts and their bush league intimidation. They were as dangerous as they were dumb. Man's inhumanity to other men. What was this all about? He thought of Ellen Wilder and her daughter and further cursed the bully boy male habit of trying to physically intimidate women. He hated thugs who picked their shots like that—a bunch of sneaks and cowards.

And how the hell did Franny figure in all of this? For that matter, where in hell *was* Franny? The big guy had pulled one of his frequent disappearing acts. Chandler had had an eye out for the largest Corbett, but the oversized lug seemed to have gone underground.

Well, Chandler figured, this was a night for rattling some skeletons. Maybe he could rouse Franny, along with a few other members of the family.

Maybe he would regret doing so.

Dead and back. Dead again.

Yeah. Anything that had happened once could happen twice.

Chandler drove along the dark road that led to Corbett Lane. In the forefront of his mind he wasn't sure what he was doing, but in the back of his mind there was a greater certainty. He was looking for any first-echelon Corbett he could find.

Paunchy, snarling shaggy-haired Wilbur.

Bandannaed, unshaven, weasel-eyed cheap drunk Ritchie.

The elusive, fade-in fade-out hulking phantom, Franny.

Maybe he'd even hit the trifecta. All three at once.

Then what?

Chandler's mental state was such that he felt half crazy. He was fatigued. Agitated. In such a state of mind that anything was possible.

Like making himself vulnerable and being shot from ambush.

He wondered as he drove, as he approached another closed door, if this was how he wanted to spend his life. How many more years would he traipse from one crime scene to another, picking through the crazed motives and explanations for why one human would take a life from another?

How many more years would it be before he was plugged from another ambush and spent the rest of his life incontinent, drooling into oatmeal, and ambling around on a walker in a nursing home? A whole lousy scenario unfurled before him in which schoolchildren who feared him and thought he smelled bad would come by once a year and pin a hero's worthless medal on him, then cower while their teachers said some kind words. The real marks of merit, the real gauge of what he had earned, would be a paralyzed arm and a colostomy bag.

What a life. What a life. Why the devil did he do it? What drove him onward? Why, for that matter, was he even messing with the Corbetts? He could have retired or gone back on disability, or opted out of this case on a day's notice.

Answers, answers, he thought. He learned all the details, but knew few of life's answers. How was he to understand his adversaries' motivations if he couldn't even figure out his own?

He kept driving. The radio in the Cherokee gave him a blast of static.

He passed through the wooded area that came be-

fore the open fields and noticed once again how one
stretch of it looked just like another. It was a lot like
snow hitting the windshield of a car during a bliz-
zard—over and over the same repetitive images, with
hypnotic effect, dulling his mind.

He drove down the road that led through the farm.
There was a mat of brown leaves on the dark country
lane leading to the Corbett farmhouse, sort of like a
slick, unwelcome piece of carpeting, again not too far
above the threshold of freezing. The leaves beneath
the tires of his car were cold and sodden and rotting.

A thousand more thoughts pursued him again. He
was coming up on the nine-month anniversary of his
shooting. Incredibly, the incident kept replaying itself
in his mind, over and over again. How had he missed
the closed closet where Tito Moreno had been hiding? How could he have been so foolish as to allow
a homicidal dirtball get a drop on him? Oh, if the
medical and psychiatric people who worked for the
state police up in Hartford had any *idea* of the things
that went through his head!

He switched the stations on his car radio.

He found some pleasant soft rock. When the music
stopped, the disc jockey started to talk about life, then
segued quickly into a bible lesson. It was a Jesus station
masquerading as a civilian one, latter day disciples in
disguise. The New Testament for New Haven, New
London, New Britain and, if the signal traveled well
enough on cold winter nights, New Rochelle. They
lured the unsuspecting suckers in with the pop culture,
Chandler mused, then ambushed them with the Jesus
pitch.

Ambush.

Oh, Lord, he thought. He couldn't get away from
that term, that concept.

That event that had once left him in the gray area between life and death.

Where would he have gone if the respirator had been turned off? Oh, sure, his *body*, his corporeal state, would have been planted in the family plot. But what about the rest of him? His spirit? His animus? Where would that part of Michael Chandler have gone?

Leave it to a near-death experience to bring these thoughts home and keep them perking in the front of a man's mind. Leave it to a pair of homicides to keep the concept fresh. And leave it to driving the back roads of central Connecticut in the evening hours to add a crazy warp to the whole thing.

He successfully drove through the gate to the farm. At night the layout looked more ominous than ever. Details, details: He counted cars and trucks parked askew for all the Corbett males. Even Ritchie's red-and-white sleezemobile was carelessly banked on the edge of the dirt driveway. Chandler pulled to a halt and put his Jeep's high beams on the door to the farmhouse.

Instantly, Chandler caught an eerie glimpse of a familiar shape in the shadows beneath a tree, legs, body and head, all askew and inverted. Chandler's heart leaped. There was a large carcass hanging on a tree in front of the house. For a moment, Chandler was startled. At first, from its size, Chandler thought it was Franny lurking in the cold shadows. Then the body took shape.

It was a slaughtered deer. A doe.

Chandler sat in his Jeep and stared at it.

As Chandler's eyes adjusted and the body took the proper form, he realized there were not one, but *two* dead deer hanging there, heels high, heads down, tongues hanging loose from lifeless, open mouths. The carcasses had been strung up on a strong oak branch to let the bodies age properly. Their stomachs were slit open, and they had been eviscerated.

There was a doe and a smaller deer, probably an adolescent. For a moment, Chandler felt as if he'd been kicked in the gut. He was certain that these were the same two deer he had admired on the edge of Lake Barbara, not long before the body of Maury Fishkin had been retrieved from the water.

Then he had a bizarre thought: The Corbetts knew he hated hunting and had hung and butchered the animals just for Chandler's sake, knowing he would present himself here. He shook off the thought.

Details, details: paranoia, paranoia.

Chandler straightened himself. He exited his Jeep and walked to the door.

Details, details, again: Hunting season had just started on November first, and already the Corbetts had enough venison to make Bambi burgers through the winter. When Chandler passed the carcasses, he could see that they had been expertly eviscerated. Still more details: The hunters hadn't been as precise as the butchers, as each animal bore maybe a dozen bullet holes. He guessed that the Corbett "marksmen" had used an automatic rifle to get the job done fast. Either that or they had all started to blast away at once. The deer had been assassinated more than hunted.

Chandler cringed and empathized with the deer. He knew what it was like to take bullets. He'd once wondered if animals had souls, and had long since concluded that they did.

Chandler continued to the front door. He knocked boldly.

The sounds of the dogs erupted from within, followed by the sound of a woman cursing. He identified the voice of Lizzie, and thought he also detected the lower rumble of Ritchie or Wilbur.

He stood to the side of the door, the cold of the night against the sweat on his face. He felt his heart kick.

Lizzie flung the door open and stood in front of him, a kitchen knife in her hand. There was no surprise on her face. She'd known exactly who her caller was.

"What do you want again?" she asked.

Chandler kept five feet away from her, close enough to know that the house smelled just as bad this time as the previous visit. He brought his hand to his weapon. If Lizzie lunged with the blade, she had the drop on him. He wondered if Lizzie had carved the deer. Chandler's fingers were on his gun, and he tried to flex them.

Complete paralysis. They wouldn't move.

He broke a steadier sweat. Verbally, he moved forward.

"I'm looking for Ritchie and Wilbur."

"Oh, kiss my fat, pimply ass."

"Want me to come back with a warrant, Mrs. Corbett?"

"I don't want you to fucking come back at all, unless you're bringin' one of them Dick Clark Ed McMahon checks."

"Ritchie and Wilbur, Mrs. Corbett. Talk to me or I'll arrest *you*."

"Me? For what?"

"I'll think of something."

"You do, and I'll claim you tried to rape me."

"Now," he said with a sinking feeling. "Ritchie and Wilbur. Tell me where they are."

"They went bowling."

"How come their cars are still here?"

"They took a truck."

"Which truck?"

"Maybe they went with friends. I don't know," she said.

"Where'd they go bowling? Wallingford? Hamden?"

"Canada somewhere."

"Don't give me bullshit, Lizzie. I'm sick of you and your whole fucking clan."

"Well, we're sick of you, too. Get off our farm, pretty boy, and watch your goddam mouth while you're at it," she said. "You got no fucking right here. We don't hardly need no Staties in Wilshire. I'm gonna file a civilian complaint if you don't stop bothering me and talking at me with your filthy mouth."

"Who was the man I just heard?"

"Nothing here but dogs," she said.

"I heard a male voice."

She grimaced. "Fuck!" she said. She turned clumsily. "Hey, Isaac," she called. "Get your sweet skinny ass out here!"

A moment later, her sallow-eyed, sixteen-year-old nephew appeared. For Isaac, it was an evening of heavy metal: He had two new pieces of jewelry on his ear, a stud through his right nostril, and had one of the German Shepherds yanking hard on a chain leash. He still had the same pudding bowl haircut, but now a touch of green dye had been added to his coif.

"Now do you believe me, Shitface?" Lizzie asked Chandler. "The only male here is my orphan nephew, so there!"

"I want to talk to Ritchie and Wilbur," he said.

"You got a warrant?"

"Not yet."

"Then fuck off."

"Tell them I was here," Chandler said. He was ninety-eight percent certain than they already knew. "And tell them I'll be back with a warrant if I think I need one."

She pushed the door. This time he moved backward and let the door close. It slammed. There followed a noisy little coda of bolts dropping and latches twirling.

His nerves eased as he stepped away from the house. At least he hadn't backed down. At least the Corbetts had received a police visit within hours after their latest bit of small-mind, tiny town intimidation, and this time it was a serious police visit—not a social call from Elmer Moore, the local law enforcement eunuch, and a sleepy eyed Corbett cousin.

Chandler walked back to his Jeep, slowly and thoughtfully. The two deer were still dead, coal black eyes seeing nothing, their slit bellies open to the night, their hearts silent. He was sure he was under scrutiny from the house, probably by the very brothers he was looking for. He scanned the vehicles and quickly reassured himself that none had come or gone since he arrived.

He had his own means of getting a message delivered. He went to each of the car windshields and laid one of his business cards across the windshield wiper.

He knew the Corbetts wouldn't be intimidated, but he also knew they would receive the message. They had thrown down a challenge, and he was up for it.

* * *

Elsewhere in Wilshire, another ominous shoe was set to drop.

"Mommy?" Sarah asked.

Ellen sat on the edge of her daughter's bed, tucking her in for the night.

"Yes, honey," she answered.

"There was a boy watching our house today."

Ellen's hand froze. "What?" she asked.

Sarah repeated.

"What are you talking about, angel?" Ellen asked.

"There was a boy watching our house. He was standing by the mailbox looking at our house."

Ellen frowned. "Anyone you've ever seen before?" she asked.

"No."

"Well," she said patiently, controlling herself. "Did he looked friendly or unfriendly?"

"I don't know. Maybe a little of both." She was frightened.

"How old?"

"Teenage," she said.

"Describe him, angel."

"I can't."

"Why not?"

"He was just staring. He had a hat and coat, so I couldn't see his face."

"Oh."

"Every time I looked close from the window, he looked away."

"Then why didn't you call me?"

"I was going to, Mommy. But as soon as I thought of it, he disappeared."

"Disappeared?"

"I was going to get you, but he read my thoughts. He was gone."

Ellen felt an uneasy flutter somewhere within her, like wings beating in her chest. She pictured the wings, and in her mind they belonged to a big, black, evil bird. She remembered too well the anecdote that Mike Chandler had told her about the teenage Corbett kid, Isaac, watching the Fishkin hardware store for the days preceding the attack. Now the vigil had begun, she thought, and the Corbetts had cranked things up another notch. Their sentry was on duty, but one of the victims couldn't identify him.

She suffered another, deeper, pang of fear. Now the Corbetts had Isaac watching her. God, this was too much.

No wonder these thugs had the whole town scared. They *were* scary. No one would stand up to them, and they came at you right away until they got what they wanted. For a moment, she felt like putting everything of value in the car and getting the hell out of Wilshire.

She couldn't, and she knew it. She drew a breath. "I wouldn't worry about it, Sarah," she said. "Maybe he was just standing there admiring our house."

Sarah was all over the lie. "I don't think so," she answered, "because he scared me. And because your hands are shaking."

Ellen abruptly hid her hands, thinking again of Isaac Corbett.

"Know what?" she lied next. "My hands are shaking because I'm tired. And you know what else? I think I know who the boy was. And I think I'm going to have that state policeman, Detective Chandler, talk to him. Okay?"

"Okay."

From the look on her face, it didn't look very okay at all. Ellen leaned forward and kissed her daughter again. She held the kiss for an extra second. Her daughter smelled and felt so sweet and pure and unspoiled. The thought of these local thugs even suggesting that they would harm her filled her with rage.

"Good night, Angel," she said.

"Good night, Mommy."

Ellen closed the door partway. In the front hall, she went to the front window of the house.

She looked down toward the street. The front light was on, and the street was quiet. She looked toward the area next to the mailbox where Sarah had said she had seen someone.

She recalled Mike Chandler's warning.

Again, she felt very vulnerable.

She went downstairs and walked to the kitchen. She put her hands on the largest knife she could find, and went to her home computer. Just so that no one could ever doubt what had happened, she began writing up the events of the day.

The house creaked. She raised her eyes and saw nothing. There was a second creak that was so loud that it caused her to get up and investigate. She thought that the sound had come from upstairs, in that damnable brown room that she could never quite get around to doing anything about.

She walked out to the dining room and again saw nothing. She went to the front window and reassured herself that the street was quiet, that no one seemed to be watching.

God, she thought. Why couldn't she live normally in this town? Why was she even spooking herself?

She tried to phone Mike Chandler. Just to talk. He was still out. She wondered how things had gone with the Corbetts. She hoped he hadn't gotten hurt on her behalf. She found herself worrying about him.

Another surge of anger went through her. This whole frightening episode had begun with the visit of the small town bullies to her paper. Well, she was *not* going to let it go. Ellen was too stubborn and indignant for that, and was not about to be pushed around by a couple of ignorant goons.

She spent an hour at her keyboard. She wrote two thousand words on the visit. She would break the story on the front page and continue it on page three, right there up front for everyone to see. It was an account of the Corbetts' visit to her newspaper. She boldly named them and recounted the dialogue. She wondered if they would threaten to sue her, or just threaten to burn her out.

"So there, you dirtballs!" she said to herself. "And why don't you subscribe to home delivery, too!" She used her modem to send the article to her newspaper.

She could barely believe her own nerve. And yet, when she was ready for bed, she was still shaken. She took the butcher's knife upstairs with her.

No, she reasoned. *Mustn't leave it there. If it's by the bed and visible, if I get an intruder, the intruder could use it on me. Better to hide it.* She placed it under a newspaper—an arm's length away, but hidden.

She couldn't fall asleep.

She moved to the front landing in the upstairs, made herself a cot, and slept there with the light on. At least she could see someone coming. At least she would have the privilege of waking up slashing.

By God, no one was going to threaten her and her family and not pay a price for it.

She closed her eyes and fitfully fell asleep.

Seventeen

Midnight arrived. Mike Chandler found it impossible to go home.

He sat by the lakeside, a solitary figure in a Jeep. The vehicle's engine was running. His line of vision overlooked Lake Barbara. His mind was a clutter of doubts, uncertainties, and suspicions.

He sipped from a freshly opened quart bottle of malt liquor—Mickey: a cheap, easy-to-guzzle brew in a distinctive, wide-mouthed Shamrock green bottle that was shaped like a mini-barrel. Meanwhile, through the verdant haze of four point four proof, his past and future alternated before him as he tried to put his thoughts in perspective.

At one moment he was a boy again, walking with his father on a cold afternoon by Long Island Sound. The next moment he had traveled through time until he had arrived at the moment a few days ago when Franny Corbett had disappeared before his eyes. Then his mind was probing into the future, to the resolution of the case before him and his potential forced retirement from the state police.

Retirement.

How he hated the word, the concept. Yet suddenly he could see all the pieces moving into place.

His arm was killing him. It spasmed sharply every time he bent it. His shoulder ached with the cold that had seized New England. How long could he hide the residual damage from the time he had been shot? Eventually, he would have to see the doctor again, and the doctor would tell the department that he wasn't physically fit for duty.

Never mind mentally fit. How could he go to the department shrinks and tell them what he had witnessed about Franny Corbett?

"Franny's not really alive, but he's not really dead, either, Doc." That would make a great opening statement. "I saw the man disappear right before my eyes. Fade-in, fade-out. Now you see him, now you don't. Happens all the time. Meanwhile, I can't find him again, and he's crucial to the case I'm working on."

Yeah, right. The arm would land him on the surgeon's table and the statements about Franny would land him on the shrink's couch. The latter would be fine except for one thing: Chandler was *certain* of what he had witnessed. By all that was holy, there *was* something unearthly about Franny Corbett. Chandler had picked up on it the first time he had confronted Franny. Now he knew what it was. That half-dead, half-alive quality.

"And those qualities are so rare in an individual these days," he grumbled to himself in bitter irony. "Franny is a man among men. Or *something* among men."

An *in-between* sort of being.

Normally when I have a dead guy on a case, he mused silently, *he's the victim, not a witness whom I keep questioning.* He laughed. "I wish to fuck that dead guys would stay in their rightful place," he said to the empty vehicle. "It would make life so much easier."

A moment passed.

"Then again, I was a dead guy, too," he continued. "And here *I* am. So who the fuck am I to tell Franny to take a hike?"

He sighed and swigged some more brew. What was there to do on this case? Where was there to go from here? Why, he wondered, had fate dropped a case like this at his feet?

Fate. Feet. He suppressed a little laugh. Words pulled themselves apart in his head and then took shape again like little subversive messages.

Fate. An old tune came back to him from his youth: "Cast Your Fate To The Wind." He played with the words while music from an unseen source played in his mind, a mind on a pogo stick, bouncing from one free wheeling association to another. He was sitting in a car by a lakeside downing a green quart bottle of Mickey and getting drunk.

Funny. He hadn't felt like getting drunk until he had been confronted with Franny and his disappearing act. Or had he gotten drunk and *then* encountered the big guy's fade-in, fade-out show?

Well, one thing was for sure. He was starting to get a bit of a buzz again right now.

Chandler was sober enough to know where else he was. He was on an edge that he never had known to exist. He knew that if he asked anyone for help it would probably cost him his job. He had to depend on himself to make his way through this case, his own ingenuity.

"Goddamned Corbetts," he cursed in his Jeep. The damned Corbett family had pushed him to the edge the same way they had long since pushed the town of Wilshire to the edge. "Fucking inbred, no-good bastards."

He wished someone would clean out the whole lot of them.

His eyes narrowed. He looked at the lake. There was a ripple of water coming toward the shore, emanating from somewhere out in the darkness.

What had caused the ripple? A duck, alighting in the middle of the night? A stray Canadian goose? A spirit walking on the water or arising from the depths? Who knew what in hell else was in the lake?

On impulse, he moved the spotlight at the window of his Jeep to throw a beam out over the lake, seeking the origin of the ripple. He saw nothing.

Was Maury Fishkin's tormented spirit rising?

Whatever had caused the ripple was invisible, at least to him.

He turned the light off and returned to his immediate problems. How to proceed?

A bunch of bad ideas danced before him, one after another.

Get some bootleg painkillers from some unethical sawbones. That'll take care of the pain.

Don't tell anyone what you know about Franny. Then no one will know you've gone crackers.

Have a few more quart bottles of booze. The brewskis make the arm and the head feel better.

Still the rage was within him. A local bully boy had shot him down in Bridgeport, and now he was faced with a whole family of them who had turned a New England town into their own little fiefdom.

One of the first principles of police work was, don't get emotionally involved. Don't take a case personally. This one he sure as hell was.

He asked himself all the important questions. Was he still useful? Was he still a good cop? Had he endured his shooting and his seven minute death with his sanity intact? All of these things were at issue here on a cold night in November as he sat sipping a big-mouth Mickey and looking at the dark, cold surface of Lake Barbara. His mental journey forward and backward in time seemed to him like a single unfinished voyage.

Outside the Jeep, the night had turned very cold. Chandler's external thoughts dispersed, and he again became aware of the radio playing in his vehicle.

No music. Just more pop chat bullshit. He closed the bottle of malt liquor, screwing the top back on with a third of the liquid left. He poked the buttons on the radio, surfing from one channel to another. Somehow he kept coming back to the strongest signal, which was the local Jesus station.

Now the man on the radio had dropped all pretensions and was talking flat-out about Christ and Salvation. The pitch was soft. Squishy soft. Never mind the fire and brimstone of that old-time religion. This was Christianity Lite. The pitchman was selling snake oil, a newer, milder variety than ever before. Stealth conversion. Soft rock evangelism.

Chandler scoffed at it. He wondered why he hadn't seen God during the seven minutes he had been dead. Thinking it further, he wished he had.

Oh, *how* he wished he had!

His father had been a religious man. Where had he lost it? *How* had he lost it? How would God have explained a cruel band of thugs like the Corbetts?

He punched another button on the radio and brought up something from New York—Something hard rock from the far reaches of FM reception, something more atheistic, something more in line with what his usual suspects listened to. Chandler turned the car and drove away from the lake.

Got to break this mood, he told himself. Got to
get my thoughts moving in another direction. Got to
be more positive.

He figured he would take one more run out toward the Corbetts' farm tonight. Maybe he'd run into
Wilbur and Ritchie crawling back from a tryst with a
whore at the local $29.95 den of assignation.

In some ways he was embarrassed and ashamed of
his own cynicism. Why couldn't he have a traditional
orthodoxy, like every other man on the force? Christ!
His heart had stopped. His brain waves had flatlined.
And now he was back. Why?

He wondered—not just today, but almost every
day—*Why did I get sent back?* What if his brother had
given permission to pull the damned plug instead of
showing the doctor some artillery?

"I got sent back," he said, reasoning aloud in the
car, "because there is some bit of unfinished business
here for me, something I have yet to do, yet to accomplish, yet to be."

It was like a mantra to him.

". . . yet to do, yet to accomplish, yet to be . . ."

He meant all this in a fatalistic, non-religious way.
It was just the natural order of things, how they were
meant to be and how they would be. Like the dream
of getting shot that recurred over and over, these
words, these thoughts, repeated themselves to Chandler.

"There is a reason that I am here. That's it. There
is a reason that I am here."

The deduction reminded him of his late father,
who used to say there was a reason he became a cop,
and a further reason that both his sons did.

"Yeah. You forced us," he answered his old man

in absentia. He managed a laugh after that one. No response from the late Captain Chandler, however.

He ran through many images and memories of his father as he was alone again in the car. Rock on the radio blasted as Chandler drove past Ellen Wilder's house. The house was dark but seemed secure. He continued through the woods toward the Corbett farm.

Yet, what was he to believe now? Mike Chandler was a man whose orthodoxies were seriously askew.

He had been dead and back. Dead and back. Dead and back. He couldn't get away from that.

Franny Corbett had appeared like a phantom, possibly passed through locked doors, and then had faded out before his eyes. What had been the explanation for that?

Deep in his heart, he knew that paranormal explanations for Franny were the only ones that made sense. So why did he decide that one minute, and then challenge it again the next?

A further thought found him. A new pattern of events emerged. Franny was an emissary from the other side of life, sent to bring Chandler back to where he belonged: the land of the dead.

Then it happened! Simultaneous with his thoughts as he drove on Corbett Lane away from the farm—

Holy Jesus!

"What's the old expression?" he demanded suddenly of himself. "Speak of the devil, and the devil appears."

Think of Franny Corbett and—

Chandler hit his brake like a madman to avoid the man standing in the middle of the road. Chandler's Jeep slid on the blanket of wet leaves, nearly fishtailing from the asphalt. As he rolled through the night he thought he had seen—he *knew he had* seen—a big, hulking figure that was all too familiar! The figure seemed to dissipate like mist, and just as quickly pop up safely on the shoulder of the lane.

Unmistakable! Out in the middle of Corbett Lane in the midst of a cold, wet night.

Franny! Standing right in the road. His arm had been upraised. Franny had been out there waiting for Chandler! It was obvious.

Chandler stared into his rearview mirror. He saw Franny's huge frame in the frostbitten moonlight and in the reddish pink reflection from his own rear brake lights.

What was this all about?

Franny had turned and was facing the policeman's car.

Chandler gunned his Cherokee in reverse, traversing the bends and bumps in the road backward, navigating toward the spot where Franny stood, hoping that no joyriding teenagers were going to be drag racing through here at this hour. If any car came fast around the bend, Chandler knew, he was dead meat for the second time this year.

He backed up all the way. Franny's frame grew larger as Chandler approached. Franny Corbett waited for him. The Jeep drew abreast, and Chandler push buttoned the side window to open it.

"Franny!" he yelled.

The big man smiled, then turned. He hulked away from the road and into a dark clump of trees which were on Corbett property. Chandler had the sense of having hallucinated. It all seemed hyper-real.

But it wasn't.

Chandler knew this was happening. He stepped out of his car and was met by a blast of wet and cold.

There was also a fetid stench in the air, one that reminded Chandler of decomposing flesh.

He called to his suspect. "Franny! Hey, Franny! Let's just talk!"

The dark woods gave no answer.

Nor did Franny.

Chandler cursed. He pulled his coat closer to him. "Come on, Franny. Come out here!"

No answer again.

Chandler reached into his car for his radio. He wanted to ask for a backup—staties, neighboring township, anything except the ineffectual locals. Just a backup. Just someone to retrieve his body in case this was another ambush, in case he was to be found dead hours from now.

He reached the phone with his left hand and the phone slid from his palm. The cold had aggravated the spreading paralysis. He couldn't grip.

He looked to the woods again, and thought he saw Franny disappearing. No time to call in. He grabbed a battery-powered search lantern from the car and then took off through the trees.

He pushed his way through cold, wet, bare branches. He felt the brittleness of them and their wicked texture as they approached frost. The branches slapped at him like little riding crops.

Franny remained twenty, thirty feet ahead of him, marching through the woods. Like a tune on his mind that he just couldn't place, Franny was there, just out of reach. Chandler noted the position of the moon and stars. It was easy to get lost in this sort of place. Unless he was going to die out there, he would have to find his way back.

Then there was an overwhelming intuition.

The thing that is before me, the creature I am following,

the beast in human form, is not human. Then another
image came back to him—that of the Manitou, the
mythical beast who lured hunters higher and higher
up a mountain, then transformed itself into something mythical and supernatural, against which guns
were useless. Immediately it turned upon its pursuer,
ripping off limbs and ears as a prelude to eating the
pursuer alive. The Unquowa and Pequot Indians, the
inhabitants of this region three hundred years ago,
had shared the Manitou in their folklore.

In several minutes, Chandler found himself in a
small clearing. It was starlit, and his eyes needed to
adjust. Large sturdy white stones were scattered
around. He blinked. He felt as if he had entered a
domain distinct from any other that he had ever
reached, a mystical sort of place.

Chandler repeated to himself of Franny, *not human.
Not flesh and blood. Not from this world.* The words were
in his mind, however—not spoken, not audible to
normal ears.

A heavy moment passed.

Then, "That's a bad thought," said a voice inches
away from Chandler's ear. "I'm not a beast. I'm human. Same as you."

Chandler whirled.

His heart walloped his ribs with two tremendous
beats, so aberrant and forceful that Chandler thought
his heart would arrest. A series of extreme palpita-
tions cascaded through his chest. Franny had materialized immediately to the left side of him, just out of
view until he wanted to be seen.

Chandler stepped back from Franny and tried to
gather himself. He raised his lantern and turned it
on. The yellow beam came upwards under Franny's
face and turned the big man's features into a gro-

tesque skeletal mask. It was all like a Halloween party gone berserk, a monstrous fantasy vision suddenly turned real.

Franny raised a hand to the lantern.

"No lights," he requested. "No lights in this place at night."

"I want a light," Chandler said.

Franny's lips made an ironic smile. "No lights."

He lowered his gaze to the flashlight. The beam waned as he looked at it. It quickly dimmed, like a doused fire. Then it was out, like batteries draining before Chandler's eyes.

Chandler lowered the flashlight. The beam was dead.

"Thank you," Franny said.

Beneath his coat, Chandler's clothes were soaked with sweat. His shirt was sticking to his ribs.

"How did you get next to me? How do you do what you do?" Chandler insisted. He was struck by the eerie echo of the ambush that had left him on a tenement floor with a bullet in his chest. Once again, he had walked right by the man, if this *was* a man, he was chasing.

"I can do a lot of things," Franny said simply.

And I can't believe this is happening, Chandler thought. *I can't believe it, but it is.*

Franny's eyes seemed to glow a little, like little white pilot lights. "That's another bad thought," Franny said.

"What is?"

"That you don't believe in me."

Chandler recoiled in further shock. He flinched at Franny's words, startled beyond belief or explanation.

"You can read my thoughts?" Chandler asked, realizing that Franny had just done it twice.

"Sometimes."

There were times when Franny's low voice seemed to come up out of the ground. This was one of them.

Chandler could see only what the moonlight and starlight allowed him to see. This place seemed empty. His eyes finally began to adjust. The surroundings came into perspective, much in the way the two deer carcasses had, and with similar results. The big white stones came into focus, a whole little army of the markers. Some were tall and narrow. Some short and flat. Some with statues on top of them.

Chandler realized Franny had led him through the woods into the Corbett family burial grounds.

"I'm over here," Franny's voice came next.

It came from directly behind Chandler. He turned and saw Franny sitting on a long stone that seemed to be worn with age. Chandler took it to be one of the oldest markers in the cemetery. It was flat and boxy, in keeping with the style of the early to mid-1800's.

Franny seemed comfortable on that deathly seat. The big man smiled. For some reason, Chandler could see Franny very well.

"Now you're my guest," Franny said. "So you sit there."

Franny poked a finger out from a big beefy hand. He indicated the tallest monument of all. Chandler understood that he was being asked to sit at the base of it.

Chandler turned, but did not yet sit. He was about six feet from Franny, facing him directly.

Franny's eyes rose, following the contours of the enormous stone at which Chandler now rested. "Impressive, huh?" Franny asked.

It was.

Still standing, Chandler looked directly above him and studied it.

The monument must have been twenty feet high. The granite likeness of a Civil War soldier stood on the top of it. The soldier was a bugler. There were two other soldiers at the bugler's side. The inscription was barely visible in the moonlight, but Chandler managed to read it. This was the tomb of two Corbett sons, Thomas and Peter, and their father, Jeremiah Corbett, who had died with the Union army at Cold Spring Harbor.

When Chandler's gaze came back down to ground level, he was startled again. Franny had moved without making a sound. Corbett was now seated at the base of the tomb, immediately next to the inscription. He held a reflective air.

"Come. Sit," Franny said.

It was midway between a command and an invitation. Chandler didn't move.

"Sit," Franny said, more insistently the second time.

Chandler moved over to him and sat.

"See?" Franny said. "Spirits. Magical place. Magical time. Don't last forever, them things. Have to take advantage."

For a moment the two beings stared into space. Franny's mood and persona had mellowed from the last time Chandler had seen him. Now he was a big, benign bear, albeit with a great, lurking sense of the abnormal.

"You watching over my Lisa?" Franny asked.

Chandler was surprised by the question. "The Lisa from the insurance company?"

"Yeah. That Lisa. My Lisa," Franny said.

"I'm keeping an eye on her."

"Good," Franny said softly. "Then I don't have to."

"No," Chandler agreed reflexively. "You don't have to go near her. Better for everyone if you stay away."

"She don't pay no attention to me," Franny said. "Maybe that's good. Maybe that's bad. You keeping a watchful eye on her."

"Yeah. She's safe if I'm watching her," Chandler agreed.

Franny leaned back. A smile crossed his lips. "Good," he said. "Yeah. Real good. Sometimes I think I scare her, anyways."

The big man seemed content. He was almost docile at the moment.

"I don't understand," Chandler said a few seconds later.

"What don't you understand?"

"Who you are. Where you've come from. Why you're here." Chandler asked.

Franny's face slackened into a cold smile. "Not the type of thing you could understand."

"Why?"

"You're alive."

"I wasn't for seven minutes."

"I know."

"How do you know?"

"I know," Franny repeated. "Sometimes I know things. I know them because they're in the air. I can see 'em. They're clear. I know you were dead."

Chandler summoned all his courage for the question that followed. "And that's why I feel something extra about you, isn't it, Franny?" the policeman asked. "You were dead, too."

"Sort of."

"You're dead now?"

"Sort of."

"Which is it?"

"Both. I'm in an in-between sort of place."

"You're dead, but you're back?" Chandler asked.

"Yeah. Same as you." Franny grinned. " 'Cept I'm not staying."

"And I am? Staying, I mean?"

"No one stays forever."

"That's not what I meant. Staying longer than you?"

"We'll see." Franny's eyes drifted upward. "I'm here for a short time," he said. "Set things right. That's what I'm meaning to do."

Franny paused as if to pick a thought out of the heavens. "You?" he said. "Can't tell. Might stay a long time. Might leave before me."

" 'Leave.' You mean, 'die'?"

"Yes."

"Do you know?"

"Yes."

"But you won't tell?"

"No."

Chandler reclined slightly. "It's all right," he said. "I don't want to know. If I knew, I'd always be keeping track of the days, the minutes—"

"Keep track of them, anyway," said the big man. "No one needs to know when they're gonna die," Franny continued softly. "They think they do, but they don't. Human bullshit."

Corbett's eyes rose again.

Chandler joined Franny in looking skyward, up into the darkness of the cold night. Above Chandler, a granite Jeremiah Corbett worked his bugle into the night sky, his final military maneuver, a mute and exquisite call to arms, one which would wail into infinity.

"I live in the real world right now," Chandler said. "I have to solve crimes in the real world."

"So?"

"Help me."

"Crimes," Franny repeated with a snort. "All your crimes, all your cases, everything will resolve."

"When?"

He snorted again. "Soon."

"Who murdered Maury Fishkin?"

"Uncle Jimmy."

"Who murdered Jimmy?"

He smiled. "No," he said softly. "You're a state pig. I can't tell you."

"Why?"

"It would wreck things."

"How would it wreck things?"

As Chandler stared at him incredulously, Franny seemed to fade a little—his way of disapproving of the question. Then for a moment, Franny seemed angry. Indignant.

"If you wanna know so much," he challenged, "ask Jimmy yourself."

Franny made a gesture with his hand. Chandler followed the line of Franny's direction. The policeman's eyes settled upon a grave so fresh that there was no tombstone yet upon it. Somehow he knew it was Jimmy Corbett's. Even if he hadn't, he knew a heartbeat later—because Jimmy rose from it.

Chandler felt a terror he had never known, so cold and startling within him that he felt as if his whole body had turned to ice. It was even more terrifying than the moments after having been shot, when he thought he was going to die.

Jimmy's specter stared at him—soundless, almost soulless, with the same wide, terrified, last-moments-of-life eyes that had given his corpse such a jolting appearance. At his neck were all the gaping wounds from the pitchfork.

"So ask him," Franny said.

Chandler couldn't find his voice. He could not bring himself to converse with Jimmy's ghost.

Franny laughed slightly. With another curt wave of his huge hand, he dismissed Uncle Jimmy. Jimmy Corbett settled back into the earth.

Chandler struggled back to time present, seeking some piece of his old reality to latch onto. He came away from the vision of Jimmy with a new spin on everything. Somehow Franny controlled Jimmy's soul. Franny was the master of it.

How? Why? Did Franny similarly control the soul of the whole clan? Again, how and why could that be?

Chandler turned back to Franny. He tried another tactic.

"Tell me how you got that scar," he asked.

"I will," Franny said. The tone of his answer suggested that an explanation was not in the immediate offing. He remained silent.

"Will you tell me now?"

"No."

"Why not?" Chandler asked.

"It ain't your time to know yet. You don't get to know nothing in life until it's your time to know."

"Then when will that be?"

"Soon."

Chandler waited resignedly for something better. Franny was like a rabbi when asked when the Messiah would come: Soon, soon. Always soon, soon. Something better as an answer wasn't forthcoming right now, either. Or soon. Chandler changed directions yet again.

"How powerful are you, Franny? What else can you do?" Chandler asked.

"Bar tricks?" he asked, his mood settling into further tranquillity. "More bar tricks?"

"Sure. Got one?"

"I got a good one." Franny grinned. "Watch," he said.

With his head, Franny motioned upwards. Chandler lifted his gaze again and scanned the heavens, fearing another ghostly appearance. Instead, his eyes settled upon the blank sky. The stars were abruptly gone now. There was just a dull, filmy moon behind some clouds.

"What?" Chandler asked.

"See anything?" Franny asked in return.

Chandler continued to scan. "No," he said.

"Do you like snow?"

"No."

Franny grunted. "Too fucking bad."

A moment later, Chandler was struck dumb. First a few big white flakes started to come out of the sky. Then, slowly, the volume built, until there was a vigorous flurry of them, enormous, solid, fluffy, cottony white ones, falling like soap flakes onto his face. A cold blanket of quiet, white peacefulness, or so it seemed.

"I love the snow," Franny said. "White. Cold. It covers evil."

"You did that, too, didn't you?" Chandler said softly. "You made it snow!"

"Yeah. You finally believe."

"Yes."

"That's good. Real good."

"Why?"

"Next time I bring someone to see you," Franny said.

"Who?"

"You come see next time."

"When?"

"You'll know when."

"I'm not following."

"Yes, you are," said Franny. "Better'n you think. You follow real good."

Chandler thought about it and came back with a different question.

"I want to know something," he said, leaning back.

The detective's eyes went skyward yet again. Up above, past the early season snow that was in Chandler's face, Jeremiah Corbett still played the bugle, forever rallying long dead troops in a conflict that ended a century and a third earlier.

A funny impulse was upon Chandler when this vision was before him. In his perspective, he was lying on the ground—or beneath the ground, far below Jeremiah Corbett's feet—and the old soldier was sounding taps for him. The image echoed the moment when Chandler had been shot in Bridgeport. He found the near flashback so disorienting and disquieting that he purposefully leaned forward. He switched the direction of his gaze and tried to focus again on Franny.

"What are you, Franny?" he asked calmly, trying to finish his question. "A ghost? A spirit? Some sort of conduit between this world and—"

The policeman felt something very cold run through him. He felt deeply chilled, as chilled as he would be, maybe even more, if from somewhere out

of the darkness in the woods behind him a pair of
cold hands had landed on his shoulders. As he spoke,
he turned slightly to check to see if anything were
going to materialize from behind him.

Nothing did.

He turned back and saw Franny scoff.

"No worry," Franny said. "There's nothing back
there but more spirits. And you can't see them."

"But you can?"

The big guy nodded. "There's one of them standing right near you," Franny said. "Maybe five feet
away."

"Franny, don't bullshit me, okay?" Chandler retorted.

"I'm not. There's another spirit there."

"Whose spirit?"

Franny stared into the darkness. He took several
seconds to answer. "It don't matter," he said.

"Yes, it does. I want to know."

"Nobody you ever met. Nobody that concerns you
none."

An icy breeze rippled through the shrubs and
branches behind him, cold as a tomb on a winter
morning. Some of the branches clicked. They clicked
the way his father had used to click sticks together
walking on Connecticut beaches on winter afternoons
two dozen years ago. Rattled, Chandler turned again
quickly, a surge of anxiety within him turning his
blood as cold as the weather.

He saw nothing. What he heard had sounded like
someone was walking away from them, pushing his
path through the branches, having been standing
there.

"Prove it. Prove something's there!" Chandler
blurted.

"I don't have to prove nothing," Franny answered.
"I want to *see* something!"

"You coulda if you'd turned when I said so."

"I want a second chance."

"I made it snow. You seen that."

"Then make this another 'party trick,' Franny," Chandler insisted.

"Nope."

"Please."

"Why should I?"

"Because I'm asking you."

The big man was leaning back fully against his great-great-great grandfather's tomb now. The question seemed to take five minutes to travel from Chandler's lips to his ears. The big man also seemed to be enjoying the very tactile touch of the snow upon his face. Several flakes fell on his cheeks and stayed there, adorning him with a benign, silvery sparkle.

"That was just some kid, anyhows."

"Who was?"

"The spirit."

"No one I knew?" Chandler asked.

"Nope."

"Then why,?"

"See, you don't figure this none," Franny said. "They're all there somewhere. You just got to want it enough."

"What are you talking about?"

Benign one moment, Franny did something horrible the next. He turned toward the policeman and caught his gaze eye-to-eye. Then he rolled his eyes upward in his sockets, exposing only the whites, which seemed to glow with a bright yellowish whiteness.

The vision jolted Chandler once again. He recognized the brightness from the time he'd been shot. Franny rolled his eyes back to their proper position, and then they disappeared again, creating two gaping cavities.

Then the eyes were back again, as normal as Franny's eyes ever were. Chandler, meanwhile, felt his heart thundering in his chest and his face soaked with perspiration. The sweat was rolling down his temples and freezing as it rolled.

"Party tricks," Franny said. "Eyes. Windows to the soul. The spirit. Huh? Tricks, tricks, tricks."

Chandler was speechless. He didn't know if Franny was friend or foe, benign or evil, human or ghostly. Or elements of all of these.

"Who'd you want it to be?" Franny finally asked.

"Want what to be?" Chandler asked.

"The spirit. The one that was behind you."

Involuntarily, an answer came to Chandler. He didn't speak it.

"Right. It's your father," murmured Franny Corbett. "Now he's there, too."

Corbett had pegged it right on the nose. A furious defensiveness sparked within Chandler. "Bullshit, Franny! Bullshit!" he raged.

"Okay, don't believe me. Your choice."

"You can't," snapped Chandler, "tell me what he looks like."

Franny's gaze flickered and seemed to focus on something over Chandler's shoulder. He spooked the policeman thoroughly, then made it even worse.

"He looks like you. But he's stockier, and a little bent over. White hair. Glasses. That's how he looked when he broke free of his earthly exist—"

The accuracy of Franny's description made the skin rise across Chandler's arms and at the base of his neck. He fought with himself again. He resisted the reality of what Franny was insisting upon.

"You've seen a picture. This is all a ruse, isn't it, Franny? You saw a picture of my dad somewhere."

"Then turn."

Chandler was afraid to turn—afraid of what he might see, afraid of the truth of what might be there, afraid to trust his own senses.

"No."

"Coward."

"This is all suggestion. Everything you're doing is suggestion. You're as real as I am, and there are no spirits here. It's a ruse and—"

"What's a ruse?" Franny asked.

For a moment, in exasperation, Chandler rubbed his eyes with his hands. When he opened his eyes again, Franny was no longer next to him. He had moved to the boxy white tombstone half a dozen paces away. He was sitting there.

"Too bad. You're *not* ready," Franny said. "You're not ready to completely believe. Too fucking bad."

He waved an arm at the darkness, seeming to dismiss what Chandler didn't believe was there.

Awkwardly, Chandler commenced an explanation, or at least an attempt at one. "A ruse is—"

"Don't matter. I don't care none," Franny said.

"A ruse is a trick," Chandler said, forging ahead. He suddenly had the nerve to turn his head. He took his eyes off Franny, turned, and saw nothing except the snow falling peacefully upon the tombstones.

"You don't even have to believe in *me*," Franny said. "Not nohow."

Chandler turned back to where Franny had been. The policeman stopped speaking in mid-sentence.

Franny Corbett was gone. Not a trace of him remained.

"Franny?" Chandler asked. "Franny?"

The snow on the ground was light, and there were no footsteps anywhere near the boxy, white tombstone or even the monument to Jeremiah Corbett. There was nothing to suggest that Franny had walked off into the night, because there was nothing to suggest that he had been there at all. Nothing, other than Chandler's memory.

"I'm not nuts and I'm not drunk," Chandler said. "I know what I saw."

The snow was relenting. A few of the branches from trees clicked together—the sound made by the wind, same as the sound made when a man pushes his way through. Chandler didn't see anyone.

Chandler spent several minutes alone with his thoughts. The snow slackened more until it began to abate completely. And why not? Franny, who had summoned it, was gone. Within a few seconds, the snow was nothing. Then it was gone from the ground quickly, too. No trace of it remained.

The detective rose. He glanced upward again. Jeremiah Corbett, a latter day archangel, was still sounding the silent trumpet. The snow, Franny's private squall, had relented completely. Ten thousand stars were visible in the November night. So was a path back through the woods, as if something large had cleared the way in front of Chandler. Chandler traipsed back through the trees and snapping branches. He found his Jeep exactly where he had left it. He wished he could say the same for his mental state.

When Chandler returned to his home, his eyes ached with fatigue. So did his back, and the rest of his body. Almost everything hurt as much as his wounded arm and shoulder now. He scrounged around the medicine cabinet and found some prescription stuff that was stale-dated but still seemed to work.

He was unable to settle into sleep, so he sat at his desk downstairs and reviewed the Corbett file for another half an hour, retracing isolated incidents and facts one after another through a clueless darkness. He traced the Corbetts forward and backward, hoping the file would tell him something new.

It didn't.

In fact, the more he examined it, the more he experienced yet another funny sensation with it. Forward or backward there was a decreasing amount of difference between the two. It was all the same journey, with presumably only one destination, one which lay ahead of him.

Or, since forward and backward meld so well these days, it occurred to him next, in this case, does 'ahead' mean 'behind'? Does the answer that I will find in the *future lie somewhere in the past*?

It was just such elliptical logic on which he had sought to close the psychological door. It bothered him that another such question had now posed itself.

Isolated fatigued thoughts suggested themselves to him. *Shot in the past, shot in the future.* He sighed.

It was 2:30 A.M. He needed to be up again at six. He still hadn't found Wilbur Corbett or Ritchie Corbett.

He called in to check his voice mail at State Police headquarters. There was one item of interest there. The computers had located a Social Security number for one Francis J. Corbett who had been born in

Ohio, not Connecticut, some twenty-eight years earlier.

This Frank J. Corbett had never worked, never filed any taxes, never done anything of record other than draw a Social Security number.

At first that struck Chandler as doubly bizarre. A Corbett who had been born in the midwest, and a man who had never held a traditional paying job. Then he realized that Franny must have been the product of a strange union, and that Franny had worked off the legal books all his life, on farms or in rural areas of Ohio. How else did one flit around the modern world without ever touching anything? An invisible life for a nearly invisible man.

Chandler went to his refrigerator and found a beer. Combined with the painkiller, it eased the overall discomfort in his body, if not his psyche. It also allowed him to grow sleepy.

He closed the Corbett file. He had put in several weeks on this now, and wasn't even sure that he had accomplished anything. He also owed his commander, Jack Lindemann, a written report on the case. An update.

He stayed at his desk and, while the events of the day were fresh in his mind, he spent a half an hour writing one, entering it into a desktop computer. He was in no mood to mince words, and thus alluded to "spiritual encounters" with one Frank Corbett, and cited "nearly metaphysical and borderline paranormal" aspects of the case, which he actually felt was understating things a bit. He hoped no one reading the report would even understand what he meant, but it was late and he wrote what was on his beleaguered mind. Hell, he had encountered ghosts that evening. He was entitled to some philosophical liberties. He had to tell *someone*.

He finished writing the report. He reread it, changed little, and thought back on the whole episode as it had unfolded so far in Wilshire. Then he sent the report electronically to Captain Lindemann, whom he hoped would ignore it, or only read the first paragraph.

No wonder, he thought to himself a few minutes later as he lay down upstairs and went to sleep, no wonder nothing in Wilshire ever gets resolved. The whole damned place, he theorized, was some sort of perverse optical illusion. The place didn't even exist, and either did anyone in it.

Random foolish thoughts, he told himself next.

There was no answer in his mind to that, for a few seconds later he fell into a deep sleep. A nightmare tried to form itself within him, but dissipated before it could take control of his mind.

The next day Wilbur and Ritchie weren't anywhere as elusive.

Chandler found Wilbur on the farm. He found Ritchie in the smoke shop. He told both that he had a potential complaint against the two of them, and all he had to do was get the complaint signed in order to come back and slap handcuffs on each of them.

"My word against the bitch's word," Wilbur growled. "You don't get no conviction on that."

"No. But I'd have the pleasure of putting cuffs on you, running you in, and kicking your ass around a cell in Bethel. How'd you like a few nightsticks across your teeth?"

"You wouldn't fucking dare," Wilbur answered.

"No?" Chandler arched an eyebrow and acted as if he were looking forward to the exercise.

Ritchie, a more contemplative soul, listened without saying anything. Then, like his brother, he lied boldly and denied having ever been to the offices of Ellen's newspaper. Similarly, both Corbetts denied with unusual vigor having posted Isaac as a sentry at Ellen's home.

Chandler listened patiently and called them both liars. Then he sought to straighten them out on how things would work in the future. He told them that if they went anywhere near Ellen, her home, her daughter, or her newspaper, he was going to put his badge in his pocket along with his name plate, slip into civilian clothing, and come looking for them when they least expected it.

"You wait till DeWayne is police chief in this town," was all Ritchie could offer. "You won't even have the balls to drive through here then."

"DeWayne's ass is going to get kicked, too," Chandler said.

"We'll see," Ritchie grumbled.

"You're right. We will."

Chandler had never laid such a threat to anyone before in his career. It seemed to take the recipients by surprise almost as much as it took him. He had no idea whether they believed him or not, or if they took him seriously. He did know, however, that their responses were fumbling and defensive. He knew he had gotten their attention, and he hoped that would prove to be an accomplishment in itself.

That same afternoon he hoped so very passionately, for the new edition of *The Wilshire Republican* appeared, complete with Ellen's front page account of the Corbetts' visit to her office, plus an editorial titled, "Bullyism in Wilshire."

Chandler had to admire Ellen's nerve and tenacity. Similarly, having encouraged her, he had to make certain that she didn't wind up in a situation similar to Maury Fishkin's. After all, visions of the half-human, half-spirit Franny notwithstanding, and even taking into consideration the inbred aspects of the typical Corbett intellect, he was dealing with murderers.

There was one more thing to keep in mind whenever he drove past Ellen's house, or even when he started his own car. If he had been shot from ambush once, he could be shot from ambush twice. He only tried to figure which Corbett was most likely to do it, and consoled himself with the fact that in drawing fire upon himself, he most likely had deflected it from Ellen.

At least temporarily.

Initially, he was proven correct.

The latest issue of *The Wilshire Republican* sold out its entire press run of three thousand, five hundred papers. Ellen sent the printers back to work and printed five hundred more copies.

The extra copies sold, too, circulating into the neighboring counties. Ellen received several messages of support at her office, at her home, and at places like the school where she dropped her daughter each morning. There was enough positive feedback for Ellen to think that there *were* other people in town who felt the way she did about the long reign of two-bit terror. These other people only needed to be galvanized.

The first reaction from the Corbetts was a long, ominous silence. Of course, a silence had greeted Maury Fishkin's early confrontation with them, also.

No battle could be judged to be over in a night. It was Chandler's contention that rather than retreating, Wilbur and Ritchie were—if it didn't stretch the use of the term—*thinking* of what move to make next.

Ellen knew what move she wanted to make. And, for his part, so did Mike Chandler.

As a gesture of thanks, and growing friendship, she invited the policeman over to dinner at her place on Saturday.

He accepted. A homecooked meal sounded like a great perk of the job, he decided quickly, and it would be much easier to keep an eye on the Sturgis Street address from within rather than without.

So he accepted—as if he needed a better reason that just the occasion to have a pleasant dinner with an attractive woman.

Eighteen

Ellen left her office at 6:00 P.M. Monday and picked Sarah up at her after school day care center. They made two stops on the way home. First they stopped in Wallingford and bought some prepared lasagna for dinner. Then they went to the K Mart, where Ellen purchased a gallon of white primer, two gallons of blue indoor paint, and some fresh rollers. Tonight was the night that she would attack the cold, uncomfortable, brown chamber upstairs that had troubled her so much by its sight, smell, and temperature.

After dinner, Sarah watched her allotted thirty minutes of television for a weekday night, then sat in the living room and looked at a picture book. Ellen spent a few minutes helping Sarah pack an overnight bag. A friend from school had invited her to a weeknight sleepover. Once the bag was packed, Ellen deposited her daughter at a friend's house five minutes away.

Ellen came home again. It never occurred to her that her house was not empty when she returned.

When she sat down at her computer it was eight-thirty. There was E-mail to answer: messages from her sister Gretchen in Boston, and two friends in New York. Ellen typed cheerful letters back to them, lying boldly by saying the journalism was exciting and that the paper was doing well. In the back of her mind she was already inventorying her friends and wondering who might contribute written features for her with deferred pay. From a business angle, things had improved a trifle recently, but there was still a long way to go before *The Wilshire Republican* was secure and solvent.

Forty minutes passed.

On the computer, Ellen also brought up the potential layouts of the next week's *Republican.* The deaths of James Corbett and Maury Fishkin were still the topics that everyone was talking about. There was nothing new on either case. With the defection of Peter Whitely, it was up to Ellen to both publish and edit the paper, as well as cover the biggest story in town. Well, she had always wanted a hands-on situation with her own journal. Now she had it.

She hit an impasse a few moments later. Nothing further came to her about either case. She made a note to ask Mike Chandler a few more questions the next night. Maybe he would give her something good.

She smirked, realizing how that sounded in her mind.

Give her something good.

"Give me something good that I can *print,*" she said aloud, correcting herself. She sighed. Floating in the back of her mind, giving her an unending sense of unease, was the incident with Ritchie and Wilbur earlier in the week. It still scared her, though her nerves had settled considerably since the day when it had occurred. She idly wished something would happen to Ritchie and Wilbur, something to take them out of the Wilshire picture. Then she cautioned herself about being careful what she wished for.

What had she been hoping for? Their deaths? Well, actually, yes.

She cringed.

The Corbett Brothers, and Wilshire, had had that much of an effect on her. She had arrived in this town with every positive feeling, and was recovering from her own bereavement. Now she was hoping that a couple of low rent brothers would get snuffed.

She shuddered. She leaned back at her desk.

Maybe, she tried to tell herself, the Corbetts weren't so bad, after all. Maybe everyone was making too much of everything. Maybe they were all bluster and threat. She thought back a few years to the only experience she had ever had with people similar to the Corbetts. . . .

She had been up in North Salem, Massachusetts, in the western rural part of the state, chasing down part of a murder story for *The Boston Globe*. She'd gotten a flat tire in the middle of nowhere on a rural road. Not a car in sight, and no houses. She was in pumps and an ultrasuede suit. Still, she'd initially figured she could change the tire herself.

She had pulled the jack and the wrenches from the trunk of the car and gone to work, but the lug nuts wouldn't budge. She jumped on them, and they still wouldn't budge. So Ellen had started walking until she reached a dilapidated farmhouse with a crumbling roof. She rang the doorbell, but no one was home. She walked on and saw a long dirt driveway that curved up away from the road. She ventured along it, and as she reached the crest three monstrous dogs came snarling at her. They were mixed breeds: part Doberman, part German Shepherd, as mongrelized as everything else in the area. They circled her. One jumped on her with muddy paws and almost knocked her over.

She held her ground as they circled and growled. Finally a hulking man with a red baseball hat and teeth that shot out in all directions came out of a ramshackle building and called off the animals. Moments later, his brother, who looked just like him, emerged from the same structure.

They were looking at her really oddly. She asked to use a phone, and they pointed to a garage. When she resisted, they guided her there by the arm. When the garage door closed behind her, Ellen had been sure she was not getting out alive. The floor was ankle deep in a green liquid that she tried not to look at. Her shoes and feet got soaked. There was a phone. She sloshed over to it in her destroyed pumps.

As the brothers watched, she called Tom Ferrara, her editor back in Boston, and left a message on his voice mail giving him the general vicinity where she thought she had broken down. She figured that at least the newspaper would know where to look for her body. Then the two brothers offered to help her change her tire. She climbed into their truck, onto the single seat littered with broken tools, dead coffee cups, candy wrappers and crumpled cigarette packs.

They'd driven her back to where Ellen had left her car, hopped out, gotten past the impacted lug nuts with a firm kick or two, and had the tire changed in two minutes. Then they wouldn't accept any money for helping her. They lived there alone with their dogs. They rarely saw strangers, and were fascinated by a woman from Boston. Ellen had never been so glad to get away from a place, but she had also learned a pair of lessons: Scary as some situations were, often even the scariest could be navigated, one could never take appearances to be exactly as they seemed. . . .

So, as she sat at her desk, Ellen pushed the Corbetts to the back of her mind and prayed for the best. She even felt a little gleeful. After all, against all odds, she was surviving another week. That was worth something.

Down below her, in the basement, the ever-voracious furnace rumbled, and somewhere in the house there was a creak. The old floorboards were jumping around again from the heat. She cast a nervous eye in the general direction of the noise, which was beyond the door to her den.

OHN's again. Friendly "Old House Noises," as she had taught Sarah to think of them. Why did she have so much difficulty sometimes convincing herself that these sounds were innocuous?

She sighed again. Sometimes she thought Wilshire was changing her personality. Other times she knew it was. She felt herself tense much of the time, dealing with a new area, being a parent, and trying to run a business.

Toward ten o'clock she went to her front window and peered out. The evening was clear and cold. She put the outside light on and looked at the front of her property. The lawn needed to be raked again, but something inside her asked, why bother?

She felt a little shudder. She didn't like the bare branches of the trees. The onset of winter now bothered her. She knew that Thanksgiving was coming and so was Christmas, and those were good holidays. Still, the change of season gave her an undercurrent of depression. She wondered if anyone else she knew felt that way. The same things had never bothered her when she lived in cities.

With another shudder, she turned off the outside light.

She checked all the locks—front door, back door, kitchen door, and garage door. She checked the downstairs windows. Everything was secure. She felt like a captain putting her ship to bed for the evening, and smiled a little at the image. She wanted to remind herself to share that analogy with Sarah the next day. Sarah would love it, and want to be First Mate.

"Sure," she mumbled to herself, reflecting on the irony of it. "First Mate on a sinking ship."

At ten-thirty she went upstairs. She turned on the radio and caught some local news from New Haven. More cold weather was in the offing; rain was forecast for the next day. The precipitation could even turn to sleet and snow if the thermometer dropped enough. Nothing much had happened in the world, though there had been a near-fatal shooting on York Street near the Yale campus in New Haven. Two days earlier on College Street, some moron had come speeding off the interstate 91 connector in a stolen car, become airborne, and put himself through the front window of Cecily's Family Italian Restaurant. When she heard stories like that she thought of her new friends on the state police and wondered if they were involved.

By then it was ten forty-five. It should have been the end of the working day for her, but she was still trying to make headway with the brown room. No matter what, she was going to take the first steps in evicting that godawful morbid—that's what she had decided it was, *godawful morbid*—aura from the room.

It would be a two step process. She would start now
with the primer. Then later, she would do the actual
painting.

Absently, she wished she had someone to help her.
A man would be nice, but decent single ones seemed
to be rather rare in this area. So like much else in
her life, she would try to make a go of it alone.

She piled the bags from the K Mart outside the
door to the room. Then she stood in the middle of
the brown room for several seconds. The strange
smell was still apparent.

Where in hell *was* it coming from? she wondered.

Then she had an idea. She had looked everywhere
except above her. Summoning up an extra bit of
courage, Ellen walked back to the hallway of the second floor. She reached upward to a rope that hung
from the ceiling of the second floor landing. She
pulled the rope and lowered a ladder that came
down from the ceiling. Then she fetched a flashlight
from her bedroom.

She returned to the hallway, steadied the ladder,
and climbed it. She went up to the crawl space between the roof and the second floor of the house,
accompanied by a twinge of fear, not knowing what
she might find.

She shone the light around in every direction. This
was a hell of a place. Tight, dirty, and cold. Off in
one corner there was an old lampshade. In another
corner were a couple of broken toys. The lampshade
looked to be of 1940's vintage. The toys appeared to
be relics of the Eisenhower Administration, most
likely untouched by human hands for nearly four decades.

Someone had tossed them there years ago and no
one had retrieved them, for a simple reason: The

ceiling probably wouldn't have supported the weight
of an adult, so why mess with it? For a moment, the
idea flickered through Ellen's head of sending Sarah
to crawl carefully along the support beams one day
to get the old discarded items. Why not tidy up the
area, after all?

Then that line of reasoning turned upon itself.
Why put Sarah at risk? If the ceiling was shaky, did
Ellen want her daughter plunging through it?

A nasty thought shot through her. *Already lost one*
child! Want to lose another? Now Ellen rebelled against
this whole jaunt to the crawl space. She wanted to
be out of there.

She shone the flashlight at the area above the
brown room. What she suspected she did not find.
She was looking for the decaying body of an animal.
A squirrel or a mouse, or a crow, something that had
entered the attic from under the eaves. Something
to account for the stench in that room.

She didn't find anything.

She clicked off the beam and went back down the
ladder. She used the rope to let the ladder rise to
where it closed.

She returned to the brown room and reopened the
door.

The room was quiet and empty.

She stepped in, almost feeling like an intruder in
her own home. With her she brought the bag that
contained her painting equipment. She now wasted
no time. She opened a can of primer, poured some
of it in a pan, and then teed up a roller. She sloshed
the roller in the primer, turned and attacked the
walls with it. She obliterated the brown with firm
hard strokes. It felt good.

She thought of going to get the radio to tune in

some music to have some company, but did not want
to lose momentum. Even though she was covering
the brown on the walls, the feeling in the room was
starting to bother her. She almost felt as if someone
were watching her. She wanted to be finished as
quickly as possible.

Ellen eventually paused. She drew a breath, exam-
ining her feelings, demanding to know why she felt
the way she did. She stood still and listened, but
heard nothing. She saw nothing. She felt nothing.
That was a good start.

She stood still again and, with a twinge of anxiety,
inhaled deeply through her nose. The odor in the
room?

The bothersome stench was gone.

"So there!" she congratulated herself. "I chased
the odor away by being persistent," she smiled.
Willpower, plus ample doses of Mr. Clean, Lysol, and
Lestoil."

After all this, she told herself further, this chamber
was an ordinary room like any other. Nothing wrong
with it. Everything had been in her imagination. She
moved to the window and opened it halfway, looking
out toward her back lawn. She wedged a piece of
wood in the window. The wood didn't fit perfectly,
but nothing fit anything perfectly in old houses. At
least the window would stay where she had set it.

She spent another half hour applying the primer
and finished the final bit of wall space. She turned
to give the room a final once-over.

She went back downstairs and relaxed for a quarter
hour. The furnace still rumbled and the odd creak
still sounded in the house. Every once in a while, she
spoke to the creaks "Get out!" or "Get out of my
home. Leave now, damn it!"

And amazingly, the creaks fell silent, allowing her to sip a soft drink in peace.

It was almost midnight. Ellen had been up since six-fifty that morning. She was tired, but she was also dead set on getting some color on the walls tonight. She went to her bedroom and retrieved a radio. She plugged it in and found an FM station from Boston which she had listened to when she lived in Somerville. Some good hard rock would keep her up and prevent her from feeling alone.

She checked the primer. She should have waited a full day, but hell, it was dry enough! She shook a gallon can of paint. With a screwdriver she pried the first can open. She picked up a wooden stick that looked as if it should have come with a four pound Hagen Dazs ice cream bar and stirred.

She poured the thick blue paint into a tin, tied back her hair, and donned a painter's cap. She selected the largest, smoothest, least complicated wall and moved the tin to it.

She began to paint. The blue went on smoothly and evenly. It resembled a sky taking shape. She finished the first wall in twenty minutes, including the trim. Ellen was filled with a sense of accomplishment. She began the wall with the window and completed half of it quickly. She carefully worked her way around the window and went to the other side. She finished.

She worked on the trim around the window. The music filled the room nicely. New stuff by Paul McCartney. More new stuff by Jewel and Sarah McLachlan.

She painted the third wall, finishing the first gallon of paint. The wall was another flat, rectangular one with no uneven areas.

Ellen paused for a moment and examined her work. She pondered whether to take a break. No, she decided. She would keep going. She pried open the second gallon of blue paint and poured a thick stream of it into the tin. The paint gurgled happily as she poured.

Ellen stopped. What *else* had she just heard? A noise somewhere in the house? She looked toward the door and a feeling was upon her—a feeling that told her she was not alone. God, this was a strange house sometimes! She turned quickly and once again was startled.

She thought she had seen a shadow cross the door to the hallway. She stood still and felt goosebumps rise on her flesh. Then she was startled a second time when she felt something cold and wet on her hand.

She looked down and saw the blue paint dripping from the roller. She set down the roller and cleaned her hand with a wet paper towel. Her eyes were still on the door.

Suddenly, as a woman alone in the house, she felt obscenely vulnerable.

She tried to be bold, yet cautious.

She called out. "Hello? Anyone there?"

No answer. The room, however, was absurdly cold now.

"Hey? Anyone?" she called again. Still no response.

Ellen heard a sound somewhere in the hallway. She went to the door and looked. Nothing there, yet the floorboards creaked again.

Rationality told her that if she could not see something, nothing was there. But she had the overwhelming sense of a presence near her. Something she couldn't see.

"No," she said softly. "This isn't happening. I'm not scared."

No. She was terrified.

First the Corbetts. Now *this,* whatever *this* was.

She decided to deny. She would go back to work, ignore everything, and prove to herself what a brave woman she was.

Fear was only in her mind, Ellen told herself, and she was damned well going to be the mistress of her own mind! She continued working and ignored whatever fears were playing in her head.

"I am going to get this room painted this evening," she said aloud, "even if it . . ."—she shuddered again at the words that had flitted into her mind—"if it kills me."

Great, she scolded herself. *Great choice of words.*

She tried to focus on the music. Eventually, she was successful, even though she kept glancing to the doorway, half expecting a male frame to hulk into view. Who would it be she wondered. Wilbur, Ritchie, or Franny?

Pick a Corbett, any Corbett.

Then the room was suddenly filled with a loud bang that nearly made her jump out of her sneakers.

The stick that she had used to prop the window open flew from where she had lodged it. The stick sailed toward her as if it had been hurled. Ellen moved fast to avoid it, but not fast enough. It whacked her across the ankle, then spun to a halt on the floor.

Her bare ankle throbbed as if it had been stung by a hornet. The stick pointed toward the doorway to the hall. Ellen's heart was in her throat. She had never seen anything quite like this. She knelt down and massaged the spot where the wood had hit her.

The contact had caused a superficial gash. She was bleeding. It was almost as if an invisible hand had whacked her for coming into the room, or was it into this *town*?

Ellen stepped back from the stick and stared at it. Her heart kicked furiously. What she had seen was something that could not have happened. The window couldn't have just expelled its prop like that. The stick had been secure. Yet now the stick was lying at her feet, pointing toward the door, as if to indicate her safe path of exit.

And that, too, caused her to think. Exit from where? From this house? From Wilshire?

She approached the window and bravely ran her fingers across it, half-expecting it to move or make a noise.

Nothing unusual happened.

She looked through the glass. It was after midnight in central Connecticut. A cloud passed over the moon.

"All right," she said softly, not even sure to whom or to what she was speaking. "Just let me finish in this room. Then I'll be out of here." Her voice was barely above a whisper.

She waited.

Silence.

Downstairs the furnace rumbled again. This room was still cold because Ellen had been unable to get the heat vent open.

"Sarah and I won't even be happy in this room," she started to tell herself. "Maybe this room should be used as . . . as what.?

Storage, she told herself. *An extension of the attic.*

Or?

A funeral parlor?

She cringed. Those words and the grisly image had jumped into her head from someplace unseen. She shivered. This room was remorselessly cold and unpleasant. It gave her bad feelings and disturbed her daughter. If she could have had it sawed off from the rest of the house and removed right then, she would have done it.

Pointless to put her or Sarah at risk.

Risk? she asked herself. What in hell was she thinking about? What sort of risk? Deep down, what was she thinking about this room? What was in it that she couldn't see? What did she feel? What was the source of her moods involving this part of the house?

She quickly finished the fourth wall. She grabbed her radio and put it in the hall, and briskly gathered up her paint, her brushes, her rollers, and her dropcloth. She fixed the window so that it would be open only a crack, walked to the door of the brown room—now the "blue room" in her mind—and looked at it.

Sarah had picked up on something. Now Ellen had, too; she just hadn't wanted to admit it earlier.

There *was* something wrong with this room. It gave her the worst feeling that she had ever had from any room she had ever entered.

A thought came to her from somewhere: *Robin's room.*

She froze and asked aloud. "What?

The phrase recurred. *Robin's room.*

Ellen felt a chill. She stepped back from the room, turned the light off, and firmly closed the door. She would have been very happy if she could have locked the door, and happier still if she never had to enter the room again. What in God's name was her subconscious suggesting? That this was the room that her late son could have used?

If she hadn't given him up?

If he were still alive?

An even worse notion came to her. *Maybe he'll use it, anyway. Maybe Robin will be there even if he's no longer alive!*

Oh, God, oh God, oh God, she thought. *Deliver me from my own subconscious! Spare me thoughts like this!*

She went downstairs. She walked through the empty house, listening to her footsteps resonate in her ears, and took the painting gear to the garage.

She *hated* that room, she now realized. That was the truth of it. She hated it. Well, at least she understood.

"Guilt," she told herself, just trying to make sense out of the crazy quilt of ideas that were in her head. "I'm upset because things in Wilshire are not going as perfectly as I would have wished. I still grieve for my son. That's what's going on. I am alone here and my mind is running away with me, and I have to control it. Yes. *Control it!*"

Yet, something in that once brown, now blue room had driven her *out*—emotionally and physically. She would never want to admit that to anyone, but that was exactly what had happened.

She would keep her feelings quiet, she swore to herself, but at least she would try to understand. She wished she had kept Sarah with her for this evening. She could have used the companionship. Sarah's love and bright smile could have been worth so much right then, even if she were sleepy.

She went to her den and sat down at her desk. She turned on her computer. Good idea. Take a look at some more newspaper work. Even though it was almost 1:00 A.M., what the hell?

"You wanted to work in journalism. So work in journalism," she whispered to herself, the only listener she could see. "It will take your mind off everything else that's happening here."

It did, but not for long. There was a sound upstairs.

Footsteps. Someone walking.

There was someone walking in the hall upstairs. Right where she had just been.

Ellen turned off the computer, but she was frozen to her seat at her desk.

She knew: this was not her imagination. This was *happening*.

She was too frightened to even breathe. Then the footsteps, or the sound, stopped.

It had stopped right at the summit of the stairs.

She listened to the silence that surrounded her. Gradually, she was aware of another very faint noise. This one was closer to her. She cocked her head and listened. As one sound followed the other, she was aware that what she heard was the sound of weight settling upon the floorboards on the main floor of her house.

Someone—*some thing*—was walking now through the downstairs of her home. Whoever had been upstairs was now downstairs. And it—or *he*—had arrived there without the benefit of having used the steps.

Second floor to the first without the stairs. Great trick. Not something that anyone human usually does.

And now was drawing closer.

Why?

She held perfectly still.

Now she *knew* that there was another presence in her house, a presence stalking her. She leaned back at her desk. A multitude of fears coursed through her. She felt the sweat break on her forehead. She felt her heart thundering, and she felt the wetness of her palms.

She told herself a final time that she would be brave. Whatever this was, she would be brave.

The worst fear was that it was a Corbett, intruding and bent on revenge. She wished she had carried the kitchen knife with her, as she had a few nights earlier, but hadn't had the focus of mind to do that this time.

Her eyes settled upon the empty door frame before her. She felt some of the cold cascade into the room, the cold that she thought she had closed in the troublesome room upstairs. In a bizarre series of associations, one she couldn't rightly explain, it occurred to her that the cold and her visitor were somehow linked.

Ellen spoke aloud, wondering if she would live to see another dawn. "Who's there? Anyone?"

Her question sounded lame even to her. She knew whoever it was wasn't going to answer. Her heart continued to race. She was glad that she had sent Sarah away, for if she were to be killed here, at least her daughter would survive.

An even worse thought accosted her. *Was* Sarah safe? Or had whoever come here to stalk Ellen already done the same to precious Sarah?

Ellen quickly yanked open the top drawer of her desk. She pulled out a letter opener, a wedding gift of a dozen years ago from her Aunt Mildred.

The noise came louder now. The footsteps, if that's what they were, seemed to show a little confusion.

They went in one direction for a few paces, then another, as if someone were looking for someone.

They were not heavy footsteps, like one would expect from a clumsy, lumbering Corbett. They were— well, there was something strange about them.

With her left hand, she reached for her telephone. She punched up Mike Chandler's phone number. The sounds continued to draw nearer.

Ellen summoned up some more courage. "Who is it?" she called again. "I'm here! If anyone wants me, I'm here! In my study!"

Her right hand was on her lap, clutching the letter opener. Mike wasn't answering. She dropped the phone and used her left hand to wrap a sweater around her fist so the intruder would not see she was armed.

She heard a voice. A low unfamiliar one, but not an overtly hostile one. *What the*— She tried to make logic of it. The voice almost sounded adolescent. All she could think of was the teenage Corbett punk, Isaac, yet it didn't sound like what she imagined Isaac's voice should sound like.

A boy's voice. Plaintive and confused. Soft as a gentle rain shower. "Mother?" it asked.

"Oh, God!" she said aloud. With an instinct unlike any that she had ever experienced before, she knew who was there. She felt her body turn to ice.

As God was her witness, she knew what was coming.

A long shadow was now apparent in the next room—the shadow of a male figure. At first she had feared it was Ritchie or Wilbur, coming into her home to kill her, but though the shadow was male, it was lean, thin. It was a youngish figure, without any question.

The room was very cold now. The light within it

seemed to change. It brightened, as if every bulb in the room were arcing brilliantly, ready to burst.

"Oh, my God!" she mumbled.

Her eyes went wide as saucers. The back of her left hand went to cover her mouth, as her right hand held a useless weapon. She felt something rise in her throat because now she *knew* what was coming.

She was bombarded by memories of a spring day in Stone Mountain when she had stood in tears at a funeral. Then there were memories of a difficult pregnancy more than a decade and a half earlier. Memories of a son whom she only had dreamed of, a boy she had loved in absentia.

She knew who this was who had come to be with her. She did not know how this could be, but she knew.

She watched the shadow creep closer to her door.

Ellen's eyes remained wide and staring. She flinched at the horror, the staggering wonder, and the visceral pull of what was about to appear before her. Her mouth was agape with a silent shriek.

No. She was not alone in her home.

Yes, the visitor was looking for her specifically. Somewhere in time, somewhere within some quirky warp in reality, things had to be set straight. Otherwise, why would he be here?

A young male figure stepped into the door frame. He was solid and substantial, sixteen years old and handsome. He looked much the way he must have looked before that horrible car accident in Georgia.

"Mother?" the young man asked again. The voice would haunt her forever, as would the vision, as would the question.

He stood in the door to her den and waited. An

eternity seemed to pass as she stared, an eternity before she could muster the courage to answer.

"Mother?" Robin asked a third time. "I'm looking for Mrs. Wilder. Are you my mother?"

Ellen's mouth was dry. Her throat felt like sandpaper. Something hard and painful caught in it as she tried to answer.

"Yes," she said. "Yes, Robin. I am. Yes."

No smile crossed his face. No look of acceptance or understanding. Only confusion. An unbanishable sense of being lost.

"Are you ashamed of me?" he asked.

"No," she said, her voice barely audible. "No, I'm not ashamed of you."

"Are you ashamed that you had me?"

She shook her head.

"Do you want to hide me?" he asked next. "Do you want me hidden away?"

"No," she answered, nearly breathless with lips that could barely register words.

"Then I want to know," Robin said softly, "why you won't even look at my picture."

She tried to answer, but the only sounds that came out of her mouth were a rushed, hysterical form of gibberish.

He gave her a final look. Disappointment. Lack of comprehension. No love. No understanding. Then the boy turned and walked away.

An instant passed. Ellen sprang from the desk. She ran to the doorway and rushed around it, expecting him to be standing there, but instead only finding herself looking at an empty house.

"Robin?" she asked. "Robin!" she called.

The next sound in her ears was a human scream. Her own.

She screamed and she screamed and she screamed, until she fainted.

When she came to she was looking up into the face of a man who was neither a husband, a son, nor a Corbett, but a man who had broken into her house all the same.

Nineteen

Michael Chandler helped Ellen to her feet. She was dazed and stunned. One moment she had been staring at the vision of her lost son. The next she had been on the floor with a man's hands on her, her brain just starting to embrace the rational world again. Then she realized that the strong hands belonged to a plainclothes policeman, a man she recognized after an instant, who was helping her up.

She felt safer, but no less confused.

"What happened here?" Chandler asked.

Ellen felt her heart still palpitating. She noticed how Chandler *acted* like a detective. He was physically supporting her as he helped her move with wobbly strides to a large red chair in her living room. As he guided her to the chair, he waited for her response. He was eyeing the premises for the details of what might have happened—that, and any residual danger.

She sank in the big red chair and felt her nerves start to settle. She had the worst feeling. Her nerves might have started to ease, but something within her psyche was doing just the opposite. Something inside her was still tingling, almost starting to gear up, and it was tender as a sore wound. Something that was within her, after what she had just seen, would never be quite the same again.

"Well?" he repeated with utmost calm. "Come on. Tell me. What happened here?"

Her eyes rose from where she sat. He stood before her, his eyes comforting, his presence reassuring.

"I'm not even certain that I know," she said after several seconds.

"Are you hurt? Injured?"

She shook her head. "No," she finally said.

"You're sure?" he asked.

"I'm sure," she said.

"Who was here?" he pressed. "Someone to threaten you?"

She made a helpless gesture that he didn't understand. It was as if, momentarily, it was obvious who had been there, and yet she couldn't quite explain it, either.

"No one to threaten me, I don't think," she said.

"Well, I got your call," Mike Chandler said, indicating the phone. "There was no message, and the receiver was left off the hook. I could tell where the call came from via Caller ID. So I came right away."

"Thank you," she managed. At the same time, in the back of her mind, she wondered how to explain a visit from a boy whom she knew to be deceased.

"You want a drink or anything?" he asked.

As soon as the question was out of his mouth, he felt foolish for having posed it. What the good would a drink do anyway? he found himself thinking. Not everyone wanted his boozy crutch.

"No," she said.

He was glad that she didn't.

"Then talk to me. Any Corbetts involved in this?" he asked.

"No."

"But someone was here?"

"Yes."

"Who, Ellen? *Who?*" he asked again.

She shook her head. "Sit down with me for a minute," she answered softly. "If you don't mind."

He didn't. He sat on a sofa directly across from her. If she kept her eyes straight ahead, he reasoned, he had her positioned perfectly.

"God, this is so crazy," she said.

"Then I'd love to hear it all the more."

It took her a moment to gather herself. She needed a final bit of courage to find her voice and explain what had transpired, or what she felt had transpired. In a few more moments, she summoned it. She felt she owed him an explanation for bringing him over.

"I lost a son earlier this year," she began. "He was sixteen years old. A few minutes ago, he was standing here. I don't know where he came from, or what he was doing here. I don't know how he found me, how he got into this house, or how he left it. But he was here. *My son Robin was here.*"

Chandler listened with every bit of professionalism that he could muster. Her tone suggested that she was still thinking this through.

" 'Lost'?" he asked.

"Lost," she said, repeating for emphasis, giving voice to the thought a second time to bring it down to earth. "I lost a son. And a few minutes ago he was standing here."

She motioned to the doorway to her study. Chandler turned to look at it. It looked very empty, but he felt a funny tingle as his eyes settled upon the vacant door frame. It was as if he were seeing or sensing something, but actually wasn't. The house was noiseless, and for the first time in his own life the silence seemed to convey a threat, a sense of the ominous.

He turned back to her.

"Lost?" he asked again. The question hung in the air. Four letters forming one small word, and one enormous question.

"Lost," she said, still trying to nail it down securely in her own mind. "I lost a son. But that was the boy who was standing there."

"I'm sorry, Ellen. I'm still not following."

"I had a child who died. A boy," she said softly.

Chandler blinked. "I'm sorry."

"And that was the boy who just visited me."

He blinked again. Ellen described the vision she had seen. She tried to be rational and straightforward. She *had* seen something, after all. She wasn't crazy.

He kept his eyes trained on her, a touch of professionalism that he couldn't throw off, a technique of using silence to induce people to talk.

She knew the procedure, too. A reporter's bag of tricks was not much different from a policeman's. Any methods that led to answers worked fine.

Her eyes found his, and when they did they found something deeper than before. "I'm going to trust you," she said. "That's not the easiest thing for me to do sometimes. But I'm going to."

He waited.

He received her words with shock. "I'm very sorry," he said.

"It's not the way it sounds," she said. "See, I, uh,

it was a bad relationship . . . I was very young and I—"

"You gave him up for adoption?"

"Yes. How did you know?"

"You had that tone of voice," he said.

"He died in a car accident earlier this year," Ellen explained. "It was a sudden, jarring thing. It caused me to—how would you say it?—reexamine my life. It made me decide I wanted to do things differently. So I quit my job, put everything I had into this newspaper, and came here."

She paused. "Maybe I made a wrong choice. Maybe I should never have put money into a failed newspaper or moved to this community. But that's what I could afford, and that's the decision I made." A moment passed and she concluded. "It was that simple," she said.

She forced a smile.

"Not simple at all," he said. "Right now, Wilshire and your newspaper are everything to you. Professionally at least. Right?"

"Right," she said.

"Very brave. Very bold."

She shrugged and tried to dismiss it.

"I had no idea what I was getting into with this town," she said. "None."

"That makes two of us," he said.

"What are you talking about?"

"Wilshire's almost off limits for the state police," he said, starting to explain the local quirks and protocol. "Have to be called in, then we're hamstrung. The locals don't help us. Makes it particularly bad with a pair of Corbetts on the police force, too—one of whom is apparently going to be the next police chief."

She shook her head. "That's just what this town needs, isn't it? A Corbett running the town police. It'll make the town even more of a black hole than it already is."

He agreed.

"And it doesn't have to be that way," she said.

He agreed again.

"Not at all," he said. "Not at all."

Chandler listened and allowed her statement to settle in the air. He moved her back to the subject that confronted them more immediately.

"So what are you telling me, Ellen?" he asked. "You're telling me you saw a ghost?"

Her eyes drifted faraway and then back again. "Yes," she finally answered. "I guess that's exactly what I'm telling you." She paused. After a long moment, she asked, "So I guess I'm loony now, huh? But something was here, Mike. Something was here, and I saw it."

His response surprised her. It wasn't even the same response that he would have given a month earlier.

"Scary, huh?" he asked.

"Yes. It was."

"This type of thing ever happen to you before?"

"No," she said. "Never."

"Where's your daughter?"

"At a sleepover with friends."

He nodded. There was a silence.

"When did it happen?" he asked. "Your son? When did he die?"

"Last April," she said. "In Ohio. He was living with the family in Georgia who raised him."

He felt a shiver go through him. He thought back to the medley of Georgia-motif songs that Franny, or someone, or something, had played for him on a snowy evening in Lorna's roadhouse. A second shiver followed the first.

"Georgia, huh?" he said.

"Yes."

"Did you know the people who raised your boy?" Chandler asked.

"No," she said, "but they were all in the same horrible car accident."

Her voice halted. He touched her hand in comfort.

"And to this day," Chandler tried, "you feel guilty that you gave him up, and that you didn't play a larger part in his life."

Ellen tensed for a moment and felt something defensive rising within her. "Why do you say that?" she asked.

"Details," he said. "Details. You had a picture of a daughter on your desk at work. No boy, and now you tell me that you lost a son a few months ago. My guess is that you're still confused about his life and death. Otherwise, you'd have a picture. He was your child as much as your daughter."

"I do have a picture," she said sadly, nodding. "It came from his adoptive relatives. The picture is still wrapped up. I can barely bring myself to look at it."

"So there's an example of your ambivalent feelings," he said. "And maybe that's why you're seeing him, anyway."

"Maybe," Ellen said again.

"If you have the photograph tucked away somewhere," he said, "maybe you should bring it out from wherever it's buried. Let it be on display."

"When I'm ready," she said. "When I'm ready." She sighed. "And thank you for not telling me that I'm crazy."

"Why would I do that?" he asked.

"Because of what I'm telling you. About seeing something."

The calm of his reaction had spread to her. She was even less aware of her heartbeat now.

"I'll tell you that you're upset and maybe stressed," he said. "Of course, who isn't these days? And with the material you've been running in your newspaper about our local band of thugs . . ." His voice trailed off and he gave her a smile.

She drew a breath. "Something *was* here," she said. "I didn't call just to get you to come over."

A second passed as he dismissed that notion, also. "I know that," he said. He aimed for a more cheerful tone as he spoke next. "Mind if I look around?" he asked.

She shook her head. "Not at all. In fact," she added, "if you want a cup of coffee or tea, tell me. I don't mind."

"Coffee," he said, "would be good."

It would be, he reasoned. And it would also give her something ordinary to do, something to keep her back in reality as he searched the house for any signs of intrusion.

He looked through the ground floor, his hand near his weapon as he walked.

What was the explanation, he wondered, for what she was telling him? His mind felt scrambled again. Was the whole world going crazy with spirits and the supernatural, or was it just Wilshire? It would have made more sense if a Corbett had appeared in her house. At least that would have fit into his traditional field of experience; at least he could have gone and made an arrest.

He reminded himself again. Police training. Detection 101. The likeliest explanation for anything is the simplest one which takes into account all the demonstrable details. But where was the simple explanation here? Where was it with Franny?

He stopped by the kitchen. Ellen seemed calm as she made a small pot of coffee.

"Mind if I go upstairs?" he asked.

"Not at all," she said.

He gave her a smile and left.

His own footsteps sounded in his ears as he climbed the stairs. The hall light was on. Something gave him a bad feeling, and with one flash he felt as if he were walking into that housing project in Bridgeport again. Behind every closet door were a thousand felons with shotguns or a single demon that defied description. His palms were unnecessarily wet as he stepped quietly from room to room. His shoulder ached, and the tingling was in his left hand again.

He flicked on lights in the master bedroom, then in Ellen's daughter's room. Nothing. Yet arguably, whatever was in the house could still be there.

He turned. His eyes settled on a final door down the hall. Details, details. There was a paint tin and a folded dropcloth outside the room. As he drew toward it, he could see dried blue paint in the tin. Ellen, or someone, had been painting.

He walked to the door that was closed.

He put his hand on the knob. The knob was firm and almost resisted him. A terrible feeling was upon him. Something that told him not to open the door.

It was, in fact, an overwhelming feeling, a heavy instinct—something almost sickening in his gut. His right hand grip squeezed on the doorknob while he held his left palm, the useless one, on the stock of his gun.

The doorknob yielded. The room was dark and cold as Chandler pushed the door open just a crack.

The feeling intensified, and something in his mind reared up and told him he was going to die soon, maybe within the next few seconds. Then that thought floated and lifted, and was replaced by another surge of foreboding. It was something similar to the one he felt when he dealt with Franny, a sense that he had crossed into another realm of reality and he was dealing with an animus that was no longer living.

He held perfectly still. He heard Ellen puttering in the kitchen down below. He heard music. Strangely, it sounded as if it were coming from within the closed room, and it nearly had a gospel sound to it. Then Chandler realized that Ellen had turned on a radio. He felt a bead of sweat roll down his left temple.

"God!" he said to himself. "What type of cop am I? Afraid to open a door to a child's bedroom!"

For good measure, he set his gun in his left hand and carried it. He used his right hand to strengthen the grip of the left.

Then he stood away from the door and pushed it all the way open. It slowly swung open wide and a swath of light from the hall rolled into the dark chamber.

The room was empty, and had a disturbing tomb-like silence. He thought he smelled something funny, but figured that it was just fresh paint on old walls.

He stepped in.

His empty right hand found a light switch, flicked it, and illuminated the room. Strangely, the place was so cold that the detective saw his breath in front of him. Then, for an instant some terrible feeling gripped him, and something moved through his bloodstream that seemed like particles of ice. He suppressed a sickening feeling. Then all of that was gone, and he felt foolish again and very small. He saw himself as a hesitant, frightened, psychically wounded, middle-aged cop who couldn't walk into a cold, unused room in a country house without drawing a weapon.

He was no longer the man he used to be, an inner voice told him, and nothing close to the brave man who would once meet any enemy head-on.

He summoned up a final surge of courage, yet the room continued to give him a bad feeling. For a second he was even convinced that there was something invisible in there with him, or maybe right behind him, but when he looked he saw nothing. He heard nothing, either.

He retreated. He turned the light off and closed the door behind him.

He finished the search of the upstairs and found nothing amiss. Several minutes later, when he had holstered his weapon and started down the steps again, he smelled the welcome aroma of coffee.

He went back to the living room and joined Ellen. He sat on the sofa and she served him a nicely flavored brew. He felt comfortable. So did she. She sat on the red chair again.

"Nothing, huh?" she asked.

He smiled. "I would have let you know if I'd found something," he said.

"Of course," she said softly. "Of course."

"Nice house," he said.

"Thank you."

He sipped. A lightly uneasy moment passed.

"You've been painting," he said. "Upstairs."

"I don't know what to do with that one room," she said. "The one that's blue now. It's a problem room. It's always cold, and it has a funny scent."

"I noticed."

Another uneasy moment. Downstairs, the furnace rumbled to life against the November cold.

A silence hung in the air between them, strange for its awkwardness.

"I'm sorry you lost a child," he said, addressing both of their thoughts at once. "That must have been very difficult."

"It still is," she said, "and always will be."

"I know," he said.

"He was a boy I never knew," Ellen said.

She drew a deep breath and made a decision. She would trust him.

"I was very young when I got pregnant," she explained. "He was born on May third, nineteen eighty-three, and I legally gave him up for adoption two days later. Signed the papers and continued my life. Except, of course, it wasn't that easy. Physically, he was not present in my life, but mentally . . ." Her voice trailed away.

"Mentally and emotionally," Mike Chandler said with understanding, "he was never too far away."

"I guess that's true," she agreed.

"What was his name?"

"Robin," she said.

Elsewhere in the house there was such a loud creaking that they were both startled. Another OHN? The floorboards responding to the furnace? Or something else? They both wondered. Mentally, Chandler reminded himself where his weapon was, not that it would make much difference against certain adversaries. And not that his left hand and arm would behave when necessary, either.

"And right now," Chandler continued, "he's still around, Robin is. Still in your thoughts, I mean."

"I ruined his life," she said.

"You gave him life."

"I walked away from responsibility."

"He probably went to a fine home."

"I'd like to think that," she said. "I wish I *knew* that."

She sipped some coffee and set down her own coffee cup. "Over the years Robin has been there so often in my thoughts," she added. "Maybe too much. Now he's in my house, too." The words, this notion, slipped out before she even knew why she had said them.

"Maybe less of the former than the latter," he said half in agreement. "We'll see."

Ellen looked at him oddly.

"Tell me something," she said. "Did the state police give you a psychology course, too? One on how to deal with agitated women?"

He smiled. "It's not that," he said. "I'm just trying to reconcile everything with the facts that we know."

"So you think I'm just disturbed?" she asked, "and I didn't actually *see* anything?"

"No. I think you're upset, and there are some emotional issues that need to be resolved. I feel much the same way in my life, but for different reasons. And I've seen things, too. Very recently. Just since coming to Wilshire."

"Seen?" she asked. "Like what?"

"Things similar to what you've seen," he answered. He opened his hands to temporarily dismiss a further explanation. "So I don't discount anything,"

Ellen thought about it. "More coffee?" she asked. He accepted.

"Then you believe in an afterlife?"

"Sure," he said. He laughed. "And you know what?" he added without thinking. "I've almost been there myself," he said.

"Where?"

"In the afterlife."

She frowned. "What does that mean?"

He told her. Bridgeport. Tito Moreno. The emergency room at the hospital. Fade to black. Life support at gunpoint. Then a tremendous brightness, then fade-out and consciousness again.

She sat riveted, listening, feeling more of a kindred spirit in this policeman all the time. The floor creaked again, even closer this time.

He turned back to her. "How's the newspaper going?" he asked by way of changing the subject.

She hunched her shoulders slightly. "Like me," she said. "I'm still breathing, and so is *The Wilshire Republican.*"

"Keep it that way," he said. "I even bought a copy myself this week."

She laughed and poured the rest of the coffee. They spent another hour chatting about Wilshire, the newspaper, the state police, the afterlife in specifics, and the present life in general. When he left later in the evening, they both held the same impression. They hadn't felt as comfortable in another person's presence for a good long time.

Later that morning, just before Ellen drifted off to sleep, a strange thought came to her. If Robin were present, why should she be frightened? If his spirit had survived death, shouldn't that be an occasion, not for fear, but for euphoria?

She turned over in her bed, a comfortable glow on her, a smile on her face.

Twenty

Late Tuesday morning, Mike Chandler ran a computerized historical check of various crimes in the town of Wilshire. What he sought in particular was an account of any sort of disturbance at Ellen Wilder's address on Sturgis Road. A violent murder. A shattered family. A tragic death.

Anything.

Something that might have evoked an unsettled spirit from the past. He recalled having heard stories about locations that had somehow been traumatized by violent or tragic events. Those events had set spirits walking ever after, according to those who were familiar with the locations. In his years as a policeman he had even heard a few stories about such houses and addresses that were just "trouble," host to inexplicable occurrences.

A fellow officer came by and asked Chandler what he was looking for. He lied. He couldn't really admit that over the course of the last month, he had turned into a latter day ghost hunter, a devout believer in the supernatural.

He spent an hour on the research and came up empty. As far as the computer told him, nothing of that sort had ever happened at the location of Ellen's home. He wondered then, was it something following her? Why? What was unsettled?

Or was it something horrible that had happened within the town of Wilshire?

He leaned back in his chair and was staring off into a different world, trying to sort things out in a new different spiritually rational context, when the phone rang on his desk..

His commander, Captain Jack Lindemann wanted to see him as soon as possible. The captain didn't sound amused.

Chandler's shoulder throbbed, and he got to his feet.

Chandler arrived in the commander's office. Captain Lindemann leaned back at his desk. His jacket hung on the back of his chair. He was in white shirtsleeves and a dark tie with a gold clip that featured the American flag. Behind him was a color photograph of himself and five other Connecticut State Police brass with President George Bush. The report on the deaths of James Corbett and Maury Fishkin lay open on Captain Lindemann's desk.

Lindemann leaned back in his swivel chair. He reached for an unopened can of Coca-Cola on the side of his desk. The can was chilled and wet with condensation. Lindemann tossed the can to Mike Chandler, who stood before him. Chandler caught it with his right hand.

"Have a cold one on me, Mike," Lindemann said.

"Thanks," Chandler said. He opened it with one hand and Lindemann watched the dexterity of Chandler's right thumb and forefinger.

Chandler sipped the soda. "Now, you wanted to talk to me, sir?" he asked.

"I did," Lindemann said thoughtfully. "I read your report to date."

"And?"

"And I'm not sure where you're going with this case, Mike," Lindemann said. "I know we got two deaths in the same town in two months, but I'm not even sure I see a connection."

"It's all in there, Captain," Chandler answered. "I like James Corbett for having killed Maury Fishkin. Then someone killed Corbett as a payback."

"What you've given me is your theory. Which is fine. But where's any piece of evidence that points in that direction?"

"I don't have anything yet."

Lindemann's eyes shifted from Chandler back down to the written reports. "Do you have anything that's moving you in that direction?" Lindemann asked. "Other than heart? Other than theory?"

A montage of images flew through Chandler's mind. Events in Wilshire: His conversation with Ellen about her late son, Robin, who may or may not have come to see her; the apparition in the Corbett family burial yard which seemed to be James himself, not live and in the flesh, but dead and in the spirit; and then Franny, Mr. Fade-In, Fade-out, make-it-snow-as-a-party-trick Franny.

"Mike?" Lindemann asked. *"Mike?"*

Lindemann was looking at him strangely. Chandler was abruptly aware that he hadn't answered his commander's inquiry.

"Yeah?"

"I asked you a question."

"Yeah, I know."

"You okay?"

"I'm fine."

"Are you sure you're up to this case?"

"Hey, it's only Wilshire, right?"

"Yes, it's only Wilshire. But it's on our logs now, damn it, and it's starting to attract some statewide attention." He paused. "I'm thinking of assigning two more detectives to the case. Could you use them?"

"No. No, I don't want them," Chandler said tersely.

"It's not your decision."

"Yeah, but I don't want them."

"Mind telling me why?"

"I think it would take things in the wrong direction," Chandler said. "It's Wilshire. It's a very intuitive case. I need to, uh, think, and, uh, make some sense out of this."

Lindemann clasped his hands and continued to study Chandler up and down. He sighed.

"I'll be honest with you, Mike. I gave you this assignment because I thought it would be straightforward and it would ease you back onto active duty after your injury. Now I can't tell what's going on in the case, and I can't tell whether I need to take you back off active duty."

"Why?"

"Your reports border on the incoherent. Or the nutty. You seem completely flummoxed mentally on this. Your attention isn't even here in this room right now. And I have questions about you physically."

"What questions?"

Lindemann clenched his teeth almost imperceptibly. A tight, impatient scowl. "I want the truth about your mental state," he said.

"It's fine."

"You're feeling okay? Not traumatized? Not feeling a little goofy. A little 'off'?"

"No."

"Everything that happens make sense to you?"

"As much as it ever did."

"You depressed?'

"No."

"Drinking?"

"A beer or two after work."

"One or two glasses or one or two pitchers?"

"Very funny."

"Okay, then why the fuck are you writing me reports mentioning spirits in cemeteries?" Captain Lindemann inquired impolitely.

"Did I say that?"

"You typed this and signed it, didn't you?" Lindemann asked, holding it up.

"I was being facetious."

"Is that right?"

"That's correct, sir."

Lindemann thought about Chandler's assertion. "What's that mean, 'facetious'?" he asked.

"I was kidding, sir."

"Kidding? Well, don't! Not in print. These reports get reviewed, and I can't control where they go. There's no way I can let this cross my desk without talking to you about it."

"Sorry."

"Now tell me about your arms and shoulder."

"Fine, too."

"Yeah?"

"Yes, sir."

"Don't lie to me. I won't be made a fool of."

"I'm not lying, sir," Chandler lied.

Lindemann studied Chandler again for another

second. Then his right hand moved quickly and he opened the side drawer of his desk. He pulled out a deck of cards. It was a fresh deck, still in cellophane.

"What's this?" Chandler asked.

"Looks like a deck of cards, Mike." The commander leaned back and steepled his fingers.

"I know that, Captain."

"I want to see you open it and deal me a hand."

"A good hand or a bad hand?" Chandler said, trying to make a joke out of it.

"*Any* five cards would be fine, Mike."

Lindemann waited. Chandler reached for the deck with his right hand. Then he realized what Lindemann was up to.

"I'd prefer not to," Chandler said.

"Of course not. And that's why you didn't care to open the can of soda in the normal, two-handed way, either. Right?"

Chandler said nothing.

Lindemann sighed.

"Come on, Mike. Don't bullshit me. That arm and shoulder are worse, aren't they?"

"There's some pain. Big deal."

"Pain you can work with, if you choose to," Lindemann said philosophically. "Paralysis is something else, isn't it?" He paused. "Can you deal those cards? If your job depended on it, could you deal those cards?"

"Maybe."

"Well, maybe your job does. So let's have a look." Lindemann waited.

Chandler picked the cards up with his right hand. With the numb, resistant fingers on his left hand, he clumsily managed to get the cellophane off the pack. Then he retained the deck in his left hand and dealt with the right. Two slick cards started to slide off the bottom of the deck. He had no sensation in his palm, couldn't grip, and couldn't feel the movement of the cards. A second later the deck fell, and four dozen cards scattered on the floor. A pair of jokers lay face up in the center, mocking him.

"That was enough to get you shot in Dodge City," Lindemann said. "Or enough to get you put back on disability in Hartford."

"The shoulder is getting better," Chandler insisted. "Give me some time. I'm fine on duty."

"Mike," Lindemann sighed and said in conclusion. "I can overlook a little. But I can't overlook a lot. Not for very long. I'd like to give you more time off with pay, but I don't want to pull you off this case if you're close to something."

"I'm close."

"Then show me some movement on this case within another fourteen days, okay? I need it."

"And if there isn't any?"

"As I said. I'll have to talk to Hartford." He paused. "I think the best you would be looking at is desk duty."

Chandler thought about it.

"That stinks," he said in conclusion.

"I know it does. That's why I'm doing you a favor by giving you two weeks. That's all, Mike. That's all."

Twenty-one

The telephone near Chandler's bedside rang insistently, jarring him from a sound sleep. It rang with the shrillness of a firebell, and was every bit as welcome. He grabbed the telephone on the third ring.

There was never any phone message that came between midnight and 6:00 A.M. that was good news, and this one was no exception. He glanced at the clock near his bed. The time was just past 2:00 A.M., Wednesday, and on the other end of the line was first a state police dispatcher in Hartford and then Captain Lewis of Homicide.

Lewis was calling from Fairfield, the state police barracks at Westport, just off Interstate 95. Calls from neighboring counties in the middle of the night were never good tidings, either.

As Chandler fought to have sleep lift from him, Captain Lewis began talking. A body had been found, and the Westport Police had called the state police barracks in North Haven. Chandler's home phone number had been issued by his commander.

"Who's dead?" Chandler asked, trying to bring events into focus as quickly as possible. "Man or woman?"

"Woman."

"Accident? Suicide?"

"Would they be calling homicide if they thought there was any question?" the voice asked.

"Point," said Chandler. "Identification?"

"We were hoping you could provide that. Plus maybe a suspect, and maybe an arrest."

He thought of Ellen. He cringed.

"Brown hair?" Chandler asked. "Woman in her thirties. Nice-looking. About five six?"

There was a pause from Captain Lewis.

"Victim seems much younger than that. Early twenties, I'd say," Lewis said. Chandler heaved an internal sigh of relief and hated himself for it. Hoping the victim had not been one person was to wish it upon someone else.

"She was a pretty girl. Dark hair," Lewis said. "The truck from Manzi Sanitation found her body in a dumpster outside of a bowling alley in Fairfield."

"When?"

"An hour ago."

Two seconds passed. "Then why are you calling me?" Chandler asked. "If it's in Fairfield County, it isn't mine."

"She had your business card in her pocket. Home phone number, too. You in the habit of giving that out or—?"

"Oh, Jesus," he said, interrupting. It took another moment for the horror of it to sink in. Then it walloped on Chandler like an emotional freight train.

"Oh, Jesus, oh, Jesus," he said again, feeling a tumbling, spiraling sensation already. *Please let there be some mistake,* he begged of a god he didn't believe in. *Please let this be a stranger.* But he knew it wasn't.

He pictured the big lurching thug who might know too much about this death, as well as some others.

Franny appeared before him, in his mind's eye. The big guy's words repeated on him.

"She don't pay no attention to me. Maybe that's good. Maybe that's bad. You keeping a watchful eye on her?"

Yeah, Franny, I was, he thought.

"Get here, will you?" demanded Captain Lewis.

Chandler set down the receiver, his emotions bottled up in his throat, a deeply sick feeling in his stomach, and a vision of Franny Corbett lurching through the central Connecticut night like a latter day monster of Dr. Frankenstein.

"Oh, Jesus . . . Oh, Jesus . . ." he cursed repeatedly. Chandler kept hoping that this wasn't really happening, that this bad dream would lift, that someone would phone back and reveal that this had somehow been a mistake.

Chandler went to his garage, still saddled by exhaustion. Mentally he was awake, but physically he was not. He raised the garage door and felt the cold air of the night pour in. He pushed the beacon onto the roof of his car. He pulled out from his garage much too abruptly, but it was midway between two and three in the morning, and there was no other traffic on his street in Guilford.

He pulled onto the main road, then had himself on Interstate 91 within a few minutes. He hit the accelerator and drove like a madman, accessing Interstate 95 South fifteen minutes later. Then, driving with the blue beacon to avoid being stopped, he hit the accelerator hard and drove southward to Fairfield at speeds hovering near ninety miles an hour. Fortunately, the Connecticut Turnpike was light with traffic. He arrived at the outskirts of Fairfield within twenty minutes.

He picked up directions from the police radio in

his car and was at the crime scene, or at least the
location where the body had been found, in another
five minutes.

It was an undignified place for anyone's remains
to be found, but a particularly unsuitable place for
such a pretty young woman. If he needed any further
indication that she was dead, he had it when he saw
that her body had been placed in a bag but not
moved. She was awaiting official identification.

Chandler walked to the body bag without speaking.
Captain Lewis was there, and moved the other cops
out of the way. A brigade of gray uniforms yielded
to the detective from upstate.

Chandler knelt and a man in a Fairfield town cop's
uniform did the honors of unzipping the bag, Chandler looked down and felt sicker than ever before in
his life.

Lisa Ann Petrillo's eyes were closed, and her head
was bent at an impossible angle. In death, she looked
like some pretty exotic bird whose neck had been
wrung. Her expression in death was midway between
benevolence and horror, but the latter emotion was
the only one felt by Michael Chandler.

"Thanks for coming down, Michael," Captain Lewis said. "No wallet, and no purse. Or at least none
that we could find." He motioned to the trash
dumpster. Some lucky souls from the Westport barracks had already been recruited to sort through the
garbage. "She had your card in one of her pockets,"
Lewis added.

With a gloved hand, the captain held up the business card, the one that Chandler had given Lisa Ann.

"So? Know her?" Captain Lewis asked.

"I know her," Chandler said softly. "Her name was

Lisa Ann Petrillo. She lived in Wallingford and worked for an insurance agent in Wilshire."

"Married? Children?"

"Estranged from her husband," Chandler answered.

"Do you like her husband for this?" Lewis asked.

"Not especially, but you never know," Chandler said, gathering his thoughts. "We'll have to talk to him, anyway."

"Yeah," Lewis agreed.

Chandler gave a nod and stood, and the bag was zipped again. There was something very cold in his blood. He hadn't even bothered to grab an overcoat. His shoulders felt as if a man were sitting on them—a big hulking man.

Chandler shifted his weight in the night as technicians prepared to pack the body into an ambulance. Rightly or wrongly, the image of the big, lurching killer was before him.

Corbetts, Corbetts, Corbetts, he thought. Every homicide he was seeing these days touched upon the family. When would someone lift this plague from central Connecticut? *Always check the Corbetts first,* a voice inside him said. *Even when you're wrong, you're right.*

"It looks like a sex crime," Captain Lewis said. "Maybe about twenty-four hours ago. We got to wait for the lab and the ME, but I'm seeing torn clothing and a lot of bruises consistent with a rape. Then there's the neck. Someone did this with a powerful pair of hands."

"Yeah," said Chandler.

Captain Lewis based his guess not on science but on thirty years in the field. "Any of that mean anything to you?"

"It might, yes," Chandler said.

"Where do we start?" the captain asked.

"Know that double homicide I'm working on? A family of thugs in Wilshire?"

"I know about it."

"This is related."

"How?"

Chandler watched the medical techies load the body bag into a boxy ambulance that was the size and shape of a dairy delivery truck. The rear doors opened and devoured the girl's body. The doors closed. For a moment, Chandler had a flashback, and he saw himself at the death scene of James Corbett several weeks earlier. There was a similar feel in the air, and Chandler was navigating in large part on feelings these days.

Then Mike Chandler raised his eyes and thought he saw a huge hulking figure standing in the shadows near the vehicle. Then he was certain that he did, but when the figure turned the man's face was not what Chandler expected. It was a New Haven cop. On closer examination, the man had nowhere near the size and girth of the man Chandler had thought he was viewing.

"How, Mike, *how*?" Captain Lewis repeated. Still no response. "Hey! Are you listening to me, or are you on another fucking planet?"

"What?" Chandler asked.

"How is it related?"

"I don't know. It just is."

Lewis flipped open a notebook. "I already talked to Captain Jennings. I hear you don't want anyone extra on your Wilshire case."

"No. I don't."

"Well you just got them anyway. Four of them."

"Great," said Chandler. It was half-past three in the morning, and he spoke with a snarl.

When the sun rose muted in a cold, gray sky six hours later, Chandler was still awake. As the morning unfurled, the news of the death of Lisa Ann Petrillo crept quickly across central Connecticut.

Another murder. Someone else dead under strange circumstances.

The radio stations in Bridgeport, Norwalk, New Haven, New Britain, and Waterbury gave it heavy air time through the morning. It was a prevalent topic on several radio talk shows, edging out extramarital sex and financial advice for at least a few hours. In factories, foundries, supermarkets and offices, the rumors flew. Lisa Ann had last been seen leaving work Tuesday evening at 5:45 P.M. She'd stepped into her car and not given anyone any idea where she was going. In the early stages of the investigation, Chandler could find no one who had seen her between the time she left work and the time she met her killer. That suggested one of two things. She had either met her killer in Wilshire, or she had gotten out of Wilshire very quickly.

Chandler took yet another trip to the Corbett farm, and the Corbett dogs were barking from the time Chandler stepped out of his Jeep.

Lizzie met him at the door again. The mutts were shoved down into the basement where they continued to bark. Lizzie was unsteady on her feet, and was wearing a frayed woolen coat in the house. There was a cigarette smoldering in her thick, yellowed fingers. Her eyes were glazed and reddish and puffy, and it didn't take Chandler more than fifteen seconds to determine that she was drunk out of her mind.

At one point the front of the coat threatened to come undone. Appallingly, Chandler had the distinct impression that she had probably been lurching around the homestead jaybird-naked when he had come to the door. Chandler's gaze drifted past her. On the table were a single can of beer, its pop top erect, and a carton of Lucky Strikes which looked as if it had exploded open—packs were lying in every direction. Beer and Luckies were apparently the central ingredients of Lizzie's breakfast of champions.

"Where's Wilbur? Or Franny?" Chandler asked.

"Franny I ain't seen. Wilbur's here."

"Get him out here."

"He's asleep, goddamn it."

"With the dogs barking like that? I don't think so."

"The dogs don't bother him none."

"Just get him, Lizzie."

She tried to slam the door in a huff, but Chandler held it. Isaac made an appearance for a moment, dressed in jeans and a New England Patriots football jersey with the number twelve upon it. It was the old style Jersey, not the splashy new kind of the last few years, but he was still a Bledsoe of the backwoods.

Chandler was surprised to see the boy. He stood in a doorway with his arms folded. Something glinted on his face. A new stud had found its way onto Isaac's left nostril.

"No school today, Isaac?" Chandler asked, knowing the answer.

"I ain't interested. I stopped going."

"Think that's a good idea?"

"Yeah," the boy said. "I do."

"Uh huh."

"Who gives a shit, anyways?" Isaac asked.

Chandler made a mental note to talk to one of the guidance counselors on behalf of Isaac, not that it would do much good. Not, he found himself thinking with increased desperation, that any of this seemed to be doing much good. How many hostile doorways could one cop visit in a lifetime? And Corbett-itis had been a disease in this part of the landscape for a hundred years. Why would it change now?

One of the dogs was at the top of the cellar steps, clawing at the door like some wild beast, and snarling. It passed hurriedly through Chandler's mind that if the cellar door gave and the animal came at him, with Lizzie drunk, Chandler might have to take out the animal with his weapon.

Wilbur came to the door next. Chandler asked if he could enter the house.

"Not without no fucking warrant, you can't, no," Wilbur answered.

"One of these days I'll get one," Chandler answered.

"One of these days you'll walk through one fucking door too many, you asshole," Wilbur volunteered. An image of Bridgeport and being shot rose up at Wilbur's remark.

"What's that mean? Some sort of threat?" Chandler asked.

"If the shoe fits, wear it," Wilbur said. He wore a pair of filthy jeans and a white, tank-style undershirt. He looked as if he had last shaved a week ago, and not very thoroughly. With the half-beard, he seemed to be developing a triple chin, as well.

"Where were you last night?" Chandler asked.

"Home. Here," he said.

"Got any witnesses?"

"Yeah, my whole frigging family, but that probably don't cut no shit with you, does it?'

"Why should it?" Chandler asked.

"He come home straight from work, Mr. Chandler," Lizzie said. "He was here with me since six P.M. So don't try to make nothing of anything."

"Where's Franny?"

"Ain't seen him."

"Where's Ritchie?"

"Did you go to his smoke shop?"

"Not yet."

"Then do that, wouldya?" Wilbur said.

"If I check all this and find that something's not true, I'm coming back with a warrant," Chandler said.

"Who the fuck cares? In a few days you're off this case, anyway."

A second passed. "Who told you that?" Chandler asked.

"Cousin Lukas heard it from Chief Moore. He learnt it from your Captain. So there, asshole."

Chandler burned. "Don't count on it. I'll be back."

"Not in my fucking lifetime," Wilbur snarled. "Now get out of here."

He pushed the door shut, but not before Lizzie leaned forward and threw a special parting barrage of obscenities at him, a little hail of verbal gunfire which would serve as his benediction this morning.

Chandler drove into the town center, parking not far from the boarded front windows of Fishkin's hardware. The sun had never completely come out this morning, and a gray, damp cold continued to grip the town center. It was such a typical morning to follow a murder. Chandler walked toward Ritchie's Smoke Shop.

Ritchie's red-and-white Chevrolet was parked in front. There were big new tires on it, Chandler noticed, four of them, the thick wide kind. The vehicle's cornering abilities had just doubled, as had its book value. The detective wondered if he could get a warrant for the car and try to find some of Lisa Ann Petrillo's DNA in it.

Ritchie was at the counter when Chandler entered. Ritchie acted surprised. He gave the detective a nervous, abrupt double take and flipped shut the December *Penthouse,* which had been open on the counter before him.

Ritchie's surprise told Chandler he had *not* been expected. In an oblique sort of way, that might have absolved Ritchie a little. The guilty tend to expect a visit.

As Chandler came through the door, and as Ritchie stashed his entertainment, the detective's gaze took a quick inventory of the place. It was the same messy, gritty smoke shop, smelling of age, tobacco, dry snack food in cellophane and cardboard cartons, and cleaning solvent. Little had changed in twenty years, Chandler reasoned, so why would much change over the last week? Yet on the side windows, someone had installed clear plastic to keep out the drafts of the impending winter. In a rack there was some Christmas wrapping paper that looked as if it hadn't sold for either of the previous two years. And on the floor at the foot of the counter, there was also still a big gap among the newspapers where *The Wilshire Republican* used to sit.

"Hello, Ritchie," Chandler said.

"What the fuck do you want?"

Chandler had no idea what Ritchie had been drinking, but his breath smelled like a mixture of coffee and kerosene.

"I just wanted to know how your day is going so far."

Ritchie missed the irony and glanced at his watch. "It's only ten-thirty. The day hasn't hardly begun."

"You got a point."

"So why the fuck can't you lay off me?"

"Because I like your family for most of the stuff that's going on in Wilshire."

"Yeah, well what's it to you, anyway?"

"Maybe it's personal now. I don't like the way you threatened Mrs. Wilder."

"Never met the woman."

"That's not what she says."

"Maybe she lies."

"Tell me about Lisa Ann Petrillo."

"Nice ass, small tits. What else you want to know about her?"

"You're not going to tell me you don't know she was murdered last night?"

"Yeah, I heard."

"Did you know her?"

"Look, Chandler, you hump, I had a woody for her, but so did half the men in this town, 'specially when she'd go trottin' around town in them tight blue jeans she used to wear. But she weren't interested in me noways, so it didn't go nowhere, okay?"

"I suppose you can account for your time after work yesterday."

"Yeah. Sure, I can, asshole. I didn't leave here till seven when I closed the store. Can you account for yours?"

"Then what did you do after seven?"

"Went to the McDonald's on Route Five for dinner."

"If I talk to the staff will they tell me they saw you?"

"I don't know. Will they?" He paused. "I went through the drive-up window. They got idiots who work at the drive-up. So who knows what they remember. They probably don't even remember their own names, which is why they wear tags."

There was a box of new NHL hockey cards on the counter near the register. Chandler examined a pack while he listened. "Actually, Ritchie," said Chandler, "driving that piece of red-and-white junk that you do, I would think they'd remember seeing you. At the very least, they'd remember hearing you coming."

Ritchie seemed uneasy with the notion that his story could be checked, or that his car might be examined by a forensics lab. It took a moment for him to answer.

"Fuck you, Chandler. That car's got four seventy-eight cube under the hood, and it'll last longer than you're gonna."

"What did you do after McDonald's?"

"Same as anyone. I went home, took a couple of Rolaids, and jerked off."

"Sort of a typical evening for you, huh, Ritchie? You probably bring one of your skin books home every night."

Ritchie started shaking his head. "You really are lookin' for it, aren't you, Chandler?"

"What's that mean?"

"You can't leave bad shit alone."

Chandler opened his hands. "Explain it to me, Ritchie."

"Lisa Ann probably got snuffed by her ex. I heard

she had a boyfriend down in Westport. Rich guy in his fifties who liked some young twat and was gettin' it here upstate from Lisa Ann. She used to drive down there all the time, and he'd hump her at a motel on the Post Road near the Ninety-five exit. Maybe her rich boyfriend killed her 'cause she was wanting to get married or have babies with him. How the fuck should I know, Chandler? I just know you're lifting your leg on the wrong tree."

Chandler thought about it.

"Do you have any idea who the boyfriend was?"

"No."

"Know anything about him?"

"No."

"Would you tell me if you did?"

"No."

"Have you seen Franny recently?"

"No."

"Have you got *anything* to tell me?"

"Yeah."

"What might that be?"

"You're going to be out of this town on your ass before you know it." Ritchie offered.

"Why is that?"

"Brother Wilbur's gonna run for the open seat on the selectman board in January. He gets elected, they vote on police chief. Then Cousin DeWayne gets appointed to Chief Moore's job by the fucking selectmen. DeWayne'll have the balls to throw your ass out of town."

Chandler took it under advisement. "We'll see, Ritchie. We'll see," he said.

Ritchie snorted and reached for a Milky Way, one of the dark chocolate ones. "Yeah. We'll see, won't we?" He bit off half of the Milky Way in one ugly

chomp, then pushed the second half in his mouth
while still chewing the first. He dropped the wrapper
in a wastebasket that was already overflowing, so it
eventually settled onto the floor.

Chandler took it as his cue to leave.

Later that day, the crime lab in Enfield processed
Lisa Ann Petrillo's car for fingerprints. There was a
whole series of prints on the doors and in the inte-
rior, but none that could be attributed to either a
living Corbett or a dead one.

Lisa Ann had had some friends at work whom
Chandler went to see, and one of the women she
worked with—the same friend Chandler had seen
with Lisa Ann at Lorna's—did say that Lisa Ann had
been "dating" a man down in Westport. She didn't
know much about him, just some basics: he was married, his name was either Jeff or Jack, he drove a
Mercedes, and sometimes took her to New York.
There, Chandler theorized as Nella rattled on, he
wouldn't be recognized.

"You don't have a last name?" Chandler asked.

"No."

"Ever see him?"

She shook her head. "I'd tell you if I did, honest,"
Nella said. "I didn't like what he was doing. If he
was still living with his wife, he shouldn't have been
seeing Lisa Ann."

"I agree with you," Chandler said. In its way, it was
the first rational remark he had heard from anyone
all week.

Nothing at Lisa's desk at work turned up anything
with a lover's name, nor did any phone numbers in
her address book or on her computer lead to a Westport phone exchange. A few friends and co-workers
knew about the affair, it seemed, but Lisa Ann

Petrillo had kept her own counsel very closely. None of her girlfriends knew the man's full name, or at least none were admitting to it.

Chandler sensed that they didn't know. The slain girl had been inordinately secretive. He figured it was her first affair with a married man. It had that look to it.

Later that first day, he turned all this over to the other detectives who had been newly assigned to the case. He left them to work the Westport angle, where they could start off by flashing the dead girl's picture to motel owners and seeing if any of the foreign car shops who serviced Mercedes-Benz's had a fiftyish Jack or Jeff. Meanwhile, Chandler worked Wilshire. In doing so, he uncovered at least one lie.

It was even a stupid-ass lie, which wasn't surprising since it had come from Brother Ritchie.

Ritchie had left his smoke shop at six, not seven. A high school kid had come in to cover for him. Chandler found that out the next day by sitting down the block in his Jeep and watching which customers came in after six. Most people, he knew, kept a similar routine each working day. Chandler stopped these customers a block away and asked if they had been there two days before. If they had been, he asked what sort of bandanna Ritchie had been wearing. What he really wanted to know was if Ritchie had been behind the counter. Two witnesses, when asked the bandanna question, said Ritchie hadn't even been there.

So that put Ritchie back in the Lisa Ann Petrillo picture, which was more than could be said for Franny Corbett, who was nowhere to be seen at all. Franny had vanished.

Chandler even drove by Franny's usual haunt, the

old cemetery on the Corbett property, both at night
and during the day. Chandler had tramped through
the damp woods to get to it and picked up the pre-
dictably macabre vibrations from the place, but had
not seen even a shadow that moved strangely, much
less the big, hulking figure for whom he searched.

And as for Ritchie's inconsistency over time on
Tuesday evening, Chandler played that card close to
his chest. He said nothing to Ritchie, and gave no
indication that he even knew of the inconsistency. He
preferred to wait and see if anything else cropped
up.

The funeral for Lisa Ann was held on Thursday
morning in East Haven, where she had grown up.
Chandler attended. So did Ellen Wilder, and several
other friends from Wilshire. Her brother delivered
the eulogy. Lisa Ann's ex-husband was a pallbearer,
and looked shattered. Chandler had already talked to
him, and had all but eliminated him as a suspect.
Nor was there anyone named Jack or Jeff who had
driven up from Westport for the occasion.

No Corbett was there, either, and none had been
expected.

That same evening, Ellen sat in the study of her
home, working at her computer. Music played softly
from the CD player in her living room. Every once
in awhile, her gaze rose to the doorway where Robin
had appeared.

Her staff had turned in all of their copy for that
week's edition of *The Republican*. She had had everything set, and then this new horror had occurred—
the death of a girl who lived elsewhere but worked
in Wilshire.

She was covering the story herself. And of course it meant uprooting the front page again.

There were many ironies these days. They took turns shuffling in and out of the forefront of her mind. The one that seemed to bob to the surface most insistently concerned moving to this town in Connecticut and having this avalanche of horrid events come her way. She had suffered her own personal tragedy. She had lived most of her adult life amidst the stimulation of New York and Boston, within the purported high crime rates of the cities, yet murder and terror never seemed to be so much at her doorstep as they were now. She sometimes thought now that the really weird, violent places in America were not the cities but the sparsely populated countryside, filled with inbred wackos and backwoods psychotics.

She wondered if she could work a mild approach to this angle as an editorial, urging people to get it together to bring a peacefulness to Wilshire. Her editorials had landed her in an uncomfortable enough position locally. She laughed. She knew she couldn't touch that subject with that approach. Her advice, to put it mildly, was not universally appreciated. It had put her in hot water before. If she persisted, it would put her in scalding water in the future.

Now this Lisa Ann was dead. Backup detectives had been assigned to the case to assist Mike Chandler, who at least was running the investigation. But the killer, whoever he was, was still out there.

Ellen fixed her layout.

Thank God for modern miracles: word processing and computerized layout composition. She wondered how the old-time newspaper guys managed, with ink all over their hands, and printing fumes in their lungs. Here, at least, she could push the ENTER button and send twelve hundred words scurrying in the proper direction. If only, she mused, she could put her life in order as easily. Well, she consoled herself, no one could.

Thump.

Her gaze rose. The noise had come from above. Upstairs. Another thump followed. It sounded like a footstep. It came, of course, from the blue room, as she now liked to call it.

Sometimes Ellen felt as if she had checked her sanity at the door, or left it on the backseat of the car. Things seemed to be happening in the house now, in the town of Wilshire now, which had once been almost unthinkable, but she had, over the last few days, come to readily accept them, so she felt it wasn't neurosis or insanity at all, if she *understood* what was going on.

Take these thumps, for example. Like footsteps.

Was there any question as to who was causing them? Sarah was in the next room at the dining table finishing her homework.

Sometimes the footsteps led out of the room and to the top of the steps. Once, when Sarah was out of the house, they had come all the way to her doorway again.

"Don't stop there, Robin," she had whispered. "I'm not scared any more. Let me see you again."

She had waited. She had wanted to see his gorgeous face peer around the corner again. She had wanted him to again manifest the fact that even though he was dead, he was still, well, *alive.* But no, playful spirit that he was, he scampered away. She even heard him going back upstairs and shutting the door.

Of course, she didn't tell anyone about this. Who would believe it? Who would understand? Maybe Mike Chandler—eventually—but for the time being, Ellen concluded, it was best not to mention anything.

She finished her work on the newspaper layout.

She asked herself the obvious question. Was she imagining this? No, she replied with the clear new logic of her mind, of course she was not. She even had a witness! Sort of.

On Monday night she had drawn up the photograph of her late son from the bottom drawer of her desk. She had unwrapped it and gazed at the handsome young face. She felt her eyes mist, but she also felt strong at the time, so she looked at Robin's picture in silence and with great concentration.

Then a child's voice had startled her. "Mother?"

Abruptly, she had raised her eyes from the portrait and stared at the door. There stood Sarah.

"Hi, Mama," Sarah said.

"Hello, Sarah."

"What are you looking at?"

"A photograph of a boy."

"May I see?"

Ellen had anticipated the question. She had her answer ready. "Of course," she said.

Her daughter had trundled over to her side and looked at the picture. "Oh," Sarah had said.

"Nice looking boy, isn't he?"

"Uh huh."

"Is he a friend of ours?" Sarah asked.

"I think so."

"Where is he now?"

"I think he's around here somewhere."

"Why does he watch us, Mama?"

"What?"

"Why does he watch us, Mama?"

"What do you mean, Sarah?"

"It's him," she said, poking a finger at the picture. "He's the boy I told you about. He's the one who was watching our house."

Ellen felt a chill, something that seemed like ice water washing over her. She rewrapped the portrait and put it away again, but it had been an instrumental moment in her acceptance of the new reality.

Robin was there with her, at least. It was fortunate now that she had an extra room in her house. It almost seemed like divine intervention that the room was there.

The room that had been the brown room,

Which was now the blue room.

Ellen also had another name for it. *Robin's Room.*

He had moved there with her following his death, after all. Hadn't he? Wasn't that perfectly logical? So why shouldn't she keep a room for him? Why shouldn't he be there with his mother, after all?

Why not?

As she sat at her desk and turned her computer off, she listened to a final shuffle of feet from above.

"Go to bed, Robin," she said softly. "Time to sleep."

As if in obedience, the sounds stopped.

Bed. She had started to give some thought on how to furnish that room. She would make it look like a guest room, but it would really be her boy's room. It would be comfortable to his spirit and amenable to his personality. It would be a room that could accommodate guests in her house, in which her son's *ghost,* if that was the right word, would also be present.

She laughed as she turned the light off on her desk. Robin's room. The haunted room in her house!

Obviously, this was how ghost stories got started, she thought. A lost spirit is made to feel welcome in one particular place, so it then can slip in and out of the various dimensions of reality, visiting the living for little flashes of time before going back to wherever it went.

Ellen had always thought of such things as preposterous. Nutty. Stuff that was amusing at best, but not to be believed.

Now she understood it much better, and she didn't find it frightening any more.

She thought of it now as sort of a *cozy* situation, one to be nurtured and brought forth. She wondered how Robin felt about it. She made a mental note. She would have to have a conversation with her son sometime soon.

How would she know anything about him, after all—how he felt, what he thought—unless she *asked* him?

Yes indeed, she told herself as she climbed the stairs and looked down the hall to the open door to the blue room. Light from the hall poured in, and she knew her son was present just down the hallway.

Yes indeed. They would have to have a chat really soon.

Twenty-two

One moment the old cemetery was empty of any life or movement. The next moment, Franny's huge body was visible to anyone who cared to look. The big man sat on the edge of an old tomb. His eyes came open with an angry start, and his gaze rose upward.

The old bugler, Jeremiah Corbett, looked down at him and winked. Half of Jeremiah's head had been blown off by a confederate cannonball at Cold Spring Harbor, and the detached bits and pieces of Sgt. Corbett's brains had been tossed into a mass grave of several black Union soldiers who fell at the same battle. This was a fine, gritty detail of mortality that had displeased old Jeremiah's surly spirit for more than a century. The bugler's ghost had manifested such wounds for decades as it flitted around central Connecticut with half a head missing, but no one sane had picked up on it, at least not visually. It had stayed in its own plane of reality, as did many kindred souls.

A couple of the more talkative residents of a psychiatric hospital in Watertown had picked up on old Jeremiah and told their nurses. Their reward had been a Thorazine cocktail, which eventually made everyone happy—or if not happy, at least placid.

Franny could see Jeremiah's ghost, of course, but he didn't care much for it. Not today. Franny knew what had happened with Lisa Ann Petrillo. In fact, he summoned up her unhappy spirit and for a moment, she stood in front of him. But Lisa Ann had never liked Franny, or any Corbett, in life, so why should she like him in death?

She had faded away of her own volition. It only made Franny angrier. A rage was upon him. A blind, urgent, furious rage. This sweet, young female should never have been here yet in the twilight world between life and the afterlife. Just like Franny, her rightful time among the living had been cut short. And as far as Franny was concerned, the rest of the cursed Corbett family had forfeited their right to be among the still living.

He came to his feet, his soul aching.

It was noon, the day following Lisa Ann's funeral. Franny kept his eye on the sky. It was bright and blue, with a heavy smattering of big, white, fluffy clouds. Franny blinked and it was night. 2:00 A.M.

Franny looked toward the sky. Although stars were present, Franny saw nothing but the darkness that surrounded them. He looked into his heart and felt nothing but anger, sadness, and an even bleaker darkness.

All around him were the tombstones. This was another bright night in the Corbett family cemetery, and Franny was the disturbed prince of the night.

He raised his voice. He screamed, emptying his lungs. Then he turned.

He trotted through the night like some strange feral beast, risen from God-knew-where. Well, he knew

what he was about this night, just as he had known
when he had surprised drunken Uncle Jimmy and
put the pitchfork through his throat.

He thought to himself as he ran. Three was a holy
number: A trinity. Father, Son, and I'll make you a
ghost. Three.

Franny ran with the steadiness of a large animal.
The moon and the stars were his compass, the pain
in his soul his guiding force. He continued through
the trees and over a pasture, through Corbett land.
Several horses saw him and fled to a safer section of
corralled land. They sensed an animal danger, same
as they would from a wolf.

Franny cursed at them. They were in his way. It
was good that they fled. When he had nighttime business to attend to, Franny tolerated nothing in his way.

How could he waste time? His hours back in this
world were so short. How could he waste any of it?
He would tear out the throats of any man or animal
who stood in his way this night, or any other night!

A pretty young thing like Lisa Ann. Why hadn't
Michael Chandler been watching her properly?

Franny ran across a second meadow, sending another pair of horses scurrying. In the light of a half
moon, the Corbett farmhouse came in sight just as
Franny crossed the crest of a hill. He leaped a split
rail fence, one foot on the top rail, pushing himself
over like a giant, six-foot-six-inch cat. The successful
jump exhilarated him. He kept moving forward.

He moved until the house was within a hundred
yards. Then he turned and went toward the back end
of the old barn.

He was so mad now that he actually had the taste
of blood in his mouth. And why not? Blood had al-

ready been spilled this week. More would follow. Franny already knew exactly whose.

He drew within a hundred feet of the south barn and slowed to a fast walk. He huffed and exhaled hard, sniffed the air.

He paused. 2:40 A.M.

The barn door was closed, but he could see there was a light on inside—not unusual when Uncle Ritchie was working late.

Franny went to the barn door. He cocked his head. There was music playing hard rock, heavy metal, AC-DC—music worthy of Lorna's, where Ritchie sometimes liked to hang out and do drugs with some of the DinCem boys.

Franny placed a hand on the door to the barn. He turned the latch, but the latch wouldn't give. He knew what the problem was because he knew this barn, and he knew what went on in it: Thievery. Bestiality. Rape. Lisa Ann's murder by a man who forced her into his car.

The barn was closed from within. A large beam had been dropped in place to secure the door. The man working within the barn was doing things, as usual, that he didn't want anyone to see.

Franny pushed on the barn door again. It wouldn't budge. He felt his rage igniting into open flames. He stepped back from the door and glared at it. Then he pulled back his huge hand and punched a hole in the wood.

He punched a second hole. Uncle Ritchie began yelling.

Franny stood back. Light poured through the two holes.

Franny saw Uncle Ritchie. He had just picked up a shotgun and was striding toward the sounds of intrusion. Ritchie Corbett's angry face appeared, bandanna across the forehead, in one of the holes for a moment. His dark, mean eyes glared through as Franny stepped backward into the cold of the November night.

"Franny! What the fuck you think you're doing?" Ritchie cursed.

"Let me in," Franny said.

"What do you want?"

"I want to come in."

"Jesus Christ," Ritchie growled. "No."

There was a long, dark stick of some sort parallel to Ritchie's face. Double barreled. The shotgun.

"I want to come in," Franny repeated.

"Well, I don't want to let you in, fuckhead," Ritchie said.

"Do it or I'll set fire to the barn."

"Jesus fucking Christ," Ritchie cursed. "You are a piece of ugly fucking work, Franny."

The big man stood back, maintaining an intense calm. "You gonna open up?" he asked.

Ritchie labored with the inside cross beam and lifted it. He set aside the shotgun. Then he pulled open one of the doors.

"Happy?" Ritchie asked.

"Happy," Franny rumbled.

The big man lurched into the barn.

The lights within were bright. Franny glared at Ritchie's work: a metallic silver 1998 Corvette, with an iron GM jack affixed to its elevated left side like a giant mosquito. The car's rear right side wheel had been lifted off.

The car was as hot as a cheap pistol. Ritchie had stolen it from behind a fraternity house at Yale University earlier that evening. The Yale parking lots at night were like a giant Toys 'R' Us to a pro grand larceny-auto man like Ritchie Corbett. By now, the 'Vette's windshield had been punched out, and its Virginia license plates had been trashed. Ritchie had been working on an adjustment to the Vehicle Identification Number and anti-theft tracking device. He'd been faceup under the chassis on a repairman's slide dolly when Franny had put his fist through the barn door.

"Stolen?" Franny asked above the music.

"Franny, you big dumb lug," Ritchie grunted. "Is the pope a fucking Polack? Of course, it's Goddam stolen."

Franny grunted. "I'm smarter'n you think, Ritchie."

"Yeah, well, that still don't make you so smart," Ritchie muttered, " 'cause I think you're dumber'n a five pound hammer."

"You ought to take it back to where you found it," Franny said.

"Take what back?"

"The stolen car."

"Horseshit, Franny," Ritchie Corbett laughed. "I can move these wheels for five grand within three days."

"You oughtn't do any of the shit you do here, Uncle Ritchie."

"Save it, Franny. I don't wanna hear it."

Ritchie got down on the ground again, irked and shaking his head. He checked to make sure the jack was secure. He needed to deactivate and remove the anti-theft electronics as quickly as possible. The device was riveted to the chassis beneath the rear axle of the car, to make the operation as difficult as possible, but Ritchie was making progress. He lay down faceup on the slide dolly again, and slid under the car with a hydraulic drill. He kept his shotgun at arm's length—just in case.

The music continued to blast.

"You oughtn'ta touched Lisa Ann, neither, Ritchie," Franny shouted. "That was somethin' you shouldn'ta done!"

"What, Franny?" Ritchie yelled from under the car.

Franny repeated, but Ritchie didn't have time to listen. Not with a pain-in-the-ass tracking device still a few inches above his head on the underside of the car. Hell, if one of those wealthy frat boys at Yale took a few moments out from drinking and fornicating and saw the car missing in the middle of the night and called the damned New Haven cops—

Ritchie turned on his drill. He never heard Franny speak again. He never heard Franny take two steps forward, either, never had any way of knowing that Franny's hands were quietly settling upon the jack.

The dream was not a pleasant one, infested as it was with guilt and pockmarked with a lack of logic.

"Hey, I'm happy you came over," the young woman said to Mike Chandler. "The sex is going to be wonderful for both of us. We're always going to remember this."

Chandler agreed, but felt some trepidation. Was it the booze that was making him feel that way as he turned in his sleep?

Lisa Ann Petrillo came to him and whispered in his ear. "Undress me," she begged. "Or do I need to do it myself?"

He turned in his sleep and smiled. "I'll do it," he said.

She stepped back and giggled. "I love to feel a

man's weight on top of me," she said. "Will you fuck me really hard?"

"I will," he said, "I will.

Lisa Ann, the dead girl, unbuttoned his shirt. She nibbled at his ear as she kissed him, the taste of the champagne on her lips. He worked his fingers around the buttons on the back of her blouse and undid them.

Her blouse fell away. Her skirt went next. Her bra and panties were black lace, just as Chandler had imagined they would be. They were very sexy, and she was enormously beautiful with her clothes off. He was sorry she was dead, and sorrier still that he might have been able to prevent it.

Some way.

"It's all right," she said, however. "I'll still make love with you. Something to remember me by."

"I'd like that," he said.

"Thanks for coming to my funeral," she said. "That was sweet of you."

Tormented, he turned violently in bed. He had the sensation of trying to cry out in the midst of his nightmare, of wishing someone would wake him.

She took his shirt from him and tossed it away. She methodically undressed him. His desire built. He was very hard. She put her hand gently between his legs and massaged him. Then she kissed him, leaned back, and smiled.

"Don't go away," she said.

She rose from the bed on sturdy young legs. She walked to a window and looked out, savoring an early winter night. Her skin was very pale in the shadows of his bedroom, lifeless and intensely white, like cold, veined marble.

Then she turned and walked back to him. Thin, young and graceful, she sat down in bed next to him.

"I'm reading your thoughts," Lisa Ann said. "I'm thin, young, graceful, and *dead*. Don't forget that I'm dead."

"How *could* I?"

She laughed, and her eyes went hollow momentarily, like a corpse with its eyes rotted away. "You never will," she promised.

"No, I won't," he thought, his arms again flailing in sleep.

"Well," she said, "are you going to make love to me?"

"I feel so bad. I got you killed."

"Yes, you did."

"Who murdered you?"

"A Corbett."

"That's what I suspected."

"Yes, but no," she said, with all her inherent lack of logic. "It's the way you think, but it's also not like you think."

He placed his hands on her breasts. The touch gave him a shock—not an electrical shock, but a double-edged charge: one of hot passion and one of chilly revulsion. He knew what he was doing, making love with a dead girl.

He stopped for a moment. The room tone seemed to change. There was another presence in the room, but he couldn't place it. It was almost as if he could hear an extra heart beating somewhere. The colors in the room seemed acute and intense.

"I'm Italian," she whispered.

"I know," Chandler answered.

"I'm also a ghost."

He laughed. "I know that, too."

"Do you?" she asked, surprised.

"Yes, but no." he explained.

"Do you believe in me?"

"Yes."

"Do you believe in ghosts?"

"I do now."

She took one of his hands and guided it to the spot between her legs.

"Tease me," she whispered.

His hand ran through her pubic hair. A finger flitted into her vagina. She moaned slightly as he discovered how wet she was, how anxious she was to accommodate him.

He turned in his dark bedroom. His eyes fluttered open, then closed again. He saw that intense bright light that had once accompanied him to a state of death and back. Then he dreamed that he was making love to Lisa Ann in her coffin, her legs wrapped around him as everyone watched from the funeral.

Then there was a funny glow to her eyes. Almost yellowish. He felt a twinge of fear. She sensed this, and laughed.

"This *is* the moment," she said again. "Ready?"

He was confused. "Of course."

"Now *I'll* tease *you,*" she said.

He rolled off of her. She stood and stepped back. He gazed at her—a lovely woman of twenty-two, completely naked, with a lovely face, pale skin, and long dark hair. Then her eyes fluttered, and again he suffered that image of having stepped from a lit path. He saw the spark of something strange on her face. Her skin, right before his eyes, was turning a horrible chalky white, almost as if she had aged fifty years before his eyes.

"Don't fuck with the dead," she whispered.

She leaned forward and found his ear again.

He felt a surge of terror. Her voice changed. It was still female. But it wasn't quite human. It wasn't quite something that was living.

"What?" he asked. "I don't understand,"

"Don't fuck with the dead," she repeated.

"I don't,"

"No. You don't. And you shouldn't. *But you do all the time.*"

"Do what?" he demanded.

"Fuck with the dead!"

"I . . . I—" he protested. His bad arm throbbed. As he turned, a nearly complete paralysis took over his left hand and arm.

In bed, he threw back his head and screamed horribly. Not just once. Twice.

He opened his eyes. The dream was finished, but Lisa Ann was still standing in his bedroom. Then her features changed. So did her body. Her shape.

Chandler flinched in shock, and he screamed again. He sat up straight in bed, sweat pouring off him. The room remained shadowy. The light was from the moon and the street lamps outside.

Franny was standing there, all seventy-eight inches tall of him. His eyes burned censoriously at Chandler. Chandler's arm wouldn't move, and there was no doubt in the policeman's mind that Franny could have killed him, or could have *already* killed him, if he had wanted to.

Franny didn't say anything. He just stared.

Chandler's mouth and lips were dry as cardboard, the consistency and feel of coarse sandpaper. He fumbled. He battled to form words.

"Are you part of my dream?" Chandler asked.

"Sometimes. And sometimes not."

Chandler considered it. "What is it?" he said. "What do you want, Franny? What are you doing here?"

"Uncle Ritchie had an accident," Franny said in a luggish, lugubrious voice that once again sounded as if it were sliding across concrete. "In the south barn on the farm. I think you should see."

Then, in the blink of an eye, the big guy was gone.

Chandler was in his Jeep ten minutes later, driving on Interstate 95 just within shouting distance of the fifty-five speed limit. The roads were clear, dry, and cold, and he made excellent time to Wilshire. Within his Jeep, the police radio crackled as an FM station from Hartford served as a backdrop.

When he arrived at the Corbett farm, he knew he was not the first, or even the second or third, or sixth, police officer on the premises.

The scene was one of organized chaos. A heavily illuminated barn stood like an historic place at the center of a surreal sea of blue cop lights and yellow front headlights. On one side, a team of Wilshire cops including cousin DeWayne, the anointed law-and-order leader of the town's future, stood at the farmhouse door with Wilbur, Lizzie, and son Isaac, all of them huddled against the cold in clumsy heavy coats over sleeping gear.

The surviving Corbetts wore boots, and were not being allowed out to the south barn. An ambulance was stationed there, as were a small fleet of mismatched police cars. Two state cars, three vehicles from New Haven, and a spare Wallingford car with a K-9 detail, the latter probably having stopped by out of curiosity. There was also one from Wilshire, but it looked as if the New Haven bulls had pulled rank on their small town brethren. The Elm City bulls just weren't letting the Wilshire men come near.

Chandler clipped his own badge to his parka and walked to the barn. He recognized two New Haven cops from auto theft, and a pair of Staties from homicide. He figured that since Wilbur was standing outside his house, it must be Ritchie, or what was left of him, in the barn.

Mike Chandler stood at the edge of the open barn door and stared. A uniformed state trooper named Benson, a tall, solid man with graying red hair, walked over to him, smoking a cigarette. Benson was about six-two and had a bent nose from a couple of breaks. He knew Chandler.

"Ever seen anything like this?" Benson asked. "I mean, outside of a traffic accident or something?"

It took several seconds for the question to sink in upon Chandler, for it took part of that time for him to recreate what must have happened. His mind was working in overdrive, restructuring the scenario and figuring exactly why troopers from auto theft were there, along with homicide, and why there was such a large puddle of blood with a body in the middle of it in the center of a rickety old barn.

"No," Chandler answered, looking steadily at the lifeless body of Ritchie Corbett. The top of Corbett's body had been crushed, particularly the skull. In fact, the skull had been crushed so much by the falling weight of a car that the head had broken open. The victim's eyes were open, too, a strange touch which reminded Chandler immediately of the details of James Corbett's death.

"Me, neither," said Benson. "Looks like he was working under the car and the jack collapsed."

"Yeah," said Chandler. "I assume it's a hot car. That's why GLA guys are here."

Benson said Chandler assumed correctly. He snorted. "Ever see a guy working under a Corvette in the middle of the night and the 'Vette *wasn't* hot?"

Chandler said that he supposed he hadn't.

The jack that Ritchie Corbett had been working with was still twenty feet away. The state police had jacked the Corvette up a second time with their own tools, primarily to slide free the crushed corpse. Homicide had been called by the auto theft squad, who had tracked the homing device to the Corbett barn. The GLA men thought there was something about the scene that just wasn't kosher.

"Apparently the deceased was trying to deactivate the anti-theft electronics when the jack flew away," Benson said.

Chandler walked to the jack and looked at it without touching it. He came back.

"How does a perfectly good, brand new jack fly free from its connecting socket and sail through the air?" he asked. "How, unless it was yanked free?"

"That's the part we're working on, too," Benson said. "It almost seems like it couldn't hardly happen. It would have to have been jerked out of its slot by some tremendous force."

"Think one man could do it?" Chandler asked.

"Nah. Woulda took the strength of three men, maybe four. That's what's wrong with this picture."

Chandler nodded. Benson was right. It would have taken tremendous strength. Superhuman. Much more than one ordinary man.

A New Haven cop named Ed Forsythe loped over to them.

"Shit, how do you figure something like this?"

Forsythe asked, bumming a cigarette off Benson in the process. "Ever seen such a mess?"

"Worst traffic accident I ever saw was on Route thirty-four in Derby," Benson offered. "This teenage kid was playing in the street and a moving van, speeding, comes round the corner on a wet road, skids. Gets the kid between itself and an oil truck that's parked. Splat, huh?"

"Yeah," Forsythe said. "Wow. Splat is right."

"I also saw one a year ago in Milford where this Mexican kid gets hit so hard it took him right up out of his new sneakers," Benson continued. "The body flew up into a tree, but a tree branch caught the neck and severed it. So we found the sneakers right in the road, the body up in a tree, and the head must of dropped down and rolled. It was next to a mailbox by the side of the road."

"That worse than this?" Forsythe asked.

"Maybe," Benson said. "That didn't resemble this at all. Here we got a guy crushed. There we had a decap."

Chandler listened and stifled a sigh. The one story that he had to tell would not have been believed. He turned to the two bulls from state homicide.

"Get the GM jack dusted for prints," he said. "Probably won't do any good. But dust the jack and the car. Inside and out. Anything else you see."

The state troopers nodded.

There was some commotion behind Chandler and he turned to see a young sawbones from the office of Dr. Verdi, the medical examiner. The young doctor had a foreign accent, and even though the stolen car had come from the Yale campus, Chandler reasoned that the doctor hadn't. Someone had to go through the formality of pronouncing Ritchie Corbett dead.

It would take five minutes, and cost the state four hundred dollars.

Chandler stepped outside and away from the barn. He stood by himself for a moment and scanned the darkness, looking for Franny but knowing he wasn't going to find him—at least, not there, not then.

Chandler's eyes drifted over the three remaining Corbetts. Father, mother, and son huddled against the night, another relative dead.

They stared at Chandler and he gazed back at them, even with a little sympathy, against his better instincts.

It occurred to him that the family had—over the last few weeks—been reduced to something very small. Chandler would forever remember wondering how long they would last, these Corbetts, and whether Isaac would live long enough to spread his own seed around and revitalize the clan.

It was hardly the type of thought that he had come to Wilshire to entertain, but strangely—as the case ground on and as the deaths mounted—it was the type of notion that posed itself to him relentlessly, both in the bright light of day as well as on dark, sleep-deprived nights like this.

Twenty-three

"It's difficult to believe some of the stuff that goes on in these small towns," Ellen said on the subject of the second Corbett death. "A lot of perverse backwoods stuff."

"You have a point," Chandler said. He stood at the doorway to the blue room in Ellen's house, watching her work.

She was a very pretty woman. He had noticed that the first time he had seen her. She appealed to him. This evening she had finished early at the newspaper and invited him over to share dinner again. He had accepted. Their dinner last Saturday had been an enjoyable time and he appreciated her sober, intelligent, sane company.

Sane?

The past few days she hadn't been quite right.

He watched her from the doorway. She wore an old college sweatshirt, a pair of paint-spattered jeans, and a scarf over her hair against the paint. She was working with a brush, meticulously touching up the window sills and trim.

"You don't think of white trash stuff happening here in the north," she said. "But it sure does." She hardly lifted her eyes. "This town's got a bigger white trash element than I thought. This is just a downright strange place, that's all there is."

"Uh huh," he said. "That's *one* reason the state police tend to stay out, if you remember. That's one reason, anyway. Protocol with the locals is the other."

"Oh, yes, yes," she said.

She lifted her eyes and gave him a wink.

"But we're *here*, aren't we?" Ellen asked. "I mean, this is where you and I and a few thousand other souls have *landed* as adults. So this is where we *stay*, and most of us don't move."

"Uh huh," he said again.

He watched her paint. She was proceeding very purposefully, as if there were not a second to waste now in addressing this particular room.

"What are you doing?" he finally asked.

She looked up and winked again. He didn't like the wink. There was an eerie subtext.

"Painting," she said.

"I can see that part," he said. "But why?"

"The room needs it."

Details again: "You seem to be in a hurry. Why the sudden rush?"

She stopped and laughed.

"Well, Mike," she said. "What *color* am I painting?"

"Blue."

"So I'm getting the room ready."

"For what?"

"Blue," she repeated.

There was another one of those OHN's. A nice big creaking on the steps. Sarah was already in bed, so it wasn't her. Ellen looked toward the noise and gave a tiny wave.

"A guest room?" he asked.

"Sort of."

Then it dawned on him with shock. "You're pregnant?" he asked.

"No, silly!" she laughed. "But I've been pregnant twice, if that helps you out. And my guest has already arrived." She went back to painting. "Keep trying," she said.

It took a few seconds. Then it dropped on him like a cold black shroud.

"Oh, Jesus," he said. "Ellen, tell me you're kidding!"

"Kidding how?"

"Robin's room," he said.

"Yes. You have it," she said without stopping work. "The blue room in my home will be Robin's room."

He felt something sickening thrash about within him. She proposed the monstrosity of this with such ease, such perverted and casual naturalness, that in many ways he found this the scariest event that he had yet encountered in Wilshire. He had known Ellen just a few short months. When she had arrived she had seemed completely sane.

"Are you shocked?" she asked.

"Yes."

"Well then, tell me," she demanded firmly. She sounded as if she were talking to no one in particular, though Mike Chandler was right in sight. "Is this so terrible? We erect tombstones and monuments for departed people. So what is so wrong with a woman preparing a special chamber for a departed son?"

"Stones in a churchyard mark someone's memory," he said, trying to confront her with traditional logic. "You're preparing a room for a spirit . . . for a ghost to . . . to . . ."

"In which to reside," she said. "And I think the latter is *much* more cheerful than the former."

She paused, then made a few deft brush strokes. Another creak sounded in the floor so perilously close to Chandler that even he, with his own rationality straining to the breaking point, found it hard to encounter.

Ellen looked back to him. "This will be our little secret," she said. "Okay? I mean, don't tell anyone else in Wilshire that I'm doing this, Mike. I don't want it to get around."

"I won't mention it anywhere," he said.

She stepped back from her window sill and looked around. "What do you think about a bed and a dresser?"

"There's going to be furniture, too?"

"Oh, yes, of course," she said. "Really, why *wouldn't* I be thinking of moving furniture in? The type of thing that a boy his age would need or would want. Pennants. Sports equipment."

"Ellen—?"

"Don't try to talk me out of it," she requested kindly. "Do you know anything about teenage boys, by the way?" Even her pace of speech was wrong these days, he noticed. There was something clipped and breathless about it.

"Ellen," he said. "Look at me. Listen to me. Robin is dead."

She scoffed.

"Not for me," she said. "He's here."

"No, he's not," he said, struggling. "You think he is, but—"

"Mike, I have my son back, don't you understand that? Why do you want to wreck it?"

"Because this can't do you any good," Chandler said. "The departed need to stay departed. God knows what we're unleashing if—"

"The departed should remain near and dear to us," Ellen said. "Particularly this lost boy."

Chandler went to a position in front of Ellen. He took her by the arms and held her.

"Show him to me!" he demanded.

"I know he's here somewhere."

"I want to see him!"

"Maybe I'll protect him," she said.

"Do you have conversations with him?"

"Not yet."

"Do you talk to him?"

She smiled. "All the time."

"And does he answer you?"

"He will."

Chandler released her. Assessing all of this, he looked at Ellen in shock. "Listen to me, Ellen," he said, "all you're doing is hanging on emotionally to something that's been lost physically. Let it go. Even if you see Robin's specter again, let it go."

Her features blurred and reassembled, from engaging and pretty to indignant and angry.

"If you're going to talk this way, get out of my home," she said with a fading smile.

"Ellen," he said again, "try to under—"

She set down her paint brush. Her expression had turned very dark. Explosive.

"I said, get out of my home!" she repeated. "Or I'll call nine one one. When they hear it's you, Mike, they'll be sure to come."

"But—"

"Leave," she demanded.

"Okay," he finally agreed. "I'm going."

Michael Chandler pulled his patrol car to the side of Corbett Lane and edged the right side tires onto the dirt shoulder. It was just after twilight of the next day. The Connecticut State Trooper stopped the car, cut the ignition, and stepped out.

Chandler felt like a fool. What the hell, he reasoned, he would probably end up doing even stranger things before his career was finished.

He stood at the roadside and tried to make sense of the jumble of bare trees and uncleared woods before him. There were no landmarks other than the physical geography of the place itself. Sometimes those seemed to shift from day to day—a fallen tree in the woods here, a wounded pine tree at this location there—and he never knew exactly where he was until he had located the cemetery. He thought he was in relatively the same place, but he couldn't be sure. The normal blanket of dead leaves and underbrush on the floor of the woods looked the same here as everywhere else.

Sometimes, in his mind, he felt that the cemetery even seemed to shift around a bit, from location to location in the woods, but he chalked that up to his own sense of disorientation, his fundamental lack of understanding of much of what was happening.

Chandler was operating by instinct again, but at least that was something he still trusted. At worst, it wasn't a bad day for a walk among the trees.

He took his first few steps. He felt dead leaves and twigs crunch beneath his shoes as he stepped into the woods. He sighed.

His head was lowered, and the toe of his shoe pushed through the brush and decomposing leaves at the base of trees. In another few weeks, he mused as he explored, another settling of snow would be upon this same ground.

"Five more minutes," he said aloud. "That's all I'm giving it."

A couple of those minutes passed. Chandler looked back toward where he had come from, trying to position himself again, and something surprised him. He had gotten very close to the Corbett cemetery without actually realizing it. He stepped through a final stand of birch trees and was within it.

He looked up to where the old bugler, Jeremiah Corbett, still presided. Today, a pair of rude crows sat on Jeremiah's shoulders. The bugler's stone hands were unable to sweep them away, but Chandler's presence was enough to startle them and send them squawking into the air.

Chandler found a comfortable stone to sit on. He waited.

"Come on, Franny," he said. "Don't play with me. I need to see you."

Darkness enclosed the cemetery. The sky remained cold and dark. The temperature would be in the high thirties again this evening, and the chill was starting to cut through Chandler's clothing.

"Come on," he repeated. "I know you're here somewhere. I want to see you."

For a moment, Chandler had a vision of himself—a wounded, middle-aged cop who had trouble with an arm and equal trouble with beer, sitting in a remote cemetery in the darkness, talking to nothing. Talking to spirits. He saw himself through the eyes of old Jeremiah, who was high above him, and he had the most unsettling and tactile sense of the old soldier being present and watching him.

The tone of the surroundings changed again. Details, details: a strange feeling much like the change of atmospheric pressure when a storm approaches. It would be imperceptible to most people, and would have been imperceptible to Chandler, too, until recently. Chandler became aware of a presence. And why not? Daylight was completely gone.

A low voice came slowly up out of nowhere nearby. "Hello."

Chandler didn't bother to look. He felt a thin smile tiptoe across his face, however.

"Hello, Franny," Chandler said.

Franny grunted in response.

"I need to talk to you about Lisa Ann Petrillo," he said.

"So talk."

"You seemed pretty interested in Lisa Ann the night we talked at Lorna's," Chandler said. "Did you see her again?"

"No."

"Did you make any effort to?"

"You told me not to."

"That doesn't answer my question."

"She was real pretty," Franny said.

"Do you know who killed her?"

"Of course I do. And you do, too."

"And what about your Uncle Ritchie?" Chandler asked.

"Yeah? What about him?"

"What'd you do? Pull the jack out while he was working?"

Chandler heard the big man laugh. A slow lurching unsettling chuckle. "Yeah," he said. "Crunch. Shoulda heard him yell. Short quick yell. Then crunch, scream, pop, silence."

Franny laughed again. Chandler grimaced.

"If I kill evil," Franny asked. "Do it make me a good spirit or a bad one?"

"That's not the point. I don't like killing, Franny," Chandler said.

"Of course not. Poor Lisa Ann."

"That's not what I meant, either."

"Killing's part of life," Franny said.

Chandler leaned back, his head upward, his gaze extending infinitely into the night sky.

"Franny, I'm in this world here. And as long as I'm in this world, I have to play by these rules."

"What's that mean?"

"I have to arrest you," Chandler said.

There was a silence. Chandler turned and saw that Franny was no longer at Jeremiah's feet. His voice came from another direction.

"Yeah. For what?"

"Murder."

Franny laughed. "No," Franny said. "You're not going to do that."

"I have to."

"Lock me up? Put me in a cell?"

"Yes."

"Can't do that. I won't stay. How would you make me stay?"

"I don't know, Franny," Chandler answered.

"I don't, either," Franny said.

Chandler gazed at the big man and then lost him as he disappeared into the darkness. Chandler jumped. He felt a force right next to him. He looked in that direction and there was Franny, seated right by his side. An iciness came with him, and a foul smell of rotting flesh and death.

"Can't you do some good while you're here?" Chandler asked.

Franny seemed to resent the question. Chandler felt the anger though Franny's voice remained in its even resonant rumble. "I am doing good." he said. "I'm doing good for you. I'm protecting people."

"Who are you protecting?"

"People."

When Franny repeated, Chandler had learned, it meant he had nothing more to say on a subject.

A silence passed between them. A fragment of moonlight illuminated one side of Franny's stark skull and momentarily made a hollow of one eye. Then the eye returned, and so did Franny's voice.

"But then at least I'll be at peace. I'll be able to sleep." He followed this with a sigh—a huge yawning sigh which, when Chandler thought things out linearly, suggested that this sleep was imminent.

"Is the sleep comfortable?" Chandler asked. "Is it good?"

"It's not anything," he said. "Not good. Not bad. It's just sleep. Sometimes we rise. We walk among you. We are seen, or we aren't. Time don't exist after you're dead, so time don't matter none." The big man shrugged.

"Are you conscious during the sleep?" Chandler asked, thinking back of his own seven minute foray into another dimension.

"I don't know," Franny answered. Chandler, thinking back, didn't know, either. He remembered the bright yellow light, but didn't know whether he had been aware of it when he experienced it or merely recalled it afterwards.

He shuddered. It was damned cold this night, and Franny was making it colder.

"Franny," Chandler began, "I'm as confused as anybody, and—"

Chandler stopped in mid-sentence when he heard sobbing. The big man was crying—long, anguished, tortured, inconsolable tears. Chandler studied the vision next to him. The big Corbett was hunched over with his face in his hands.

"Franny?" Chandler asked. "Franny?"

"She was such a pretty girl" he said. "Lisa Ann. She wasn't due to die yet."

"I know."

"The whole damned Corbett family. Got to be eradicated."

"Franny, I don't like talk like that."

"The damned whole Corbett family. Got to be eradicated."

The vision of Franny leaning over was replaced by one of him leaning back against the headstone. Chandler's eyes had become accustomed to the darkness. He could see long streams of tears gliding down the big man's face, like little glistening rivers on a craggy rocky landscape, springing from eyes that were wells of sorrow.

"What is it, Franny?" he asked. "Tell me. Please."

The sobs were long and almost uncontrollable. "I don't like sleeping in no grave," Franny said. "I like this earth. This earth is beautiful."

"I know."

"I have to go back when I finish here."

"Back to your grave."

"Yes."

"What more do you have to do?"

"Some things."

"Can you tell me?"

"I already did."

"Tell me again."

"No."

"More killing?"

"The whole damned Corbett family. Got to be eradicated."

"Franny, I'm telling you. If you keep speaking like that, I'll have to stop you."

Franny snorted. "Yeah? How?" Franny held out a wrist. "Go ahead," he said.

For a moment Chandler was puzzled. He wasn't certain what he was supposed to do. Then he pulled out a set of handcuffs. He knew he could never hold Franny, but he would go through the motions, anyway.

He clasped one manacle on Franny's right wrist. He snapped it shut, checking to see if it was firm. It was.

Franny smiled. He looked like a big dumb kid who had learned a simple game. Another one of Franny's bar tricks followed, this one even better than the times he had gone to Lorna's with his uncles and been content to just *break* a set of cuffs.

"Watch," said Franny.

Before Chandler's beleaguered eyes, Franny pulled his wrist from right to left. Chandler felt a little tug. It might have been imperceptible to almost anyone else. But it was the motion of Franny's arm passing through the cuff.

Chandler had witnessed it, but he hadn't witnessed it. He had seen something once again that he could barely believe had happened, even though it had transpired before his own eyes. He exhaled and tried to pull away from it. He felt something icy on the back of his neck and supposed it was fear.

"It wasn't fear," said Franny, reading his thoughts again. "It was real hands. Hands of others."

Chandler's body recoiled in a fear that was now amplified. "Others?" he asked. *"What* others?"

"Take a look," said Franny.

Chandler's eyes focused in the near darkness. He

was startled for a moment. He saw movement and then he realized: "We're not alone here, are we?"

"We're never alone."

"Who else is here?"

"Others. Those who are restless. People who died too soon. Children. A lot of lost children. Boys and girls." He hunched. He was still crying. The sound was heart-wrenching.

"What spirits can you call?"

He hunched over again. "Almost any."

"Will I be able to see them? Communicate?"

"If the spirits want. Maybe."

"Franny, if I don't arrest you, can I bring a friend?"

"Where?"

"Out here. To talk. To settle a spirit."

"You could try."

"You'll be here?"

"Unless I'm resting."

"What's that mean, Franny?"

"I ain't going nowhere till I'm finished what I have to do."

"What's that you have to do?"

"I have to put my spirit in order," Franny said, sounding strangely philosophical.

Chandler was about to add something, but turned to him slowly and cut him off in mid-thought. "Just like you do, Mikey Boy. You have to put your life in order, don't you? *Help put the lives of other people in order and you'll put your own in order at the same time. Huh, Mikey Boy?*"

Franny's eyes were older, and scolding.

Chandler's heart was kicking like a boot. "That was a message, wasn't it?"

"Yeah."

"You're here with a lot of messages, aren't you?"

Franny looked away. "I'm settin' a lot of things right," he said.

"I hear you," Chandler said. "I hear you."

"Come back with your friend," Franny said. "And don't mess with what I got to do."

Twenty-four

Responding to the knock, Ellen opened the front door of her home. She closed it slightly when she found herself looking at a man she liked, but at whom she was angry.

"Yes?" she asked.

"How's the room going?" Mike Chandler asked.

"What room?"

"The blue one," he said. "The one we discussed."

She tried to push the door shut. Gently, he put out an arm and held it open.

"I'm on your side, Ellen," he said. "I want you to be at peace with your son, also."

He felt her pushing against the door, and then he felt the force from her arms ease. She opened the door again and he stopped holding it.

"Why did you come here?" she asked.

"There's someone you should meet," he said.

"Who?"

He shook his head. "You're a reporter," Mike Chandler said, "you have to respect the confidentiality of sources. Particularly police sources."

She gave him a faint smile. "You think I've lost my mind, and you're trying to pull something on me," she said. "I won't fall for it."

"The request was an invitation," he said. "If you're not interested, by all means close the door, and I won't bother you again."

She thought about it.

"Good," she said. *"Don't* bother me."

He stepped back. He allowed her to close the door in front of him.

He didn't move. On the other side of the door, she didn't move either. He waited. A full minute passed. It felt like an hour.

She opened the door again.

"Why aren't you leaving?" she asked.

"If you have a question about whether or not to come with me," he said, "ask Robin."

She blinked. "Ask Robin?"

He nodded.

She looked at him curiously. "Wait here," Ellen said.

She left the door open a strip as she retreated to the stairs. Sarah came to her and asked her something that Chandler couldn't hear. It looked as if it had to do with homework.

Ellen went upstairs and Chandler assumed she was going to the blue room, the haunted chamber in her house, the room claimed by her departed son. He waited longer in the cold. As the seconds passed he felt like a strange sort of suitor, one who had come to ask for permission to take a lady out. Instead of asking her parents, by the inverted logic of the hour, she had gone to ask her son.

Life traveling in the wrong direction? he wondered. *Time out of kilter?* The cold began to cut into him. His shoulder ached again. His fingers felt as if they weren't attached to his left hand any more.

He turned and looked at the flagstone path behind

him. He gasped and blinked. There was a woman standing there with no coat. She was plain and dark-haired, and Chandler knew where he had seen her before—in the brightness that had accompanied his near death, and in his occasional dreams in the months since.

The brown-haired woman offered him a slight smile. The detective gasped and held his mouth open in shock, because in another second he knew she was an hallucination.

Janine Osheyak. Whoever she was.

He heard Ellen coming back downstairs and turned toward her door. He glanced toward the woman behind him, and she was already gone. She had only been there for him to see.

"I can go," Ellen said.

Chandler, mildly shaken, fumbled for words. He was as loony as Ellen, but at least he knew it.

"You, uh, *spoke* to him?" he asked. "To Robin?"

"I received a general feeling," she said.

"Would you *prefer* to speak to him?"

"Of course," Ellen said. "That hasn't happened yet." She paused. "Where are we going? And when?"

"Tomorrow evening when it's dark. Maybe nine P.M."

Sarah came to her side and hugged her. "I'll arrange a sitter for Sarah," she said.

"I don't think you'll be sorry," he said. "I'll pick you up in my car. I suspect you'll be back in an hour."

"I'll be ready," Ellen said.

She was still speaking with that tone that sounded both distant and euphoric at the same time. He didn't like it, and wondered if that tone would be

following them the next night. He wondered idly
what Franny would make of it if it did.

As he walked back to his Jeep, he searched the
darkness for the brown-haired woman, whom he now
felt was circling him. He did not see her again, but
somehow knew he would.

Chandler's next and final stop of the day was in
the town center of Wilshire, where he presented himself at the emporium of the recently departed Ritchie
Corbett.

Wilbur Corbett, unshaven, with bloodshot eyes,
looked up from his position behind the counter of
his late brother's smoke shop. Today, there was nothing but morbidity and animosity in his eyes when he
saw Chandler entering.

There was a short, stout woman on the paying side
of the counter, engaged in a twenty dollar transaction
that had become more complicated than it deserved
to be. She wore a down vest and a bulky sweater and
was buying lottery tickets, a big fistful of them, along
with three soft packs of Pall Malls. The cash register
drawer was already open, and Wilbur folded the
twenty into the drawer without ringing the sale, the
better to skim profits and keep some extra dollars
out of the avaricious hands of the I.R.S.

The woman passed Chandler at the glass doorway
as he entered. It was half past five on a dull, cold
afternoon following the funeral of Ritchie Corbett.
The smoke shop was a low maintenance cash business, and Wilbur was keeping it open to keep the
cash pouring into Corbett pockets.

Chandler spent a moment watching the woman
leave. Once inside, he was alone with Wilbur, who

continued to eye him with intense animosity, along with a newly conceived jumpiness, but didn't say anything.

Chandler closed the door and nodded to the last living adult male Corbett—for the time being, anyway—of his generation. Still, Wilbur refused to offer anything. He had a cigarette perched on the inside edge of the counter, ignited end out, filter end on the Formica, as he stood near the cash register.

Chandler scanned the newspapers. Wilbur had all the local Connecticut ones, again with the glaring exception of *The Wilshire Republican*. He also had the national tabloids, a couple of football weeklies, and that day's *New York Post*. Outside, in the coldness and the grayness of the uneven parking lot, the short fat woman sat in the front of a Toyota with its engine running, scratching the coating from the lottery tickets. There were two children in the backseat who appeared to be fighting with each other. The woman got to the end of her lottery tickets, and there was no hit. She crumpled the tickets and dropped them out the car window. She lit a smoke and pulled away.

"You again, huh?" Wilbur Corbett asked.

"Me again."

Chandler turned back and eyed Wilbur, who was staring at him.

"Ain't you done enough to our family?" Wilbur asked. "Both my brothers been killed, and you still come around to kick my ass."

"I'm trying to understand events," Chandler said. "And I'm starting to. Maybe you can help me with the rest."

"Maybe you can take some of them magazines over there and jam 'em sideways up your ass," Wilbur suggested.

Chandler smiled and didn't take the bait.

"So what's the drill, man?" Corbett finally asked. "You didn't come in here to stroke me, so what is it?" The remaining Corbett brother seemed inordinately jittery—understandably.

"There really isn't a drill, Wilbur," Chandler said. "Unless you want to make one with me, which would be as smart a thing as you'd ever done."

"Fuck yourself, Chandler," he said acidly. "Then fuck yourself again for Ritchie, who can't be here to tell you for hisself."

"I was afraid you'd take that position," he said. "See, I could actually help you, maybe. But only if you helped me."

"Nothing I can do for you. Nothing you can do for me," Wilbur said. He was a man of simple pronouncements.

"I know who killed Lisa Ann Petrillo," Chandler said. "It was Brother Ritchie. I know who killed Maury Fishkin. It was Brother James, maybe with an assist from your nephew, Isaac. I don't know that part."

Wilbur laughed nervously. "Horseshit," he said. "Every time something bad happens in this town a Corbett gets blamed."

"Usually one is responsible," Chandler said. "But thanks to the ineptitude of local law enforcement, nothing ever happens."

"I'm not afraid of you, Chandler. So why don't you just get lost?"

Wilbur made a little motion and his hands went to the edge of the counter.

"I know your brother kept a twelve-gauge shotgun under that counter, Wilbur," Chandler said. "Suppose you keep your hands where I can see them so that no one has an accident."

Wilbur didn't move. The hands remained where they were, just out of sight.

"See, your prints are all over that shotgun," Chandler said. "All I'd have to do is blow you away, push the twelve-gauge onto the floor as you're bleeding to death, and claim you drew it."

Chandler shrugged.

"Fuck you," Wilbur said—a favorite theme—but he placed his hands on the counter.

"Much better," Chandler said.

"So what's the drill?" Wilbur asked again, convinced that there was one.

"Not much. Your family has been intimidating and murdering here for decades," Chandler said. "You've had this town by the short hairs. We both know that. It's going to stop."

"What do you want from me?"

"Some information. An explanation."

"I don't have nothing for you."

Chandler sighed. "There was flesh beneath Lisa's fingernails, from scratching her killer or killers. We're going to do DNA testing on it, Wilbur. I know it's going to match Ritchie's. But when it comes back from Dr. Verdi's lab, I'm also going to compare it with yours. Maybe I can hang an accomplice thing on you in the Petrillo murder. If so, I'm going to take great pleasure in arresting you."

Wilbur was starting to sweat. "Ritchie went nuts for that girl. That ain't my concern. So get out of my face with it," he said.

"Of course," Chandler said, continuing unbothered. "That's if you're still alive."

"What the fuck are you talking about?"

"Well, it seems to me that there's a trend going on in this area, Wilbur. Open season on the Corbett brothers. Open season on the whole Corbett family, it would almost appear."

"Yeah. Does seem that way."

"And you're the last one left."

"So who protects me? Other than me?" Wilbur asked.

Chandler shrugged and smiled.

Wilbur's eyes narrowed. "See, Chandler, that's what I'd figure you to say. So I got a legal shotgun under this counter, like you know. It's loaded right now. Anyone comes for me, I use it."

"Won't do you any good."

"The fuck it won't."

"You know as well as I do that we're dealing with something not quite human."

"I don't know nothing of that sort," Wilbur said bravely.

"Yes, you do. It's your darkest fear, isn't it, Wilbur? That someone whom you might have harmed would come back to even things up."

Wilbur said nothing again. He had a faraway, frightened look in his eye but he wasn't divulging anything.

"That's all bullshit," Wilbur said. "It can't be happening the way I think it's happening."

"No?"

"No."

"What can't be?"

"You know. *Things.*"

"Like someone coming back from the dead? Isn't that what we're talking about, Wilbur?"

Wilbur looked away. "I don't believe in that shit. I *don't!*"

"Then why can't you convince yourself of that?"

Chandler asked softly. "You wouldn't be quite so frightened if you truly believed that."

Wilbur cursed again, long and low. The sweat was pouring off his brow now.

Wilbur looked out of the window. A car arrived, a long, old sedan with four battered doors and a teenage boy driving.

A pair of teenage girls emerged from the car and came into the store. They were about sixteen, Chandler guessed as he watched them giggling to each other. They were blond and pretty, with clear, pink complexions. They wore sweatshirts from a Catholic high school in New Haven, mid-thigh skirts and knee socks. The taller one wore a green Phish cap and asked for Red Kamel cigarettes.

Wilbur said he was out and reached for the Winstons, instead.

"You girls have age ID?" Chandler asked from the side.

They looked at Chandler as if he were mad. Wilbur's hand carefully left the tobacco.

"Screw off," the taller one said. "We buy here every day."

"Is that a fact?"

"That's a fact, asshole," the shorter girl said huffily.

"I've never seen either of them before," Wilbur said.

The girl in the hat looked at Ritchie Corbett's brother without comprehension.

"You were here yesterday when—"

"Get out of here," Wilbur said to them.

"Why?"

"Trying to get me in trouble, you little bitches?" Wilbur snapped. "This man's the law. Go on. Get your asses out of here! Don't come back."

They looked at Wilbur, then at Chandler. They turned indignantly and stalked to the door. The girls shot each of them a filthy look, and went back outside. They shouted something rude in Chandler's direction and jumped into the old car, slamming the car doors.

Chandler watched as they related what had happened to the boy who was driving. He looked angry and opened his door to come in to continue the disagreement. Chandler glared at him. The boy backed off. He said something angrily to the girls and hit the accelerator. Chandler got the full license number and filed it in the back of his mind. He figured the kids were on their way to a gas station down the road and would score their butts there.

"You're real good for my business, aren't you?" Wilbur said. "Used to be the law was ours in this town. Now there's you hanging around all the time."

"Plus Franny," said Chandler.

"What's that got to do with it?" Wilbur asked.

"Well, that's where we started, isn't it?" said Chandler. "Franny. I'm hoping you'll tell me." He paused. "Now talk."

"No," said Wilbur.

"Who *is* Franny?"

"My nephew."

"Who was his father?"

"Dixon Corbett. Died in 'seventy."

Chandler smiled. "But he can't be, can he?" Chandler asked. "Not by anything we believe in."

Wilbur paled.

"See, I want to know what happened in concrete terms," Chandler continued. "I want a real life, honest down-to-earth explanation for everything I see around here."

"Not from me, you won't get it."

"That Franny. He hardly seems human, does he?" Chandler pressed. "And how about that scar on his neck? What should I make of that?"

"What the fuck do you want to make of that?" Wilbur snapped, quite furious and quite frightened all of a sudden. "Jesus Christ! You know everything, man? Then what're you asking questions for?"

"Because I want facts that exist in this world, not another one," Chandler said.

"Yeah," Wilbur snorted. "Don't we all? Well, Franny got raised out in the midwest, then he come back. It's that simple."

"I don't know about that, Wilbur. I've heard it, and I don't believe it. That's the problem. I think Franny's history is a little different."

"Like how?"

"That's the part I don't know. That's for you to tell me."

"Well, I ain't telling you nothing."

"I can see that." Chandler paused. "Brother James ended with a pitchfork through his neck. Brother Ritchie died under a car. A stolen car, not to press the point."

"So?"

"What do you think Franny's got in mind for you?"

"Why would he have anything in mind for me, fuck it?" Wilbur snapped. "And if he does, goddamn it, you're a cop. It's your job to stop him."

"I will if I can. But I don't think I'd be able to."

"Lock him up. Shoot him. Or something."

"Not possible."

"Well, why don't you damned well try! Instead of fucking around with me."

"Because you still haven't answered questions for

me," Chandler said. "So until I have answers, I can't do anything."

Wilbur blew out a long breath. He labored over a long, complicated thought. "You tell me something, Chandler," he said, "without making it official that I asked, like. Okay?"

"Okay."

"What do they call it in legal talk, when you can't get charged with something you done cause you done it too long ago?"

Chandler took a moment trying to decide what Wilbur meant.

"Statute of limitations?" Chandler finally said.

"Yeah. That's it What is it? On something big."

"How big?

"Real big."

"Murder?'

"Maybe."

"There isn't a statute of limitations on murder. Murder's murder. Whether it happened in nineteen eighteen, nineteen sixty-seven, or now."

"How about attempted murder?"

"Same thing."

Wilbur looked far away. "Oh," he said. "That's what I thought. That's what I reckoned."

"Nothing to say?"

"No."

"What murder?"

"Jeez. As if you don't know. A scar on his neck, and you don't know?"

He reached down and checked his shotgun.

"Sorry, Wilbur. But it won't do you any good if you don't explain it better. And we both know it."

Chandler turned and left the smoke shop. He climbed back into his Jeep. His eyes drifted upward and he saw the out-of-date sign above the door.

Ritchie's
Smokes Cold Drinks News

"Not any more, Ritchie," Chandler mused to himself. "Not any more."

He was putting the key in the ignition when he saw the front door of the smoke shop open again. Wilbur, minus the shotgun had something final to discuss.

"If'n I ask you a question, can it be off the record, or does it got to be on it?" Wilbur asked,

"You're not in a great position to make deals, Wilbur," Chandler said. "So why don't you ask, anyway?"

A surly expression crossed Wilbur's face. His mind seemed to travel a long way, then come sailing back again. Even in the cold night, he was sweating.

"I ain't admitting nothing with this, huh? All right?" he asked.

Chandler gave him a curt nod which suggested that whatever followed was in the gray area between on and off.

"Talk to me, Wilbur," he said. "It might do us both some good."

"Suppose one of the brothers had a kid born illegitimate out west somewhere," Wilbur said. "And suppose the mother of the bastard kid kept looking for money or a payoff or something from the family. And suppose this one brother, late Brother Dixon, drove the other brothers out there to take care of things."

"Take care of them how, Wilbur? The right way or the wrong way?"

Wilbur gave him a curt nod, which meant the wrong way. That being a Corbett way of doing things, Chandler had guessed as much, anyway.

"Ritchie, Jimmy and me," Wilbur said, "we didn't

know what was gonna happen. Honest, Dixon was just
nuts. We went out to the west to show some muscle.
Get the girl and her family to lay off."

"And when would this have been?"

"A long time ago."

"Dixon died in nineteen seventy," Chandler said.
"I know what swings from your family tree better
than you do."

"Yeah, well, it was shortly before he died. Autumn."

"So maybe the fall of nineteen sixty-nine?"

"Yeah, maybe. If this happened at all, understand?"

"Continue."

"Well, he made the mother disappear. And then
he went and cut the bastard kid's throat with a fucking kitchen knife," said Wilbur softly.

Chandler cringed.

Wilbur seemed ill at ease with his statement. For
a moment, Chandler was not inclined to help him.

"Killed him, you mean?"

"That's what we thought," said Wilbur. He motioned off into the darkness of the Wilshire evening.
No cars in either direction. The main road through
town was vacant, leading nowhere. It was as if somewhere someone had called a Time Out. Strangely, a
few small flakes of snow started to fall, reminding
Chandler of the evening in the cemetery when
Franny had willed it to snow. He wondered if somehow Franny were listening to this, the account of his
own murder.

"That's what we thought 'till the same kid turns
up last summer telling us he's our nephew. Then we
figured, hell, since we didn't *see* it, we must of
thought wrong all them years. The kid was alive."

"Uh huh."

Wilbur grew quite animated on this point.

"I mean, Dixon was long gone and, well, we were just as happy the kid had survived," Wilbur said. "Gave us another close kin here." He snorted and gave an ugly little laugh. "We been sorta feeling surrounded sometimes, you know," he said. "Us against the rest of the town. So if Franny was kin, we was glad to welcome him."

"Uh huh."

"What about Franny's mother?"

"What about her?"

Chandler sensed Wilbur faltering. For the first time, Wilbur Corbett seemed troubled about the consistency and the implications of his story.

"Did Dixon murder her, too?"

"I just know she disappeared."

" 'Disappeared,' as in 'died'?" Chandler asked.

"I don't know the details. I only know that Dixon took care of the problem."

"So she could have been murdered when all four of you wonderful guys were in Ohio. While the infant's throat was being cut."

Wilbur edged back. He stiffened and straightened. He acted like a man who has suddenly realized that he has said too much.

"All I know is that she disappeared. And the boy survived. Thank God, huh?"

"What was the mother's name?"

"Don't know."

"Think harder, Wilbur."

"I don't—"

"Come on," Chandler said easily. "I'm going to ignore this story officially, Wilbur. I just want some help understanding."

"It was a funny name," Corbett admitted. "Janey

something, maybe. Then an ethnic name. An 'O', a 'K', a 'Y', maybe, and some funny vowels."

Chandler picked it out of the air.

"Janine Osheyak."

Wilbur's face illuminated, then darkened. "Yeah. Sounds like that."

"I thought it might."

Wilbur stood watchfully and looked at Chandler in the car. He shrugged. "I don't know how you got that out of me, Chandler," he said. "But that's what I remember."

"What do you want me to do?" Chandler asked.

"Well, I don't know," he said. "But seems to me you maybe got some sort of suck with Franny. Maybe you can talk to him. I think he killed my brothers."

"Do you?"

"Yeah."

"Sort of evening up the scores and all? That sort of thing?"

"Yeah."

"It can't be that way, Wilbur," Chandler said.

"Why not?"

"You were right the first time."

"How's that?"

"My information has it that the boy whose throat got cut in nineteen sixty-nine died. So that can't be the same kid, can it?"

Wilbur didn't have an answer.

"I don't know," he said. "No, it can't be unless . . . unless'n—"

"I don't think I can help you, Wilbur. Unless you want to officially admit everything and let me take you into custody."

Wilbur bristled and blanched. "I ain't admitting nothing," said the remaining Corbett.

"I know."

"So then?"

"God help you, Wilbur. I can't."

Wilbur leaned back. An expression of fear came across his face, and he retreated a few steps from the Jeep.

"See," Chandler said, "there seems to be some system of laws and justice other than mine. I don't understand it. Can't control it. It's almost like the way things have been here in Wilshire for so long."

Wilbur listened and didn't move an eyelash. He stood uncomfortably but motionless, and the snow abated.

"You tell that Franny thug to stay away from me and my farmhouse," Wilbur said. "He ain't welcome there no more."

"I'll tell him."

"If he comes close, I'm using the shotgun."

"I'll mention that to him, too."

"See that you do."

"Do you really think the gun will do any good?"

Wilbur strained to block out the thought: If he had killed a boy once, how could he kill him a second time?

"I'll blow his ass through the wall," Wilbur answered crudely. "Double barrel. One after the other. He wants to be a ghost, I'll make him a fucking ghost."

"God help you, Wilbur," Chandler said. "Because I don't think I can."

Twenty-five

On the edge of the Corbett farm, past the tree from which Jimmy Corbett had been pushed to his death, Mike Chandler pulled to the side of the road and stopped his Jeep.

"Okay?" he asked.

"I'm not sure that I understand this," Ellen said, almost distrustfully.

"You don't have to understand it," he answered. "You just have to leave your mind open. Let your spirit loose. And believe in what you're doing."

"Are you a policeman or a spiritualist?" she asked.

He found what little humor he could in her question. "Today I'm a little of both," he said softly. "So come with me."

He locked his car. He offered her his hand, and she took it. It felt trusting in his, and his hand felt secure and trustworthy as it held hers. All right, she decided, she would have faith.

The moon filtered through the branches of the trees. Ellen wondered how Michael Chandler had any idea where he was going or what he was doing, but it soon became obvious that he had been in this place before and could find it at night.

She kept gazing upward. The woods were scary at

night, and she considered the moon her friend. If she kept in mind its position, she could find her way back to the road no matter what.

"Careful of the branches," he said.

They were like little whips, little switches, as they snapped backward. Michael pushed past a number of bare trees, and their spidery little branches were like fingers as they poked at Ellen.

God, she couldn't believe what a personality the woods could have on a cold night. She saw her breath in front of her face as she walked. The cold seeped through her coat minute by minute.

"How much longer?" she asked.

"Not much at all," he said comfortingly. "We're almost there."

"Not a moment too soon," she answered. She wondered whether this was an experience she could write about for her paper.

Michael led Ellen to a little clearing and stopped her. "Now," he said. "We're here."

"Where's that?" she asked.

Part of the woods became alive. It startled her so greatly that her heart felt as if it were going to explode. She was suddenly in an area where the trees gave way to large markers. It took a moment, but when her eyes adjusted to the moonlight she could see many old tombstones. She almost thought she saw movement among the stones, and was startled with the realization. Then she saw the high monument with the bugler upon it—Jeremiah Corbett, blowing an endless reveille for the dead, a call that was never answered, or always answered.

Franny Corbett was sitting under one of the larger trees that remained in the burial yard. His back was against the tree. The moonlight was on his face, strips of shadows across it from the branches of the trees above. He looked like some feral beast in the forest, like a brown bear with his back against the trunk of the old oak.

Chandler stopped short when he saw him. More than seeing their eyes lock, the policeman *sensed* that their eyes had locked.

"Hello," Chandler said.

"Hello. Hello, Mrs. Wilder," a low voice said.

She jumped so hard that she pulled away from Michael. Her hand came away from his. A body stood and extended itself in the moonlight to six and a half feet tall.

Franny.

"Where am I?" Ellen asked.

"You're in the Corbett family graveyard, Ellen," Chandler said. "But you're also in a place that's magical. At least for a short time."

Franny grunted his agreement.

It could have been like a nightmare, but it wasn't.

"How can that be?" she asked. "You're talking gibberish, Michael. Get real. Explain."

"It's the way you want it to be," he said. "This is an in-between type of place. Midway between heaven and hell, maybe. Midway between life and . . . and another life, maybe."

"Maybe," Franny concurred.

"Wilshire, out in the woods at night."

"But why did you bring me here?" she asked.

"I thought you'd know." Chandler said.

"No, I—"

She was interrupted by another voice. A boy's voice.

"Mother?" the voice asked, plaintive, questioning, like a lost child.

She turned and gasped. The moment froze in time
for her. There was her son. Or his spirit. Or something of him. Looking at her. Translucent in the
moonlight, his arms extended, becoming solid. Fading in. The Franny trick. A handsome boy turning,
as Franny had, from spirit to reality for a few heartbeats in eternity.

"No," she said, terrified. "No, it can't be."

"There's nothing to fear, Ellen," Chandler said.
"Just let this play out. It will only happen once in
your life. For most people it doesn't happen at all.
Go with it."

She looked at her son again. It was one thing to
see him flitting through her house, on the edge of
reality and on the periphery of her consciousness. It
was quite another to go face-to-face, heart-to-heart.
She tried with everything she could muster to put a
lid on her fear and found she was able to do it.

"Robin," she said softly. "Robin."

He smiled. "Hello, Mother," he said again.

She fought back sixteen years worth of tears. There
were still some left over.

"I'm so sorry," she said.

"For what?"

"For . . . for everything. For giving you up. For
not being with you. For not having you part of my
life. For—"

The boy was shaking his head. Amiably.

"I know you loved me," he said.

"I did."

"I was happy. I had a wonderful home."

"Your parents?"

"I'm with them. Just as I'm with you."

She sighed, and felt her lower lip quiver. Chandler
gave her hand a squeeze of encouragement.

"It's what was meant to be," her son said. "It's neither good nor bad, but it's what was meant to be. You have to believe that."

The light shifted. She saw elements of his life unfolding before her. She lost track of the minutes.

"Where are you?" she finally asked.

"On the other side."

"Of what?"

"Of life. From you. From where you are."

"Then there *is* another side?" Ellen asked.

"If you wish there to be one."

"Stop leading me in circles."

"There are only circles," her son answered. Strangely, it was a response worthy of Franny.

Her son's voice was like a whisper, like something riding or tumbling on a cold breeze. They talked for several minutes, Ellen knew, because a little cloud above the statue of Jeremiah Corbett drifted slowly toward the moon and passed it.

Her conversation with her son moved quickly, however, without any real measurement in time. The cold breeze became a wind, very cold. Intense. Forbidding. Chandler watched. For some of the time, he could see Robin. At other moments, he thought Ellen was talking to an empty darkness, but he knew better. He knew her son was there.

Somewhere. Somehow.

More time slipped by. A low voice was suddenly coming up from the earth, a voice that was now like warm fudge. Franny was speaking. "It's time."

Time somehow seemed out of joint. Chandler could have sworn that he was aware of Franny's voice before he heard it. The more time he spent in this place, the less he understood it.

"Robin!" Ellen said. She extended her arms. Chandler looked to Franny. The big man gave a shrug. Touching was permissible.

The image would stay with her forever.

She opened her arms and her late son walked into them. She closed them around him and he was a warm, strong young man in her arms for a few final heartbeats. For the rest of her life, she would not be able to remember how long she held him.

What she would recall, was tears and sadness, and then a sudden, rushing joy that she did not think possible. Then she was aware how the shape of the male in her arms changed. When she released him, it was almost as if she were waking from a trance, and she realized that she was holding Mike Chandler. He was looking at her with understanding in his eyes. His eyes were not as moist as hers, but they were damp.

"Enough," Franny said in a low voice.

Chandler looked at him.

"It's my time, too," Franny said. "I have to finish."

It took Chandler a moment to realize what Franny meant. Chandler broke away from Ellen and turned toward Franny. Franny gave a little parting glance in Chandler's direction and stepped through the stand of trees.

"Franny, stay here," Chandler insisted.

The big man grinned. "No way," he said. "It's my time tonight. I got things to do."

Chandler moved quickly to block Franny's path of escape. Chandler tried to hold one of the big man's arms. Franny only laughed at him, and he picked up Chandler with his other arm, all one hundred and eighty pounds of state policeman, and threw him over backward like a rag doll. Chandler landed hard against a cold bush.

Chandler's left ankle twisted and instantly throbbed.

Franny stood above him. For a moment Chandler thought he would be killed, but then he thought better of it. He knew that other mayhem was on Franny's agenda, but not that.

Franny leaned downward.

"I got a little bit of magic left, friend," Franny said. "Not much, but some. I done saved it for you."

Franny's huge hand reached forward. He placed it on Chandler's left shoulder. The big man's eyes locked on Chandler's, and the gaze was like an electrical connection.

Something Chandler would never understand happened next. He felt something else like electricity flow into his left side. This was like a surge, a jolt. The energy poured into him.

Then Franny leaned back. He didn't say anything, but Chandler knew it was good-bye. Franny turned and retreated into the woods.

Ellen moved carefully to stay out of his way, then went to Chandler and helped him. His ankle ached. As he climbed to his feet, it was tender to step on, providing Franny all the head start that he needed. When Chandler flexed his fingers, the feeling was back in them completely. Amazingly, the pain was gone from his shoulder.

"Are you all right?" Ellen asked.

"Yes. What about you?"

She nodded.

He motioned for her support. He put an arm around her, and she helped him clomp through the trees back to the Jeep. The walk was labored and slow.

As he unlocked the vehicle's door, a distant roar sounded in the stillness of the night, then a second.

They both froze.

"What was that?" she asked.

She turned and looked toward the center of the Corbett farm. They were about half a mile from the farmhouse.

"Shotgun blast," he said softly. "Twelve-gauge. Probably Wilbur's."

"What's he shooting at in the middle of the night?" she asked.

As soon as the question was out of her mouth, she knew.

She hopped into the Jeep.

The pain in his foot eased, and with only slight discomfort he managed to drive. The gate to the Corbett farm was closed, but he steered his Jeep around it, cut across a meadow, and then cut back to the driveway.

He drove at a mad speed, more out of instinct than anything else. He knew that a resolution to these affairs in Wilshire had already been written. There was nothing he could do to stop it or prevent it. It was enough just to be able to understand it.

The moon was marginally past its three quarters phase, and its glow allowed just the amount of illumination he needed. The Corbetts' house stood by itself, and not surprisingly the front door was open, even on such a cold night.

Chandler pulled his Jeep in front. He reached to his police radio to order a backup. Then he put the radio down.

There was no point. Nor did he want anyone else to come. Not just yet.

"You can stay here or you can come in with me," he said to Ellen. "I guarantee you, however, that it won't be pleasant in there."

She thought about it. "I'm the only reporter on the scene, right?" she asked.

"It's your story if you dare to print it," he said.

They stepped out of the Jeep together.

They walked to the front of the farmhouse. When they reached the door, the house was quiet. The first thing that Chandler recalled was the dogs. The two big guard dogs were conspicuously absent. Or silent.

He drew his pistol out of habit more than anything. He pushed the door farther open, reached in, and turned on a light. Still no noise. No sound.

He started to sweat, even with Ellen behind him. Once again, he pictured the time he had been shot in New Haven. Here he was, repeating the whole damned procedure, in the darkened home of another trigger-happy felon whom he knew to have a loaded weapon.

He wondered if he had five minutes to live. He tried to envision where the bullets would come from that would end his life. He kept his gun raised, felt his sweat soak through his shirt, and vibrated with the sound of his heart.

"Stay behind me," he said to Ellen. "If shooting starts, get down."

The inside of the Corbett home was dark, condemned, cramped, and dirty. The furniture dated from the 'sixties, with the exception of the television. The whole house smelled of age, the carpets were badly worn, and once again Chandler could smell the dogs even if he couldn't see them.

Lizzie's housekeeping was nonexistent, it seemed, and Chandler had difficulty making sure he was seeing an unkempt house and not the signs of a struggle.

He went through the downstairs, finding no one.
No dog moved, either.

He motioned to Ellen to stay back and he went to
the steps. He called upward.

"Police!" he shouted. "Anyone home?"

If anyone was, anyone wasn't answering.

He drew a breath, kept his weapon raised, and
started up the steps. He was halfway up when he saw
the first body.

It was the boy, Isaac. He lay on the floor in the
doorway of his room, just steps from the upstairs hallway. His body was slumped and crumpled, but there
was surprisingly little damage.

Chandler went to it and felt for a pulse. None.

Closer examination suggested that he had been
killed with one or two blows to the head and neck.
Probably enough to cause a brain hemorrhage or a
broken neck.

Chandler raised his eyes. There were two large
shapes on the floor beyond Isaac. At first, in the
shadow as they were, he took them to be blankets or
bedrolls of some sort. He gagged, however, when he
realized what they were.

The two dogs. They were not breathing. Their necks
had been broken. Something incredibly strong—and
there wasn't much question what it was—had overpow-
ered the two animals, breaking their necks, one by one.

Chandler turned on a room light and looked at
the floor.

Details again: No blood.

The dogs had probably attacked Franny when he
had come through, but he had been impervious to
their bites. The frantic animals, lying dead with their
tongues hanging from their mouths, much like the
dressed deer that Chandler had once seen in the Cor-

betts' yard, had not even understood what their opponent was, and why they were powerless against him.

Chandler stepped back into the drafty hallway. He pointed himself toward the master bedroom. He knew Wilbur—or what might be left of him—had to be somewhere. He expected Franny to lurch into view at some time, too.

A voice called his name. "Mike?"

It was Ellen, calling from downstairs.

"Yes."

"Are you all right?"

"So far."

"I don't like it down here. May I come up?"

"Yes," he said. "But be careful."

The stairs creaked as she climbed them. She came to a spot behind him and cringed when she saw the dead boy. At the same time, Chandler's eyes settled upon the partially open door of a closet in the hallway. The closet was halfway toward the master bedroom. It was the same layout as the time he had been shot.

Well, he decided to himself, he wouldn't get shot the same way twice. He would investigate the closet before passing it. If he didn't know better, he would have thrown a shot into it to be certain.

He moved toward it, Ellen behind him. Ten feet. Five feet. Then he saw the front part of a foot on the floor jutting just an inch or two past the door frame. It was a large, thick foot, and appeared to be in a sock.

"All right," he said. "I see you there. Come out."

No answer. No movement. Then, as if pushed by an unseen hand, the door started to move. It swung open and the body behind it started to move, too.

"Down!" he yelled to Ellen, who screamed and

went down low. Chandler went into a crouch and pointed his weapon straight forward.

The body only slumped, and then fell. Then it sprawled. Lizzie was already dead, her hands bound with clothesline and a plastic bag tied around her head and neck. She hit the floor with a sickening thud.

Ellen cringed and looked away. Chandler only had a moment to study the dead woman. He knew there was still Wilbur to account for, not to mention Franny.

He raised his eyes and focused on the dark doorway to the master bedroom. Every instinct within him told him that this was where the long line of troublesome Corbetts would end.

Here Chandler proceeded cautiously, even though he knew he was not going to find anything living. As he drew closer, he saw that through part of the door there was the evidence of a shotgun blast. The buckshot had sprayed into the hallway.

He drew within five feet of the room and signaled for Ellen to remain behind him. Then he moved close to the doorway. The room was dark and shadowy. It smelled musty and unkempt with the scent of dirty laundry. It also had the unmistakable stench of fresh death.

When he stepped inside, he also found the evidence of another shotgun blast against the wall. Wilbur Corbett's gun lay on the bed, empty, discharged, and as useless as Chandler had known it would be. Wilbur had fired twice point blank, it appeared, at someone who had come to kill him.

Details again: There was no evidence of any intruder's blood on the wall, no sign of a wound or a partial hit. Yet Wilbur could not have missed at that range. The blast had passed harmlessly through his assailant.

Chandler took a second look at the shotgun. The killer had grabbed it away from Wilbur and broken it in half—once again, raw, superhuman strength.

Wilbur probably never understood it completely either, this other ledger in which debits and credits were tallied. When Chandler found him lying by the bed, his eyes were still open and alive with terror, much as brother Jimmy's and brother Ritchie's had been, and perhaps, Chandler considered, much the way Dixon Corbett's probably were back in 1970.

Eyes open or eyes closed, Wilbur was dead, and this one was messy. Something savage had reached to Wilbur's neck and torn it open. There was a river of blood cascading from it, and the neck looked as if it had been twisted almost all the way around.

Brute strength. The killer had not even used a knife or a weapon. Just his powerful hands.

Chandler drew a breath and went back out to the hallway.

He and Ellen drew a breath together.

"Don't go in there," Mike said.

"Where's Franny?" she asked. "Here somewhere?"

"Maybe. And maybe he's gone," Chandler said. "I doubt if we'll ever see—"

A startled look swept across Ellen's face as her gaze alighted on something behind him. Her hand rose in shock, her eyes went wide, and she pointed.

"Mike!" she suddenly blurted. "Oh, my God, Mike, look!"

He turned his head in the direction that she indicated. He felt his heart catch, and nearly stopped. Ellen pressed right against him and held his arm with hers.

There was on the floor, shimmering, opaque, and perceptible only to eyes and minds trained to register such things, a very small child. It was a ghost child, probably about two years old. Its skin was as white as its clothing, and across its neck were two monstrous slashes, the type that might be inflicted by a kitchen knife.

The wounds were open and bleeding, but there was no blood. The bleeding and the wounds seemed to exist on their own plane of reality, as did the wounded child.

Then something even more extraordinary came into view.

The child was standing, crying, clutching its neck and its wounds. Neither Ellen nor Mike could hear it, as though they were watching a silent movie, or an aging black-and-white television with its sound off. Flickering with light as it was, they could not see the vision perfectly, though neither had any doubt what it was.

Behind the child was the figure of a woman. She was a ghost, too, opaque and shimmering. She was very plain looking, with a kindly face. Her hair was dark and short. She had a sixties midwestern look to her, and Chandler knew who she was.

He had seen her in his mind, and her name had been written on the scratch sheet of his soul. Chandler had seen her in the brightness that had come to him as he had teetered between, and beyond, life and death earlier that year. He had seen her in his dreams; he had felt her haunt his subconsciousness. And now he understood how she served as a link, an angel of sorts, between life and death: for him, for the boy that Ellen had lost, and for *her* son, who had been murdered—the son, Franny, who she would now bring back to her own place in eternity.

Chandler spoke aloud. Not to Ellen, but to the spectral woman.

"You're Janine Osheyak, aren't you?" he asked.

She smiled and didn't say anything. She leaned over and picked up her child. Janine also conveyed a thought to them: *I've come for my boy. I've come for my lost child.*

She opened her arms and picked him up. Franny was no longer in the immense hulking form that he had returned in to bedevil those who had taken his earthly life. Instead he was small again, vulnerable, a child.

The Franny-child seemed immediately comforted by his mother. The slash marks on his throat closed. The hot pain left the scene before them, and Ellen bit her lower lip so hard that it almost hurt.

She clutched Michael's arm. It was as if something—or many things—had been set right in some distant universe or some unknowable book of laws.

A wave of peace swept across the scene of the carnage. Janine Osheyak held her son tightly. A small piece of time elapsed, and they gently faded from view.

Chandler watched very carefully as the spectral images disappeared. He knew he would never see Franny Corbett again. Not in this form, or any other.

"Had enough for one day?" Chandler asked.

Ellen nodded.

He had a slight limp as he walked, so she steadied him as they went back down the steps. They went back out of the farmhouse and to his Jeep.

He reached in and radioed for the state police to come to the scene. Wilshire cops would arrive eventually, too. Late, as was their habit. Useless, as was their tradition.

Chandler would make a perfect witness as to what he had found here. He could speculate on how it happened, and they could put out an all points bulletin for Franny.

The full explanation would never reach print, as it would never be believed. Never.

The case would be lodged into the perfect files for an in-between type of place like Wilshire—forever open, but forever closed, wedged into a little corner of reality which few people who hadn't been there could possibly understand.

Twenty-six

The mass murder on the Corbett farm put Wilshire on the front pages of the newspapers throughout the northeastern United States. Camera crews from television stations arrived, shot their footage, and left. Wilshire ceased to be an isolated, sleepy place, at least for a few weeks. Meanwhile, *The Wilshire Republican* continued to operate. Several wire services picked up Ellen's initial accounts of the carnage at the Corbett farm. The royalties from the story put the small paper in the black for the year, paid off its debt, and guaranteed that it would survive into the next year. In a backhanded way, Franny had done Ellen more than one favor.

A frigid cold wave arrived, as did a steady blanket of snow. Chandler could never look at the white stuff coming out of the sky again without thinking of Franny Corbett, but as the events in Wilshire receded, as the attention given to the case by the state and local police began to wane, Chandler quietly tried to put the events in order.

By any orthodoxy he had previously believed, he failed.

He could not define what Franny Corbett had been. Benign demon? Avenging angel? Had there been some perverse warp in reality that had allowed a lost boy slain long ago to return to this plane of existence to set records straight? Chandler tried to believe in this interpretation, but was unable to set all of the details in order.

If Franny had come from beyond the grave, who or what had sent him? Had Franny sent himself? As logic turned a mirror image upon itself and presented itself to Chandler, he wondered anew why he himself had returned from the dead.

Chandler had spent seven minutes on the other side. Franny had spent thirty years. What was the difference, if any? Did time have a measurement when heartbeats were not involved? Time never seemed to pass traditionally in the quirky Corbett cemetery, so why would it pass that way for spirits that were departed?

Chandler had to finally concede that many of the details of this sort of event were unknowable, and let it go at that, but letting it go was not something he did willingly. In the same way, having his name as the chief investigating officer of the Connecticut State Police on a mass murder file that would never close also troubled him. He took comfort in the fact that for him personally, the case *was* closed.

On cold winter days in the weeks that followed the eradication of the Corbett family, when he had the time and when the spirit moved him, Chandler was given to driving past the spot where Jimmy Corbett had died and visiting the old burial ground. It was a sinister yet peaceful place under the snow, and occasionally Chandler found footprints in the freshly falling white carpet. Who had visited? Kids from the local high school? Thrill seekers?

Or was there a darker explanation?

Once, on a day in the following January, Chandler trudged through the snow near the tombstones, looked up to Jeremiah the old bugler, and asked him aloud if there were any questions he cared to answer. Jeremiah, wearing his own white coat and hat that day, did not flinch, nor did Chandler expect him to, but when the state policeman turned he saw a second set of footprints in the snow—the only others besides his own.

Details, details. He saw no one standing near him, and was quite certain that the footsteps had not been there when he'd made his own. He would have noticed, he was certain. He noticed that the footprints were large, as if made by a huge, hulking man.

He felt a surge within him, then thought things through a little more. Maybe, he concluded, it was better to leave the dead where they lay. Maybe it was better *not* to pose certain questions. He left the burial ground and did not visit it again until spring.

By that time, other aspects of his life had changed, too.

Chief Elmer Moore had been finally nudged into retirement from the Wilshire police force. Chandler had been offered his own retirement package by Hartford. Though the nerve damage in his fingers, hand and arm had stopped tormenting him, some aspects of the injury continued to show up on medical exams.

So retirement was forced on him—somewhat. In January, Ellen had managed to get herself elected to the Wilshire Board of Selectmen. She had put up Chandler's name for the position of chief of police. With no Corbetts still alive other than DeWayne and Lukas, the nomination sailed through by 5-0. A week after Chandler took the office, DeWayne and Lukas "retired." For some reason, they chose not to work for their new chief.

Mike Chandler also felt as if his heart, once closed so glacially, had begun to open again. He began seeing Ellen socially. Eventually, their lives intertwined to the point that there was never a formal arrangement as to when they would see each other. She would call him whenever she desired, and he always stopped by her house on his way to his own home. Sometimes, he wouldn't get to his own house at all.

At the same time, the lovely photograph of her late son emerged permanently from its wrapping in her desk drawer and took its place on her desk, not far from that of her daughter. The mysterious footsteps upstairs ceased at the same time.

The Corbett farm, a victim of "bad publicity"—as the real estate brokers termed bloody, high-profile multiple murder—would sit idle for several years. The remaining livestock was sold off, and other assets went into a fund held for next of kin. Lukas and DeWayne were the closest, and their claims would kick around the courts for years, with no one in too much of a rush to get things settled. Franny might have had a claim, too, but no one really expected him to show up and make it.

Spring finally came. It came late, but it finally came.

One day Ellen and Chandler took some extra time together. It was a weekend in May and Sarah was at a school activity. They sat in his Jeep with the sunroof open at the edge of Lake Barbara, sharing a late lunch. It had been one of those warm, brilliant springtime days.

A cold front rolled into Wilshire, and with it, a thunderstorm.

They sat at the lake watching the storm roll down from the hills. They noted the darkness of it, the violence of the storm, and the way it resolutely rolled forward until it had taken the brightness away from the day, shrouded the blue of the lake, and obscured the sky.

They had seen it coming. They had watched it and been powerless to stop it or in any way change its course. Later, in a discussion that seemed to come out of nowhere, Ellen and Mike realized that they had looked upon their belief in ghosts much the same way.

Many spirits had been sitting there at the edge of their consciousness, eternally poised and ready to take possession of their day. Looking back, they knew how inevitable their acceptance had ultimately been. The spirits had rolled in with darkness, but had been bracketed by a brilliant light, one which had a yellowish-white glow to both of them, and had resolutely rolled forward until neither Ellen nor Mike had had any choice but to acknowledge their presence.

Now the knowledge of ghosts was with them, the belief in spirits and perhaps even the triumph of the spirit over the flesh. Like the aftermath of the storm, the realization had led to a greater brightness that illuminated both their lives.

There was a final footnote.

On the anniversary of her son's death, Ellen went back down to Georgia, this time accompanied by Mike Chandler. There she joined Harold Duperry and other family members at a memorial service marking the passing of the three loved members of their family. The occasion was bittersweet, but at least was not as tragic or gut wrenching as the funeral service a year earlier.

Harold had put together a few more things for Ellen, odds and ends that he wanted her to have. There were some schoolbooks and some letters, some pictures, and a bracelet.

There was also a book of music, popular jazz and blues songs. Robin had been learning piano when his life had ended. In the book there was a single piece of sheet music.

Ellen was startled when she pulled the music from the book and examined it. Harold was present as she looked at it.

"What's this?" she asked. "This tune's been on my mind for a year."

The music was for "Midnight Train to Georgia."

Harold Duperry smiled. "Your son *loved* the tune," Harold said. "He was learning to play it when the accident happened. Played it real well, too."

"Sort of a favorite piece?" Chandler asked.

"Yes, you could say that," Harold said with a wide smile. "I would say that. Yes, sir, it *was* Robin's favorite, without a shadow of a doubt."

Ellen held the music tightly in a hand that was not completely steady.

"I knew that," she said. "Don't ask me how, but some way I knew that."

It was one final "in-between" sort of thing for a woman who had chosen to live in an "in-between" sort of place, and who was feeling more at home there with every day that passed.

Readers may contact Noel Hynd at
nhy1212@aol.com